GINA
IN THE
FLOATING
WORLD

GINA IN THE FLOATING WORLD

A NOVEL

BELLE BRETT

She Writes Press, a BookSparks imprint
A Division of SparkPointStudio, LLC.

Published 2018

Printed in the United States of America

ISBN: 978-1-63152-407-3
978-1-63152-408-0
Library of Congress Control Number: 2018937081

For information, address:
She Writes Press
1563 Solano Ave #546
Berkeley, CA 94707

She Writes Press is a division of SparkPoint Studio, LLC.

For my husband and life partner, John Louis Heymann,
whose belief in me and whose love inspires me
to reach for ever greater heights

and

In memory of my sister, Beth Brett,
whose creative spirit continues to hover
over me and nourish me.

In 1981, the same year Dolly Parton's feminist hit "9 to 5" reached number one on the charts and Sandra Day O'Connor was sworn in as the first female justice on the Supreme Court, I became a whore in Tokyo. At the time, it seemed like the natural thing to do.

CHAPTER ONE

"Ah, Miss Falwell, how could we at the American Bank of Tokyo justify paying you?" Mr. Yamaguchi focused on a pile of pristine manila folders on his sleek, Plexiglas desk. He swiveled the top folder ninety degrees and patted it. "You are here to be trained, yes?"

My throat tightened. The voice that came out was high-pitched, alien. "Yes, but the brochure from Wharton specifically said that internship stipends would cover living expenses."

"I am not familiar with this brochure," he said. "Perhaps you are not interested in continuing with us?" He glanced up at me, his bushy eyebrows arched.

Interested? Interest didn't begin to describe my feelings. This summer internship was only going to transform my sorry life. But without a stipend, I wouldn't last long. Even my crappy hostel cost a fortune. I pictured myself living on plain rice, begging in the streets, or cleaning out those ceramic holes in the floor they called toilets, my mother berating me, "Miss Dorothy Thinks-She's-Better-Than-Us, I'll bet Joliet looks pretty good right now."

I shuddered and stared out the picture window at the Tokyo skyline. Mist shrouded the tallest buildings, amputating their upper floors. Raindrops splattered on the glass. *Stay calm,* I told myself. *Everything is going to be okay.* "Of course I'm still inter-ested," I blurted out. "I just got here." I felt wet spots form under the arms of my jacket.

"Good," Mr. Yamaguchi said, turning the folder on his desk back to its original position. "Tomorrow after you have gone through the papers I gave you, I will give you a company tour."

I thanked him and bowed slightly for at least the tenth time since 9:00 a.m. Later, when the offices opened, I'd call Wharton to sort it out. Surely it was all a big mistake. I ambled to my cubi-cle and attacked the stack of papers until the charts and graphs morphed into squiggly blobs.

At 7:00 p.m., I lurched onto the teeming sidewalk, dodging the maze of dark-suited people with umbrellas. Stupidly, in my excitement at starting my internship, I'd left mine at the hostel. But it was warm out, and I didn't care. Maybe a walk would clear my head, still fuzzy with jet lag. I ducked under a doorway and consulted my city map. If I kept walking straight, I wouldn't get lost.

I briefly thought about calling Mark, my Asian Commerce instructor and one-time lover, who'd hastily arranged my intern-ship just a month ago with Mr. Yamaguchi, his old Wharton buddy. He paid for my round-trip plane ticket and then a week later dumped me so he could screw around with another one of his unsuspecting graduate students. I'd loved that man, and I thought he loved me. But at the end, all he said was, "You're smart. You're going to do just fine." My mother had been right about Mark being a jerk but for the wrong reasons. She thought he was put-ting big ideas in my head, like encouraging me to go east for an MBA. That was the best thing he did for me. But I wasn't going to get off the wait-list for Wharton's international business pro-gram if I didn't complete this internship. For once, I had to figure things out on my own. No parents breathing down my neck, no nuns guilt-tripping me at every turn, and no boyfriend telling me lies. I would show everyone how resourceful I could be without their help.

Energized by my new resolve, I walked vigorously until I began to feel faint. My stomach grumbled, and I realized the only things I'd eaten that day were some tiny tea sweets. It was getting dark now. The glare from the traffic was blinding. I shielded my eyes with my hand, and a cluster of chattering women almost knocked me down.

"*Gomen nasai!*" one of them said. They all giggled as they dashed in high heels and short dresses with no raincoats toward the glass door of a six-story building, its multiple signs winking. One sign said KITTY KAT KLUB. Another, HONEY SNACK BAR, which sounded promising. I followed the women inside, where they waited for the elevator. Two of them looked Japanese, one was darker-skinned, and the fourth one was blond and a good six inches taller than the others. All had fluffy perms and wore heavy makeup.

Reflexively, I touched my long, mouse-brown hair, now damp and stringy. "Honey Snack Bar?" I asked, pointing up.

"Fourth floor," the blonde said.

Another growl from my tummy, this one even louder. One of the women muttered something, and all the women giggled again. They got off on the third floor at the Kitty Kat Klub. On the next floor, the door to the Honey Snack Bar was locked, but I could hear music and voices. I pushed a buzzer next to the door, which an elegant middle-aged Japanese woman in a kimono opened. Behind her was a dimly lit, smoke-filled room. I saw the silhouette of another woman in a long red gown pouring a drink.

"Member only," the kimono-clad woman said. She eyed my outfit and frowned.

"Oh." How odd. I wondered how many restaurants in Japan had membership requirements. The woman in the red dress lit a man's cigarette. He reached toward her breast, but she grasped his hand midair, whispered something in his ear, and smiled sweetly.

Holy cow, I thought. At home that would have earned him a slap. Were customs that different here? Then a waiter brought them a steaming plate of plump pink shrimp. I salivated.

As I headed back to the elevator, I caught a glimpse of myself in the hallway mirror and gasped. No wonder the woman in the kimono frowned at me, with my hair stuck to my cheeks, my striped Oxford shirt clinging to me like I'd just come from a wet T-shirt contest, and my pumps caked in dirt. Was that drool on my lips? Preoccupied with my hideous reflection, I almost bumped into two white guys in suits staggering off the elevator in the direction of the Honey Snack Bar.

"Hey, darlin', want to join us?" one of them asked in an American accent, his speech slurred. He wore a gold cross around his neck. He reminded me of my Uncle Guido, who, like the men in his family, enjoyed his booze. But he got me. He was the only member of my family who encouraged me in my career ambitions, who thought it was cool that I wanted to be a hotshot in business. That is, until I announced I was going to Japan. "How can you do this to your father, who lost his leg fighting that damn war in the Pacific?" he'd asked. I didn't have an answer for him. It's not like I purposely chose Japan. And it's not like Dad even cared what I did. He'd been in an alcoholic daze since I was five, when my older brother Robert died in a motorcycle accident at age eighteen, and that was pretty much most of my living memory.

I smiled weakly at the men.

"We're real lonely for a nice girl who speaks English," the other one said. Patches of red scaly scalp peeked through his rust-colored hair.

"And who has big boobs," the first guy said, glaring at my chest.

I crossed my hands over my breasts.

"And who fucks in English," the second one added. He slapped his thigh. "How much do you charge?"

My heart raced. "Excuse me?"

"Excuse me?" the drunk said in a squeaky voice and laughed. "She thinks she's too good for us," he said to his pal. "Well, fuck her." He blocked my path to the elevator. "Fuck you, you little whore." Then they headed toward the Honey Snack Bar.

I flew down the stairs and bolted for the nearest subway station.

I was still breathless after my encounter with the two American assholes. What nerve those guys had. I should have responded, "Too high for you," when they asked me how much I charged.

When the train arrived, people surged into the coach, sweeping me along. I couldn't reach a strap or a seat back to hold on to, but the force of the packed bodies kept me standing. A man in a pin-striped suit on my left was reading a comic book. In one panel, a horned beast with a giant penis appeared to be having sex with a yellow-haired woman, who struggled, her face contorted. Why would a grown man read such gross junk? Then I felt a sharp pinch on my backside. I hoped it was an accident, but it happened again a few seconds later. I tried elbowing the alien arm, but I couldn't locate it amidst the tangle of limbs and torsos. I edged closer to the comic book guy. I noted that the horned beast, his erect penis leading the way, was now chasing two women with bare breasts as big as beach balls. Something hard rubbed against me. A briefcase? Probably not. Yuck. Another pinch.

"Cut it out," I spluttered in English. I wished I knew some appropriate Japanese phrase, but all I'd learned so far was "please" and "thank you." This was no time for useless politeness. A few people glared at me as though I was the ill-behaved one, and I became scared that the crowd might suddenly turn against me. This trip was nothing like the Chicago El, the only other subway I knew. I felt trapped in the steamy, but silent, car.

A hand tapped my shoulder. Startled, I jumped and turned around as far as I could to see a cherubic face with almond-shaped eyes and a pudding bowl haircut grinning at me. Using his duffle bag like a battering ram, he wedged himself between me and any probable suspects.

"How nice to see you," he whispered.

How could he know who I was? Was this a teenage pickup line? My first instinct was to move away, but I had nowhere to go.

"Are you having nice day?" he asked, continuing to whisper.

Uneasy, I shifted from foot to foot and pulled my bag to my chest.

"Do not worry," he said. "It okay."

It took me a few more moments to catch on that I was being rescued. Did I seem that helpless? I looked up, forced a smile, and said in a loud voice, "Oh, hello. How are you?" Heads turned.

"You English?" he asked.

"American," I said, quietly this time.

Close up, his cheeks were chubby and smooth, with just a few whiskers sprouting from his chin.

"I like Americans. Yankee Doodle Dandy."

He stood close to me as the train hummed along the tracks. When our bodies brushed against each other, he would step back a little, as though respecting my space. We didn't talk anymore, but I liked having him nearby. He made me feel as though I could handle all this strangeness. I just had to be patient and open, and something good would occur. Isn't that what my mother always said? Of course, she was referring to nabbing a well-heeled Catholic guy and living the life she wished she'd had. My mother was convinced that all the bad things that had happened to her were God's way of punishing her for marrying a Lutheran.

After two stops, a seat opened up, and the young guy leaped in front of it to reserve it for me. I had no choice but to take it. He remained standing.

I decided to break the silence, to show that I was grateful. "Thank you for your help."

He leaned down. "Welcome you. You know judo?" His breath tickled my ear.

"No, I don't."

"I show you things. I like speak English. Good to practice."

"Are you a student?" I asked.

"Yes. Student at cram school. Prepare for test to go to Tokyo University. Very hard. Much study," he said, frowning. "You student, too?"

"Yes. A business student." A stretch, since Wharton hadn't officially accepted me.

"I will be business student, too. Maybe next year. I twenty years old."

Only three years younger than me. And I thought *I* looked young for my age.

"You in Japan long?" he asked.

"I'm here for four months—until late August."

"I be your guide. I good guide. Not cost anything."

"That's kind of you, but I won't have much time to be a tourist. I'm working." The concept of internship was too hard to explain.

"Must see things!" He reached into the front pocket of his bag and pulled out a business card. One side was in Japanese characters; the other, in the Roman alphabet.

"That my number. That my name. Hiro. You call anytime."

Ha. Hiro, my own superhero of sorts.

"You name?"

"Dee Dee," I heard myself saying. The way I pronounced my name when I first started to speak. Until Robert died, even my mother called me Dee Dee, but after that I was Dorothy again, named after the girl in *The Wonderful Wizard of Oz*. In fact, the only family trip we ever took was to Kansas. I think my mother was in search of the fairy-tale Dorothy, so she could replace me with her. Or maybe she was hoping we'd all be whisked away to Oz by a tornado, where we would find Robert, and life would be hunky-dory again.

"Dee Dee. Nice name. We maybe go for ice cream now?" he asked.

I was taken aback by his directness. "I have an appointment," I lied.

The train slowed, and I craned my neck to check the name of the station. Fortunately, the names were in Roman letters as well as Japanese characters. Just three more stops.

"Where you from?"

"Chicago." Chicago sounded worldlier than Joliet, the place I wanted to forget.

"Chicago. Gangsters," he said and made a mock gun with his thumb and forefinger.

I laughed. "You must have watched a lot of old movies."

He looked at me, puzzled. "We have gangster in Japan. Called yakuza. You know yakuza?"

I nodded. The word sounded familiar, and I didn't want to appear dumb.

"Name yakuza mean eight-nine-three. Very bad. How you say? Small toss game, with number?" Hiro cupped his hands together, shook them, and swung one arm as though he was throwing a bowling ball.

"Oh, dice. Roll of the dice." I felt like I was playing charades. "Eight-nine-three is a bad throw?"

"Yes, most bad. Yakuza bad. Very bad men." He raised his arm and made a sharp chopping motion with the side of his hand. "That what I do to yakuza."

I cringed. Did I have to worry about gangsters, too?

The train arrived at Ikebukuro, and I rose from my seat.

"Promise you phone," Hiro said.

I nodded, but it seemed unlikely. I had a career to jumpstart.

I welcomed the sight of my antiseptic youth hostel with its ungrammatical signs in English and several other languages on the otherwise bare cinder block walls. No flush after 11 p.m. Wear toilet slippers in toilet. Door lockings from 10 a.m. and 4:00 p.m. And my favorite: Be wary of personal bee-longs.

But the youth hostel allowed only a week's stay, and I was already on night three. The brochure, the one that Mr. Yamaguchi claimed not to know existed, stated that internship supervisors would help with housing. Fat chance of that happening. And what if they couldn't pay me? I had exactly two weeks' cash, *if* I were careful.

As I approached the reception desk, I heard the bark of the sandy-haired Danish sergeant major who manned it. "Ten o'clock curfew strictly enforced. No exceptions." He was talking to a guy, maybe a little older than me, signing his name in the giant ledger.

I checked my trusty watch with its large, glowing hands, a gift from Uncle Guido when I left my job at the medical supply plant he managed and where I'd worked since college. It was now 9:10 p.m. At home, it was fifteen hours earlier. Everyone would just be getting up.

"Relax, Leif, I know all about the rules. Don't you recognize me?" the guy said with an American accent. "It's Gabe." Gabe had a stocky build and was dressed neatly in khakis and a crisp blue shirt that bulged slightly over his round tummy. Thick, wavy brown hair framed a face with a little bit of stubble.

Leif patted his own clean-shaven cheeks. "You don't look like Jesus Christ anymore." As I walked by the desk, Leif glanced at me. "Hello, Dorothy." I was surprised he remembered my name.

Gabe turned around. He smiled, a sweet dimpled smile. "Hey. Lose your umbrella?"

I'd almost forgotten how wet I was. My skirt clung to my legs, and dirt dotted my panty hose. Somewhere my jacket button had popped off. I didn't want anyone else staring at my now transparent wet shirt. I waved and clambered up the metal steps that reverberated through the stairwell like cymbals clashing.

The girls' dorm was on the second floor—eight as yet unoccupied bunk beds in two rows on a yellowing linoleum floor. Lining one wall were the "toilet slippers," four incongruous pairs of pink flip-flops decorated with oversize plastic daisies. I kicked off my pumps, and, too exhausted to remove my wet clothes, fell down on my lower bunk, and shut my eyes. I awoke in the middle of the night, chilled and with the urgent need to pee. I wedged into the pink flip-flops and headed to the bathroom. While positioning my feet on the ceramic footprints on either side of what was a hole lined in ceramic, one of the flip-flops fell into the void. I panicked. It's not like I was going to stick my hand down there, so I stepped off the footprints and attempted to flush the shoe down. The water backed up, almost flowing over the top of the hole before receding. I thought I saw the slipper staring back at me. I walked back to the dorm barefoot and hoped that no one would discover my indiscretion.

Before changing out of my suit, I remembered that I still needed to phone the intern office at Wharton. I stumbled to the lobby pay phone and managed to reach the USA. A Ms. Roxanne LaTour told me that while internship sponsors were encouraged to provide some kind of compensation, it wasn't required. Then she scolded me for not doing my "homework." Besides, she added, I wasn't officially a student there anyway. I felt her scorn traveling the seven thousand miles from Philadelphia, but my brain was too fried to make my case.

I dragged myself back to bed, making sure to hang my clothes on the metal bed frame to dry. After tossing for a while on the thin mattress, I dreamed of toilets overflowing with pink daisies. My mother made me eat them to teach me a lesson for coming to Japan. In the next room, my dad stared at a rerun of "Father Knows Best." My brother Robert's ghost hovered over all of us.

The deep clang of a bell woke me up at seven o'clock. I heard groans from two of the neighboring bunks. While hosing myself down in the communal shower, I replayed my brief conversation with Ms. LaTour. Although she'd been mean to me, she was also right. I'd messed up by not doing my research. But I would figure out something. Soon. *Think positively,* I told myself.

After dressing in my other navy-blue suit, I headed to the cafeteria on the first floor and picked up a tray of food prepared as though from an assembly line. I'd skipped breakfast the day before. Empty from hours of not eating much, even the pickled vegetables, small bony fish with the head still on, bowl of murky brown soup, white rice, and cold egg looked passably edible. I sat by myself at the far end of one of the long picnic-style tables and poked at the slimy-looking vegetables. At least the egg wasn't strange. I whacked it on the edge of the tray, expecting it to be hard-boiled. Instead, clear goo and runny yellow oozed all over my tray. I gagged and shoved away the tray, rescuing only the green tea. I could see that my eating preferences needed adapting. I would try harder when I was more settled. I retrieved a pad of paper and a pen from my purse and began creating a list of things I needed to do, starting with "find a place to stay."

"Okay if I sit here?"

I looked up and saw Gabe, who looked much more alert than I felt. "Suit yourself." I took a sip of the tea and winced. It was bitter. I returned my attention to my list.

"You're the one in the suit. Not the usual get-up for a youth hostel."

Self-consciously, I examined my outfit, heavily rumpled since I'd left it in my suitcase as a precaution against theft. "I guess not. I'm an intern at a bank."

"Ah, yes. The purposeful American." He nodded his head at my list.

I put my pen down and watched Gabe crack his egg on the edge of a bowl, empty its contents into the hot soup, and stir vigorously. The egg began to cook.

"What do you mean?" I felt attacked.

"I meet Australians or English people or Germans, and they're just traveling, but Americans always have a project. They're going to learn Japanese, research Buddhist temples, study tea ceremony. So many items on their to-do lists."

"So, what's wrong with that?" I asked, practically hissing. I turned over my pad of paper so that the list no longer showed.

"Whoa!" Gabe put up both his hands like I was holding him at gunpoint. "Nothing's wrong with that. I don't mean it as a criticism. I'm just making an observation about different approaches to life."

"Sorry. I just had a hard day yesterday." But I didn't want to talk about my problems. "So, what's your approach?"

"Just a wanderer, I guess." He laughed, triggering those dimples again. "No purpose at all. I've been meandering around Asia for eight years since college, the last three in Japan."

"Wow." An eight-year vacation was beyond my imagination. I wondered how Gabe got by. Maybe he was a rich boy. I didn't know too many of those.

"Having spent the first five years stoned, I could be wrong about the amount of time."

Drugs weren't my thing. I liked being in control of my mind. But determined not to sound too wimpy, I snapped back, "So, you did have a purpose."

"You got me there. The search for the perfect hash."

"Did you find it?"

"Oh, yeah. Many times," he said. "But I've gone straight now, more or less."

"You've been wandering around Japan for three years?"

"Nah. I've been teaching English in Kyoto."

I felt relieved to learn that Gabe was doing something legitimate. "What are you doing in Tokyo?"

"R and R." Gabe slurped his broth, holding the bowl near his mouth.

"From what little I've seen, Tokyo is hardly the place to rest and relax," I said, recalling my disastrous outing of the previous evening.

"Oh, but you're wrong. You just need to know where to go."

"I'm not sure I trust the judgment of someone who *chose* to stay *here*." I looked around at the sterile room, no art on its walls, no personality.

He laughed. "I love this place. It's so . . . basic," he said. "It makes you appreciate everything else so much more."

I laughed too.

"But what's a banker like yourself doing here?" he asked. He deftly pulled apart a pair of wooden chopsticks and attacked the slimy vegetables. I screwed up my nose. "Seaweed," he said, pointing to the dark green mass.

"I'm not a banker yet, and I can't afford anything better, even this. I just learned my internship doesn't pay." Why was I bearing my soul to this stranger?

"Rough luck. By the way, Gabe's the name," he said as though reading my mind.

"I'm Dee Dee." It came out easily this time.

He stretched his large hand across the table to shake mine. His grip was firm, but his fingers were warm and soft. "I thought I heard Leif call you 'Dorothy.'"

He'd been paying attention. "My mother's obsession with all things *Wizard of Oz*."

"And now you're a long way from home."

"That's the idea," I said.

"I hear you. Don't want to hit your folks up for money, huh?"

"I'd rather stab this in my eyeballs." I brandished my fork. "They don't approve of my being here." The fork flew out of my hand onto the floor. I picked it up.

Gabe nodded. "For the banking internship, which you are doing because . . . ?"

"I need evidence of something called 'cultural adaptability' to get into this special international MBA program."

"So you can become an international banker."

"Not necessarily. But something international." I pulled my

tray near me and poked at the seaweed, spearing some on my fork. I nibbled a small amount. It wasn't so bad.

"Woman of the world."

"Are you making fun of me?" I tore the paper covering off the set of chopsticks on my tray. I tried snapping them apart the way I'd seen Gabe do, but they broke into two uneven sections. I slapped them onto the table.

"No. I admire your focus," he said. "So, is there some cultural adaptability scale they rate you on?" I shook my head. "There should be, and then you could keep track."

"How about a point for eating this seaweed?"

"Half a point. Eating raw squid legs without throwing up— that's one point." He extracted a black, slithery morsel from his soup and waved it in front of me.

I backed away. "Raw squid legs?"

"This is a mushroom," he said, popping it into his mouth. "Raw squid legs was just an example of weirdness you may encounter."

"Very funny." I stood up. "I have to get going. Nice talking with you."

"You, too. Hey, if you want, my old college friend, Suki, may be able to help you find something to pay the bills. She's well connected." Gabe grabbed my pen, jotted down some information on a paper napkin, and handed it to me.

I shoved it in my purse along with my pen and pad of paper. "Thanks."

"She's nice even if she is a bit bossy." Gabe winked. "But don't tell her I said that."

As I left, I made a mental note to add "create cultural adaptability scale" to my list.

As promised, Mr. Yamaguchi took me on a brief tour of the bank, introducing me to several men he identified as bank officers. They wore almost identical dark blue suits. Near each suite of offices, a group of women about my age occupied a large open space.

They sat in front of computer keyboards and monitors all at the same angle, looking like a row of fashionable robots. As I passed by with Mr. Yamaguchi, a few of them giggled and covered their mouths.

I spent the day in meetings in a conference room with an enormous mahogany table and large chairs with arms. Mr. Yamaguchi assigned me a seat in a corner away from the table so that I could "observe." A stream of men paraded in and out, accompanied by much bowing with each entrance and exit. Although the presentations were in English, between the accents and the new material, I had trouble following the speakers. The constant smoking didn't help either. The room became shrouded in a fine blue veil despite the steady hum of the ventilation system. My eyelids grew heavy, and I wished I could stomach the strong coffee that everyone else consumed continuously. I kept myself awake by figuring out how many points each new experience or action would earn me on my new cultural adaptability scale. The day had to be worth at least a two.

At four thirty, Mr. Yamaguchi shook my hand, wished me a good weekend, and ushered me out.

It was raining again, but this time I'd brought my umbrella. I stood under the overhang of the post office next door, unsure of what to do next. The American Embassy, where I might have found some helpful information, would close soon, and it was too early for dinner. As I watched the growing parade of well-dressed people scuttle past on the sidewalk, I wondered whether I'd overreached myself. The fact that I'd graduated from college at age twenty with straight As didn't matter now. Thank God I had two days to regroup.

I polished off the crisp biscuits I'd bought earlier from the tea lady and fished around for a tissue to wipe my mouth. Instead, I found the napkin with the phone number of Gabe's friend, Suki. I supposed I had nothing to lose if I phoned her.

CHAPTER TWO

I followed Suki's directions carefully, changing subway lines, and found her place. Streets in Tokyo did not have a logical numbering system, and the row of houses on her street all looked alike. Hers was third from the corner directly across from a café, distinguishable only by the large white noodle bowl in its window. Surely, my latest excursion to an unknown part of this huge, foreign city was worth at least one point.

The entryway to the building was unlocked. When I rang the bell for number one, a woman, who appeared to be Japanese to my untrained eyes, opened the door. Her hair was piled casually on top of her head and secured with an ivory ornament, a few wisps escaping its grasp. She wore a pastel kimono with large coral-colored flowers and small white socklets on her feet.

After greeting me, she ushered me into a hallway. Two tiers of footwear—strappy high heels, woven sandals, black leather boots—lined one side. Above the shoes on a silk scroll, delicately painted egrets stood on spindly legs, wings spread. I dutifully removed my pumps and placed them nearby. Suki dropped my dripping umbrella into a bamboo stand. She then led me into a small, simply furnished room with straw-like carpeting. Purple velvet cushions surrounded a low table of polished wood. Against the wall another taller table held a lone vase with a perfectly balanced arrangement of flowers and twigs.

"What a lovely room," I said. It was nothing like my parents' living room, regularly vacuumed but stuffed with worn furniture, the television at center stage and always a beer bottle or two on the floor next to my father's recliner.

"Thanks. Get comfortable, and I'll make some tea." Her American accent seemed at odds with her space and appearance. She disappeared into her kitchen.

I sat down on one of the cushions and picked up a book lying on the table called *Portraits of the Floating World*. The name conjured up images of clouds scudding across a bright blue sky. Instead, I found woodcuts of Japanese women in kimonos fussing with their hair, applying makeup, or tying their sashes, each action meticulous as though preparing for an important date, each woman frowning in concentration. Personally, I didn't spend much time on how I looked. I never went to a hairdresser, and I'd worn the same style for years. But I was intrigued by these ladies and the loving way the artists rendered them.

Suki returned with a brown ceramic teapot edged in a shiny blue glaze, matching cups, and a few small morsels, all arranged artfully on a lacquered tray. When she knelt and poured the tea, it was as though a page from the portrait book sprung to life. She handed me a plate of food. "Try one of these. They're filled with sweet bean paste."

I obediently took a bite of the pastry. It was delicious.

"Do you like those woodcuts?" she asked, gesturing to the book still in my lap, open to a print of a woman downing a large glass of wine while holding a crab in her other hand. It was called *The Hussy*.

"Yes. I love art, but I'm afraid I don't know much about Japanese art. What's the 'floating world'?"

"Oh, theaters and brothels. You know, places associated with the pleasure-seeking life of Edo, the old Tokyo." Her eyes appeared to focus on something at a great distance. "A lot of great Japanese art draws on inspiration from the floating world."

"Why is it called that?"

"I think it's Buddhist—the idea that our time on earth is temporary, maybe even an illusion."

I nodded. Suki seemed to know a lot. "So, does that mean you are supposed to spend your time enjoying yourself? That seems a little self-indulgent." Suki smiled but didn't respond.

I glanced down again at *The Hussy*. The woman's arm hid an obviously naked breast.

I closed the book and asked Suki how she came to be in Japan. She explained how she'd quit City University of New York after her junior year and had come to Japan to learn more about her heritage.

"Did you ever finish college?" I asked.

"No. Once I'd stopped, it was hard to think about going back."

It never would have occurred to me not to graduate, as much as I felt stifled by my women's Catholic college in Milwaukee, the only one that offered me a full scholarship and met with my mother's approval. Once, I took the bus to the big university in Madison, found a dark lecture hall where some professor was showing slides of Dutch landscapes, and pretended for a moment I was a student there. Afterward, I bought fries and a chocolate shake and arrived back at my college in Milwaukee before curfew.

"So, what are you doing in Japan?" she asked.

I told Suki about the course in Asian commerce that had inspired my interest in international business and my need to get some experience abroad, but not about my doomed affair with Mark or my wish to be as far away from home as possible. I was anxious to get to the point of my visit. "To be honest, I've got a problem." I sucked in my breath. "I learned that my internship doesn't pay, and I need to earn some money. Gabe said you knew people."

Suki studied me for a minute. "Ever been a waitress?"

"Just the local burger joint during high school. But I wasn't a real waitress, carrying trays. I just yelled out orders and collected money." In college, I'd held numerous part-time jobs, but most involved limited interaction with the public, like shelving books in the library.

"No trays. If you can pour a drink, you can do the job."

"But I don't speak Japanese."

"No matter. They love gaijin women here. Foreigners. They consider them exotic."

"I don't know, Suki. I'm not the exotic kind." I wasn't sure what kind of waitress job Suki had in mind, but I couldn't afford to be picky.

"You don't have to be. It's all in the eye of the beholder. You've got what it takes." She sat up straight, thrusting out her small breasts.

"Thanks, I guess." I shifted on my cushion and stared down. When I first started to develop, I was thrilled, as I'd been a late bloomer. Now it bothered me if guys didn't see beyond the size of my chest.

Suki patted my arm. "The point is you get to earn money, learn about Japanese business practices, and delve into this wonderful culture. What could be better for your future?" She was quite the saleswoman. "I know a Mr. Matsumoto. He has a small club in the suburbs, and he's always looking for hostesses. I've worked for him."

"Hostesses? Like the women who seat people at a restaurant?" I asked hopefully.

Suki poured me another cup of tea. "Not exactly." She leaned over to grab the phone, which was on the floor near me, and started dialing before I had time to protest. After two rings, a male voice answered. Suki spoke rapidly in Japanese. The only word I recognized was my name. She asked me if I was free that evening. I nodded. After just thirty seconds more of conversation, she hung up, slamming down the receiver in triumph.

"Done," she said. "You're going to meet Mr. Matsumoto at a restaurant. He said to please order dinner."

"What have I just agreed to?" I asked.

"You're going to be just fine," she said. "Trust me. He's going to like you."

The waiter at L'Italiano Restaurant showed me to a booth and gave me a menu all in Japanese. The place was empty except for a guy and three women, all about my age, two booths over. The women stared at me and giggled, hands covering their mouths. Was the sheer blouse Suki lent me too revealing? Did the blush she applied to my cheeks make me appear clown-like? I turned the menu over, hoping to find photos. I skimmed the room for those wax models of plates of food I'd read about. But there was nothing to give me a hint about what to order.

The guy from the group sidled over. "You want spaghetti?" he asked kindly.

"Is there anything else on the menu?" I pictured red sauce running down my chin.

"Mostly spaghetti. You want spaghetti and meatballs. It number six." He pointed to the appropriate place on the menu. I thanked him.

When the waiter returned, I ordered the number six and a coke, which arrived quickly. Anxious to be finished, I gobbled down my meal, even though the sauce was overly sweet. Soon, a short, solid Japanese man with black, slicked-back hair approached. He wore a long-sleeved blue shirt and a striped tie.

"Miss Falwell?" he asked with just a hint of an accent. He held out his hand to me, and I stood up to shake it. As I did so, he looked me up and down, not in a lascivious way, but as though he were buying a horse at market.

He ordered a cup of coffee and cut to the chase. He explained that working conditions were "outstanding" and that my hours would be from 8:00 p.m. to 2:00 a.m. every night but Sunday. The pay was ¥7000 a night plus bonuses. Less than $200 a week. Since I hadn't found a place to stay yet, I wasn't sure whether that would cover my expenses or not.

"You got something else to wear?" he asked.

"Just a long skirt," I said.

"Not a problem. We have a couple of dresses at the Club fit you nice."

I opened my mouth to thank him, but Mr. Matsumoto kept speaking.

"Now your name. I don't like it. Dee Dee sounds like baby talk."

"How about Dorothy?" I suggested reluctantly.

"Doloti?" He laughed, showing his two gold teeth. With the addition of a bandana, he'd look like a pirate. "That's how all my Japanese customers will say your name." Then his brow wrinkled in thought. "I know. Let's call you Gina, like my favorite actress, Gina Lollobrigida, born on your country's Independence Day. Very sophisticated name. Easy to say. In Japanese, Gina means 'silvery.' Okeydoke?"

"I guess." I hadn't even agreed to the job yet, and Mr. Matsumoto was already managing my life and changing my name.

Again, he stared at me, narrowing his eyes. "How old are you?"

"Twenty-three. Almost twenty-four."

"Say you're twenty. Japanese like young ladies. Makes them feel young, too. You start tonight."

The four people who'd been sitting near me strolled past. The smallest of the women was wearing a Chicago Cubs baseball cap, except Chicago was spelled "Chickago." She turned, caught my eye, and said something to her friends. As they headed toward the door, I heard their laughter.

I shifted in my seat. "I need to think about your kind offer."

"What's to think about?" Mr. Matsumoto set down his cup and smiled a closed-lipped smile. "I give you a good job. You don't want it, I give it to someone else."

I couldn't argue with his logic at that moment. "All right. I'll take it. But not tonight. I have to be back at the youth hostel by ten o'clock."

Mr. Matsumoto shrugged. "No big deal. You work and then sleep tonight in the room above the Club. For free."

The waiter brought the check. Mr. Matsumoto reached for it.

"Tomorrow would be better," I said.

"I need you this evening. I pay you in advance." He took out his wallet and removed ¥7000.

I eyed the crisp bills. "I don't even have a toothbrush with me."

Mr. Matsumoto shrugged again. "We have toothbrushes. Everything you need."

What did I have to lose? Just a night out of my life. The next morning was Saturday. This would be just another adventure. I nodded my consent.

"Okeydoke. And, Gina, you can call me Chief from now on." He gave me a big grin.

After about a half hour's drive, we arrived in Wakoshi and pulled up in front of a wooden house with no signs to indicate it was a club or any other kind of establishment. We entered an unlocked door and climbed a narrow staircase to a large room. An empty floor covered in straw mats, like at Suki's, and a closet lining one wall were its only features. Chief opened the sliding doors of the closet. Hanging on one side were half a dozen of the most hideous frocks I'd ever seen, with garish colors, frills, sequins, and gathers in strange places. They looked like costumes from a failed Broadway musical about prostitutes. From this assortment, he retrieved a simple yellow brocade shift and held it against me. Other than the color, which I was certain would make my skin appear jaundiced, the dress was the least offensive of the lot. He then opened the other side of the closet to reveal the bedding and left me alone to change. The shift fit too snugly and rode up my thighs. My navy-blue pumps looked all wrong with the dress, but they were all I had.

I slinked downstairs. The main room of the Club was dark. It held an odd assortment of furnishings: a faded blue sofa, a booth with cracked plastic cushions, and two Formica tables with mismatched chairs. The low-pile, charcoal-gray carpet, worn in spots, bunched up around the furniture legs. An old jukebox stood in one corner, and a scratched metal Coca-Cola sign served as the only wall decoration. A mirrored disco ball hung down from the ceiling, serving no purpose since the lighting was too poor to allow it to flash. The room reeked of stale smoke and beer.

As I was surveying this sorry scene, Chief appeared, holding a large knife in one hand. I shivered. He gave me the once-over.

"Ah, Gina. I need you to wash some glasses. Customers will be here soon."

I heaved a sigh of relief and followed him into the kitchen. Where the main room had merely been dowdy and in bad taste, the kitchen, a narrow galley behind the main room, was a hellhole. The stench of forgotten leftovers made me gag. Dirty dishes crusted with remnants of meals overflowed the sink. Chicken bones, wrappers, lemon rinds, and empty bottles dotted the limited counter space. An overturned beer bottle had leaked its contents down the side of the cupboards, leaving a sticky trail in its wake.

I located a soiled, stiff cloth, peeking out from under a saucepan on the stove. A large black roach popped out, and I leapt back, hitting the counter and knocking a teetering glass to the linoleum floor, where it smashed into pieces.

Chief rushed in. "What's the matter?" he snapped.

I pointed to the shards and apologized. He handed me a broom. "Be more careful," he said, seemingly oblivious to the kitchen ecology, which could not be disturbed without upsetting its delicate balance.

I heard the front door open.

"Chief! I have arrived," boomed a loud, brassy female voice with an American accent. "You can rest easy now."

Chief snatched the broom from me and shooed me into the main room. There stood a tall, fleshy woman, with a head of curly platinum blond hair and a cigarette dangling from her bright pink lips. She was dressed in a long, green flowing chiffon top, with matching loose-fitting satin trousers.

"Aren't you a cutie," she said when she noticed me. "I'm Berta, the reliable." Then she shouted, "Got that, Chief?" She blew a big smoke ring in his direction and returned her attention to me.

"Hi, I'm Dee…uh, Gina. I'm Gina," I said. I'd almost blown my cover. "It's nice to meet you. I assume you're one of the hostesses?"

"Bet your ass. Numero uno. They love me more than those scrawny Asian chicks. I got something they can hang on to." She grabbed her substantial rear end and wiggled. "And at least I show up," she added, again loudly.

From the kitchen Chief yelled, "Pipe down, Berta. You'll scare Gina."

"You new at this?" Berta asked. She took a large drag from her cigarette, tapped the long ash in the nearest ashtray just as it was about to fall, and stubbed out the butt.

"Kind of," I said. "I've done a little waitressing."

"This ain't waitressing, honey. This is sucking up to a bunch of horny dudes who'd love to get into your little gaijin panties." If I was on the runway after the scene in the kitchen, I was ready to take flight now.

"Don't mind me, honey." Her voice softened. "I just had a difficult day. You'll be fine. Just watch me. I've been doing this for years."

Wow, I thought. *I'd shoot myself if I had to be in a place like this for long.*

Another hostess came in shortly. She was stick thin, with sunken cheeks and Asian features. I couldn't tell how old she was. Berta exchanged a few words with her in Japanese and introduced her as Hana. Hana bowed her head and giggled. She slithered into the kitchen.

"His favorite," she said, rolling her eyes and snorting. "She's the 'head' girl." She pulled a small gold case from a cavernous green purse that matched her outfit, removed another cigarette, and lit it with a jewel-encrusted lighter.

"You speak Japanese?" I asked, hoping to take my mind off of my growing anxiety.

"Not if I can help it. My daughter, Penny, thinks in Japanese."

"How old is she?"

"Fifteen. The little bitch is the reason I'm here," she said, not bothering to remove the cigarette from her mouth. Smoke escaped in puffs as she spoke. "I got knocked up by an air force officer about to be stationed in Japan and followed him. My mistake."

"So, you live on the base?"

"Not anymore. That whoring bastard left us nine years ago to rot on our own."

"Why didn't you go back to the States?" I asked, intrigued that in three days I'd met three Americans who'd made Japan their permanent home.

"Penny likes it here. You want something to drink? I'm parched. We could be waiting all night for someone to show up at this dump."

Berta, Hana, and I sat in the booth and talked, with Berta translating when it suited her. She and Hana both knocked back a few shot glasses of a clear liquid while I sipped my coke.

At nine thirty the doorbell finally rang. Chief, who'd stayed hidden in the kitchen, answered it and ushered in three Japanese men in dark business suits. They looked like the bankers.

"Tambuki-san," Chief said to the shortest, but most handsome of the three, a note of reverence permeating each syllable. He bowed low, holding the posture for what seemed like ages. "Sansui-san. Yakumasei-san," he said to the others, giving them each a more perfunctory bow, which was returned.

"*Irasshaimase!*" Berta and Hana said simultaneously as they rose from their seats. I also stood up.

Tambuki-san bowed. "Ah, Miss Berta, Miss Hana, good evening," he said in carefully enunciated English. He walked over to the table, took Berta's puffy hand, and kissed it. "Don't you look radiant tonight?"

Berta patted her coarse hair, which in the low light had a green tinge. Now I could see it was a wig. "Tambuki-san. You are such a flirt. You look pretty good yourself."

Indeed, his suit, made of an expensive-looking charcoal-gray textured cloth, fit as though it were made for him. A crisp white shirt, a tie with a delicate geometrical design, and gleaming black shoes completed the ensemble—seemingly effortless in its perfection. His features were symmetrical, and his smooth black hair was flecked with gray, especially near the temples. Although not tall, he held himself erect. The only odd thing about him was his lack of expression. The stereotypical word *inscrutable* came to mind. I was no expert at flirting, but a flirt, he wasn't.

"Meet our new girl, Gina," Berta continued, pushing me forward. "Gina, this is Mr. Tambuki. He's an important businessman."

Mr. Tambuki bent very slightly at the waist, a bow of mild acknowledgment. I hesitated a moment and bowed back.

"Miss Gina. Lovely," he said. In contrast to his previous blank look, his eyes widened ever so briefly, and a trace of a smile flitted across his lips. Mr. Tambuki nodded to the other men, who were talking to Chief.

"These are my associates, Mr. Yakumasei and Mr. Sansui." More bowing. Mr. Sansui was clearly the youngest. Plainer than Mr. Tambuki, with thinning hair and crooked teeth, his eyes bulged under the thick lenses of his black-framed glasses. Whereas Mr. Sansui's appearance was almost comical, Mr. Yakumasei's pockmarked face was bordering on frightening. A lumbering older man, his shirt strained to stay buttoned over his paunch.

Chief whisked up our half-full glasses and retreated to the kitchen.

"Gina, you show Mr. Yakumasei a pleasant time," Mr. Tambuki said. I cringed.

We all squeezed in the booth after much deliberation about who should sit where. I was wedged into the corner with Mr. Yakumasei's substantial girth pressing into my side. Hana immediately lit Mr. Sansui's cigarette. Berta, who took the desirable end seat, wandered over to the jukebox. Chief emerged with a whiskey bottle, ice, three glasses, and a bowl of green pods. Mr. Yakumasei gestured to me and pointed to the bottle. I noticed then that a part of his little finger was missing. I had to try not to show my revulsion although every fiber of my being longed to escape.

"Gina, Mr. Yakumasei would like to buy you a drink. Would you care for a whiskey?" Mr. Tambuki asked.

"Oh, thank you. I'll have a coke." After watching my father handle his problems by drinking too much, I associated alcohol with weakness. In college, I got drunk once on some dreadful purple punch to see how it would feel. The evening ended with me making out with a guy I barely knew and then couldn't face later. I also felt like shit the next day.

"Mr. Yakumasei wants to buy you a *real* drink," Mr. Tambuki said, as though he were a teacher correcting my grammar. Mr. Yakumasei hadn't spoken a word. Chief hovered, shifting from foot to foot.

"How about a vodka and orange juice?" I ventured, hoping that would pass the test. Maybe the orange juice would cut the impact of the alcohol. Berta filled the men's glasses with ice, whiskey, and a little water. In a few minutes Chief returned with my vodka and orange juice and two more glasses of the clear liquid for Berta and Hana. Mr. Tambuki gave another order to Chief in Japanese.

"A toast to our gracious hostesses." Mr. Tambuki turned back to us and raised his glass. "*Kampai.*"

"*Kampai!*" we all said.

Mr. Yakumasei tossed back his drink in one go, and Hana refilled it.

"And a toast to our distinguished guests," Berta said. "*Kampai!*"

Mr. Yakumasei muttered something in Japanese, and everyone nodded and laughed, except me. I looked at Berta quizzically.

Mr. Tambuki said matter-of-factly, "Mr. Yakumasei compliments your beautiful breasts."

"He said, 'Beautiful *big* breasts,' honey. Mr. Tambuki is editing," Berta said. "Tell him, '*honto?*' It means 'really?'"

My face felt hot. "*Honto?*" I said, my eyes lowered. I couldn't look at him.

Mr. Yakumasei said something else.

Berta translated. "He wants to know whether all American women have such big breasts." Berta spoke in Japanese to the men and cupped her own large breasts. Mr. Yakumasei and Mr. Sansui guffawed; Mr. Tambuki emitted one brief chuckle. Mr. Yakumasei then reached across the table toward Berta's right bosom, looking at Mr. Tambuki and Mr. Sansui as he did so. Berta smacked his wrist playfully.

Mr. Sansui gestured at Hana and contributed something to this inane conversation.

Berta translated again. "He said, 'In contrast, Hana's breasts are like ping-pong balls, like a child's.'"

I thought it inappropriate to call attention to the small size of her bust, but apparently, no one else did, even Hana. She giggled and brought Mr. Sansui's hand to her breast. He snatched his hand away, as though the breast were a living monster, and said a few words to the men. More laughter.

"He said, 'Maybe she has a big vagina instead.'" Berta blew a puff of smoke at Mr. Sansui and poured Mr. Yakumasei his third whiskey. Mr. Tambuki still nursed his first drink.

This intimate talk confused me; I concentrated on my vodka and orange juice. When I glanced up, I saw Mr. Tambuki observing me. I realized then that although he had joined briefly in the laughter, he had contributed nothing to the crude conversation other than a translation, which he delivered as though reading an article from the newspaper.

Chief brought out a plate of chicken legs and some French fries. The men left most of it for us to eat. Hana didn't touch any of it. After chowing down a couple of the legs, Berta hopped up to choose another song on the jukebox, "Brown Sugar" by the Rolling Stones. She gestured to me to join her on the dance floor, and I was relieved to leave the confines of the booth. Mr. Yakumasei extricated himself and barreled toward the restroom. Berta swayed her considerable hips, and I did some modest gyrating.

"Get used to the trash talk, honey," Berta said. "It doesn't mean anything. You can't let it get to you." The brass was temporarily absent from her voice. I nodded and gave myself over to the dancing. I was almost having a good time. The others watched and clapped. We returned to the booth, breathless.

"Very charming," Mr. Tambuki said.

When a slow song came on, Hana and Mr. Sansui got up and danced. He held her close, his eyes shut, his cheek against hers. Berta, who swigged one drink after another, and Mr. Tambuki talked in Japanese despite her earlier protests about using the language. Every so often, he would gaze at me, always expressionless. Everyone chain-smoked, except for Mr. Tambuki, who'd take a puff or two before stubbing out his cigarette. Chief placed a small, noisy fan in the corner, but it only chased the stench around the room.

Faint from the fetid air and achy from being wedged against the wall by Mr. Yakumasei, I wasn't sure how much more I could take. Chief brought out a new bottle of whiskey and instructed me to refresh everyone's glass. Because of my awkward pouring angle, some of the liquid spilled onto Mr. Yakumasei's lap. He seemed too drunk to care, but I let out an "Oh, God." Chief, who was heading back to the kitchen, dashed back and barked at me to dance with Mr. Yakumasei while he cleaned up.

Mr. Yakumasei had trouble standing up, much less supporting himself on his two feet. He hovered over the table while I slid out and then he staggered after me. On the dance floor, his large arms encircled me in a boa constrictor's grip. We swayed to the music, and he loudly whispered in my ear, "Gi-na. Gi-na. Gi-na," while groping my rear end. When he planted an oily kiss on my neck, I stiffened. Stone-faced, Chief watched us for a couple of minutes before returning once more to the kitchen. Mr. Yakumasei lost his balance, which had been tentative at best, pushing me onto a table and almost collapsing on top of me. Somehow, I managed to disentangle myself and get us both back to the booth. Chief reemerged with coffee. The evening came to an end not long after. It was only eleven o'clock, but it felt like the middle of the night.

After final bows, Mr. Tambuki said something to Chief. I thought I heard my name. Then, he turned to me. "I will see you again, Gina." It sounded like an order, not a statement of hope or even intent.

Hana and I picked up the cups and glasses and wiped down the tables. Berta was now minimally functional and let us do most of the work.

"How you doin'?" she slurred.

"Mr. Yakumasei was slobbering all over me."

"Yeah, he's more of a pig than some. Most of them are all bark."

"And he doesn't speak a word of English," I replied, realizing that was a silly thing to say. After all, I was in Japan.

"If you're lucky, they'll use the few words of English they remember from grade school." Berta took one last swig from her glass before Hana removed it.

"Mr. Tambuki was quite fluent."

"The exception in this boondockland."

"He seems different from the others, and he's kind of cute for an older guy."

"You can have him. They all look the same to me." Her eyes were at half-mast.

"You seemed to be enjoying his company."

"Pffff," she said. "He's Mr. Tambuki. Whaddya going to do?"

I had no idea what she meant, and I didn't ask her to elaborate, given her state. Chief had to shake her when it was time to lock up. He didn't say anything to me.

I slipped upstairs to the refuge of the futon, which I pulled from the cupboard and fell on after yanking off my clothes. I knew I couldn't do that job another night. Besides, it was hardly something I could include on my resume. Surely, I could find other ways of making money that didn't involve drunken men.

CHAPTER THREE

I didn't wake up until after noon, and I couldn't wait to leave the Club. There was no shower, just a tiled toilet hole and small sink on the first floor, the same facilities the clients used. I put on my navy suit and my two-day-old underwear. As I walked downstairs, I heard someone rustling in the kitchen. I ducked into the bathroom first. It smelled of piss, and the floor was sticky. I splashed my face with cold water.

When I emerged, I almost ran into a young woman wearing a thigh-length turquoise blue cotton robe tied with a matching sash. She headed into the main Club room, holding a plate of rice, vegetables, and some kind of meat.

"Oh, hello! You're new, aren't you?" she asked in accented English. With her free hand, she pushed her long sun-streaked hair away from her face.

She plopped down at a table in the Club, the ashtray still brimming with cigarette stubs, and shoveled vegetables in her mouth with a pair of chopsticks.

"I was just here for one night," I said, still standing.

"Oh, you're not working for Chief?" She looked up from her food, her chopsticks two elongated pincers poised in the air, still grasping their prey. Her large green eyes, rimmed with dark liner, and her violet-shaded lids gave her the appearance of an alert, nocturnal animal, even though it was daytime.

"Oh, no," I said, perhaps a little too quickly. "I'm here on a banking internship."

"I haven't heard that one before. You're from America, aren't you?"

I nodded. "And you're from?"

"Australia. I'm Victoria."

"Dee Dee." I eyed her full plate.

"Say, are you hungry? I have way too much food here." She laid her chopsticks down.

"That's okay."

"No, really. If I eat all this, I'll get fat." Victoria dashed to the kitchen and returned with another plate and, much to my relief, a fork. "You're not vegetarian, are you?"

I shook my head. My first night home after my freshman year at college, I consumed only the mashed potatoes and canned peas on my plate, leaving the meat loaf with its slimy gravy untouched. Bad idea. My mother yelled at me that if that was what they were teaching me at college, maybe I shouldn't be allowed to return. I shut up and ate the damn meat loaf. I vowed that one day I would eat whatever I wanted.

"I was a vegetarian when I was in India, with cows being sacred and all, but here it's just easier not to be too fussy." Victoria slid food from her plate onto the second one, which she placed across from her seat.

"Thank you." Grateful for the friendly attention, I sat down. "You were in India?"

"Among other places. Let's see, Singapore, Malaysia, Indonesia, Thailand, Burma, Nepal, Vietnam, Hong Kong, and now here." Before settling into her chair, she paused to count on her fingers. "Ten months total."

"That's a long time to be moving around." I put a hunk of chicken in my mouth. It was a little dry.

"Not really. Lots of my friends from Australia do this after school. I'll stay here a while and then maybe go back to India and camp at the beach in Goa. Perhaps America after that."

"Are you planning on college?"

"No, I just want to get married and have a family."

How could someone who seemed so adventurous be so conventional at heart? She reminded me of my sister Carol, who at sixteen used to sneak out at night and cruise around with her boyfriend in his convertible. Two years later, barely a year after Robert died, she married a guy who took over his father's Oldsmobile dealership and settled into her life of church suppers, PTA, kids' soccer games, country club membership—the whole nine yards of boring, suburban life. I guess she was happy. We weren't that close.

But I could make polite conversation with Victoria in exchange for the meal. "Are you working for Chief?"

"At his wife's Snack, two towns over. Today is my last day."

"What was it like working for Chief?" I asked.

"It was fun."

Fun? "You didn't find the men rude?"

"Nah. Nothing ever happened I couldn't handle. In Singapore, I worked for an escort service. That was more of a nail-biter."

"An escort service?" I once saw a notice for an escort service in a men's magazine that someone's boyfriend left in our dorm lounge. "Luscious ladies. All shapes and sizes, all nationalities." We all had a laugh. We couldn't imagine what kind of low-life woman would sign up for what surely was a cover for a prostitution ring. Now my face must have shown my surprise.

"It's not what you're thinking. You just sit in a room with other women, and if a guy chooses you, you go out to dinner and maybe dancing with him." She bit her upper lip. "Some of the blokes tried to get sex for free. But mostly, it wasn't so bad. I've met kids here doing all kinds of things."

"Oh?" I asked, leaning forward.

"Yah, I had a friend who worked in a no-panty coffee shop here in Tokyo." Victoria looked around like she was making sure no one else was listening. "They have mirrored tables, so the blokes can see the girls' private parts, and then they get so hot and bothered, they have to be jerked off in special booths in the back of the shop." She shook her head.

"Wow." I couldn't believe what I was hearing, but I felt intrigued, like the time I found a copy of *Peyton Place* stashed at the back of my parents' bookshelf. I was twelve. My parents, who professed to be so religious and made me go to church, owned dirty books. Reading it by flashlight under the covers at night, I was both horrified and titillated. It was the first graphic description of sex I ever read.

Victoria concentrated on her rice and then glanced up at me. "One of the blokes she met set her up with her own apartment, so she didn't have to work there anymore."

"Like his mistress?"

Victoria gripped a piece of chicken between her chopsticks and nibbled at it. "I hadn't thought of it like that. Here we are, so far away, and no one knows us. We can do whatever we want and make money however we want to make it. It's not the same as at home. The rules don't apply." Victoria abandoned the chicken and stood up. "I'm going to make myself some tea. Want some?"

"Sure," I said. I needed something to wash down all her perplexing comments.

She picked up the plates and left the room.

The rules don't apply? I wondered. *Doesn't everyone have a personal moral code? Okay, sometimes we regret our bad decisions, like mine in taking this horrible job. But that indicates our moral code is still working.*

Victoria returned with two chipped mugs without handles. She checked the large clock on the wall with the cracked face. It was one o'clock. "Oh, God. I've got to be somewhere at two." She chugged her entire mug of steaming tea and dashed up the stairs.

"Thanks for the meal," I called out. I took a sip of my tea, which seared the roof of my mouth. I poured the rest of it down the kitchen sink.

It was almost two thirty by the time I returned to the youth hostel. I wanted to phone Suki and yell at her, "How could you send me into this lion's den?" But she didn't know me. Maybe she thought she was doing me a favor.

As I entered the hostel, I saw Gabe in the lounge reading a book and puffing on the remains of a cigarette. He blew out a cloud of smoke and looked up. "The prodigal banker has returned. Excuse me if it's not my business, but where have you been?"

"I've been to hell and back, thanks to you and your friend Suki," I said, exaggerating for effect. But secretly I was glad to see him.

"I can see that," he said, checking out my rumpled suit. "Do you want to tell me about it?"

I was relieved to have at least one temporary friend. "Maybe after I take a shower and reenter civilization."

"I'm planning on going to a tea ceremony later. Want to come along?" He closed his book without marking his place.

"I thought you didn't approve of Americans studying tea ceremony."

"I'm not studying it. I'm experiencing it. They're very soothing. This one is supposed to be the real deal." He took a last drag on his cigarette and extinguished it in a green ceramic ashtray, the only remotely artful object in the place. "Anyhow, you can't be in Japan and not go to a tea ceremony. It's good for a cultural adaptability point."

"I think I've earned a boatload of points in the last twenty-four hours, thank you very much."

He nodded as though he knew what I'd been through. "You can tell me all about it after the ceremony. You need to be in a calm state of mind, and it seems like talking about whatever you went through might get you in a state of agita. Am I right?"

"Agita?"

"Agitation." He patted my hand. "It's okay."

Of course he was right, but I was bursting to tell him.

The tea ceremony Gabe took me to was offered by a school that taught the "art of *chado*," as they called it. A young woman in a cream-colored kimono ushered the dozen guests into a small teahouse inside a neatly landscaped garden. Gabe and I were the only Westerners. The room was unfurnished except for a simple flower arrangement. The woman kneeled and leaned back on her feet. We all copied her position. My pants felt too tight. After bowing, our host, a bespectacled man in a plain sea-green kimono, also kneeled. A tray of implements covered in a purple silk cloth rested in front of him. I watched him wash a bowl, ladle, scoop, and whisk, even though all appeared to be clean. My attention drifted through the following painstakingly precise and slow ritual of the tea preparation. My thighs ached, and my feet became numb. I looked over at Gabe, who was perfectly still. When I was finally offered an opportunity to sip from the communal bowl, I almost spit out the bitter tea. But I managed to swallow it and wipe the rim as had been demonstrated. Even the little sweets we were served didn't remove the unpleasant taste.

After it was all over, I stood up and massaged my legs. My circulation returned. Gabe waited patiently, not saying anything.

"Did you actually enjoy that?" I asked.

"Enjoy is the wrong word. I feel spiritually clean. Don't you?"

I shook my head. "To each his own. I don't think I'll be doing that again, but thanks for the opportunity."

"One and a half points. I've given you a bonus half point," Gabe said. "Now we'll go have some fun."

I was dubious. And I was tired. I looked at my watch. It was only six o'clock.

He smiled that dimpled smile of his, and I gave in. "Okay. But just for a while."

First, when I told him I'd never tried sushi, Gabe took me to a small, brightly lit *sushiya* with four small wooden tables. He ordered in Japanese. Behind a low glass barrier, the sushi chef deftly sliced fish and shaped rice balls. Gabe urged me to try a deep-red piece he said was tuna. When the morsel slipped from my chopsticks and fell to my plate, Gabe demonstrated how to use them properly, grasping the top chopstick between his thumb and index finger and bracing his other fingers against the bottom chopstick to hold it steady. Then he mixed some of the spicy green wasabi with soy sauce on a small dish. He dipped the sushi in this concoction, swiftly bringing the fish to his mouth. "Don't think, just do it," he said.

The next time, I was more successful, even with him watching me.

"Do you like it?" he asked. I nodded. A little soy sauce seeped from the corner of my mouth as I chewed. Gabe caught it with his finger and laughed.

After the sushi, we went to a place Gabe called a "coffee house," although it seemed more like a bar. The tabletops were sawed-off, shellacked tree trunks. We sank into giant velvet cushions on the floor. A thick cloud settled around us even before Gabe lit up another cigarette. I realized I wouldn't get very far in Japan if I couldn't tolerate a little smoke.

"Want some saké?" Gabe asked.

"I'd rather have a coke, but I'll try it to see what it's like." I didn't want to seem like a complete drip, and I had managed to stay in control after the vodka and orange juice of the previous evening.

Gabe gave the young man dressed all in black our order and turned back to me.

The saké arrived in a small carafe. Gabe poured the warm liquid into two tiny cups. "*Kampai!*" he said as he raised his cup.

I raised my cup as well. "*Kampai.*" I took a tiny sip. It was not unpleasant.

"So, spill," he said and sat back, his arms crossed over his chest.

I explained how Suki had gotten the ball rolling. Then I gave him an abridged, somewhat sanitized version of my evening, mentioning the key players and the basic flow of activity. I included one interesting detail to get his reaction. "One of the customers was missing part of a finger."

Gabe leaned forward, his eyes widening. "He could have been a yakuza. Now I'm really impressed."

"Yakuza—like a gangster?" I flinched. I remembered how Hiro had described them as bad men.

"Yeah. If they do something to upset their bosses, they cut off part of a finger as an apology." Gabe made a slicing gesture.

"Yikes! Now you've really got me freaked out. Thanks a bunch."

"You don't want to mess with them. But it's no big deal. I hear they come into the clubs all the time. They even own some of them."

"It doesn't matter. I'm not going back."

"Why not? Didn't you tell me that this was worth a shitload of cultural adaptability points? Isn't that why you're here?"

I took a larger swallow of the saké. "I'm here for a banking internship."

He shook his head. "That's just your cover. Like teaching is for me."

"That's not what you want to be doing?" I asked.

"It's good for now."

"Oh?" Was I the only foreigner in Tokyo with aspirations?

"You sound like you don't approve."

Once again, I had to rein in my judgmental side. "No. It's just different from the way I think. I need to know where I'm going."

"I used to make big plans," he said, turning serious. "But I learned that life is short, so why not take some chances and see what happens? My dad taught me that."

I downed the rest of the saké in my cup, letting its gentle heat flow through me. "How did he do that?" Taking chances for my parents meant trying a different brand of coffee.

Gabe was silent a moment. "My father had a delicatessen with big barrels of pickles. He always smelled of brine no matter how hard he scrubbed his hands. I loved that smell. Still do." Gabe's face lit up. "Sometimes, when I was small, I would help him at the shop, and he'd let me choose three cookies from a big stoneware jar he kept on the counter. Always three."

He paused and refilled both of our cups. Outside a siren screamed.

"Except for the day of my mother's funeral. I was ten," he continued. "The deli was closed that day, but dad led me by the hand through the back, took the lid off the cookie jar, and told me to help myself. I chose three cookies, as I'd always done." Gabe pantomimed laying out three cookies. "Dad upturned the jar. A whole mess of cookies tumbled out. I'd never seen him eat his own cookies before, but we both sat there shoving them into our mouths until we were beyond stuffed."

I teared up.

Gabe rested his warm hand on my arm. "It's not meant to be a sad story. It's about doing what feels right at the moment. Anyhow, my dad had the good grace to wait to die until two days after I graduated from college. I had a bad draft number, so I took off for Canada before coming here."

"Oh, I am sorry, Gabe."

"Because I was a draft dodger, or because my folks died prematurely?"

I shrugged, tears flowing more freely now.

"It's okay." Gabe removed his hand from my arm and refilled my empty glass. "My parents loved me, and they loved each other. Not everyone is so lucky. And President Carter gave me amnesty, so everything is fine." He eyed me as though he knew I was hiding something.

If my parents loved me now, they had a funny way of show-ing it. They treated me more like their ward from one of those nineteenth-century British novels than their flesh and blood child. Born so many years after my brother and sister, I figured I'd been an accident, and not a happy one at that. "Do you ever miss home?" I asked. I swilled the entire glass.

"This is home now," he said, gesturing to the room in general.

I looked around at the other customers. One couple about our age was sharing a dessert. At another table, three men were drink-ing coffee. All had straight jet-black hair and almond-shaped eyes. "You don't mind being different from everyone around you?"

"I like being different. In New York they thought I was a nutcase. Here I'm excused because I'm a gaijin, even though I'm fluent in Japanese. I can be more me than I ever was in New York, or less me if I want. It doesn't matter."

I felt light-headed now and not entirely in control of what I was saying. "So, back in Kyoto, does the gaijin have a girlfriend?"

"I have lots of girlfriends. I'm very popular with the local ladies. At least in the bars, where they treat me like royalty." He gave my hand a quick squeeze. "But no, no one special at the moment. Why? Do you want to be my girlfriend? You're a bit GU." The flip Gabe I'd met yesterday was back in action.

"GU?" My cheeks felt warm. I could picture them as red as two beets.

"Geographically undesirable. I live in Kyoto—you're in Tokyo. It could get costly. Plus, I'm not really into phone sex." Gabe cocked his head. "How about you? Boyfriend back home?"

I laughed nervously, thinking of Mark. I shook my head.

"So, you left with a clean slate? Ready to take on someone new."

"I don't think so. I'm going to be too busy for a relationship."

"Don't give us so much credit. Some of us only want sex." Gabe grinned. "I'm not talking about myself, of course. But it has been said about the male species."

"So I've heard. But I've decided to be celibate on this trip. Much easier." Was he flirting with me? I didn't mind, but I was tired. I looked at my watch. It was close to midnight. "Gabe, I really have to get to bed."

"I'll resist the temptation to comment on that remark."

We walked back to the hostel holding hands. Gabe's completely covered mine. When we arrived at the grated door, he pulled me around to an unlocked back entrance near the garbage dump.

"I have to catch an early train, so I probably won't see you," he said.

Then he kissed me. And I kissed him back with the smell of yesterday's food as our backdrop. It was more a sweet kiss than a passionate one. But that was as far as it went.

As we parted to go to our separate dorm rooms, Gabe said, "Remember, Dorothy, you're not in Joliet anymore. But the yellow brick road is waiting. Japan is your Oz. Maybe think about going back to the Club?"

"I will," I lied.

"And Dee Dee, give yourself a couple of cultural adaptability points for tonight. You were a trooper, hanging out with me."

"Thanks for showing me your Tokyo," I said, sad to see him go. He was as close to home as I would probably get in the next few months and as far away as I could imagine.

CHAPTER FOUR

The next day, which was Sunday, I had to search for a place to stay for the next few months. I spread out my Tokyo map on the coffee table in the lounge. On one side the tangle of colored subway lines resembled a complicated circuit board. On the other, the impossibly sprawling city, pocked with names all ending in vowels, spilled off the edges of the paper. Shinjuku. Bukyoku. Minatoku. I called a bunch of hostels and boarding houses that sounded reasonable, but no dice. Several didn't even answer their phones. One didn't understand me.

I felt panic setting in, but I wasn't ready to give up. I thought of Suki. Didn't she owe me one?

When I phoned her, I was surprised that she sounded angry. "Chief told me that you didn't show up last night on his busiest night of the week. He's really pissed at *me* now."

I guessed I hadn't thought that I'd get her in trouble. I was so eager to forget the whole episode, I'd focused only on my own feelings. I apologized and explained how I couldn't go back, how I couldn't even pour drinks correctly, didn't know the language, and couldn't stand the overbearing and rude customers.

"Yes, Chief said you seemed like you were in over your head. But he's still willing to try you out again. At his wife's Snack. It's less formal."

"He still wants me back? He behaved like he thought I was useless."

"One of his other gaijin girls just quit."

I remembered Victoria telling me she worked at the Snack and was leaving. How cavalier she was about the whole job. "Suki, I don't know." I twisted the phone cord around my finger.

"There must have been something about you he liked, that he thought his customers would like."

Maybe it was the big boobs. Men were the same everywhere. "At the moment I need to find a place to stay."

"Chief lets his hostesses stay in one of the rooms over the Club. With the other girl gone, there's a vacancy. It's simple, but it's comfortable enough."

"Yeah, I know. I stayed there Friday night."

"Okay. Then can I tell him you'll be back tomorrow? They're closed on Sunday."

I wondered why this was so important to her. Was she scared of Chief? "I'll have to think about it."

"Can you come on over now, and we can discuss it further? I know it's hard to talk about an important decision over the phone."

I felt cornered but not quite ready to cave in.

"Have you been to an *ofuro*—the public bath?" she continued. "You might find it interesting, and it's very relaxing."

In my situation, I had every right to be anxious. A part of me resented her interference. But I was desperate, so I agreed.

The bath building, which was around the corner from Suki's, looked from the front like any other building on the street. If any signs existed, they were too small to be noticeable. Maybe you just had to know.

After paying a small fee in the lobby, we entered the locker room to undress. I didn't normally mind getting naked among other women, but I hesitated in this unfamiliar environment. Suki wasn't at all self-conscious. As she stripped, I noticed a yellowing bruise on her upper arm. I peeled off my clothes, placed them in a basket, and locked up my shoes as instructed.

The actual bath room was steamy with many faucets low to the ground. Several older Japanese women with drooping breasts and sagging skin were seated on tiny stools, soaping themselves up and rinsing. We sat down on stools, too, and I copied their actions, trying to act as though I'd been doing it all my life.

After we hosed ourselves down, Suki led me to the first of three pool-like tiled tubs. She told me that each one was progressively hotter. I eased halfway into the scalding water, wondering how anyone could tolerate the higher temperatures in the other tubs.

Suki fully immersed herself without hesitation. "So how can I make you feel better about this job?"

I blurted out. "Is Chief yakuza?"

"Chief? Oh, heavens, no. Is that what's worrying you?"

I splashed some of the hot water onto my arms. If she wasn't scared of Chief, then why was she trying to talk me into this job? "I hear that gangsters come into the bars all the time. Is that true?"

"Who told you that?" She looked me right in the eye. "It's perfectly safe. Really."

I guess I wanted to believe her. I finally dunked down so that water covered my shoulders. We stayed there for a few minutes, just breathing in the steam. I felt my muscles untangle.

"I just don't know if I can behave in such a phony way," I said. "Berta was flattering these guys, and she doesn't even like them."

"All the men want is a few sweet words. Don't you see?" Suki sounded impatient. "They don't hear those kinds of things from their wives. It's why they come there—to be in another world for a while."

I wasn't quite ready to feel sympathy for these guys, but I did understand that they might be lonely. I knew all about not getting what you needed at home. About feeling neglected and longing for something else.

Suki rose up from the tub, water dripping off her body, and entered the second tub. I followed. It was searingly hot, but I didn't want to appear cowardly. This time, I plunged in as quickly as I could.

"Have you ever been in a play?" she asked.

"In the sixth grade, I was Aunt Em in *The Wizard of Oz*." I thought I would be chosen to be Dorothy, as seemed only fitting, but the part went to a freckle-faced redhead.

"Just pretend you are Dee Dee, the starving actress, playing the role of Gina, the darling of the club scene. It's your chance of a lifetime."

"A drama or a comedy?" I tried to make light of the situation.

"Whichever you choose. Have some fun with it. What do you have to lose?"

"My dignity? My membership in the National Organization of Women?" I wasn't actually a member of NOW, but I did believe women had the right to be treated civilly.

"It's just a paycheck, and it's just for a little while."

My skin was bright pink when we emerged from the second tub, and my knees buckled. Thank God Suki didn't suggest going into the third tub. I was fairly certain I couldn't stand the heat.

Back in her apartment, after we drank our tea, Suki fished in a cupboard and returned with a set of cassette tapes, a portable tape player with earphones, a Japanese-language textbook, and a Japanese-English dictionary.

"Learn a bunch of words and forget about the grammar. What you hear in the clubs from the men isn't the way you, as a woman, would speak in polite society anyway."

"I'll say. All that talk about breasts. It's so juvenile." I recalled the compliment about my own pair. I'd been embarrassed, but also flattered.

"It's just a piece of their ritual."

"What if I made fun of their private parts?"

"Oh, don't ever do that. It ruins the illusion. But you could say, 'You are so manly. You must have a very big penis.'" Suki laughed. "I can teach you that. You'll be surprised at how little you need to know to get along. We can practice together, too, if you want."

"That's nice of you. I'm just not sure." I felt I was being railroaded again.

She was silent for a minute and clenched her jaw. Then she said, "There aren't a lot of options for evening work for foreigners. Do what you have to do. But take these anyway. You can use them in your internship." She popped the books, tapes, and tape recorder into a green shopping bag and thrust it into my hand. "Let me know what you decide."

I thought I saw a flash of fear in her eyes. Maybe in my own tentative state, I imagined it, but it unnerved me.

On Monday, I was back at my internship. Mr. Yamaguchi gave me another stack of background reading. He said he'd be tied up in "confidential" meetings all day. He told me that I could leave when I'd finished as he didn't have anything else for me until I was more familiar with bank operations. The reading consisted of an out-of-date textbook and photocopies of some cases from the *Harvard Business Review* that I'd read in my graduate course. I completed the reading by lunchtime.

I was disappointed that there wasn't more to do, but perhaps it was for the best. The clock was ticking, and I needed to find another place to stay by tomorrow night.

When I left the bank, I wandered around the streets in the Ginza with its fancy shops and restaurants. I spied a handsome leather briefcase in the window of one of the department stores. I wanted that briefcase, but I knew it was beyond my means.

I thought about my main goal—to have a successful internship. I should be welcoming any opportunity to let me realize that goal. I remembered that one semester in college, I wanted to take six courses because a favorite professor was leaving, and I wouldn't have the chance to study with him again. My advisor eased my worry about the load by saying, "It's only a few months out of your life." I survived and did well. That same mantra would work for me again. If things were occasionally uncomfortable, I would weather them. With some money and a roof over my head, I could enjoy some of what Japan had to offer, couldn't I? Working at the Snack would buy me time. I could always quit when I found something better.

I found a phone and called Chief. He was curt with me but said he'd give me another chance. He told me that he was closing the Club for a while but that his wife could use me at her Snack. When I asked about it, he offered me a room above the Club, as Suki had mentioned. He said he'd leave the door of the Club unlocked for me, pick me up at six o'clock, and take me to the Snack.

I returned to the department store and bought a box lunch in the basement cafeteria. After taking a seat at a table in the corner, with my back to the room, I opened the container. I swiftly snapped apart the pair of chopsticks without breaking them, speared an unidentifiable bite-sized chunk with the end of one of the chopsticks, and wolfed it down.

After lunch, I returned to my hostel, checked out, and took the train to the Club to drop off my things and change.

But as I pulled the smelly brocade dress over my head, a pulsating knot that began in my stomach expanded into my other organs, pushing down on my bladder and weighing on my lungs. A roach as large as a small mouse flitted by my bare feet, its legs rustling against the tatami-matted floor as it headed for the door. I couldn't even bring myself to unpack.

At six o'clock sharp, I heard the front door open and someone tear up the stairs. Chief burst into my room without knocking.

"Are you ready, Gina?"

I nodded and followed him downstairs to his sedan. A crate

of dead chickens, plucked and headless, but with their feet still in place, lay on the back seat. I shuddered.

Chief and I didn't speak on the thirty-minute ride. He glared at the road, driving so fast I had to clutch the seat. I guessed he was mad, but I didn't know what to say to him. Finally, we stopped on a semi-commercial street. Unlike the Club, which was nameless and furtively situated among private residences, the Snack announced itself with a blue neon sign, blinking HAPPY SNACK.

We entered through a glass door. Inside, sunlight poured in through a large window. Nearby, a jukebox, like the one in the Club, glinted and cast a long shadow across the spotless linoleum floor. More than a dozen red leatherette stools surrounded a Formica-topped, horseshoe-shaped bar. It looked almost like the diner we used to go to in Joliet, where my dad took me on my fifth birthday for a root beer float. I remember how special I felt sitting high up on a stool and, unbeknownst to my mother, eating forbidden foods. After Robert died, he never did that again.

A tiny, attractive woman, a cloth in her hand, emerged from a door in the back. She wore a kimono with delicate pink flowers on a beige background and a wide sash in a deeper shade of pink.

"This is Mama-san," Chief said, the first words he'd uttered since picking me up. "The Snack is her place. You will do what she asks." He turned to her. "Mama-san, this is Gina."

Mama-san smiled and bowed her head demurely, hands clasped in front of her. White makeup covered her face. Her chestnut brown hair, pulled back tightly into a bun, stretched the skin of her cheeks. I smiled, too, and bowed my head. Mama-san pointed a finger at me, and said, "Pretty." It was the only English word she would ever utter. Despite being unsure about the job, I was glad I had her approval. I wanted to restart on a positive note. Then she said something to me in Japanese.

Chief translated. "Mama-san said, 'Welcome to her Snack.' She said you will like it here. Nice young people like you." Hulking his crate of chickens, he retreated to the kitchen, where he'd stay put all evening. The front of the house was Mama-san's roost.

She took me by the hand and led me inside the horseshoe bar. There she pointed to the two mainstays of the place and named them for me: *bieru* and *uisuki*. Beer and whiskey. Then she handed me the cloth and made a circular motion on the counter to show me what she wanted me to do. As I began wiping, Berta sidled in. She wore another flowing outfit—this one in bright turquoise, its embroidered edge woven with golden thread.

"Shit! I was wondering what happened to you. So, they persuaded you to work here for peanuts, huh?" She threw her purse on a stool.

"Peanuts?"

"And I ain't talking about the food, honey. This low-class joint don't pay the big bucks of the Club." Berta snorted and took a drag on her ever-present cigarette.

"Oh?" Chief hadn't mentioned any reduction in my salary.

"Yeah. But never mind. You won't get bored here, and there is this nice little barrier between you and any loose-pawed drunks." Berta gave the counter a fond pat.

Business was light for the first hour. Mama-san presided at one end of the counter, guarding a glass of a clear white liquid, which Berta explained to me was schnapps. She asked Hana to refill it from time to time. Customers paid their respects to her there and sometimes engaged her in conversation. She seemed at home in this role.

I watched Berta masterfully open beer bottles and pour them so there wasn't too much of a head. Around ten o'clock, three young guys wearing khakis and open-necked shirts came in and sat near us. They asked for *bieru*. Berta scooped up three bottles from a big barrel filled with ice. After uncapping them, she gave me one. I held the glass at an angle so the beer didn't foam up and served it to the one with a shock of hair slicing across his face and covering one eye. He pointed to me.

"You drink?" he asked. I looked to Berta for guidance, remembering Friday night's awkward exchange on the same issue.

"He wants to buy you a drink," Berta explained. The customer nodded. "You get a bonus for each drink they buy you. Instead of tips. Then they get the pleasure of your company."

"*Arigato-go-zi-mas*," I said to the guy, attempting my first Japanese "thank you." I bowed my head. He seemed delighted and elbowed his friends, who were yakking to each other.

"You speak Japanese?" he asked.

"A few words." On the subway I'd listened to one of the tapes Suki had given me. "My name is Gina." If I said it often enough, maybe it wouldn't sound so alien to me.

Berta magically placed a drink in front of me. "Vodka and orange juice," she announced. And aside to me, she said, "That way One Eye will know you're getting a *real* drink."

One Eye smiled approvingly, and he and his buddies raised their glasses to us, laughing.

One of his friends, who wore a mustard yellow T-shirt with the dubious slogan "Lick My Hot Dog," inserted some coins in the jukebox. Patti LaBelle belted out "Lady Marmalade." The guys laughed again. I must have blushed, thinking they were being suggestive, particularly given the T-shirt.

"Relax. They have no idea that song is about a prostitute. They're just having a good time." Berta, soberer than the other night, was clearly watching out for me.

Licker asked me if I wanted to dance. Berta nodded to me. The Snack had no real dance floor, but there was a small space in front of the jukebox. We did some chaste swaying; he kept his distance. Then, he picked up a microphone attached to a box with speakers and handed it to me. "You sing!"

I shook my head. I was strictly a shower singer, where the noise of the water disguised my voice.

"Gi-na. Gi-na. Gi-na," the three guys chimed in chorus.

Berta hustled to the floor and yanked the microphone from Licker's hand. "What do you know, honey?"

"How about Frank Sinatra?" I asked, figuring that would be Berta's speed. My parents had a giant record collection. I was weaned on Sinatra, Perry Como, and Nat King Cole.

"Good choice. We'll do 'I Did It My Way.' Cue up the karaoke!"

Of course, I didn't have a clue how to operate this strange machine, but Licker came to the rescue.

Berta, as it turned out, had a damn good voice—she was full-throated and could keep a tune. She pretty much drowned me out, but at least it looked like I was trying. The boys at the bar clapped and hooted.

Then the third guy, who hadn't said much up to this point, rose from his stool. After laying his wire-rimmed glasses on the counter, he ran his fingers through his hair until it fell over his forehead and undid two more buttons of his blue Oxford shirt, revealing some of his hairless chest. His friends egged him on. "El-vis. El-vis. El-vis." I began to see the resemblance now. He headed over to the karaoke machine. Clutching the microphone with both hands, he closed his eyes and began singing "All Shook Up," word perfect, with only a hint of an accent, complete with hip thrusting, appropriate pouts and sneers, and the occasional wink at me. The other customers gave him a wild round of applause. He bowed and headed back to his stool, where he smoothed his hair back, put on his glasses, and buttoned up his shirt all the way to the top. The only lingering signs of his performance were his pink face and the light sweat on his brow.

"Wow. That was great. The King." I loved Elvis. My friends were singing "Hey, Jude" and "Love Child" while I raided Carol's old 45s for Elvis's original hits. His sultry voice filled me with nostalgia for a time I didn't know, a time of bobby sox and poodle skirts, where "going all the way" was something a girl didn't do lightly. Yet, the Elvis I knew best was the sexy man with the black leather jacket, the "comeback" Elvis of 1968, the year I turned ten. I sensed something very forbidden about that Elvis.

Licker and One Eye nudged this Baby Elvis and guffawed.

He cast his eyes down, his shyness returning. "*Bieru*, Gina?"

I fetched him another beer. He pointed to the item he wanted on the menu card and said "shrimp" in Japanese. I repeated the word and walked over to the kitchen counter.

"Chief! *Ko-ebi!*"

More clapping. With their limited English vocabulary and my few new words of Japanese, the guys and I pieced together a primitive conversation. We cheered after each successfully understood phrase as though we were scoring goals at a soccer match. Berta kept our glasses filled.

After a while, Mama-san rose shakily from the stool where she'd been firmly rooted. She led me by the hand to a well-dressed older woman, the first female customer I'd seen in the Snack all evening. The woman pointed to her whiskey bottle in the tall cabinet in the center of the bar. Berta had already shown me that some customers purchased entire bottles of whiskey for their future consumption. We marked their names on them in black magic marker, and they sat in a row like library books waiting to be checked out. I stood on tiptoe and reached for her bottle. When I poured her a glass, she made a motion to let me know I should have one, too, so I gave myself a small shot. She patted my hand and raised her glass to her lips. I raised mine. The whiskey burned a little. I sipped it slowly. We drank in a comfortable silence, two women acknowledging each other in this man's world.

Eventually, I had to leave her to serve other customers. She pressed some bills into my hand. I squirreled the money into the small pocket of my dress. I felt buzzed now but more confident. Although almost everything I did was a cause for others' amusement, I didn't mind. The occasional reference to breasts seemed less threatening in this brighter, livelier environment. And no one slobbered on me that night.

By 1:30 a.m., the last customer had left. Mama-san's head lolled on the counter, a dreamy smile lighting her face. Hana wiped down the countertop while Chief lined up clean glasses on the small ledge of the window that separated the kitchen from the bar. They clinked against one another as he wedged them in. He barked at us to put them back in the cabinet. Berta stuck her tongue out at Chief as he disappeared from our view. I stifled a giggle, and we both restocked the shelves with glasses.

"You did okay tonight," she said.

"Yeah. That wasn't so bad." The Snack had a nice rhythm to it and seemed to attract a largely innocent crowd. I was feeling good and remarkably in control given the amount of alcohol I'd consumed.

When all the glasses were clean, and we had swabbed down the counters and the floor, Chief emerged from the kitchen, drying his hands on a towel. "I take you home now."

At the Club, he handed me a small packet of bills. "Buy yourself some new shoes, Gina."

CHAPTER FIVE

The next morning my alarm screamed at me at what seemed like an ungodly hour. My head throbbed, and my throat felt dry. I washed down a couple of aspirin with some flat soda water from the fridge. I had to rush to figure out the trains and still make it to the bank by nine o'clock.

When I arrived at the thirty-ninth floor, one of the bank officers greeted me. "Miss Falwell, I am afraid that Mr. Yamaguchi is not in today."

"Is he ill?"

"I do not know," he said.

"Is there someone else I can work with today?" I asked.

"I think not. Come back tomorrow. That is best." He turned on his heel and trotted away.

I thought it strange that Mr. Yamaguchi hadn't made other arrangements for me in his absence. Maybe he didn't want to burden anyone else with his American intern.

With my head still thumping, I wasn't entirely sorry to have the day away from the navy-suited men and the robot women.

"Shoe shopping it is," Suki said after I showed up on her doorstep and gave her a rundown of my life the last couple of days, including Chief's last order. "I don't know about you. But shopping always gets my mind off my woes."

Now that I had some money in my pocket, I warmed to the idea. And Suki knew shoes. She encouraged me to try on at least two dozen pairs. A pair of silver open-toe sandals was surprisingly comfortable given the outrageous height of their heels.

"Silver shoes, and I don't even have to kill a wicked witch to get them." I giggled. In the mirror, I admired the way they made my calves look shapelier.

"What?"

"Dorothy in *The Wizard of Oz.* When her house lands on the Wicked Witch of the West, the Good Witch tells her to take the dead witch's silver slippers."

"Weren't those shoes ruby-colored?" Suki asked, as she stroked a thigh-high leather boot with a three-inch platform.

"Only in the movie version." I twirled around.

Suki nodded her approval. "Silver shoes for the silvery Gina."

The shoes were an extravagant price, but Suki convinced me they would be a sound investment for my evening job. She said that more men would buy me drinks and that would mean more money for me. We also each had makeovers at a cosmetic counter, and I ended up buying mascara, a set of eye shadows, and two new shades of lipstick.

I was conflicted about using my sexuality to line my pocketbook. But I wasn't doing anything illegal or even unethical. Besides, it was all play acting, wasn't it?

When Chief picked me up that evening, he didn't comment on my makeup job, the more revealing full-skirted dress with a stretch sequined top I'd chosen from the Broadway wardrobe, or my new shoes. But Mama-san cooed approvingly when I arrived at the Snack. She put me to work refilling the napkin holders. Berta sashayed in about ten minutes later wearing a bright fuchsia outfit. Accompanying her was a big-busted teenage girl with short butterscotch-blond hair that encircled her round face. She had on tight blue jeans, a T-shirt that said, "Let it all hang out," and about a gallon of eye makeup. What she lacked in beauty, she made up for in confidence. They stopped near the jukebox, not acknowledging me.

"You got any cigs, Ma?"

Berta reached into her bag, pulled out a cigarette, and popped one in her own mouth, as though she were the defiant child. "Why should I support your unhealthy habits? Get your own fucking cigarettes, Penny."

From the cavern of her large bag, Berta unearthed her jewel-encrusted lighter, lit up, and took a long drag, blowing the smoke in her daughter's face. This was a routine that had clearly played itself out before.

"Mu-ther! You're setting a bad example."

Berta relented and gave Penny a cigarette. She even gave her a light and then headed in my direction.

"Come meet my new co-conspirator," Berta said over her shoulder to Penny, who gripped the sides of the jukebox, her eyes scanning the song selections.

Penny didn't budge. Berta marched over and guided her to the counter by jabbing her hot pink nails into the small of Penny's back.

Penny rolled her eyes. "Geez, Mom. I'm not a puppet."

When they reached me, I put out my hand for Penny to shake. "Hi, I'm Gina."

"You don't have to be formal with the kid," Berta said.

Penny shook my hand vigorously and stuck her tongue out at her mother. She leaned over the counter, her ample boobs brushing the surface. Ash hung from her cigarette and fell off onto the clean Formica.

"Hi, I'm Penny. Cool dress. Can I borrow that sometime?"

"It's already borrowed, I'm afraid," I said.

"Then one more borrower won't matter, will it?"

Berta joined me behind the counter. "See? Uncontrollable." Then she pursed her lips and emitted a breathy wolf whistle. "Look at you all dolled up. Hoping for some hot action?"

I half expected that reaction from Berta, and I was determined not to get embarrassed.

"I think you look nice," Penny said before I had a chance to respond to Berta.

Berta took out her wallet and removed several bills. "Go get yourself some dinner, and don't go over to the barracks tonight. I'm warning you. I'll smack your hide off if I hear you've been over there again."

Penny snatched the money from her mother and headed back to the jukebox. She inserted a coin. As the invitation in French to sleep with "Lady Marmalade" boomed out at top volume, she waltzed out. I wiped the ash off the counter.

"I know she's fooling around with some army fellow," Berta said.

I opened my eyes wide. Even though some of my friends at Catholic school were sort of slutty, I didn't have sex until I was twenty and just finishing up my senior year of college. This friend of mine, a smooth-cheeked kid from Milwaukee Technical College, also wanted to shed himself of his burdensome virginity. By then everyone seemed to be doing it. The first time was awkward and not very satisfying, but it did the trick. By the time I met Mark a couple of guys later, I didn't feel quite so new at it. "Uh, isn't she kind of underage?" I assumed that messing around with a teenager was illegal in the army.

Berta shrugged. "Chip off the old block. But I swear I'll disown her if she gets knocked up."

Even though it was only Tuesday, the crowd kept us busy. One batch of guys, already drunk when they staggered in, were a handful. Only one of them spoke even minimal English. He had to translate everything I said to the others. The other two kept glancing at me and laughing.

Berta came to the rescue. "You stupid, provincial idiots!"

"I don't think they understand you," I said.

"Yeah, they're too stupid."

Apparently, they knew that word and hurled what I assumed were insults in Japanese. They met their match in Berta, who continued sparring.

"No, she doesn't speak Japanese. She has better things to do with her time, like get an education, which is something you drunken farts wouldn't know about." She said this in English for my benefit, followed by a Japanese translation, I guessed.

Berta kept whisking away our drinks when they were only half empty and filling them again. The men would be obliged to pay, and they wouldn't complain about the bill, Berta explained later. Eventually, one of them apologized.

"I thought we were supposed to cater to the customers," I said.

"That's your job. Mine is to let them know who's boss. Anyway, they love it, and I feel a helluva lot better. Don't you?"

When Chief took me back to the Club that night, he asked me. "The Snack is good, yes? Lots of young customers, like you. Many tips from drinks."

"Yes. It's fine." I had only a two-night sample, but so far, it felt manageable under the bright lights. Even tonight's crowd seemed tame in comparison to my experience at the Club.

"Mama-san says you do well with customers."

"Thank you," I mumbled. Since Mama-san seemed nonfunctional after nine o'clock, I wasn't sure what her judgment was based on.

"You will stay, then? I need reliable girls."

"Yes. Sure."

"Okeydoke." Chief nodded. "All settled." As I opened the car door, he added, "Wear those shoes again, Gina."

I felt pleased to have Chief's approval. With a secure job, now I could walk up that yellow brick road to my dream.

But the next morning my yellow brick road ran smack into a wall. I donned my business suit, gulped my yogurt standing over the filthy kitchen sink, and caught the commuter train into town. This time I was greeted by another bank officer, a younger man, whom I remembered from one of our meetings because he seemed more junior than some of the others. He wore his hair parted in the middle.

"Miss Falwell, I have been asked to tell you that Mr. Yamaguchi has been transferred to our Dubai office. He will not need your services anymore."

"I don't understand," I began. "He didn't say anything about this to me last week. Is there anyone else I can work with?"

"I am afraid not. Mr. Yamaguchi did not leave further instructions and apologizes for the inconvenience. It was beyond his control."

My face grew hot, and my breathing quickened. "Yes, this is inconvenient. This internship is very important to me. I would appreciate it if you could refer me to someone more senior who can help me." My voice edged on hysteria, but I was proud of myself for not taking this man's word that nothing could be done.

"Again, I am most sorry. I will see what I can do," he said.

"Thank you. I will wait here," I said, hoping that my persistence would pay off.

"I am most sorry, but I cannot do anything right now."

"Then I will come back tomorrow."

"If you wish," he said. "I will do my best." But he didn't sound convincing.

When I left the bank, I felt at a loss. I bought a cocoa at a coffee bar. I had no idea what to make of what had happened. Why hadn't Mr. Yamaguchi contacted me himself? Of course, he didn't know my phone number, and perhaps he was urgently needed abroad. But wouldn't he have made an effort to take care of any loose ends? Either he was incompetent, or he didn't want to strap his colleagues with me, the foreign girl. But I didn't plan on being a burden. I wanted to be useful. I was smart. They would have seen that if I had been given a chance.

I thought of phoning Suki, but she knew nothing of banking.

Instead, I walked back to the subway station. As I crossed through a small park, I heard clapping and noticed a group of people surrounding two boys in white judo outfits with black belts. As I moved in to have a look, I recognized one of the boys as Hiro, my rescuer from the subway. I was happy to see another familiar face.

His companion held up a sizeable wood plank. Hiro frowned in concentration and then gave the plank a sharp whack. It broke into two pieces. A gasp from the crowd and from me and then clapping. Hiro bowed several times.

After his demonstration, the crowd dispersed. I approached. When he saw me, he beamed. "Dee Dee. Yankee. How nice to see you. Big surprise."

He remembered me. "Yes, for me, too. That was spectacular what you just did."

"Spectacular?"

"Amazing, fantastic, terrific." I mustered up various synonyms that described his feat.

"Oh. Thank you. Just practice. Where you go now?" He eyed my suit.

"Nowhere." I had no plans, and I felt unmoored.

"I know places you never find on own. Real Japan places." His English, which was somewhat better than the variety I was hearing at the Snack, tumbled out.

We spent a couple of hours walking around, with Hiro pointing things out and naming them for me in Japanese, and me repeating them, like an obedient schoolgirl.

As we passed a restaurant, he asked, "You eat *tonkatsu*?"

"What is *tonkatsu*?" I asked.

"Very good stuff. Meat stuff. You will like. We go tonight?"

"I have to work tonight," I confessed.

"What kind of place you work at night?"

"I'm a hostess at a snack," I said, making a point of looking at him directly.

"A nice snack?" He sounded horrified as though I had just told him I murdered babies for a living.

"Nice enough." I cast my eyes to the ground.

Sensing that I might have crossed some line with my revelation, I decided I wouldn't describe brassy Berta, drunken Mama-san, or some of the rude customers. I didn't need to.

"Not good job. Bad people. Drink too much. Not behave."

"It's okay. I can handle myself." I tried to sound confident, but I felt bruised by the disappearance of my internship.

"Bad ladies work there, too. Ladies see mans. Mans pay money."

"Prostitutes?" Surely not Berta, but Hana? It hadn't crossed my mind.

He nodded. "You need help, you call me anytime. Anytime! Yes?"

I wondered whether I gave off some damsel in distress vibe that inspired Hiro's bravado, but at least I didn't feel he was judging me. He asked if we could get together again on Sunday, my day off, and I agreed. He was sweet, and seeing him had cheered me up. As we said goodbye, he shook my hand. His fingers were chubby, like a child's.

When I went to work at the Snack that evening, I chose a third dress from my meager selection. It was a long floral print, not exactly me, but not completely preposterous either. Before any clients came in, Berta, in royal blue silk pants with a matching stole, draped herself over one of the stools on the client side. I thought I would get her take on Hiro's comments about our clientele.

"Your little friend got that right," she said. "All that seeming politeness gone when they're shitfaced. They can do or say anything and get away with it."

"Should I be worried?" I asked.

"Nah. They're like annoying bugs. Here's what you do." Berta flicked an imaginary insect off her arm.

Hana trundled in. I surveyed her with a fresh eye, although I didn't know what a prostitute was supposed to look like. Hana seemed perfectly normal, if a little more hard-edged than your average Japanese woman. Her limbs were angular, and her lips had small creases around them. But her dresses weren't any sexier than mine, and the male customers didn't treat her any differently than Berta or me. She wore expensive-looking jewelry sometimes, but it could have been paste for all I knew. I whispered to Berta, "My friend also said that prostitutes work in clubs. Is Hana a prostitute?"

Berta wasn't having any of it. "I mind my own business, honey. People do what they must do. But how sweet that your little guy wants to protect you."

I was about to protest when Mama-san appeared. She didn't like to see her staff idle, even when there was nothing to do. She shooed us with her hands to let us know we should at least appear to be doing something useful.

"Sorry bitch," Berta muttered.

As I cleaned up a beer spill behind the karaoke machine, the door chime jangled. Out of the corner of my eye, I saw a man, overdressed in a gray suit, enter the Snack. I stood up, clutching the wet ball of cloth. With his back to me, he positioned himself on a stool, owning it, yet seeming out of place. Mama-san took rare leave of her perch to greet him. "Gi-na. Gi-na," she sang out, her voice cracking, and beckoned me to come over.

The man turned around. It was Mr. Tambuki from my first night at the Club. Much to my surprise, my heart skipped a beat. Soiled cloth still in one hand, I smoothed my skirt with the other and approached him.

He stood up. "Gina. We meet again. You are looking lovelier than before."

I bowed slightly. "*Arigato*, Mr. Tambuki."

Mama-san smiled and took her leave.

"You remembered me. I am flattered. And you have learned some Japanese?"

I decided to play it cool, but I could feel the muscles in my stomach tense. "Yes, a little. What can I get for you?" I went behind the bar and dumped my cloth.

"Start me a bottle of whiskey." He sat down. "Get yourself a drink, too. A real drink." He winked at me.

I thanked him and fetched a fresh bottle of whiskey from the shelf. I wrote his name on it with a marker, poured a shot in two glasses, dropped in a couple of ice cubes, and added some water. I had to concentrate to keep my hand from shaking.

"I see you are drinking whiskey now. I like that in a woman."

My tongue stuck to the roof of my mouth. I took a swig. It burned less than before and rocketed warmth through my veins.

"We did not get to talk much before, I regret. You are American, yes?"

"Yes, I'm from the Chicago area."

"A very interesting city. I've been there often. So, what brings you here?"

"I could ask you the same, Mr. Tambuki." The whiskey was doing its work quickly.

"A clever answer. Very good. Perhaps we are just two people in search of something. Let us drink to that." Mr. Tambuki raised his glass, and we toasted each other.

I wanted to let Mr. Tambuki know I was more than a bar hostess. "I'm going to business school in the fall. I'm here for a banking internship, to get some experience in the international realm." It sounded good. Too bad it wasn't happening.

"I thought there might be more to your story. And which bank is it?"

"The American Bank of Tokyo."

"And what do they have you doing?" Mr. Tambuki took out a cigarette and held it expectantly. His question threw me off course, and I momentarily forgot my job. Magically, Berta passed her jeweled lighter to me. Mr. Tambuki curled his hand over mine to direct the flame. His fingers were warm but not sweaty. He sat back, took a puff, and studied me.

It took me a second to remember that he had just asked me something. "Well, it's unclear. It seems that my supervisor has been transferred to Dubai, and no one is available to take his place."

He blew a perfect smoke ring away from me. "Dubai. How unfortunate. And what will you do now?"

"I'm going to look for something else, I guess."

"I have connections. I may be able to help you." Mr. Tambuki took one more deep drag from his cigarette and stubbed it out. "But what do you want from this internship, as you call it?"

"I'm supposed to be acquiring something that Wharton— that's the school I'm going to—calls 'cultural adaptability.'" I wasn't sure I should be telling Mr. Tambuki all this, but if he could help me, I thought he had a right to know the details.

"And are you not acquiring 'cultural adaptability' from this job?"

"I don't think this is what they had in mind exactly. I believe they meant it in more of a business sense."

"Ah. Perhaps. But you should broaden your definition. Japan is a very complicated three-dimensional puzzle for outsiders. If you view it from one side, you will miss the other faces of it, yes?"

"I guess so. I've been in Japan just over a week. I've learned so much already," I said, wondering whether I sounded sincere.

"I can see that," he said without any sarcasm.

"Gi-na!" Mama-san called out from her perch. She held out her empty glass. As I refilled it with her schnapps, I heard the door chime again and saw Mr. Tambuki leave. He turned around and bowed slightly. I nodded. When I went back to where he'd been sitting, I found two ¥10,000 notes under his glass.

I didn't see Mr. Tambuki again for the rest of that week, but I felt more hopeful. I threw myself into cleaning up my new nest, as meager as it was—just my one room upstairs and the kitchen and toilet room that were both part of the Club downstairs. I tossed out all the garbage, including all the questionable contents of the fridge, washed the dishes, scrubbed the floor on my hands and knees, and polished the counters and sink until they were spotless. A black roach scuttled across the floor and disappeared under the stove. I wasn't fazed.

I also looked for another internship with renewed gusto. I vowed that each day I would dress in my business attire and visit at least three banks. But the first day, without specific names or an official appointment, I couldn't get past the guards at the front door of any of the banks. I worried that I didn't look professional enough. Later, I bought myself the expensive briefcase I had admired earlier, using up most of the money Mr. Tambuki had given me.

By Saturday, I felt discouraged, but the Snack was so busy, I didn't have time to feel sorry for myself. Chief drove me home at the end of the long evening. Mama-san slept in the back seat, with her mouth open, snoring gently.

"Gina, starting Monday, you need to go to the Snack on your own. Take the train to Shujiku and change for Chibaya train. Two stops. The Snack is just up the street past the market."

"Two trains?" I asked for confirmation.

"Easy trip. No problem. And Gina, be sure to come by six thirty. After-work crowd during the week." I hadn't noticed men trying to break the door down on a weekday. "Of course, I will take you home since it is late. Okeydoke?" How could I argue? I had a free room. If I had a long commute to work, so be it.

When we arrived, he leaned across me to open my door and then handed me a small brown envelope folded in half. "Your first week of pay. Many bonus points for drinks customers bought you." I thanked him and said goodbye.

At last I would see regular money coming in. I raced up the stairs and tore open the envelope, spilling the contents onto my futon. I counted out only ¥8000, all in ¥500 notes to make it look like more. I peered inside the envelope, but the only thing left was a folded piece of yellow paper with two neat columns of handwritten numbers. On the income side, ¥3500 a night for six nights, just half of what Chief had promised to pay me originally, plus ¥7000 for my one night at the Club and ¥4000 for bonus drinks, for a total of ¥32,000. But on the debit side, in red ink, the ¥7000 advance pay from my first night, ¥10,000 he'd given me for shoes, and to my horror, a weekly charge of ¥7000 for the room. I'd spent most of the cash I'd brought from the States, and this paltry ¥8000, just over thirty-five dollars, was supposed to cover my train trips and food for the week." With Berta's persistent help, I'd wangled twenty bonus drinks this past week. I wasn't sure I was capable of much more.

It was all carefully accounted for, but I'd been hoodwinked.

I could already picture Chief arguing that at ¥7000 a week the room was a bargain. It was true. I dropped to my knees on the futon and pummeled it a few times with my fists before slumping onto my back. I had no other prospects for an internship or paid work. In short, no negotiating power.

I didn't feel much like doing anything on Sunday, my day off. But I'd promised Hiro I'd meet him for *tonkatsu*. I hadn't talked to Suki since our shoe-buying day. Because she knew Chief, she might have some advice for me. She sounded happy to hear from me and suggested an ikebana exhibit.

The exhibit was held in the entrance hall of a small museum on two long tables covered in white cloth. The tables stood away from the wall so that visitors could see the displays from both sides. Rather than pots of assorted flowers crammed together in colorful bunches like my mother favored, the arrangements were often spare, with blossoms and leaves bent to the will of the artist.

I gave Suki an update on my internship situation and Chief's bait and switch. "I'm just so mad. At him. At the bankers."

"Try to stay calm," Suki said. "The Japanese don't like visible displays of emotion. If you keep your feelings under wrap, they'll listen to you better."

I was silent for a moment as I studied a series of arrangements featuring orange and purple birds-of-paradise. The first one looked like foxes' snouts. "How can I be calm when I've been so badly screwed? The Snack is a lot of work for so little money."

"Some of the girls have found other ways to make more money," she said.

"You mean by getting the customers to buy you drinks? I already do that."

"That's just small change. I meant Date Club."

I glanced at the next arrangement. The stems of the birds-of-paradise were entwined as though they were necking. "Date Club?"

"Yes. You get customers to take you to dinner first and then bring them to the Snack afterward. You have a nice dinner, and Chief will pay you for the time you miss plus another ¥3000 bonus."

"That's it?" I asked, suspecting it wasn't as simple as she described.

"Look pretty, laugh. These men just want an attractive, attentive woman on their arm. And a gaijin woman is prestigious. If you were working in a downtown club, it would be expected."

"How does one get these so-called dates?" I asked.

"Chief has a whole phone book of men who used to come to the Club. He'd love to get them to the Snack. I'm sure he'd be thrilled to give you their numbers."

I pictured Chief as a villain out of a Dickens novel, copying names from a leather-bound ledger, handing me a lengthy list, and gleefully ordering me to go forth into the night. "So, I have to do the asking?"

"Not necessarily. If someone from the Snack asks you out, that's legit. It can even lead to bigger things. That's how I met

Bento-san, my patron." Suki squeezed and rubbed her hands as though she had arthritis.

"You have a patron?" This was news to me, but it did explain how Suki was jobless yet still had a lovely apartment and nice clothes.

"That's what I call him. I go out with him regularly, and he helps me out. A lot."

My gaze landed on four strands of birds-of-paradise that appeared to be engaged in conversation, or maybe they were bickering. "And there are no strings?" I asked.

"Nothing of consequence."

"I don't know. Every time I think I've learned Gina's lines, someone adds some more to the script."

"At least think about it? I'm just trying to help you out here." Suki pulled out a delicate pink handkerchief from her pocket. She turned away from me and gently blew her nose.

"Sure." I didn't want to dismiss Suki's suggestion outright, but I was certain I wasn't about to phone men I didn't even know to see if they would go out with me. The nonsense at the Snack was bad enough without the expectations of a possibly lascivious man who had just bought me dinner. How would he behave when we were alone in his car? Or more to the point, how would he misbehave?

At least I felt safe with Hiro. His purity was a welcome contrast to the crudeness of some of my nighttime customers. As promised, he took me to a restaurant to eat *tonkatsu*, which turned out to be a batter-fried pork dish, edible enough, though greasy. He was as proud of the cuisine as though he had made it himself. I asked him about his studies.

"Not much to tell. I work hard, I pass, I go to Tokyo University. The best."

"You passed?" I asked, thinking I'd missed something. A piece of *tonkatsu* fell from my chopsticks. I was successful with them only when I didn't hesitate.

"No, not yet. Tests next month."

"I'm sure you'll pass, but what would happen if you don't?" Hiro clenched his fists.

I regretted the question the moment it escaped my lips.

"Must pass. Last chance. Must not disappoint mother. She wait long time for this."

I understood that sentiment, although I felt I'd lost that battle. "Aren't there other universities?"

"Not like Tokyo." Case closed. "You want to go to whiskey house? Many young people. Nice place."

The whiskey house was a dimly lit bar, with private booths of wood. The odd flash of neon imbued it with an air of unmemorable trendiness. Hiro had his own bottle of whiskey, with a little necklace around it marked with his name.

"Not like Snack?" Hiro asked.

I wasn't sure what the correct answer was. Was he hoping that he had brought me to a higher-class place than the Snack, or was he looking for assurance that the Snack was comparable in style? I was never a good liar, so I gave an ambiguous answer. "No, it's very different."

"Good. I show you the best. Next Sunday we go to Kamakura. Very beautiful."

Hiro accompanied me back to the Club. When we reached the door, he moved in a little closer.

"I would like to kiss you. Okay?" he asked.

"Oh." I was surprised at his forwardness, and I hadn't thought of him that way. "Okay."

He leaned forward and kissed me lightly on the lips. Then he placed his hands on my upper arms and kissed me with more confidence. It wasn't a sexy kiss, but it was soft and lingering, almost expert. He knew just when to pull back. I missed kissing. That had been one of Mark's strengths.

"Thank you. You make me happy," he said.

"I had a good time."

"Thank you." Hiro reached into his pocket and retrieved a small, exquisitely wrapped box, which he held in front of me. "Here, I want you to have."

I took the package. I unwrapped it slowly, respectful of its art-like quality and apprehensive about what was inside. It was a double-stranded bracelet of pink freshwater pearls, and it looked expensive. A personal gift. It was too much, too soon. "It's beautiful, but you shouldn't have."

"It go with your skin," Hiro said proudly, as though he'd taken a color chip to the store where he bought it. "I help put on."

He struggled with the clasp. When it was closed, he took my hand and admired my newly adorned wrist. My hand was clammy.

That night, I took the bracelet off, laid it carefully back in its box, and placed the box on a high shelf of my cupboard.

CHAPTER SIX

The following Tuesday evening started out slowly. I talked to Penny, who'd been mooning around, writing the name "Jimmy" on her hand with a pen, and then rubbing it out before Berta saw. She showed me a photo of a serious-looking black man in glasses and told me all about him. "He's the best," she said. I didn't think it was my place to lecture her about getting involved with an officer, who was not only married but who had a new baby on the way, so I just let her babble on.

Then Baby Elvis showed up by himself. I gave him a beer, poured myself a watered-down whiskey, and stood near him. He focused on his glass as though it were a crystal ball that would tell him what to say, glancing up at me with his long-lashed eyes. After a few minutes, he asked me what I did back home. When I told him in my fledgling Japanese that I was going to be a student of international business, he sat up straight. "*Parlez-vouz français?*" he asked.

I'd studied French for four years of high school, and although I was hardly fluent, my French sure beat my Japanese. "*Oui!*"

"*Une femme des affaires internationales,*" he said.

Of course, the literal translation of *affaires* was business, but I chuckled at the alternative translation, the double entendre he hadn't intended.

I wanted Baby Elvis to know that even in Japan I was not just a hostess, but a woman with ambition. I told him about my internship at the bank, about my long-term goals. He listened intently, nodded, and said he thought it was important for women to have careers outside the home. He explained his work in computers, although I am not sure I fully grasped the technical language in French. I also learned that he temporarily lived at home but was saving up for his own apartment, which he told me was very expensive in Tokyo. I told him about my family and how they didn't understand why I wanted to come to Japan.

"*Tu veux voir le monde? Choisir ton destin?*" He was excited now, and so was I.

"*Oui. C'est ça.*" He knew I was curious about the world and wanted to choose my own destiny. I was so thrilled to have someone here get my essence that I ignored his use of the familiar form of *you*. Since arriving, I'd made new friends, but except for Gabe, they knew little about me, even Suki.

I touched him on the arm to acknowledge the connection. He stared at my hand. "*Koepi?*" He ordered shrimp in Japanese.

As I pulled my hand away, I looked up to see Mr. Tambuki watching us. I didn't know how long he'd been standing there. I didn't remember hearing the little chime of the door as he entered. When our eyes met, he gave me an almost imperceptible bow. I nodded.

Mama-san, who had been in the back with her books, swooped in. "*Irasshaimase,* Tambuki-san." We never bothered with that greeting at the Snack. He took her hand and kissed it. I could see her blush beneath her white makeup. "Gi-na!" she snapped at me. "Tambuki-san! *Uisuki, ne?*"

"*Hai!*" I said, the sharp sound of that "yes" word making me feel like an enlisted soldier responding to the sergeant's bark.

I was happy to see Mr. Tambuki, if somewhat thrown off by his timing. He settled himself on a stool a few seats away from Baby Elvis. I ordered the shrimp for Baby Elvis, smiled, and wished him a good evening. He had to understand that I had a job to do.

Mr. Tambuki told me to fetch two glasses, and I poured us each a drink.

"Your boyfriend?" Mr. Tambuki asked, jerking his head toward Baby Elvis.

Hana had already taken my place and was laughing at something Baby Elvis said. I felt a small kernel of jealousy.

"Him? No, no. He's just another customer. We both speak French."

"Ah. A linguist."

"Hardly. But my French is better than my Japanese."

"So, Gina. I've been thinking about your two challenges—to be culturally adaptable, as you say, and to find a banking internship."

"I'm listening." While enjoyable, my brief conversation with Baby Elvis now seemed trivial.

"I need someone to accompany me on a business dinner tomorrow night with some guests. Entertaining is an important feature of business in Japan." In contrast to Baby Elvis, Mr. Tambuki looked directly at me as he was talking. "It is also the way to make contacts, which must be carefully tended to, over time, not all rush-rush as in America. Would you do me the honor?"

I couldn't believe my luck. I felt like a junior high school girl being asked to dance by the football captain.

"I will inform Chief, so he does not think I am stealing you away," he continued. "He will be fine with it."

"I'd be delighted."

"Excellent. And wear something special. This is not a time for dowdy business suits."

I pictured my wardrobe of hideous dresses. The brocade now needed cleaning badly, the sequined number was too gaudy, and the floral print wouldn't do for a business event. I would need something new. I'd have to borrow against my income, like buying a stock on margin, but the investment would more than pay for itself if the date were successful.

"Now as for your other concern," he continued. "I believe you need some fundamental grounding in one of the roots of Japanese personality and culture. The way of Zen."

"Zen. That's Buddhism, isn't it?"

"Yes, but it is so much more. It is a way of life, a way of seeing things, a way of being." Mr. Tambuki's eyes lit up for a second.

"Okay. How do I learn this?" I ran my fingers through my hair. It felt greasy.

"You cannot learn it from books. You need a master, a teacher. If you will permit me, I would like to be your teacher."

"Oh." I took a big slug of my drink to quell my rising excitement. "Thank you."

"We can work out the details later of how this will happen." Mr. Tambuki raised his glass. "*Kampai.*" Before I had a chance to hoist my own glass again, he took one sip out of his mostly full glass and left.

Later, Chief took Hana, Mama-san, and me out for a late-night sushi run. As Mama-san and Hana giggled and chatted with each other and downed their saké, Chief told me that he was pleased with my work at the Snack and knew he'd made the right decision in hiring me. I thanked him. He leaned forward as if about to share a secret.

"Gina, I have some good news. Mr. Tambuki asked me if you could accompany him to a special dinner meeting tomorrow. He is a very important person. This is an honor."

I decided to play it cool and not let Chief see that I shared his enthusiasm for this new development. I also wanted to let him know I was aware that this was a business proposition. "Oh. Suki told me you ran a date club. Would it be through that?"

Chief sucked in his breath as though he'd been found out. "Of course. All on the up and up. More money for you. Date Club pays well. All set, okeydoke?"

I knew this was not a question requiring a response, so I sipped my saké and let the good news sink in.

"And Gina, you bring him back to the Snack afterward. Okeydoke?"

The next morning, I woke up early, like a child anticipating a field trip. I caught the train downtown and spent at least two hours trying on dresses. Some of them were beyond my means, and unlike in the States where everything is perpetually on sale, nothing was marked down. I finally settled on a long black sleeveless dress, with a slit up to the knee on one side, a fitted bodice, and a scoop neckline that was sexy without being slutty. The dress hugged in all the right places and made me look taller and slimmer. It proclaimed elegance. My silver shoes seemed gaudy, so I bought some black slingbacks with spike heels. They felt comfortable as long as I didn't have to walk anywhere. To complete my outfit, I purchased a small black evening bag covered with tiny beads. My wallet was now empty of all the money I'd brought from home, but the effect was worth it.

Just prior to eight thirty, I changed in the back room of the Snack. When I made my entrance, complete with appropriately bright red lips, I noticed heads turning to gawk at me. Two guys whistled loudly. I was Eve, finally able to take over the part for which she'd been an understudy. I was Mata-Hari. I would make men weep.

"Wow," Berta exclaimed. "That's a fuck-me outfit."

"Oh, God, you think so?" I said, dismayed that maybe I had overdone it.

"No, doll, but it should net you a few extra yen. Just watch your tits don't fall out."

The guys watched this exchange with rapt interest.

"What are you looking at, you fucking morons?" Berta barked at them.

"Berta, they're paying customers," I said, pretending to be shocked.

"They don't have a clue what we're saying, do you boys?" she switched to her most flirtatious voice.

The guys were all smiles. One leaned forward. "Gina, I touch big breasts?"

I pulled away from him. His friends laughed. One of them pointed at me.

"You fuck?" he asked.

Berta chuckled. "I apologize. I guess they understood at least one word."

Mr. Tambuki arrived shortly after. When he saw me, he bowed but remained without expression. However, he said I looked lovely.

We drove off in a midsize black sedan. I thought he'd have a classier car, like a Mercedes, though it did have leather seats and his own driver.

The dinner took place in a private dining room with sliding paper doors and low tables. There were three Japanese men—Mr. Tambuki, Mr. Sansui, and a Mr. Muriachi, plus two American men, two Japanese women, and me. The women wore short cocktail dresses and chatted comfortably with the men. I wondered whether they were also in the banking business. It was hard to tell.

The meal was the best I'd eaten in Japan. A virtual army of waiters scuttled in and out, removing plates, bringing new dishes, and filling glasses and cups. The Japanese women giggled a lot. I was surprised at how relaxed I felt, especially since I drank only a little. Not that I worried that I would behave inappropriately with Mr. Tambuki.

The conversation at the table ranged between interesting and entertaining. Although no actual business was conducted, we did discuss the comparative states of the Japanese and American business climates. Mr. Tambuki told some amusing stories and skillfully navigated the conversation, even while translating, so that everyone had a chance to shine, including the other women. Occasionally, he would ask for my opinion, although never on any subject in which I might embarrass myself because of ignorance. At the end of the dinner, he invited everyone to a hostess bar in the Ginza and insisted that I come. The other women did not accompany us.

Bar Diana was a far cry from Chief's club or Mama-san's snack. Polished wood tables and velvet-cushioned chairs nestled in dark corners on a plum-colored carpet. Scrolls depicting scenes from nature—birds in flight, snowcapped mountains, and puffy flowers—decorated the walls. The Mama-san, in an intricately patterned kimono, greeted us at the door, complimented Mr. Tambuki in English, and led us to our own table. Three Japanese hostesses, dressed in floor-length gowns, joined us. Young men brought whiskey bottles, not the standard Suntory we served at the Snack, but single malts from Scotland. They placed these on the table along with crystal glasses and a silver ice bucket with tongs. The hostesses poured drinks and lit the Japanese men's cigarettes. The American men didn't smoke. Surprisingly, the hostesses were as attentive to me as they were to the male guests.

"You are so very lovely," said Nagomi, who was taking care of my needs. "Your hair is the color of new-mown hay. Your dress is like midnight. May I touch it?" Her English was flawless, poetic. Words gushed from her mouth.

"Thank you," I said. "Yes, you may touch it."

Nagomi stroked the bodice. "So shiny and smooth. You have such good taste. It must be very expensive."

"Your dress is also very beautiful," I said. It was a lovely shade of blue.

"This is just an old rag, not like yours. It did not cost half as much, I should think."

I would not be able to beat her at this game.

"And your dress makes your *breasts* look even bigger," Nagomi continued. "They are like two Mount Fujis." Apparently, it wasn't just the men who noted breasts. Like Pavlov's dog, one of the Americans turned my way, eyes quickly alighting on my chest as though he had somehow missed his cue earlier, and then resumed his conversation with his hostess.

"You must be very good at golf," his hostess said to him. "You have such strong-looking hands." And she patted the hand that wasn't holding the drink.

Nagomi focused on my untouched drink. "You do not like whiskey? You would perhaps like something else?"

"Whiskey is fine. I just like to drink slowly."

"I can get you anything you like. You must enjoy yourself in the company of these handsome men." Nagomi looked around to be sure that at least some of the men had heard this last compliment. "You are very lucky. But they also are lucky."

I glanced over at Mr. Tambuki, who was on the other side of the table, talking to one of the Americans, a Mr. Barker, and a hostess with Japanese features but ash-blond hair.

He gave me one of his half smiles. "Gina, have you tried the Glenfarclas whiskey? It is one of the best from Scotland. Do you know it?" I detected a slight slur to his speech.

"Yes, the Glenfarclas. The best," Nagomi echoed. "You deserve the best. Very expensive."

The conversation did not improve, but neither did it degenerate. If I was totally new to the culture, I might have expected Nagomi to proposition me. But I knew she was just doing her job.

At eleven o'clock, Mr. Tambuki rose from the table, steadying himself by holding on to its edge, and announced that regretfully he had other business to attend to and that Muriachi-san would assure that they continued to have an enjoyable time.

As he rounded the table, he said, "Gina, you need to come with me."

Nagomi crossed her hands over her chest and registered disappointment. After the obligatory bows, we left. When I returned to fetch my forgotten purse, Nagomi was already deep in conversation with Mr. Barker.

I assumed that Mr. Tambuki would take me back to the Snack as Chief had requested. We climbed into the back seat of the sedan.

"Ah, Gina, Gina, I am glad that we no longer have to do business."

"I didn't mind. That was much more interesting than I expected. Especially the dinner. I learned a lot."

"There is so much more I could teach you," he said. He put a hand lightly on my knee. His usually impassive face had softened, and the tip of his nose was a deep pink. "You are very sexy, you know."

"Thank you," I said. This time I was the expressionless one. Mr. Tambuki was obviously drunk. His hand moved to the slit in my dress and slithered under to find my leg. I noticed then that the car had pulled up in front of a three-story hotel. A large heart, with the word *Love* over it in English, flashed in red, green, and blue neon.

"Should we go in?" he asked politely.

"I'm not sure I understand," I replied. I full well understood, but I was confused by the turn of events.

"Oh, Gina. Of course you do. This is a 'love hotel.' You know what I want."

"This wasn't part of our deal, Mr. Tambuki."

"No, it's not part of the deal. I don't pay for sex. I thought you liked me." His hand, which had been lightly kneading my pantyhose covered flesh, now rested precariously close to my private parts.

I grabbed his fingers and removed them. "You are very good company, Mr. Tambuki, but I don't do this."

"Gina, you don't have to play hard to get with me." He lunged for me in a most ungentlemanly fashion, pulling me against his chest, and kissing me hard.

I struggled, but he maintained his hold. Finally, I pushed him away. "Please, Mr. Tambuki. Take me back to the Snack." I was shaking.

Mr. Tambuki released his hold and sat back in his seat. He straightened his tie and smoothed his hair back. "You surprise me, Gina."

"What on earth did I do to encourage you?"

"Look at that dress. Those shoes. Those breasts. What did Nagomi say? Like Mount Fuji."

Berta had been right about my fuck-me dress. "I just wanted to look nice for your engagement, so you would be proud to be with me."

"You have so much to learn about Japan. So much. I don't know if it can be done."

"You won't say anything about this to Chief, will you?"

Mr. Tambuki took a deep breath and stared straight ahead. "It is not his business."

He took me back to the Snack but did not come in, much to Chief's dismay. I covered for him, mostly to keep from hearing one of Chief's harangues. Before I started work, I changed back into my other outfit. I was feeling very let down. I trusted Mr. Tambuki, and he had proven himself to have no more class than the guys Berta and I had tussled with prior to my date. I had to remind myself that I was no worse off than I was before. I would just have to do it all myself now with no help.

When Sunday arrived, I looked forward to seeing Hiro, who had none of the rough edges of the barroom crowd, nor the unpredictability of Mr. Tambuki. He was taking me to Kamakura, a popular day trip out of Tokyo. The weather was initially very warm, and I wore a summer shift and sandals. Kamakura itself was more rural than I expected, but it was still difficult to avoid the crowds. We visited several of its temples, including one that was reachable by climbing up many steps. We decided to take a more difficult way down along a steep path. Hiro took my hand most of the way, guiding me around rocks. At one point, the path became very muddy. I hesitated, and Hiro scooped me up and carried me across the worst part. Suddenly, it began to pour. We dashed under a tree, but by then we were already drenched. My thin dress was clinging to me like saran wrap and was probably just as transparent. Hiro had a lightweight jacket with him that he put over our heads to keep the rain from falling on us through the branches. He pulled me in toward him, so we would benefit from the makeshift umbrella. The closeness of our wet bodies and the beauty of the rain on the green hillside made me feel happy.

We kissed, the water dripping from our hair and eyelashes to our lips. Hiro put his arms around me, leaving the jacket to balance on its own. It fell off onto the soggy ground, where we left it. His kisses were sweet, sensual, and salty and became deeper and more intense as we stood there embracing. He tentatively touched one of my breasts through my damp clothing and massaged my nipple until it was hard.

The rain subsided. I put on Hiro's now wet and dirty jacket to make myself more decent. Before returning to Tokyo, we stopped at the island of Enoshima, which was connected to the mainland by a long causeway. We wound our way around a maze of souvenir stalls and up escalators to the top of the mountain with a lovely view overlooking the sea. When we finally returned to Wakoshi, Hiro did not ask to come in, and I didn't invite him. We kissed one last time, now familiar with each other's mouths, and said goodnight.

As I lay in bed that night, I wondered what Hiro wanted from his relationship with a gaijin. And I wondered what I wanted when my time in Japan was so limited. Would Hiro read too much into it if we were to take the next step? I needed a brief primer on Japanese views on sex. I would consult Suki, who had become my go-to expert on most aspects of Japanese culture. Fortunately, we had tickets for a Bunraku show. I chuckled at the notion of discussing sex after seeing puppets, which I associated with children.

The puppets were unusually large marionettes, manipulated by three puppeteers. Two were dressed head to toe in black, but the main puppeteer was clearly visible. It created a fascinating effect where you alternated between being taken in by the realism of the lifelike puppets and being aware that someone else was carefully orchestrating all the action. The male narrator acted out all the parts. Another man accompanied him on an eerie-sounding string instrument. The story was about a blind man who commits suicide so as not to be a burden to his wife. In her despair at losing him, she also commits suicide. It had a happy ending, but only after one tale of woe after another.

Later, Suki explained to me the complex rules of Bunraku.

"Are there also complex rules to Japanese love life?" I asked after ingesting this information.

"What do you mean, Dee Dee? What's happening?"

"I think things are heating up between Hiro and me. I wonder if he thinks I'm easy because I work at the Snack."

"Are you?"

A part of me wanted to confess all of it—my flirtation with Gabe, my wrestling match with Mr. Tambuki, my attraction to Baby Elvis. It was so much less confusing at home where I engaged in serial monogamy—one boyfriend at a time. Even if I didn't see a future in the relationship, I honored it for the moment.

"I made a rule for myself that I wasn't going to get involved with anyone on this trip. I'd hate to lead Hiro on. For me, it would be just a summer romance."

"The Japanese aren't as hung up about sex as Americans,"

Suki said. "They don't have all this Puritan baggage. He's a big boy. Do what feels right to you."

It seemed simple enough. My instincts seemed to be in good working order, even with a drink or two in me. I had staved off Mr. Tambuki. I hadn't jumped into bed with Hiro after our make-out session. Maybe I didn't need my rules anymore. I just needed to stop thinking so much.

CHAPTER SEVEN

L ater that week, I had an appointment at a bank. A very nice Human Resources man spent about a half hour describing the structure of the bank. He ended by telling me that they couldn't use temporary people without substantial banking experience. Since I didn't have that, they wouldn't be able to help me. I should reapply when I was more seasoned. I tried to get across the nature of what I was looking for, not so much a job as an opportunity to learn. The Human Resources person repeated himself and thanked me for coming. I knew he was giving me the brush-off. I was disappointed and frustrated, but tomorrow I would work out my Plan C.

That evening before the Snack opened, Chief was unloading groceries with Penny. After his first trip into the kitchen, he poked his head out of the counter window.

"Gina, Mr. Tambuki wants you to escort him again," Chief said like a proud father as he plunked down a large plastic bag of raw chicken wings. The bag burped as the air inside escaped.

"Oh?" I said. I was surprised that Mr. Tambuki should want me after I rejected him. I also was sure I didn't want to put myself through that unpleasantness again. But I didn't know what to say to Chief. I wondered whether I was risking my job, but I did have a little integrity left. Chief retreated into the kitchen and then returned to his car through the front door.

Penny traded places with him and set a box of fresh produce down on the counter. She looked disheveled, and her eye makeup was smeared.

"Jimmy's wife is coming home today from the hospital with the baby. I'm really bummed out. I like him *so* much."

"You knew he was married, Penny, and now he has a family." I was irritated that she failed to see the obvious.

"I can't help it. I love him, and I can't get enough of his gorgeous, big dick."

Berta entered noiselessly. She was very light on her feet for a large woman. If she heard this last exchange, she didn't let on. But she figured out quite correctly that Penny was up to no good. "Penny, where the hell were you last night?"

"I was over at Yasuko's, Mother. I told you that."

I could tell that Berta wasn't buying it, but she let it go. "You're a mess. Go fix yourself up. I'll take care of these."

Penny disappeared into the back room. Berta lit a cigarette, her usual refuge when she was worked up over something, which was pretty much most of the time.

"Think twice before screwing a guy. That is the consequence." She pointed her thumb at Penny, picked up the box of produce, and headed back to the kitchen.

The Snack was busy for midweek. Hana hadn't shown up, and we had to all cover for her. I had my back to the door when I heard the carrion cry of Mama-san, her speech already slurred.

"Tambuki-san!" I looked over my shoulder and saw Mr. Tambuki bowing to Mama-san. She rose shakily off her throne and guided him to an empty stool near me.

I acknowledged him with a small, stiff bow, and fetched his whiskey bottle off its high shelf.

"Good evening, Mr. Tambuki," I said, with only the briefest amount of eye contact. I poured him a shot.

"Good evening, Gina," he said formally, like we had just been introduced. "I trust you are well?"

"I'm fine, thank you," I said. *Despite you and your love hotel,* I thought.

"Pour yourself one," he said, gesturing to the bottle.

I knew he was doing me a favor, but it felt like an order. I hesitated. He was scrutinizing me, like he was trying to get inside my mind.

"Go on," he continued. "I'm not going to bite."

I poured another glass, but I let it sit on the counter.

"I owe you an apology," he said. He leaned in just a little, hands folded in his lap. "Please pardon my presumption the other day. I had a little too much to drink, and I was rude to you. Am I forgiven?"

It was so simple and direct. How could I not forgive him? I was in his country now, and he was only playing by the rules he knew. It's not like anything really happened. Just one slipup. Still, I didn't want to show him I was too pliable.

"Maybe," I said. I looked up at him now. He had sincerity tattooed on his face. I had liked him and wanted to like him again.

"You are different from the other girls, or should I say 'women.' I can see that. You know just what you want, don't you?"

"About some things," I ventured. I could feel myself melting from his charm.

"So, international woman of business, will you accompany me again? Mr. Muriachi, from the other night, was very impressed with you. I believe he will be able to help you with this elusive internship of yours."

This was an offer I didn't want to refuse. "I will accompany you on the condition that you promise to behave yourself," I said.

"I promise, but then you must not look so beautiful and tempt me."

"I won't make the mistake of wearing that dress again."

"Oh, no. You look like a queen in that dress."

"Queen of tarts?"

Mr. Tambuki laughed, a rare response for him. His teeth were very even and white except for one gold-capped tooth. "I am pleased you are able to put what happened behind you. That, you see, is very Zen. So, you have already learned one important lesson."

Before he left, he gave me Mr. Muriachi's card and told me to contact him.

The next morning Suki and I went window-shopping. I told her all about my adventures with Mr. Tambuki.

"Mr. Tambuki?" Suki asked when I first mentioned his name. She stood up straight from where she had been peering at a display of cashmere sweaters with kitschy designs, like tennis players and small dogs.

"Do you know him?"

"I might have met him at the Club once or twice."

Suki suggested that I try to erase the memory of the black dress by looking at clothing that felt more like me. After rejecting at least two dozen different outfits, I tried on a short-sleeved, slightly below-the-knee dress in a delicate pink that matched the bracelet Hiro had given me. It had a high neckline with a Chinese-type collar. Normally, pink isn't my color, but this dress had a beautiful texture and sheen that took on different hues depending on how the light hit it.

"Do you see Mr. Tambuki as a possible patron?" Suki asked me as I appraised myself in the mirror.

"I'm not looking for a patron, Suki. I just want to do this internship, and he has connections. He also offered to teach me about Japanese culture—the way of Zen." I walked out from the fitting room to get Suki's opinion.

She motioned for me to twirl around. "Zen. That will be tough. We should go to tea ceremony. *Chado*. The way of tea. That's very Zen." She screwed up her face in concentration and then nodded. "Very nice."

I ignored the tea ceremony suggestion. If that was Zen, I had a long way to go. "Do you think I can trust Mr. Tambuki now?"

"Just because he made a pass at you? Some men think they have to at least try."

"Has your patron ever made a pass at you?" I went back into the fitting room to take off the dress. I had no money to buy it with.

"He's contented if I let him play with my feet," she said matter-of-factly as though she had just said, "He eats rice every day."

"Your feet?"

"He has a foot fetish. It's harmless enough."

The picture in my mind of a man making love to a foot sent me into convulsions. Suki started laughing, too.

"He likes to buy me shoes. I have more shoes than I know what to do with. And he gives very good foot massages."

"Sign me up. After an evening standing in high heels, I could use one of those."

"No, you'll have to find your own foot fetishist," she said. "Maybe Mr. Tambuki will indulge you."

"I think I should leave it as 'you can look but not touch.' You know, Hiro is starting to look better and better. Maybe he'll give me foot massages."

Hiro had the following day off from school. Since he couldn't see me that Sunday, we had arranged to meet for a martial arts movie matinee. That kind of film wouldn't have been anywhere near the top of my "must-see" list at home, but he told me it was his favorite genre. How could I refuse? He offered to do a real-time translation.

The matinee crowd consisted mostly of older men. We sat in one of the rear rows of the movie house. About three-quarters of the film was an excuse for various scenes of fast-paced kicking, chair throwing, and assorted choreographed mayhem, with one man able to fight off dozens of others at a time. I always wondered why evil men were depicted as such incompetent fighters.

It seemed to me they wouldn't last long in the business of evil-doing if they weren't more skilled. But then our on-screen hero wouldn't win.

In the dark theater, Hiro whispered his truncated version of the script in my ear. His warm breath both tickled and excited me. The hero was fighting one shirtless man covered in tattoos and another one missing the tops of two of his fingers. There was a minimum of talk. Hiro took my hand and held it in his.

"He say the man is bad. Yakuza. Japan gangster. He fight him."

I was riveted as the hero brought down both men with two fierce kicks, one with each leg, and then turned to face a whole other round of combatants. Furniture flew. The hero ducked. Walls broke apart. Hiro was beside himself. He squeezed my hand so hard it hurt. Then he let go and started to make karate chop motions in the air.

"This the good part!" Hiro had practically memorized the movie. He was able to deliver lines before they were spoken.

Three more evil characters were knocked off in turn, each bout more difficult than the last. Finally, our hero prevailed. He lifted a beautiful woman, who had been cowering in the corner, and spoke to her softly.

"He say, 'You be safe with me.'"

The movie ended abruptly after this final act, and we exited the movie hand in hand.

"You like movie?" Hiro asked.

"I've never seen one of those kinds of films before. It was impressive. Can you do that stuff?"

"Sure. Different stuffs, too. *Ken* sword. That my favorite. I show you sometime." With his free hand, he slashed at the air with an imaginary sword.

"I remember you broke a board in two at the park. Do you do that much?"

"Can do, but it not about the breaking. It about, how you say? Concrate, but not concrate?"

Hiro often searched for large words. In me, he seemed happy to have a living dictionary. I could usually figure out what he was trying to communicate. "Concentrate," I suggested.

"Yes. No other thinkings. Empty mind. Believe in self. Believe in board. Work hard." Hiro frowned in mock concentration.

We walked to a nearby ice-cream parlor and ordered big, gooey ice-cream sundaes. They were overly sweet, but the sugar was satisfying.

"Those yakuza were scary, with those tattoos all over their bodies. Do they all do that?" I wanted to know.

"When belong to group. Show belonging. Different group have different *izebumi*. How you say it—tattoos?"

Hiro understood and recognized more than he was able to comfortably reproduce. I smoothed out his translation. "They wear the tattoos of their special clan?"

"Clan. Yes. Some yakuza not belong to clan. Work on own. All bad. Big danger."

"What do they do?"

"Have bad business. Drugs. Drive fancy car, like Mercedes. Kill people!" Hiro had become all worked up again, conjuring up images of armies of criminals roaming the streets in their expensive vehicles.

"How would you know if someone was yakuza?" I asked.

"May not know until too late," he said, thumping his chest gleefully.

My spoon full of ice cream, whipped cream, and sauce was poised to enter my lips. I held it just one second too long, and the contents fell into my lap, staining the front of my khaki-colored slacks with a deep brown. Hiro asked for a glass of water, dabbed it on a handkerchief, and began rubbing the spot at the top of my thigh. It was an unusual kind of foreplay. Although it was still early, he was eager to take me home.

We stood in front of the Club. He took both of my hands in his.

"Thank you for introducing me to so many different things," I said.

"It my pleasure. I like make you happy. Learn Japan." He looked down at his feet and then added as if it were a throwaway line. "I like make love to you now. Is okay I come up? I have condom."

I knew things were heading in that direction, but I thought they would take longer, moving up a notch from week to week. "You are sweet to ask. You're a polite young man."

"Maybe not polite to ask at all?"

I wondered whether this was his first time. Maybe he saw me as the older, experienced woman. "It's fine," I said, reasonably confident that I was doing the right thing, that the sugar had not loosened up my judgment the way alcohol did. "I'd like to."

"Oh, I am so happy!" Hiro said.

Hiro was more aggressive than I expected, perhaps because of his eagerness. After we lay on the futon, he quickly helped me get undressed and then took his own clothes off, careful to remove the condom from his pocket and place it near the bedding. Despite his athleticism, his limbs were round rather than muscular as though he had recently shed his baby fat. His uncircumcised penis was a first for me. We kissed. Because of what I thought was an inequality of experience, I took more control than I usually did. I caressed him, working my way down his body. He did the same to me. When we finally made love, he came quickly but was not embarrassed. He thanked me. We held each other for a while. Then he started kissing me all over, went down on me until I came, and entered me again. Perhaps he knew what he was doing after all. But I didn't feel any fireworks.

I didn't have time to go to the *ofuro* before work. Although I washed myself as thoroughly as I could in my small sink, I worried that I still smelled of sex. I sprayed myself with an extra squirt of perfume.

That evening I wore my bracelet to the Snack for the first time. Nothing slipped by Berta.

"You're glowing tonight. You get some? Mr. Tambuki?"

"Berta, I'm not that kind of girl." I pretended to be shocked.

"No? Then why are you working in this hellhole, and where did you get that expensive bracelet?"

Berta grabbed my wrist and examined the bracelet more carefully.

"A friend," I said.

"Uh huh. If I were a betting gal, which I'm not, I'd say you have a male friend who's been humping you or hoping to."

"Maybe." I knew Berta would tease me mercilessly if I gave her too much information.

As if on cue, Chief came out from the kitchen with a crate of beer bottles. He glanced at me and hustled by, so he could unload the bottles into the beer barrel. Berta and I looked at each other and muffled a laugh. Chief sidled back to the kitchen.

"The little guy who offered to protect you?" she asked.

I nodded.

"Well, I'm glad one of us is getting some," she continued. "It's been such a lean year that the pathetic losers that come in here are starting to look good."

Just then, a group of five guys, wearing matching black taffeta bomber jackets emblazoned with a roaring lion, stormed into the Snack. They were already wasted.

"Hold on to your britches, honey," Berta said. She crushed out her cigarette as if in anticipation of needing both hands. "We're in for a wild ride with this bunch, and they've got money to burn."

Berta was right. The guys knocked back whiskey as though they were in a drinking competition. Two of them ordered us around. Berta, cigarette dangling from the corner of her mouth, leaned over the counter. She scrunched up her face in her best dragon imitation and puffed a cloud of smoke in the face of the obvious ringleader.

"Listen, you pinheads," she said in English, "get this straight. You are on my turf now, and you'll do what I want. Got it?"

This harangue only prompted one of the thugs to be bolder. He reached out and gave Berta's left breast a good squeeze. His comrades laughed. Berta caught his wrist and pinned it to the counter.

"Try that again, and you're dead meat," she said as she twisted his wrist. Another guy jumped off his stool and thrust his pelvis at Berta. Berta unhanded the first guy and busied herself fixing us drinks. If we had to endure this nonsense, we were at least going to reap some rewards from it. I stood by, helpless. We had some crude creeps come here, but they usually only appeared in twos or threes and were manageable.

One of the fellows nodded at me and beckoned me over. "Name?"

I edged in but not too close. "Gina."

"Gina. Gina. I want my penis in you. Good English, yes?"

Berta shoved a glass of whiskey in my hands. She chugged her own in one swallow, prompting applause from the guys. "I don't know about you, but I can't face these pricks sober. Drink up." Berta prepared two more drinks for us.

I wished the bar had more customers, so I could excuse myself. Berta told me to go order a pile of food, although the boys hadn't requested it.

"It doesn't matter," she explained. "It will give them something else to do with their hands."

I downed my whiskey and placed the order with Chief. When the food arrived, it only made matters worse. One of the guys, who up to that point had been quiet, picked up one of the chicken legs and ran his tongue along it in a sexual manner.

"Gina, lick his dick! Lick his dick!" the one with the best English said. That set up a chorus of "Lick his dick! Lick his dick!" from all of them. Then they each picked up a chicken leg and imitated the first guy, who handed me a chicken leg. I took it and stared at it. Berta grabbed one from the plate and tore it apart with her teeth.

"That's what I'll do to your dick if I get a hold of it," she said.

The guys loved this stuff, and Berta was good at dishing it out. I gave her my chicken leg, and she gnashed at that. She was enjoying herself, and I thought I should try to get in the spirit of it, too. How much trouble could they cause in a public place?

I reached over and took a handful of French fries. The ringleader picked up one long one, leaned his head back and slid it in his mouth, pulled it out partway, then popped it in and chewed. More applause. Berta wolfed a whole mass of French fries and then stuck her tongue out covered in masticated potato. The guys were hysterical. The grosser the humor, the better. Berta made sure our glasses were always full. I could feel the alcohol lowering my inhibitions.

When a plate of shrimp arrived, plump and pink with their tails still on, one said, "Hey, Gina. Shrimp?"

I did love Chief's shrimp. I was about to take one when the guy stood up and shoved one down my chest along with his greasy fingers, which he then licked one at a time. I fished out the shrimp, broke off the tail, and made a show of eating the succulent flesh. The other guys drummed on the table. Shrimper asked his neighbor for change, which he deposited in the jukebox. A fast number with a strong beat bounced off the walls. I danced in place behind the counter. The customers always seemed to like that. Shrimper returned, held his hand out, and beckoned me to the patch of linoleum that passed for a dance floor. We danced apart for a few seconds before he took my hand and twirled me around. In my high heels, I lost my balance, and he caught me without letting go. He planted his other hand on my backside, started grinding himself against me, and forced his tongue in my ear before I pulled away. Then he took my free hand and placed it on his clothed, but now very hard penis. The guys were hooting. I considered kneeing Shrimper but opted for stepping on his foot with my sharp heel, making it look like an accident. He emitted a "youch" and released me.

I put my hands up to my mouth in mock horror. "I am so sorry," I said. "I just got so excited."

I don't know if he understood, but the guy who spoke English catcalled at Shrimper, who slunk back to the counter. One of the other guys slapped Shrimper on the back.

Meanwhile, Berta had replaced my almost full glass with another one. I reckoned I had about a six-drink bonus, a personal best, and I earned every yen of it. Eventually, other customers came, and we left the fivesome to fend for themselves. They soon became bored. Berta gave them their bill, followed by a complicated exchange of money. The English speaker asked for a kiss. He was quite insistent. Since I just wanted him to go, I leaned over to give him a quick peck, but he moved his head, so our lips met.

"Next time we screw," he said, thrusting his pelvis for the last time.

I laughed, both relieved to see them go and yet, like with whitewater rafting, which I'd only done once, exhilarated at having survived the rough spots. I remembered a time my freshman year when a friend talked me into going to a Delta Upsilon party at Marquette. The high-ceilinged frat house was old and smelled of stale beer. The atmosphere was distinctly meat market, with the upper-class brothers grading each girl as she walked through the door. I was just coming out of my high school wallflower phase. The new attention was flattering and overwhelming. After one dance, too close for comfort, the guy told me he wanted to show me something upstairs. I excused myself and never went near a fraternity house again. In contrast, DU now seemed tame. The only difference was there I felt threatened, and at the Snack, I felt oddly safe.

CHAPTER EIGHT

A s the woman with excellent English had instructed me over the phone, I took the elevator up to the fifteenth floor at the New Bank of Japan. A large desk dwarfed a well-coiffed receptionist, with a crown of golden letters above her head spelling out the bank's name. She led me to a smaller front office and told me to wait until Mr. Muriachi's secretary came. Soon an attractive young woman emerged from an inner office. She wore a perfectly fitting beige suit, matching heels, and a scarf arranged around her neck with a studied casualness.

"Hello. I am Keiko, Mr. Muriachi's personal assistant. You are Gina?"

I put my hand out to shake hers, and she limply took a few fingers. "I'm pleased to meet you," I said. "As I explained over the phone, my real name is Dee Dee. Gina is sort of a stage name." I realized the complication of mixing up my two lives.

"Mr. Muriachi asked me to give you a tour of the bank now. He is very busy." She swiveled on her heels and headed down the hallway. I trotted after her.

Keiko whirled from one pod of offices to another, briefly announcing their functions. Each pod contained one larger central room where a pool of a dozen young Japanese women sitting at computer monitors tapped away. Dark-suited men strode in and out of doors separating the central room from private offices. A few women occupied desks in front of these offices like security guards for their occupants. Keiko showed me conference rooms with leather chairs and state-of-the-art technology, which she briefly demonstrated by pushing various buttons. One button unfurled a large white screen. Another brought a projector down from the ceiling. Everything was clean and modern, with soothing color schemes of gray and mauve, curtains with pleasing patterns, and sleekly framed canvases of scenes from each continent on the walls. It was the American Bank of Tokyo's richer cousin. We ended in the cafeteria. In the hallways, young women pushed carts from office to office, offering tea service and snacks.

After the tour, Keiko led me to a desk that she said was mine. It was on the edge of one of the large rooms with the pools of women. She handed me a notebook in English about bank policies and operations.

"So, do I have the internship? I thought I was just meeting Mr. Muriachi to discuss it."

"All settled," she said.

It seemed almost too easy after the runaround I'd been given at the other banks. I guessed this really did demonstrate the power of knowing people.

I read the policy book, which had many awkward constructions. "Please be to arrive timely manner." Most of it wasn't interesting except for the fact that the bank had a lot of real estate holdings with names like Edo Towers and Imperial Business Hotel. I finished it in an hour and a half and went back to Keiko's office.

"I've gone through this," I said. "What should I do next?"

"I have these numbers that need to be checked," Keiko said, handing me a folder of papers. She opened a drawer and took out a small adding machine along with an extra roll of tape. "This will make it easier," she said. "If you need help, just ask one of the girls on the floor. Most of them speak at least a little English."

I was surprised at being asked to use something as primitive as an adding machine when the bank had access to the latest technology. Even back at the medical supply company, we used our computer for complicated calculations.

"Um, will I get to meet with Mr. Muriachi today?" I asked, trying not to sound too eager.

"Mr. Muriachi is a very senior man. He is very busy. Perhaps tomorrow?" Keiko said, not looking up at me.

"Okay. Thanks." I was disappointed, but I was grateful to have any kind of position, so I said nothing more.

"Oh, Gina, you can take your meal at noon in the cafeteria I showed you. The food is very good there," she assured me, her voice as soothing as the colors of the walls.

"It's Dee Dee," I said.

For lunch I bought a *bento* box with some unknown morsels and the usual rice and miso soup. Since the strange hostel breakfast, I had developed the habit of trying whatever was put in front of me. I didn't have to like it, and I didn't have to finish it. Each new food attempted was worth one point on my cultural adaptability scale.

The cafeteria brimmed with chattering women, with an occasional man dressed in the working clothes of someone whose job involves dirt. I felt like a stranger and didn't have the nerve to sit down at one of the tables of established relationships. I would try that tomorrow or the day after when I was more familiar with my surroundings. So, I sat alone and enjoyed the new textures and tastes of the *bento* box. Definitely one point.

The afternoon was much the same as the morning until my adding machine jammed. I struggled with it for a few minutes and noticed that some of the "girls" were watching me. Indeed, they did all look like girls, younger than me even. I asked the one who seemed to be most senior to help me. She was patient and businesslike, but after she fixed my machine, and I thanked her, I saw her give a look to another "girl" and stifle a giggle.

At five o'clock I went straight to the Snack, a change of clothes in my bag. On the train, I convinced myself that the internship would get better. At least I had the opportunity to prove myself. Once they saw what I was capable of, they would offer me some experiences that were more suited to my abilities. I felt good.

To add to my buoyancy, that night Baby Elvis arrived at the Snack with Licker and One Eye. He ordered his usual beer and shrimp. I watched him pull off their little legs and pliant shells and then pop them in his mouth. He gestured for me to take one.

After he finished his first beer, the chorus swelled for his Elvis act. "El-vis. El-vis." He assumed his Elvis demeanor and strode to the karaoke machine. Tonight, it was "Teddy Bear." I did a little dance behind the counter. At the end of his song, he looked right at me, pointed in a theatrical way, and winked. I felt that familiar fluttering in a very private place. It was silly. I had a nice Japanese boyfriend, whom I liked a great deal and had made love to. But as sweet as he was, as competent as he appeared to be in bed, Hiro didn't give me those feelings. Baby Elvis returned to his seat, beads of sexy sweat on his brow and upper lip.

To show my appreciation for his friendship, I decided to deliver my own rendition of an Elvis favorite, "Return to Sender." I fixed my gaze on him so that he would know this was a gift to him. When I was finished, he clapped but not as enthusiastically as the others. His face was blank, unrevealing. And he left before I even had a chance to retreat to my station behind the counter. I was embarrassed, like the time I'd been paired with my big crush at an eighth-grade dance and then stepped all over his toes. Was it because of my terrible singing? Was Elvis his exclusive domain? Did he not like my song choice?

As I wondered what I'd done wrong, Chief called me over.

"Mr. Tambuki is coming to pick you up in half an hour. Go fix yourself up, okeydoke?"

"I'm not finished work yet," I protested. I didn't mind going out with Mr. Tambuki, but I would have preferred doing it on my terms. Why didn't he ask me himself?

"Doesn't matter. Berta can cover for you," Chief said.

I was a new lamp, with Chief trying to decide whether I would fit better in the living room or the dining room. But I wasn't going to let him have the last word, and I was still upset about Baby Elvis leaving. "And you'll pay me for this time?"

"Sure, sure. No problem."

Mr. Tambuki couldn't have been more pleasant. He took me to dinner at another expensive restaurant and thanked me politely for coming out on such short notice.

"I was happy to take a break," I replied.

"Some of those guys are very juvenile, aren't they?" he noted.

I was glad he understood what I had to deal with each night. "Yes. Such silliness."

"They are letting off steam, so to speak." His eyes appeared to fix on a nonexistent horizon. "The rest of the time they must be on their best behavior."

"Were you like them when you were younger?" I asked. I saw Mr. Tambuki as a highly polished stone that didn't easily chip.

"Maybe now and again. But I had a very different life. I was a Buddhist monk."

"A monk?" I tried to picture this man, who wore designer suits and ordered the best whiskey and dined on Kobe beef, in saffron robes, living a Spartan life and praying all day long.

Mr. Tambuki read my mind. "It is perhaps not what you are picturing. Monks here can be more of the world. But it was a very focused existence."

"Why did you leave?" I asked.

"In some ways, I have never left the monkhood, at least its principles, which inform what I do every day. But I did develop other interests."

"And have you succeeded in doing what you want?"

"It would be unwise for me to rest on my laurels at this stage of the game. There is always more to know and to experience, Gina. The more we humble ourselves to that fact, the more will come our way."

The waiter placed a plate containing a small white fish in front of each of us. As on our previous dinner date, Mr. Tambuki did the ordering. He hadn't let me down with his choices. I flaked off a small piece of flesh with the edge of my chopstick. The fish melted in my mouth.

"I started working at the New Bank of Japan today," I said to show Mr. Tambuki that I, too, was open. "Thank you for helping to make that happen."

"You are most welcome. I hope it will prove to be rewarding."

"I hope so, too."

"You sound uncertain?"

Damn! I thought I had squelched my tone of doubt. "It did start a little slowly. I didn't get to talk to Mr. Muriachi today . . ." I stopped before completing a full account of my tedious day and sounding ungrateful. I concentrated on my fish.

"Gina, you must embrace this opportunity, own it, be patient. It is what you wanted." He said this more as though he were instructing rather than scolding me.

"You are entirely right, Tambuki-san," I said. That was the first time I had used the Japanese form of respect with Mr. Tambuki.

Again, his trademark non-smile smile. "Gina, I can see that we need to have more time for your instruction in the way of Zen. You will find it very helpful both in your daily negotiations in Japan as well as in framing a bigger picture in which these disturbances are no longer troubling." He stared at me with those dark eyes, those opaque screens that kept me from peering in. "We should set aside three evenings a week. How does that sound?"

One remaining morsel of fish eluded my chopsticks. I chased

it around the plate. "Oh, I'd like that, but I work at the Snack six nights."

"I have already alerted Chief to this possibility. He is agreeable."

I poked the fish between the chopsticks with a finger, hoping that Mr. Tambuki didn't notice. "I need the money, Tambuki-san. It's the only way I can afford to stay here."

"Of course. This is a reciprocal relationship. I need you to help me with my business relationships. You will be handsomely compensated. I am sorry if I did not make that clear."

As I brought the fish to my lips, my chopsticks parted, and the fish fell back onto the plate. "Oh."

"In any case, I want one night to be Sunday. No work obligations for either of us."

I set my chopsticks down in defeat. "It's my only day off." And my only time to see dear Hiro.

"Then we'll plan on having fun, too. But you must meet me halfway." Mr. Tambuki wrote a figure down on a business card and handed it to me. "This is what I will pay you for your time, in addition to some fine meals, of course."

I was stunned, as the figure was several times my nightly pay at the Snack, even with bonuses.

"And this is just for accompanying you?" I asked, wanting to be sure I hadn't misunderstood his intentions.

"I expect you to be good company and to open your mind for your instruction."

"Why me, when I assume that a man in your position could have his pick of women?"

"Do not underestimate yourself, Gina. I see great potential in you. You are smart, curious, and adventurous, yes? And you are different from Japanese women. You bring a fresh perspective. With some additional schooling in our ways, you might make a great ambassador one day."

"An ambassador?" A greater goal than even I imagined for myself. Ambassador Falwell. I liked the sound of it. "I suppose flattery will get you everywhere." I paused so as not to sound too eager. "Okay. I agree to your terms."

"You won't regret it," he said. He took my free hand and kissed it to seal our deal. "Since we went out tonight, I will see you Thursday then. And here is a little extra. Buy yourself something nice to wear for our next business outing."

He gave me enough to purchase something more than nice. "Thank you, but I don't think I should take this in case I make the wrong choice like I did the last time."

"I am sure you will use your best judgment. But you were beautiful in that dress, and we have an understanding now, don't we? I am good for my word."

Mr. Tambuki's faith in me gave me more energy for my internship. The next day I was sure I would meet Mr. Muriachi and find out about his expectations for me. Maybe even land a serious assignment. I arrived early. Keiko was not yet at her desk, and Mr. Muriachi's door was closed. Either he was with someone, or he was not in. It would be rude to knock.

I walked over to my desk on the other side of the open room. On it was a new stack of papers, larger than before, with a note. "Your work for today. Please finish by end of day. Thank you. Keiko." It was more of the same. Pages of numbers to double-check. Maybe I was being tested. After all, as an intern, I was at the bottom of the ladder. Eventually, I would be supervising people doing these kinds of tasks. It was important to understand the work at all levels. I sat down, took my adding machine out of the drawer, and pecked out numbers.

At eight thirty the room suddenly filled with secretaries and the high murmur of female voices as though the doors had just been flung open at a special department store sale. The women settled quickly, and soon their fingers were flying over their keyboards.

The tea lady came through with her cart at ten o'clock sharp.

I bought a tea, which was served in a china mug with a saucer, and two packets of cookies wrapped in cellophane. My short nights made me hungrier during the day. I noticed that the young woman in the desk next to mine observed this transaction, which I conducted with the few Japanese words I knew. She had a narrow face and a pixie haircut. She bought nothing but continued to watch as I unwrapped the cookies and devoured two in quick succession.

I made the first move. "Would you like a cookie?" I asked her in English. Once again, she lowered her eyes but then looked up again as though filled with a new revelation.

"Please. Yes," she said. I handed her the half-eaten packet. She nodded. "Thank you," she said and began to nibble eagerly at the edges of the cookie, like a small mouse.

"My name is Dee Dee," I said, trying to sound friendly.

She stopped chewing, swallowed, and quickly swiped her finger over her crumb-filled lips. "Pardon," she said, startled as though she had been discovered in the middle of an unseemly act. After a moment, she regained her composure and, in the deliberate manner of a student in an English class, said, "I am Midori. I am pleased to make your acquaintance."

"You speak very good English," I said.

"Thank you. I study now in night school for three years," she said. "You are from America?"

"Yes. I am doing an internship here for one month and then will study business back in America."

"Please. What is internship mean?" Midori asked.

"An internship is when you learn about a career or type of job by doing parts of that job. Someone supervises you and teaches you," I explained.

"You want to be secretary?" she asked.

"No, I want to be an international banker," I answered.

"Oh. But you are doing work of secretary, not banker," she observed, crinkling up her face.

"I am just starting. In an internship you learn many different things," I said, but as I spoke, I started to doubt my own words.

I decided to work hard and show Keiko and the elusive Mr. Muriachi how reliable I could be. Then they would increase my responsibilities. I moved so little for the next few hours that one of my feet went to sleep, and I had to massage it to revive the circulation. It was one o'clock before I took a break. Midori and some of the other secretaries were just returning from lunch.

Walking down the hall to the cafeteria, I passed by an elegantly carved door with a brass plate engraved with both Japanese characters and the words Executive Dining Room. I hadn't noticed this room before. As I stopped, the door opened, and two dark-suited men exited. Other dark-suited men sat at square tables with white linen tablecloths and bone-white china while waiters in white jackets served them from platters of steaming food. In the far corner, I recognized Mr. Muriachi, who sat with two other men.

Suddenly, I didn't feel like eating lunch. Instead, I went for a walk outside. The heat of the day ricocheted off the buildings and sidewalk. I found a small park nearby and sat on a bench. Was I really just a secretary? Would this job impress anyone at Wharton?

When I returned, I marched straight over to Keiko's desk, which was devoid of any semblance of activity beyond one pad of paper and a pen.

"Good afternoon, Keiko," I said, trying to sound normal. "I am making good progress on the work you gave me and wondered if I could schedule an appointment to see Mr. Muriachi."

"I can answer all questions," she said sweetly. "We do not bother Mr. Muriachi on such matters. Are you not comfortable at your desk?"

"It's fine," I said. "That's not a problem."

"Do you not have enough to do?" she asked.

"It's not about my desk or the work you gave me. I would like to see Mr. Muriachi about my internship. I thought I might be able to attend meetings, observe the bankers, and even carry out some research."

"Oh," said Keiko. She fiddled with her bracelet, which was gold with tiny pearls. "I will check if Mr. Muriachi has any open appointments next week."

Keiko removed a large leather-bound appointment book from the shelf behind her. "Tuesday, seven thirty a.m. is the first time."

"Next week? Okay, if that's the first time he has available," I said.

With a fountain pen, she painstakingly entered my name on one of the book's vellum pages. As she closed the colossal volume, I felt the whoosh of air across my face.

"The work you are doing is very important," she said. "The bank cannot run without it. We are very grateful for your assistance."

I felt helpless to combat such appreciation, and I had only myself to blame for not negotiating the terms of the internship. As I looked around, I observed that gender stereotypes were fully in operation. I might have to play by some alternative rules. Maybe the idea of a young woman seeking to move up the corporate ladder was new for them. I would need to introduce the idea slowly so feathers wouldn't get ruffled. I would need to earn acceptance, even if it took a little time. At least now I was on Mr. Muriachi's calendar, and by next week, he would see what a stellar worker I was. That day I stayed until the last possible minute to finish up all the number checking.

The rest of my first week passed uneventfully. Each day on my desk I found a stack of papers, which I dutifully completed by the evening. I became more efficient at the task so that by the end of the week I was finished by five o'clock.

For my next engagement with Mr. Tambuki I wore the pink dress I'd bought with the money he'd given me. We went to dinner with Mr. Sansui and two Chinese men. With my increasing vocabulary, I was able to converse in a primitive manner with Mr. Sansui. At nine o'clock, Mr. Tambuki indicated to me that it was time to leave. He wanted to show me something, but it was to be a surprise. He left his guests in the charge of Mr. Sansui. On the way there, I asked him where Mr. Yakumasei was.

"Mr. Yakumasei is a very valued colleague, but social situations are not his best strength. If you like, I can invite him along sometime."

"No, I was just curious. He seems less refined than Mr. Sansui, for example."

"Ah, so. Yes. Mr. Sansui is a well-educated man. He makes a good impression. Although he does not speak much English, he can converse in German and Chinese quite well, you know."

"Do I make a good impression?"

He laughed. Neither a laugh of derision, nor of acceptance. Just a laugh, but it put me at ease. "Gina, you are pushing for compliments. You need to believe in yourself and your power."

"I have followed your advice at the bank and asked for a meeting with Mr. Muriachi, but I am also being more patient."

"That is good. You are an able student. It will make my job easier." He laughed again.

The car stopped at a small gallery in the Ginza. The gallery was closed, but Mr. Tambuki had a key. We went to a small room in the back, where he donned some white gloves, unlocked a drawer, and took out a series of prints.

"Hokusai's *Thirty-Six Views of Mt. Fuji*. There are only sixteen of them here. Do you know them?"

"I saw one or two in a world survey of art class I took as part of my core requirements at college," I said.

"He actually did forty-six views. An interesting man. Prolific. He produced more than thirty thousand pictures in his lifetime. He changed his name several times. He is said to have lived in more than ninety homes. He also changed his style, his subject matter. He captured human nature in all its aspects. Yet always he stayed true to himself. A true master." A flicker of light passed through Mr. Tambuki's eyes.

"These are lovely," I said. "I didn't know you were interested in art."

"I am sure there is a lot we don't know about each other, Gina. When it is time, we will know it."

"Ah." I didn't really understand what he was talking about, but that was nothing new.

"Japanese arts and their creators exemplify the Zen spirit. Now Hokusai's work might not technically be classified as Zen arts, as say, brush painting and calligraphy are, but I believe the way he listened with his eyes and made his art his practice, so to speak, was very Zen."

"I am not sure I am following you, Tambuki-san. I thought that Zen was more of a meditation-type thing."

"Yes, of course, sit meditation is an important kind of Zen practice. But the way of Zen is an integral part of other traditional Japanese pursuits, such as chado—the way of tea, ikebana, and the martial arts."

"Tea ceremony and martial arts?" The two seemed utterly incompatible.

"Perhaps you have seen too many kung-fu films? The martial arts represent the highest form of discipline and practice. Just like Hokusai, who worked tirelessly in his practice. Today, it is sufficient for you to understand that in modern life, Zen practice can be applied to many activities."

Mr. Tambuki pulled out another set of prints showing small sketches of a beefy, almost naked man engaged in the activities of daily life—bathing, cutting off the head of a fish, preparing food. "Hokusai was not just about the ideal or the lofty. To live a Zen life does not mean eschewing all but the life of the mind. But one can develop a whole new appreciation for these ordinary activities through cultivating a Zen approach. It is all about the moment.

The here and now. Do you see?" He held out one print, cocking his head to one side, as if noticing some fresh detail for the first time.

"I think I get your point," I said.

"I have done too much talking." He placed the new stack of prints near the Mt. Fuji pictures and gave me my own pair of gloves. "I should just let you look."

I studied the first set for a while, noting the rich use of colors, the way Mt. Fuji appeared from different perspectives, with its prominence varying from scene to scene. Sometimes filling up the frame. Sometimes in the background as it was in a frightening picture of a wildly frothing wave with a tiny Mt. Fuji behind it. Yet it always seemed to maintain its essential Mt. Fuji-ness.

"I will take you there sometime," Mr. Tambuki said. "Everyone should see Mt. Fuji."

"I would like that."

Afterward, we went back to the Snack. Mr. Tambuki ordered one drink and an order of chicken, which neither of us ate.

"Gina, we meet Sunday night then?"

I would have to lie to Hiro about Sunday night. But I didn't feel I could turn down Mr. Tambuki. He was being good to me, and I was enjoying his company. At home, I never spent time with older men, other than men of my parents' generation, who treated me like their daughters. Mr. Tambuki respected my opinions or at least was ready to entertain them. And I was curious about what else he would teach me. Wasn't that openness to experience part of what Zen was all about?

CHAPTER NINE

On Saturday I'd promised Penny I would meet her in a park near the Snack. I was now her confidante regarding Jimmy, and she was regularly bursting at the seams to tell me the latest twist in their turgid and secret affair. When I arrived, she was on a swing. I gave her a big push, and she soared up and down a couple of times. Then suddenly, she dragged her foot along the ground on the downward pass. The swing lurched.

"Oh, God. I think I'm gonna throw up," she said, turning pale. She flew off the swing and dashed for the nearby public toilets. Concerned, I followed her and waited outside. I heard her retch violently, held my breath, and entered to find her hanging over the hole in the floor toilet, the door to her stall swinging open.

"Penny! Are you okay?" Dumb question. Of course she wasn't. I rummaged around in my bag for a tissue and ran it under the tap. Penny sat back on her heels, took the damp tissue from me, and wiped her mouth with it. She stood up on wobbly legs.

"Are you going to be all right now?" I asked.

She twisted the soiled tissue in her hand. "Gina, I think I'm pregnant."

I was hoping she was just being dramatic. "It was probably something you ate."

"No, I'm pretty sure. I skipped my period, and I'm real regular normally. I've been sick every day."

I didn't know what else to do, so I hugged her. She held me tight and started crying.

"I'm so scared," she said.

"I know." But I didn't know. I could only imagine.

"Have you told Berta?"

"Are you kidding? She'd skin me alive. You won't say anything, will you?"

"No, but have you used one of those home pregnancy kits to be sure?" Were they even available in Japan? I had no idea.

Penny nodded, although not convincingly.

"I assume it's Jimmy's?" I asked.

"I've been faithful to him!" Penny seemed hurt that I could possibly think she'd been cheating on her adulterous boyfriend.

"Does he know?"

"No, but I'm gonna tell him soon. Then he'll have to leave Donna and take care of me."

"Oh, Lord. Penny, it's not that easy. She's his wife, and he's already got a kid he's responsible for."

"He has to take care of me. He has to. I'll kill myself and this baby, right at his door."

At that moment, Penny seemed capable of such an extreme act. I felt this huge crush of responsibility to land her safely in reality, as though she were a hijacked plane in my command.

"It's okay. We'll think of something." But I was out of my league here.

Penny's announcement and the pressure of keeping it from Berta gave me a headache through most of the evening rush at the Snack. Berta gave me two aspirins and assured me I would feel better if I had a couple of vodkas and orange juice. "Vodka will cut the pain, and orange juice has vitamin C." She found the perfect victims to buy me drinks—One Eye and Licker, who was wearing his preferred "Lick My Hot Dog" T-shirt. I was disappointed that Baby Elvis wasn't with them.

"Gi-na, how are you this evening?" Licker asked slowly in English.

"I am fine, thank you," I said just as slowly. "Thank you for asking. Beer?"

The boys nodded, and as I poured two beers, Berta placed a vodka and orange juice in front of me.

Licker leaned over and whispered in my ear. "My friend want know—what color your hair down there?" He pointed to my crotch.

"Green," I said. It was a small price to pay for a free drink.

"Ah, so?" Licker said. I think he believed me. He must have translated for One Eye because I recognized the word *green* in Japanese.

One Eye nodded solemnly and pushed the hair off his face, revealing that he actually had two eyes. One was the usual brown, but the other was almost green. "Like this?" he asked.

Berta ordered me two more vodkas with orange juice and some *yakitori*. We didn't hear any more trash talk from them that evening, and they left by ten.

At eleven o'clock, Baby Elvis appeared alone. He looked disheveled—shirt unbuttoned, face flushed, and no glasses. Through my three-drink haze, I felt my knees go weak. Since his abrupt departure on Tuesday, I found myself fantasizing about him at odd hours, while adding up numbers at the bank or shopping for groceries. Maybe it was his seeming lack of interest in my sexual being, compared to the rest of the bar crowd, that made him so desirable. As he plopped himself on the stool and called out, "Bonsoir, Gina," I felt self-conscious. I smiled and turned my attention to the beer barrel, taking somewhat longer than usual to fish out a Sapporo.

"*Tu es belle ce soir*," he said.

I wasn't used to compliments from him. "Thank you," I said.

I tipped his glass and poured the beer so it wouldn't foam up too much. But my hand shook, and the beer flowed over the rim of the glass onto my hand and the counter.

As I was about to fetch a rag to wipe up the spill, Baby Elvis said, "*Attende.*" He brought my wet hand to his lips and licked off the beer with short, gentle laps. This act was far more outrageous than any of the verbal crudity I'd been subjected to in the past few weeks. But I didn't mind. His sparkling eyes locked onto mine, and I realized he was completely drunk. He held my hand a few seconds longer than necessary. My pulse hammered against his thumb.

He ordered the barbecued chicken wings, second only to Chief's shrimp in popularity. When they arrived, he said. "*Pour toi,*" indicating that the wings were for me. I wasn't sure how to attack them in all their glorious messiness. Baby Elvis picked one up and held it to my mouth. I took a nibble, its spiciness singeing my lips and tongue. He finished it off and urged me to try another one. With our fingers and faces covered in the red sauce, we both laughed. I wet a couple of napkins. After Baby Elvis dabbed my face, he wiped his own face and stained fingers. Staggering over to the karaoke machine, already in Elvis mode, he grasped the microphone and crooned "A Little Less Conversation," eyes fixated on me the whole time. He sneered, fondled the microphone, ground his pelvis, and fell to his knees. The Saturday night crowd, who did not know him, went wild.

When he came back to the counter, he gestured at me to lean toward him. Cupping his hand over my ear, he whispered, "Gina, *es-tu libre ce soir?*" I was free tonight. His breath tickled my earlobe, and the smell of his aftershave mixed with his Elvis sweat sent a surge of raw energy through me. Other than Mr. Tambuki, with whom I had a clear and contractual relationship, I had never been out with a customer before. But this was different. Baby Elvis and I were friends. And now the attraction that had been brewing for me was apparently mutual. I eagerly agreed, fairly certain how the evening would end. Baby Elvis arranged to pick me up at 1:00 a.m. after my shift.

Having downed two whiskeys in the past half hour, I was sufficiently drunk myself to leave any self-censoring at the door. During the taxi ride, we didn't say much, but Baby Elvis held my hand, moist from anticipation. He lightly circled his fingertips around the soft cushion of my palm. It drove me crazy.

The taxi stopped at the Hotel Twist in Shibuya. The main sign was in English, its neon H and T hissing and spitting. The hotel was old, and from the look of it, the limited décor hadn't been changed in a couple of decades. The lobby was poorly lit, dimmed further by dark wood paneling and a faded wine-colored carpet. With his hand burning the small of my back, Baby Elvis guided me down a long hall with identical doors except for their dull brass number plates.

At number sixty-three, he bent down and removed my shoes and then his own. The door was unlocked, and we entered what could be described only as a shrine. The walls were covered in fading burgundy velvet. On them were hung at least a dozen portraits of Elvis, also on velvet, punctuated with replicas of gold records with the names of his number one hit songs. In the middle of the floor was the pièce de résistance, a giant model of a pink Cadillac convertible with exaggerated fins. Rather than seats, the interior was outfitted with a mattress covered in zebra-striped fur, two large matching pillows, and an oversize steering wheel in the middle of the dashboard. Across from the car was a large television with a VCR playing a mute version of "Viva Las Vegas." I stood in the doorway while Baby Elvis stopped to push a button on a mini jukebox situated next to a karaoke machine. Soon the stale air of cigarettes and past lovers was filled with the sound of Elvis crooning "Help Me Make It through the Night." Baby Elvis looked at me proudly.

"*C'est bon?*" he asked, eyes twinkling.

"It's good," I said, stifling a giggle. It was a ludicrous place, but I felt strangely happy. Baby Elvis opened the convertible door for me. I sat down on the fake fur, my legs dangling outside. The red and pink spotlights dotting the edge of the ceiling weren't bright, but they were hot. Baby Elvis poured us drinks from a bottle of whiskey from the bar that was tucked into a cupboard. After handing me my glass, he downed his own and went to fiddle with the music. The real King serenaded us with "Are You Lonesome Tonight?" Baby Elvis sat next to me on the mattress and took my hand again. We watched the silent Elvis on the television. As Elvis was kissing his leading lady, Baby Elvis leaned in and kissed me. His full lips were soft and inviting, and I returned the kiss. He lost some of his awkwardness, and we fell back on the fuzzy striped surface. My dress rode up, and the fur tickled my thighs. Soon we were tangled up in each other, unable to distinguish one beating heart from another. By now, I was in such an alcoholic haze, I was ruled only by desire. While Elvis spat out the lyrics to "I Want You, I Need You, I Love You," Baby Elvis reached up under my dress to pull down my underpants. I wiggled out of them. I unbuckled his belt and undid his zipper. He tugged at his trousers and briefs until they released his hard penis. It was bigger than Hiro's and also uncircumcised. I reached out to touch it, and Baby Elvis put his hand on top of mine to stop me. He massaged my own wet genitals. I could hear myself moan with each stroke.

After donning a condom, he was inside me. Elvis sang "It's Now or Never," and the car started rocking back and forth, the mattress vibrating, and the headlights flashing, as if cued by our heat and urgency. On the screen, Elvis, as large as life, mouthed another song and egged us along with his own gyrating pelvis. I closed my eyes. Our bodies undulated in perfect rhythm to the jukebox Elvis and to the pitching and throbbing of the convertible. Baby Elvis shuddered at the last refrain. The car grew still, and he rolled off me. I had not yet come. As I lay there staring at the ceiling, I saw for the first time a large mirror. I realized that, minus my underpants and Baby Elvis's belt, we were both still dressed, a couple of wide-eyed teenagers discovering each other in the King's car, not entirely sure what to do. Across from me on the wall, the Elvises smiled from their serene velvet perches. Baby Elvis kissed me on the forehead.

"Merci," he said.

I must have drifted off for the entire night because when I awoke, the clock on the wall said 10:00 a.m. Baby Elvis was gone, and in his place was an envelope addressed to me. Inside, wrapped in a plain piece of paper with the words "THANK YOU" printed neatly in English, were ¥20,000 in crisp ¥500 notes. With my racing heart and pounding head, I couldn't make any sense of this. Why would he leave me so much money? And then it dawned on me. He thought I was a prostitute.

And I believed we had something real.

I was due to see Hiro in two hours. Instead of washing first, I scrubbed myself thoroughly inside the heart-shaped tub and used all the products available—bath oils, soaps, lotions, and powders. My mind went in circles over what had happened and what it meant. The money part wasn't my fault. I had neither done nor said anything to give the impression that I was for hire, but maybe it went with the territory. I would give the money back, plain and simple. But why had I so readily agreed to this liaison? Sure, I liked the guy, and he was awfully cute. Yet, didn't I have my hands full with Hiro? Of course, we hadn't made a commitment to each other. For all I knew, he had a Saturday girlfriend, a Friday girl-friend. Was I really hurting anyone but myself? I decided that this was just a one-night stand fueled by alcohol in my fake Gina world, and maybe it didn't count.

I returned to the Club and changed into shorts and a T-shirt. I wanted to be as asexual as possible for the time being.

My head still ached when Hiro knocked. Sweet little Hiro.

"Dee Dee, I teach you *ken* sword today. I bring practice sword." In both hands, as though performing a ceremony, Hiro held out a several-foot-long replica of a sword made from bamboo. It had a wrist guard about one-third the way up.

We went to a miniature park near the Club. The day was sunny with a light breeze that bent the thin stalks of red and yellow flowers newly planted around the edge of the green.

"First, I teach you correct breathe. We sit."

Hiro sat down cross-legged on the grass. I was stiff, but I managed to assume the posture. The grass felt cool against my bare legs.

"Breath from stomach," Hiro said, pointing to his abdomen. "In. Out." He demonstrated, eyes closed, counting slowly with each breath in and out, filling his stomach. He opened his eyes again. "You try. Count so no thinkings. Sit up," he admonished.

I straightened my slumping back. "One-two-three-four." Breathe in. "Five-six-seven-eight." Breathe out. "One-two-three-four." Breathe in. "Five-six-seven-eight." Breathe out. I wondered how long we would do this. I wasn't good at sitting still. Would I ever be able to break a brick? A board? A twig?

"No thinkings!" Hiro scolded.

Breathe in. Breathe out. Breathe in. Breathe out. I was starting to feel calmer. I lost sense of the time.

"Good," said Hiro finally. "Now I teach you *ken* sword." Hiro stood up, holding his sword out in front. "Sword is soul of samurai. First, important to remember. Sword kill. But you not fear death."

"I am not supposed to fear death?" I asked.

"No. If fear death, sword not work. No thinkings about what sword doing."

"Whoa, Hiro. You're going too fast. I don't understand. You don't fear death?"

"No. Not think about death, so I not fear it. That is what teach us."

"Oh." I could see Hiro was several lessons ahead of me.

"But no talkings. I show." He went through a series of deliberate but balletic movements.

Later, he stood behind me like a male golf pro helping an attractive lady perfect her swing. The sword felt heavy after I'd held it a few minutes. I had some trouble coordinating the movements of my legs with those of my arms, but eventually I mastered the routine to Hiro's satisfaction. His praise was spare but sufficient to maintain my interest.

"Is good. Don't forget breathe." He stood in front of me and demonstrated correct breathing again. "Okay. Breathe in ... breathe out." And I breathed in and out as he had taught me, feeling like a child who had just learned to put her head under the water.

"You very good student. You like *kendo*?"

I didn't think it would be my next hobby, but I was happy to have some understanding of one of Hiro's chief avocations. It obviously meant a lot to him. The good news was that I spent two hours not obsessing about my incident with Baby Elvis. And my head finally felt clear.

"Okay. I be student now. You help with English for test?"

As we headed up the path to the door at the Club, I noticed Chief's car parked nearby and behind it, Mr. Tambuki's sedan.

"I think there are people in the Club." I said. "We should be extra quiet so they don't see us."

"Like little mouse," Hiro said, putting his finger to his lips.

We crept in, but the jukebox was playing and drowned out our footsteps as well as the voices from the Club room. Mr. Tambuki's back was to me, but I saw an unidentified arm pass him a small package wrapped in brown paper. Hiro followed my gaze. Chief was clattering in the kitchen. We tiptoed, hoping he wouldn't hear us, but he came out with two mugs of coffee just as we were starting up the stairs. He glared at us. I was relieved that Hiro didn't ask me about Chief, nor the men in the Club. Even though my relationship with Mr. Tambuki was quite innocent, I wanted to keep my two lives separate. It was easier that way.

We spent two more hours going over the finer points of English grammar and doing some vocabulary building exercises. I acted as a task master, but Hiro was a willing and able student. As I suspected, his grasp of the language was better than his everyday delivery of it. He was so often in such a hurry to get his thoughts out, he wasn't as careful with his words.

Then I had to figure out how to tell him he needed to leave so that I could get ready for my engagement with Mr. Tambuki.

"Hiro, I am afraid I have to work tonight, so you need to go."

"Work on Sunday? No time to make love?"

"No. Sorry, not tonight."

"Oh. I cannot see you next week. Must study for test. But then we go to Nikko. Magic place. Lots of temples. Big celebrate."

"That would be nice."

I quietly opened the door and listened to make sure we were alone again. When I was assured that we were, I gave Hiro an especially warm kiss, so he wouldn't feel like I was slighting him in any way.

"Good luck on your test. I will keep my fingers crossed." I demonstrated, as it occurred to me that might be a Western custom. Hiro imitated me and smiled.

"Thank you for helping me. It will make a big difference." It was probably the first fully grammatical sentence he had uttered, and I was touched. I hoped it would do the trick and allow him to pass.

Mr. Tambuki came back at seven thirty. I didn't ask him what he was doing in the Club earlier. We went out to a small local restaurant that specialized in *okonomiyaki*, a cross between a pancake and an omelet with vegetables. We cooked it ourselves on the grill at our table.

He tantalized me by saying, "Gina, I have decided to share something about myself that not many know."

When we returned to the Club, he retrieved a large portfolio from his trunk as well as a rectangular wooden box with a metal handle. He ushered me into the main room, and we sat down in one of the booths. I was glad that I had washed down the tables in my cleaning frenzy.

"Do you remember the woodblock prints I showed you? I am a bit of a collector myself." Mr. Tambuki pulled from the portfolio a sheaf of prints. "These are called ukiyo-e, pictures of the 'floating world.'"

"Oh, yes. My friend Suki told me about the floating world—life in the pleasure-seeking quarters?"

Mr. Tambuki flinched. "Yes. But these prints are so much more. At one time, they were considered very ordinary in Japan, but they were very popular in the West and had a great influence on Western art of the nineteenth century."

He showed me one of two women elaborately dressed in kimonos. One of them was fanning herself.

"That one is very much like a painting Monet did," I said, remembering that Monet had been influenced by the Japanese prints he'd seen. I was pleased with myself for making the connection as I thought it made me sound intelligent.

"Very good."

"Are they part of my Zen instruction?" I asked.

"Not directly. I just thought you might enjoy them as you seem to like art."

Mr. Tambuki carefully turned over each print. I recognized some of them from Suki's book. Only these were the real thing. In most of the pictures, the women were fully dressed, with the occasional breast and nipple appearing as a kimono drooped casually off a shoulder.

"Utamaro is one of the finest of the ukiyo-e artists. That one is amusing. It might be translated as *The Drunken Courtesan*." A woman held her cup upside down; her eyes were slitty and unfocused. "Utamaro captured women of all classes. Is he not a master?"

"This is very impressive, Tambuki-san. Thank you for sharing these with me."

"I have a few other sketches to show you." He took some smaller sheets of white paper from the portfolio. These were simple line drawings in black ink, also of women wearing traditional-looking garments. However, in most, the clothes were open or draped in such a way as to reveal a fully naked body underneath. But the lines were so spare that the drawings were elegant and sensual. "What do you think?" he asked.

"The gesture is so perfect in this one." I said, pointing to one with an outstretched hand. "With just a few lines, they manage to capture a pose and an expression."

"I did these," Mr. Tambuki said.

"Wow. No kidding? They're really good. You *are* a man of hidden talents." I was stunned. I thought of Mr. Tambuki as a businessman. First, he revealed he was a monk and now, an artist.

"Thank you." He put the pictures back in the portfolio. "I would like to sketch you, Gina. You would make a lovely subject."

"Oh, Tambuki-san. I'm flattered, but I've never been a model before. I don't do well at sitting still."

"That doesn't matter. I will pay, of course. Model's fees."

The thought of additional money increased my interest, and I had to admit I was intrigued at how Mr. Tambuki would represent me on paper. "Now?"

"Yes, I have taken the liberty of bringing my sketch pad and pen."

"Oh. How should I dress?" I certainly had no intention of taking my clothes off.

"Why don't you wear that dress you wore when we first went out?"

"The Queen of Tarts dress?"

"Yes. That's the one. Would you like a drink to relax you first?"

"Please."

This time Mr. Tambuki served me. He poured me a double whiskey and himself a single shot. I chugged it back, and the warmth coursed through me.

After putting on the dress, I returned to the main room. He began by having me stand with a hand on one of the tables. Then he had me sit, leaning forward. I was surprised at how quickly he worked.

"Gina, I would like to do some with you lying down on your futon. I will be a gentleman, I promise."

Once in my room, he had me rest on one elbow as I sprawled across the futon. Then he asked me to bring my knee up toward my chest and show a little more leg. Next, he wanted me to push my dress off one shoulder and cover a part of my face with my hair.

"A little more?" he asked, pointing to my shoulder.

I did as he asked.

Mr. Tambuki continued to draw. After about a quarter of an hour, he asked, "Would you think I was rude to inquire if you might show me one of your beautiful breasts?"

He made the request sound so chaste and reasonable. In the name of art, I unzipped the dress partway to allow the shoulder to slip a little further so that my right breast was exposed as far as the nipple.

"Perfect," he said.

"Tambuki-san, why do Japanese men talk about breasts all the time?"

"Perhaps it is a mother fixation?" he suggested. "Perhaps it is because breasts are so uniquely female. So round and sensual and comforting." There was no tone of lasciviousness. No lustful gaze.

But I found myself getting aroused by the act of exposure and Mr. Tambuki's intent regard of me as he sketched. He didn't ask me to remove my clothing further, although I might have if requested.

When he completed several more drawings, he announced that he was finished for the night. I asked to see his work. The drawings didn't look like me. Rather they captured an essence, an attitude. The later drawings were very sexy with a come-hither expression and a very ample bosom.

"Oh my, I could get myself in trouble with these," I said as I struggled to zip up my dress.

"You were perfectly charming. May I help with that?"

Mr. Tambuki zipped me up, and the hair on the back of my neck stood up as a finger lightly grazed my neck.

"Gina. I should go now. You have work tomorrow, and so do I. I thank you very much for humoring me."

"Not at all. Your drawings are wonderful," I said.

"I am glad you think so. Next Sunday, I would like to take you to Nikko."

My heart raced as I remembered Hiro's offer to take me there. "Oh. I kind of promised someone else I would go with them."

"You could go to Nikko a thousand times and not be bored. Twice will not matter, will it?"

"I suppose not. Thank you." What else could I say to my benefactor? And no doubt he was right. That would be the Zen way—to see it from different perspectives.

I walked Mr. Tambuki down to the front door just as Chief was leaving the kitchen with a grocery bag. He bowed to Mr. Tambuki and nodded to me, still in my long black dress.

That night I fell asleep as soon as my head hit the pillow. I dreamed I was in a room filled with men grinding and bumping against me. I couldn't move. Every time I turned around, another one was in position. One of them started kissing me while another one pinned my arms to my side, so I couldn't push him away.

I woke up suddenly to find my nightmare was real. A man was on top of me, slobbering all over my face. I tried to scream, but no sound came out. His weight was fully on me, so that I had no leverage. I could smell the familiar stench of alcohol.

"Stop it. Please stop," I whimpered. I was wearing a short summer nightie. I could feel his naked flesh against mine, his erect penis rubbing against my thigh, trying to find its way into me. I squeezed my legs as hard as I could. When he shifted positions to find a new angle, I toppled him off balance until he rolled off me. I sat up, breathing hard, and pulled the cover over myself tightly. When he managed to sit upright, I saw to my horror in the shaft of light from the street lamp that it was Chief, clad only in a T-shirt. I could feel my strength temporarily return.

"You! Chief! How could you?"

"I'm so sorry. So sorry."

"Get out! Now!"

"I am so sorry. Excuse me."

Chief got up to his feet and then fell again as if in defeat. He seemed so helpless, unable to control his limbs. After a few moments, he stumbled over to his clothes, which were in a heap near the edge of the futon. He grabbed them and padded out of the room as fast as he was able. Shortly after, I heard the front door close.

I shook uncontrollably, my teeth chattering up and down like the keys of a player piano. Even though it was a warm night, I swaddled myself in the sheet, to add a layer of protection against the outside world. No specific thoughts went through my head, just waves of emotion. Finally, when the worst of the shock subsided, I took some deep, measured breaths and rose to put the small lock on the door. It wouldn't hold against anyone who really wanted to enter, but I would be alerted sooner to any intruders. I also put on some underwear. I couldn't begin to process what had happened.

I sat staring at the blade of light from the window until it softened with the early dawn. Only then did I feel safe enough to shut my eyes again. But it was the kind of sleep where you believe you are awake. I felt strange people looming over me, dark ghosts about to suffocate me. Then, in my dream I would wake up, and they would still be there. In reality, I willed my paralyzed body to move, looked around to assure myself I was alone, and fell back into slumber, to experience the same pattern all over again.

CHAPTER TEN

I called in sick at the bank and went back to bed. They wouldn't miss me. The internship was going nowhere. The work was dull and repetitive, the secretarial pool had little interest in me, and Keiko patronized me with her saccharin voice. I couldn't imagine that meeting Mr. Muriachi would displace my doubts. At least that was the way I was feeling after my dreadful night.

Around noon, I got off my futon and plodded downstairs. I splashed water on my face and squinted at myself in the mottled bathroom mirror. I didn't look different except for the dark circles under my eyes. I shuffled into the kitchen and made myself some tea. The thought of food made me ill.

When my head had cleared sufficiently, I tried to make sense of the situation. What could Chief possibly have been thinking? Had he planned this, did the urge creep up on him, or did he have some spontaneous itch? Did he ever try this with any of the other hostesses, or was I fair game because I was a gaijin? Twice yesterday, he had seen me in potentially compromising situations, although both were innocent. He had noticed Hiro and me going upstairs and Mr. Tambuki coming downstairs, with me in that infamous low-cut black dress. What worried me was that Chief had a key, and he could try again. My situation was clearly untenable. I couldn't take the chance, could I? And, in any case, I couldn't face him again. It would do no good to complain. I remembered what Berta told me—that none of the rules apply when Japanese men are "shitfaced." And it would be his word against mine.

I assessed my finances. Of course, I kept careful records, but I wanted to be sure I hadn't miscounted. I reached to the back of the closet where I hid the envelope with my money. Most of what I earned at the Snack went to my daily expenses. The few extra tips I'd received I'd spent on makeup, clothes, and shoes so that I could be a good hostess. Mr. Tambuki had paid me for our first week of engagements, but not our second. And then there were the ¥20,000 from Baby Elvis that I swore I would return. I didn't even have enough cash for a ticket home, but in my passport case was my emergency credit card. Surely, this constituted an emergency. When I put the money back, my fingers passed over the box with the bracelet. I opened it, but I didn't take it out. That would be another chapter of my life hastily closed.

In the afternoon, I went to the *ofuro* to cleanse myself of both my literal and figurative dirt. I'd already scrubbed the spot where Chief's penis had touched me until the skin was almost raw. After I completed my soaping and rinsing, I sank into the second hottest tub, hoping that the searing water would complete my physical purge of Chief. For supper, I had cereal and yogurt since those were the only foods I kept in the house. I ate upstairs in my room with the door locked.

At six thirty I phoned the Snack to say I wouldn't be coming in. Mama-san answered. I tried to explain in my minimal Japanese that I wasn't feeling well, but she handed the phone to Berta, who got all motherly on me.

"It wasn't because of that little guy who speaks French, was it? I'll personally cut off his dick if it was." I assured her that wasn't it. "Well, drink plenty of fluids, and call the doctor if it isn't gone by tomorrow," she said. "Don't worry about us, honey."

Because of my new schedule, I hadn't seen Suki in over a week. I needed a friend right now and arranged to see her. She would be shocked when I told her what had happened. On the way to her house, as the early evening light bounced blinding slivers off the glass buildings, I stopped in a park with a red lacquered bridge over a small pond. The reflection of the overhanging trees dappled the pond's surface, and the fading sun spotlighted the koi as they darted after each other. One was bright orange; another, steely gray; a third one, stripy. I watched them for a while. They seemed content with their simple life.

Suki, hair pulled back messily, answered the door in her kimono robe. I was too preoccupied with my own problems to ask why she looked pale and red-eyed.

"Dee Dee! I haven't heard from you in a few days. I hope that means you've been happily busy."

"No. I came to tell you I'm leaving." My words were unplanned and spilled out.

"What? You can't. What about your internship? You've only been here a few weeks." Her voice had an edge to it.

"It's not what I expected."

"You must give it time. Business relationships don't happen overnight here." She seemed to be scolding me.

"It's not just that, Suki." I took in a deep breath, having made the decision that I would tell her about Chief. After all, she had told me he was harmless, and he turned out to be evil. "I don't belong here."

Suki stared at me a minute before inviting me in. The conversation was becoming too intimate for the front steps.

As she served me tea, her hand shook. Some tea missed the cup. It was then that I asked her if she was all right.

"It's Bento-san," she said, as she mopped up the spill.

"Your patron." She didn't say his name often, so I wanted to be sure I knew whom we were talking about.

"Yes. He said that his mother-in-law needs my apartment. But I think maybe he wants to be rid of me, and he's just saving face."

"What will you do?"

"I'm too old for the downtown clubs. I guess I'll go back to work for Chief. It's all I'm any good at."

"Where will you live?" I asked.

"I don't know yet."

"You could share my space at the Club until you find something else."

"I thought you were leaving."

"I forgot. I am." For one moment my mind had erased all that had happened, and someone else's problems seemed more important than my own.

"Would you stay?" Suki squeezed the fingers of her right hand with her left and then reached out and touched my hand. "It would mean a lot to have a friend there."

"I want to help you, I do." I said hesitantly.

"Why not stay? You've got everything going for you. A roof over your head, a nice boyfriend, regular tips, a potential patron, and a life to go back to." She made things sound pretty good. Except for the one piece of information I hadn't yet shared.

"I feel like such an object at the Snack," I said. "All they see is Gina. They don't even know Dee Dee."

"So, men get to live their fantasies through you for a while. Is that so terrible?"

I took a big swallow of tea so I could get the rest of the words out. "I can't go back, Suki. Chief tried to rape me in my bed last night."

I thought Suki would be horrified. Instead she sounded like a lawyer for the defense, and I was the victim on the stand. "Oh. Was he drunk?"

"Yes. I could smell alcohol on his breath, and he stumbled a couple of times."

"I assume you asked him to stop?"

"Of course!" I sat up straight as though good posture would save me from this unexpected haranguing.

"And did he?"

"Yes, more or less. But it was so gross. He was half naked, pushing at me, trying to get my legs apart."

"And was he sorry?"

"He said he was." I slammed my cup down. "But that doesn't excuse it."

"No. But think about it from Chief's viewpoint."

"That's ridiculous, Suki."

"Please hear me out. Here you are a foreigner, working in his bar as a hostess. Harmless enough. Then you agree to Date Club. He makes some assumptions about the kind of girl you are, right or wrong."

I bristled at her use of the word *girl*. "Suki, you were the one who suggested I do Date Club. I didn't know there was a stigma attached."

"I thought you wanted the money. Does it really matter what Chief thinks?"

"Yes, if it leads him to think it's okay to rape me."

"The point is he didn't. He has a marriage that's a sham. He's lonely and desperate. One night he has one too many, maybe without even realizing it, maybe to get up his courage, maybe to forget. Who knows? This isn't something he routinely does. Have you ever even seen him drunk before?"

"No." It was true. Only Mama-san drank night after night.

"He has a key to your place. He's thinking, why not give it a try? Maybe Gina likes me. Then he's rebuffed. He apologizes. It's forgotten."

"Not by me it isn't. I did nothing to suggest in any way I was interested. At home, I could prosecute."

"This is Japan. There are some rules that can be broken under some circumstances. I'm afraid this falls under the shades of gray category."

"I'll never understand this country." I curled my back and shrank into the cushion.

"Yes, that's true. But you know how to get by."

"Is that really enough?" So much for cultural adaptability and all the points I'd awarded myself. This latest misunderstanding was evidence of how large an ocean I still had to cross.

Suki fixed me a snack of edamame and played me a tape of traditional Japanese music. It was slow, and the voice was high and almost whiny, yet haunting and cheerful at the same time. We sat and listened. I munched on the edamame and didn't say anything for a while. Maybe I was being a spoiled American. Maybe I did have a lot going for me. But attempted rape? Was my goal worth the price?

As I was saying goodbye to Suki on her doorstep, she took both my hands in hers and held them tightly.

"It will be okay with Chief, I promise. He won't try that again. But don't bring it up. To regain his own self-respect and yours, to save face, he has to pretend it never happened."

"How can I forget?" I asked.

"You probably won't, but one man's foolishness and pride doesn't have to rule your life and your decisions."

"Yes . . ."

"I wish you'd consider staying."

I realized then that Suki was asking me for support as she dealt with her man's foolishness and pride. "I'll give it another try," I said. "But you must come stay with me if Chief doesn't object. I don't know that I want to live there by myself anymore."

"Oh, he won't object. He owes you one. Milk it."

When I arrived at the bank early the next morning, it was open but quite deserted. As I considered the opportunity I had before

me and refocused on my long-term goal, I regained some of the
optimism that the incident with Chief had shredded. I strode with
confidence to Mr. Muriachi's office. Keiko wasn't there yet, so I
knocked on Mr. Muriachi's door. No answer. I sat near Keiko's
desk, reading over the questions I'd prepared on the train ride. At
8:20, Mr. Muriachi arrived. He cast me a quick glance and entered
his office, without closing his door. I gave him a moment to get
settled and then knocked again.

"Yes?" He regarded me with no flicker of recognition. "What
do you want?"

"I am Dee Dee Falwell, your intern, and I had a seven thirty
appointment with you?" I said more as a question than a statement.

Mr. Muriachi continued to look at me blankly. "I am sorry.
I had other business," he finally said, as though I should have
known this. "What is it you would like?"

"I've been here over a week now, doing some number checking
that Keiko assigned me, but I was wondering if there were some
other aspects of the bank I could learn about, if not from you then
someone else?" I had rehearsed this part, but now I sounded like a
petulant child who is ungrateful for vanilla ice cream because she
wanted chocolate.

"Oh. What is it you hoped to learn?" Mr. Muriachi asked.

"About the different bank operations perhaps. Or the special services you offer. Or your investments. Or your relationships
with other international banks. I want to learn about all of it, any
of it." I babbled on.

"Miss . . ." Mr. Muriachi began.

"Falwell," I offered.

"Miss Falwell, I suggest you go back to your numbers and
when you have something more specific in mind, we shall see.
Good day to you." Mr. Muriachi reached for the top sheet from a
small stack of papers on his otherwise pristine desk.

As the other secretaries filed in, I plodded back to my space.
Slumping in my chair, I replayed my conversation with Mr.

Muriachi. I wasn't sure what I had done to earn such flagrant disapproval. Maybe it was a test to see how I held up under stress. Or maybe I just didn't have enough focus for this kind of work. Or maybe Mr. Muriachi didn't like me, or perhaps Keiko didn't like me. I had to remind myself that I was smart, a straight A student, who had done well not only in school but also on the job. I needed to prove myself, but I wasn't being given the chance to do so except through the tedious number-checking tasks that bore no relationship to the real world of international banking. I needed another strategy, or it didn't make sense for me to stay.

I found it hard to concentrate on my work. Every time I added a column of figures, I would think of one other reason to leave Japan. Did I want to work for a rapist? Would he fire me? Would he try again? It wasn't as though the job at the Snack had many benefits. The pay barely covered my expenses, and many of the customers were rude. Moreover, I had embarrassed myself with the one customer I did like, Baby Elvis. Sometimes I drank too much. I'd come to Japan for an internship that wasn't panning out. And then there were other people's problems when I had enough of my own—Penny's pregnancy, Suki and Bento-san. If I was honest with myself, I'd realize that I wasn't going to understand this culture any time soon.

I wanted to make a list, but I was afraid of committing too much personal information to paper. Then the tea lady appeared. I rummaged around in my briefcase for my purse. Some tea might calm me. Midori appeared at my desk with a cup and a small pastry.

"These are for you, for your kindness," she said.

I thanked her, and she returned to the tea lady for her own cup of tea. I wondered what kindness she was referring to, and then I remembered the cookies I'd given to her. It hadn't been any big deal. I cradled the warm cup and observed its simple but elegant shape. I ran my finger around its silver rim. Was I shortchanging my experience by just listing my misgivings? I guess there were some good things about my life here. Mr. Tambuki was paying me well and teaching me about Zen. He took me to nice restaurants that I couldn't afford myself. He had good connections, even if the referral to Mr. Muriachi wasn't quite what I'd wanted. Both Hiro and Suki were exposing me to new activities. Maybe I would never be an expert in the culture, but I was getting a glimpse at it, even at the Snack. I was already here, and I would feel like a failure if I left prematurely. I had nothing waiting for me back home, and I didn't need my mother's "I told you so." Staying would show I was adaptable, wouldn't it? And if I framed it right, I could make the internship sound positive. I was working in "special operations." The Wharton people didn't need to know that meant adding and subtracting. I chuckled at my cleverness.

"Something is funny?" Midori asked, looking up from her computer screen.

"The world is funny, don't you think?"

She looked puzzled. "It is a big world. Some parts are funny. Some are sad. But it is good to smile. When you smile, the sad parts do not seem so sad, yes?"

"Yes. Yes!" I had an epiphany then. "Thank you, Midori."

"You are welcome, but I did nothing."

It was all in my attitude. I needed to capitalize on opportunities that presented themselves. I had to see everything as a potential learning experience. I wasn't here forever.

I picked up the next sheet in my pile and clicked away on the adding machine. The recording paper inched its way out with each strike of the keys. There were solutions to all my "problems," which were not very serious in the big scheme of things. Of course, the culture was challenging—wasn't that the whole point of being here? I'd been putting up resistance where I didn't need to and consequently not getting the full value from any experience. Mr. Tambuki was a gift from heaven, a door to possibilities, as well as a source of income. He was a wise man, a former monk. I must listen to him. I no longer felt like Sisyphus climbing the mountain with his boulder, only to slide down again. *I* would be the boulder—a rolling stone, taking whatever path was in front of me.

Wearing my pink dress, I went back to the Snack Wednesday evening. Berta was doing her nails as Penny filled the ketchup containers, seemingly mesmerized by the thick blood-colored substance as it flowed from the larger vessel to the bottles. She was remarkably accurate in her aim, not her usual random self. She didn't look pregnant, and I wondered if she'd made it up.

"Well, looky who it is," Berta said. "We'd about given you up for dead. Or maybe gone off to the ball with your prince-fuck-ing-charming." She gave one stubborn nail a last whisk with the emery board.

"I've been gone only two days," I protested.

"I've got so much to tell you, Gina." At least Penny was happy to see me, like a child coming home from her first day of kindergarten.

"Oh. You can't tell me everything?" Berta asked in her best scorned mother voice.

Penny rolled her eyes. I suppressed a giggle. I don't know why I found the two of them so amusing. Their relationship was kind of sad, each needing and loving the other, but unable to show it.

"Mu-ther!"

"I feel fine now. Thank you for asking," I said, pretending I didn't catch Berta's tone.

"Ooh, a new dress," Penny said.

"You look like a goddamn princess. Don't break your nails or anything." And as if to make her point, Berta took out her nail polish, gave it a little shake, and began to apply a bright purple to each finger.

"Are you mad at me, Berta?" I asked in a hurt voice, tread-ing the fine line between going along with a joke and taking her seriously.

"I only had to deal with all your customers. 'Where Gina?'

'Gina so pretty.' 'Gina got nice titties.' 'Gina blow job better.'" All of this was said with a very good rendition of a Japanese accent.

"They did not say that," I said in mock disbelief.

"You'll never know. And Chief has been moping around without you. 'I wish my Gina was well.' 'Why can't you be good like Gina?' 'Gina's the best girl I ever had, and I've had a lot of my girls.'"

I was embarrassed into silence. I'd hoped to bury the sordid event of three nights ago into the recesses of my mind, but it wasn't going to be easy, even with my new attitude. I caught Penny eyeing me.

"Mother, he never said all those things."

"Whose side are you on anyway? I'm trying to get a little sympathy here." She blew on her freshly painted nails and then waved them in the air.

"Okay. Tell me what to do." I said cheerily, trying to change the subject and the mood.

"You forgotten how to do your job already?" Berta asked.

"Now who's being impossible?" Penny said, clapping her hands. "Hey, Gina, you want to meet me before work tomorrow in the park?"

"Sure," I said, happy to have the diversion, no matter how frivolous.

Chief strode in with a sack in each hand. I glanced up briefly. He didn't try to make eye contact with me, so I busied myself swirling a damp cloth over the already clean counters.

"Penny, get back here and start preparing the chicken," he barked as he disappeared into the kitchen, loudly thumping the sacks on the counter. He always spoke to Penny in English, even though her Japanese was flawless.

"Yes, sir!" Penny said, saluting as she marched into the kitchen stiff-legged like a toy soldier.

"It wasn't the same without you. I just don't like getting sentimental in front of the kid," Berta said. "She already thinks I'm a pushover."

"I missed you, too. And strangely, I sort of missed this place."

"Ah, shucks," Berta said.

I moved in to hug her.

"Watch the nails. I didn't miss you that much," she said, her arms outstretched as though she were about to take flight.

On the way home that night, Chief had Hana sit next to him while I sat in back next to the dreamy Mama-san. Hana chatted away merrily, oblivious of Chief's stony mood. Mama-san stroked my cheek, smiling at me, like we were sisters sharing a quiet secret.

"So pretty," she said. I caught Chief glancing at us through his rearview mirror. I wondered if he was considering firing me. But whatever happened, I would go with the flow.

When I met her at the park, Penny was sitting on top of a picnic table, sucking desperately on a cup of orange slush. As the drips slid down her chin, she caught them with her now stained fingers, which she then licked. Penny could turn the most innocent of activities into X-rated fare. After she waved to me, I bought myself a small cup of ice cream from the snack shack and joined her at the table.

"I've found a way to keep seeing Jimmy," she said, her mouth rimmed in orange.

"Are you still sleeping with him?" I asked, trying to make it sound like idle curiosity rather than judgment. I didn't want to know how she was managing this feat.

"Oh, God, yes! He makes me feel so good."

"What about Donna?"

"I can't help it if she can't keep her man happy. I love him so, Gina. And he loves me." She took a large bite of the ice and winced at the cold. "So, you have a guy?"

"Yeah, I guess so."

"You fucking him?"

"Penny!" I thought I was used to the way Penny spoke by now, but her directness caught me off guard.

"Hey, man. You asked me. It's only fair."

"Just once so far."

"You gonna fuck him again?"

"I don't know." I realized that I although I'd thought about Hiro these last three days, my thoughts weren't sexual. Our brief encounter had been overshadowed by my confusing tryst with Baby Elvis, my scary moment with Chief, and my surprisingly sensual experience as a model for Mr. Tambuki.

"He's no good?"

"No, he's lovely." It was an odd choice of word. He wasn't necessarily the best lover I'd ever had, but he was more than competent. Yet, his sweetness overpowered his sexuality, at least for me.

"Lovely? That's an odd word for a guy. Go ahead and fuck him, though. Or what's the point of it all?" Penny had discovered her own magical abilities to keep a man's attention and obviously couldn't imagine why someone with this sorcerer's knowledge wouldn't use it.

"I think I'd rather have him as a friend," I heard myself saying.

Penny paused momentarily from her loud sucking and licking, a young woman in perpetual heat.

"Wow. You're weird."

The topic of Penny's pregnancy never came up, and I didn't ask. I guess I didn't want to know.

I met Mr. Tambuki at a restaurant in Shinjuku. He'd promised me a meal I wouldn't forget. I was happy to see him as he was now the linchpin in my master plan for Japan.

"Gina, we both look like bankers today." I was still in my business suit as I'd come right from my internship. Mr. Tambuki's suit was also navy blue, although of a much better quality and cut.

"I'm sure you have more of the skills of a banker than I do."

"Things have not improved at your internship? Would you like me to have a word with Mr. Muriachi?"

"Oh, no thank you," I said. "You've done enough. I think they just aren't used to having interns, but I've found a way to make it work. I'm going to do more than is asked of me and show that I am worthy."

"Excellent. That is the Zen spirit."

"Speaking of Zen, are you going to give me another lesson?"

"Perhaps when you least expect it. Zen is taught in a nontraditional way. If I tell you I am teaching you Zen, then it will not be Zen. Do you see?"

"Not really. But whatever you say. You're the boss."

"You are your own master, Gina, or should I say 'mistress.' But I will monitor your progress and adjust my lessons accordingly."

Although I didn't remember Mr. Tambuki having ordered, a waiter came with two plates of what I assumed was a kind of fish, arranged on the plate like a flower with white, almost transparent petals. On top of this design were two other foods, something that looked like shaved pieces of skin and the other, a mystery. The plate came with condiments—a lemon, an onion type of stalk, and chopped scallions along with a bowl of soy sauce. There were other little delicacies as well in yet another set of dishes. It was not a vast amount of food, just overwhelming in its unfamiliarity. I looked to Mr. Tambuki for guidance as to how to tackle this strangeness. He obligingly showed me how to prepare the sauce with the scallions and soy, roll the fish petals around the stalk, dip this creation in the sauce, and eat. Although by now I was much more proficient with my chopsticks, the fish was slippery. When I managed to locate my mouth, I found that the taste was not unpleasant, but the sharp sauce made my lips pucker.

"Don't watch me," I said when I noticed Mr. Tambuki looking at me.

"Sorry," he said with no hint of contriteness. "I was just curious how you would like it."

"It's very interesting. Delicate. Nice texture. What is it?"

"It's *fugusashi*. A fish, sort of a sashimi."

"I figured as much, but what sort of fish is it? I don't believe I've had it before." I tackled another piece.

"Fugu. Blowfish."

I stopped chewing, wanting to spit it out. "Blowfish? Isn't that a poisonous fish?"

"Yes, technically. One fish has enough poison to kill thirty people. An agonizing death. But that is only if it is not prepared properly."

"You haven't touched yours."

Mr. Tambuki picked up the piece he had prepared as a demonstration and popped it in his mouth. "There. See? We will both die then. Just like in a Shakespearean tragedy."

I stared at my plate. The fish appeared to grow spikes, like a porcupine.

"Fugu is a great delicacy. Gina, you must empty your head and try to be one with this experience, even if it means facing your death."

"You are making fun of me."

"Yes, a little. But I am quite serious about not thinking so much. Just use your senses. Here, put your chopsticks down. Now breathe in. Breathe out. Count to distract thoughts from entering your head."

Mr. Tambuki put his hands in his lap and demonstrated just like Hiro had shown me. Breathe in. Breathe out. I began to feel calmer. I could do this. I picked up my chopsticks and prepared another piece of the *fugusashi*.

"That's good," Mr. Tambuki said. "Because there are two other courses of fugu, prepared differently. You wanted something uniquely Japanese. This is it."

The next course was *fugu karaage*, deep fried fugu with vegetables. It was tastier than the *fugusashi*, with a crunchy texture. The final dish, *fugu-chiri*, was fugu with vegetables cooked in a broth at the table. We finished our main meal in silence by eating rice added to the broth along with an egg. Mr. Tambuki concentrated on each bite, each slurp. I tried to focus on my sight, my smell, my taste, even my touch. I'd brought myself to the brink of death and lived to tell the tale. Another adventure I couldn't share with my family.

"There you did it," Mr. Tambuki said. "I hope you enjoyed it as well. You have about thirty minutes to live."

"Tambuki-san!" I was not used to Mr. Tambuki making jokes. He was usually so serious. "I did enjoy it. I liked the fried part the best."

"Closer to what is familiar to you perhaps. But you were willing to try this. That was very laudable. Many foreigners would have shied away once they found out what it was."

"Tambuki-san, what do the Japanese really think of foreigners?"

"What do you mean?"

Mr. Tambuki was always cautious about answering questions whose intent was not entirely clear. Even then, he often didn't answer directly.

"I get treated differently here than at home, even at the bank, so I was wondering whether World War II influenced people's views."

Mr. Tambuki took a sip of his tea. "Ah. That was a difficult time, of course, but it was many years ago. Japan has proven that it could be an economic giant on the world stage."

"But it's still not a very diverse country. Do Japanese mistrust foreigners?"

"Gina. You ask such big questions. There are no simple answers. We have a unique culture with a long history of traditions, as I have said before. We do not expect outsiders to understand us."

"Not even people who have lived here a long time?" I thought of Berta. If she ever tried to understand the culture, she seemed to have stopped somewhere along the way.

"It is difficult for people to lose their original frames of reference, their native lenses, as it were. It is perhaps better not to wear glasses at all, to be a little blind for a while?"

"I am trying very hard to do that—to be a rolling stone, just feeling the ground beneath me."

"A rolling stone without glasses. Very good. I like that. Remember that a rolling stone does not gather moss. It does not pick up debris of excessive thoughts. It does not focus on its past, where it has been, nor does it ponder its future. It is very much in the moment. And in that state of being, the stone will become enlightened."

"There is hope for me yet?"

"Perhaps."

CHAPTER ELEVEN

Nikko surprised me. It was both a place of great beauty and serenity but also obscene commercialism. I could understand the merchants just on the outskirts. But even on the walkway up to the entrance of a stunning temple, with its tall leafy trees hanging over us like umbrellas, salespeople hawked everything from the godly to the blatantly kitsch to the downright insalubrious. Worse, people bought these things. I'd given myself credit for becoming open-minded, but sometimes it was impossible not to judge.

"I don't understand how these people can be allowed to spoil this beautiful place with all this junk." And to illustrate, I picked up a T-shirt with a picture of Mickey Mouse smelling Donald Duck's butt and held it against myself.

Mr. Tambuki, who for him was dressed down in khakis with a silk open-necked shirt, Rolex watch plainly visible, chuckled. "Ah, Gina, and you, a future woman of commerce."

"I hope not this kind. Don't you agree that this makes no sense—having this reeking commercialism engulfing this spiritual mecca?" I threw the T-shirt back on the table. The salesperson folded it neatly and placed it carefully on top of the stack.

"And you do not have this in your country, with its billboards smack against a peaceful mountain backdrop?"

"That's different. This is a religious place. I thought things would be more sacred, more traditional, and that people might want to keep them purer," I said.

"Oh, yes. We are rich in traditions. Some of them good, perhaps some of them not so good? But we value progress, and commerce is a part of progress. We cannot be a quaint little country trapped in another century, just because it does not meet your fairy-tale standards."

"Oh my. I didn't mean to offend you," I said, not too apologetically, because I still thought I was right.

"No offense taken, Gina."

"You are very proud of Japan and being Japanese, aren't you?" I asked.

"All the more so because I have traveled widely and tried to understand what I see. I know what I am embracing, warts and all, as you might say."

I didn't know how to respond to that, so I asked Mr. Tambuki to tell me more about Nikko. The extent of his knowledge about its history, its architecture, and its religious traditions didn't surprise me. I learned how intertwined Buddhism and Shintoism were. In my world religions course, they had always seemed very distinct.

Near the Shinto Toshogu Shrine, with its Buddhist-like pagodas, was the Sacred Stable. Inside, the famous carving of the three monkeys demonstrated "hear no evil, see no evil, speak no evil."

"What about 'do no evil'?" I wondered out loud, without considering how Mr. Tambuki would leap on this opportunity for a lesson.

"How do you define evil?" he asked me. I thought maybe it was one of those rhetorical questions, but he was waiting for my answer.

"Oh. Something that isn't ethical, I guess," I said.

"By whose standards?" he wanted to know.

"Well, there are certain accepted standards in society. It's wrong to kill people, for example," I said. I realized I hadn't given the question much thought in recent years. When I was young, the nuns had defined my thinking on the subject. To them, everything was evil. Later, their puritanical views became a source of ridicule among those of us who saw ourselves as worldlier. "Wearing red and black excites the boys," Sister Archangel had told us when we were in the eighth grade. So, in defiance, underneath our uniforms we wore black bras and red panties. But no creed had replaced the mores of the mother church on more substantial questions of wrongdoing.

"Always?" Mr. Tambuki pushed back. What if you were on the edge of a cliff, and someone was trying to shove you off, but the only way you could escape would be to push your attacker off. Is that wrong?"

"Well, there are extenuating circumstances," I said. "Like self-defense."

"Ah. So, ethics are not so black and white. How should one decide what one will and won't do for money, for example?"

"Again, there are things that are clearly wrong, and some where you'd have to evaluate the situation," I said, hedging. The "hear no evil" monkey seemed to be staring at me. I felt the need to leave the Sacred Stable and turned toward the entrance.

Once again on the path, Mr. Tambuki walked briskly, and I had to trot to keep up with him. "What about people taking money for sex?" he asked. "Do you think that is always wrong?"

"What are you driving at?" Just as I was getting comfortable with Mr. Tambuki, the conversation took an odd turn.

"You know, if you go into business, you will be faced with many ethical dilemmas as well as people whose ethics you may question." Mr. Tambuki's stride seemed to lengthen every few yards.

"I suppose. But I think I'm a good judge of character. I'll have to trust my instincts."

"And what do your instincts tell you about your friend Suki?"

"How do you mean?" I asked. I felt short of breath as though we were climbing a mountain or walking at a high altitude.

"I mean, do you think that your friend Suki is bad because she has taken money for sex?"

"Suki doesn't do that. And how would you know that?"

"I *know* Suki." Mr. Tambuki emphasized the word *know*. "She did not tell you?"

"No." I was struggling to make sense of what he was saying, and then I remembered the night he groped me in his car. I stopped abruptly. "Wait a minute. I thought you told me you didn't pay for sex."

Mr. Tambuki turned around but didn't walk back to me. "I don't pay if I don't need to. I thought you were one of those free-love American women who like to collect foreign men and have adventures. I was wrong. I was also intoxicated. Or perhaps you did not find me attractive."

I was still trying to get my head around this news about Suki. "You've slept with Suki?"

Two young Caucasian men, holding hands, headed toward us. Mr. Tambuki returned to stand near me and quietly asked, "And who do you think less of now—her or me?"

"I don't know. Perhaps both of you."

Mr. Tambuki nodded at the two young men as they passed us. One of them had a maple leaf stitched on his daypack. "That is very sanctimonious of you, Gina, especially when you tell me that circumstances count. We both got what we wanted. In Japan, these things do not have quite the same stigma as they do in America."

"American men aren't as pathetic." I don't know why I said that. It was rude, I suppose, but I was mad at Mr. Tambuki for shaking me up. I didn't really care what he did, but I would rather not have known about Suki.

"I'm sorry you feel that way." He walked away but at a slower pace. The path split, and he chose the one that sloped down.

"Not you," I said, following him. "I didn't mean you. Just some of the boys at the Snack." It was a weak recovery.

"So, tell me, how do you decide what you will and won't do for money?" he asked.

"I don't think I'd sell my body, if that's what you mean."

"Ah, the body is your temple. But you are not a virgin surely?"

"Mr. Tambuki! That is none of your business." I wasn't really shocked, but I had to continue to hold some cards close to me.

"Fair enough. But let's suppose that someone you were attracted to offered to pay you handsomely for sex. Surely, you would not give it away for free, especially if you needed the money?"

My feet felt heavy as they sank into the spongy covering of wood chips and pine needles. "I'd rather not talk about this anymore."

"I'm sorry. I'm making you uncomfortable. That is thoughtless of me. But I so enjoy talking with you, Gina. You are not like anyone else I know."

"Because I put up with your nosiness? Oh, I didn't mean that." I tripped on a root buried under the ground cover.

Mr. Tambuki caught hold of my arm. As soon as I regained my footing, he let go. "You are right. I was out of line, as you say. You do strange things to me. You are very beautiful even when you are angry. But you must know that I respect you."

From an American man that would have sounded fake, but I genuinely believed Mr. Tambuki, and I was flattered that he was willing to pay to be with me. I couldn't deny I found him interesting, and he was so much more sophisticated than the men I dated at home. I still had the money Baby Elvis had left me. Lightning hadn't struck me dead, nor had the blowfish. Maybe it wasn't such a big deal. Maybe I needed to empty my mind of the Catholic teachings and begin over.

Mr. Tambuki and I ambled in silence for a while through the dark, cool woods. We climbed steps to a terrace with stone lanterns and one revolving bronze lantern. On the ceiling of the Honjido Hall was a huge dragon. Mr. Tambuki told me to clap my hands to hear the dragon roar. At the top of the stairs to the highest terrace was the most ornate gate I had ever seen. I was engrossed in seeing how many different birds, flowers, dragons, and other things I could find, when I heard a familiar voice. I turned around to see Gabe with a petite and pretty Japanese woman. "Gabe! What a small world." I was happy to see him. Suddenly, I felt more grounded.

"Dorothy Falwell," he said. "How's that trip down the yellow brick road?"

Mr. Tambuki swiveled his head sharply. The cat was out of the bag about my real name. I hugged Gabe, his round tummy pressing softly against me, and introduced Mr. Tambuki as a "friend" from Tokyo. I could see that Gabe was dying to make one of his humorous but sarcastic comments, but he kept his mouth shut. He introduced me to Tamiko. "Rhymes with Nikko," he said.

"So, what are you doing in Nikko?" I asked.

"Same as you, I suspect. Soaking up the sights," Gabe said. "I'm heading to Tokyo for a couple of days. Tami's cousin just moved there. I was going to look you up."

"I sent you two postcards. You didn't answer," I scolded.

"I'm not very good that way. Sorry. But I was glad to hear you met up with Suki and found a roof to put over your head," Gabe said.

"How do you know each other?" Tami asked, nodding at me and then Mr. Tambuki. She spoke slowly, enunciating each word. She smiled at Gabe.

"*Dorothy* and I met through her work," Mr. Tambuki replied, emphasizing my given name. "Apparently, I am the only one of her customers she can understand."

"Customers?" Tami asked. "You are a shop girl?"

"A hostess," I answered without thinking. Then to Gabe, "I can speak a little Japanese now. You'd be proud, Gabe."

Tami moved in closer to Gabe, her eyes downcast. I bit my lip as I realized that being a hostess was not such a high-class job.

Maybe Tami wondered how I knew Gabe. Mr. Tambuki didn't express any curiosity. I had visions of Gabe saying, "Oh, we kissed in front of the garbage dump at the youth hostel. Another day and we would have been lovers. The first of many, I'm sure." Of course, he didn't, but I still felt awkward. I was grateful when Mr. Tambuki suggested that we all have an early dinner together at a café we'd passed on our way in.

The restaurant was decorated in a traditional style, with paper sliding doors and lanterns. We had plenty of saké and simple food. Mr. Tambuki couldn't have been more charming. After learning that Gabe had been living in Japan for three years, he wanted to know more about his experiences as an expatriate. Gabe was his usual entertaining self. When the two of them were caught up in some discussion about sumo wrestling, Tami and I chatted. I explained my reasons for being in Japan and my need to earn money by hostessing. Tami seemed satisfied with my answers. She told me that Gabe had been her teacher. "I am very good student," she said, followed by a giggle.

"You talking about us?" Gabe asked.

"Girl talk. You men think we have nothing better to do than talk about you," I said.

As we left the restaurant, Gabe walked next to me. I figured that Mr. Tambuki would be happy with Tami, a beautiful woman, by his side. It started to rain. I pulled my small travel umbrella from my bag. Gabe moved in closer to share it with me so that our hips touched.

"Are you and Tami an item?" I asked.

He put his hand to his lips, feigning shock. "I don't sleep with my students. At least not until they are finished with the course. So 'no' is the answer."

I knew I had no claims over Gabe, but his answer pleased me.

"So, what's the deal between you two?" He nodded toward Mr. Tambuki, who was several yards in front of us, engaged in conversation with Tami. "Or shouldn't I be asking?" His deep voice dropped even lower.

"It's okay to ask. There's not a lot to tell. I haven't been seeing him all that long."

"Is he the tin man, the Wicked Witch of the West, or the Wizard? He's definitely not the lion because you can see he's no coward, and he's not the scarecrow because he clearly has a brain."

I'd forgotten how much I enjoyed being with Gabe. Talking with him was so effortless in comparison with Mr. Tambuki. "I think he's the Good Witch. He's been helping me a lot."

"Let's hope so. So, you like him?"

"Gabe, you're not jealous, are you?" I secretly hoped he was.

"Only if you've broken your vow of celibacy."

"Oops."

"Ah. Did I prime the pump?" he asked.

"Perhaps."

"And the waters are now gushing."

"I wouldn't put it quite so crudely, but there was more than one," I said.

"Good for you. At the same time?"

"The same week." Had I really? So much for vows.

Gabe glanced over at Mr. Tambuki. "Does he know about the others?"

"Nothing going on there. It's more of a business arrangement with Mr. Tambuki."

"Oh? Could have fooled me."

"You know how Japanese businessmen are," I said.

"You're a long way from business here in Nikko, I suspect."

"He wanted to treat me to something fun."

"Fun. Is that on your to-do list?" Gabe zigzagged away from me as though I had just farted.

"I'm through with lists, Gabe. I made my last list a week ago, and then I had a breakthrough. I'm trying to be Zen about things."

"What am I hearing? Is it aliens?" Gabe banged his hand against the side of his head as if clearing his ears.

"I'm the alien here, I think," I said, laughing at his comical gesture.

"The gaijin perhaps, but not an alien. I can see the change already."

"Good or bad?"

"Interesting . . . More confident maybe? Less uptight? Less judgmental?"

"I was a complete dweeb?"

"More or less, but a nice dweeb. Now you really are a woman of the world. Going out with Japanese businessmen. What next?"

Mr. Tambuki and I drove Gabe and Tami to the train station later that evening. The rain was falling steadily now, enhancing the fresh scent of evergreens. Everything looked ten shades darker here than Tokyo, where streetlights and neon created the illusion of permanent day. We said our goodbyes and made our promises to keep in touch.

Mr. Tambuki and I were alone again.

"So, Dorothy, is it?" I could see he'd been dying to confront me with my little secret.

"That's not so unusual, is it, hostesses having 'stage' names? But please don't call me Dorothy. It's not a name I use anymore. I prefer Dee Dee."

"Whatever you like. But now I have to wonder, who is the mistress of whom? Is it Gina or is it Dorothy-Dee Dee?"

I wished I didn't get so tongue-tied with Mr. Tambuki. There he was conversing in my native language, and I didn't have a ready response for him. But he made me think, even when I didn't want to. As I was considering his question and becoming mesmerized by the steady sweep of the wipers, the sky opened and lightning lit the forest like a flashing disco strobe. Mr. Tambuki slowed the car down and frowned at the now flooding road ahead.

"Gina, I don't want to drive anymore in this weather. Would you mind staying in a nice Japanese inn? Separate rooms, of course, and my treat."

I couldn't very well ask him to plow ahead in this storm, but I felt awkward, and it must have shown.

"I didn't plan this. Honestly, I didn't," he said.

I had to laugh.

The *ryokan* we found seemed like a luxury hotel. My room was large and had its own deep tiled bath in a recessed area. A blue-and-white *yukata* robe hung nearby on a hook, with slippers underneath. The futon was already laid out next to a coffee table with a small vase holding one exquisite white flower. Mr. Tambuki bid me good evening, but since it was still early, he suggested having a drink together after we both had a chance to relax.

I took off my damp clothes, sponged myself, rinsed, and eased into the steaming water. The wet heat penetrated every pore and muscle. Enjoying the rare privacy of my bathing experience, I probably stayed in too long. When I finally emerged, skin glowing pink, I felt weak. I dried off, and just as I wrapped my robe around me, there was a knock on the door. Mr. Tambuki stood there in his *yukata*, his dark hair slicked back. He held a tray with a carafe of saké, a large bottle of water, two glasses, and two porcelain cups. Dressed the same way as me, he looked more human, softer. His skin was also pink.

"I lost track of the time," I said. "I'm not used to having the bath all to myself." If it had been Gabe, I knew exactly how he would have replied. I had a knack of making remarks that left the door wide open.

But all Mr. Tambuki said was, "I hope it was pleasant." He set the tray down on the coffee table and asked my permission to turn on the radio. Sitting down on a floor cushion, he poured two glasses of water, telling me how important it was to "rehydrate" after the bath. We sipped our water in silence, listening to the eerie yet comforting sounds of stringed instruments playing traditional Japanese music, with the rhythm of the rain as a background accompaniment. I became aware of my heart thumping against my chest, adding a percussive beat to the arrangement.

Mr. Tambuki spoke first. "Gina, of all the choices you could make as an American woman, why international banking?" Mr. Tambuki poured saké into the cups and handed me one.

"It seemed exciting." The warm saké contrasted with the coolness of the water. I felt it travel down my esophagus to my stomach, where it radiated through my body.

"And you want more excitement in your life?"

"I did when I lived in Joliet." I pictured the neat little houses with their neat little gardens, lined up like good children along our street. "It's not where I want to spend my life."

"And how do your parents feel about your choice?"

I chose my words carefully. I didn't want Mr. Tambuki to think I had no respect for my family. "My father was less successful than he might have liked. My mother left high school before graduating."

"And you want them to be proud of you," he said.

"Yes. I'm the first person in my family to finish college. They were proud of me then." My eyes misted up at the memory of this rare occasion. Both of my parents had attended and watched me deliver the valedictorian speech. Even then, their words of praise were few. I overheard my mother say to another parent, "That was my girl up there." But to me, all she said was, "That was very nice, dear. I wished you had smiled more." My father commented on my "fancy" words.

"And how do they feel about this trip to Japan?" Mr. Tambuki asked.

"They don't understand why I had to go so far away." That was an understatement. Travel to them meant driving a few hours to spend a week in a small mildewed cottage by a lake in Wisconsin, where Mom cooked and cleaned and Dad zipped through a few beers, as if they were at home. They would sooner have endured a month-long fast than go to a place where English wasn't spoken and where the food was unfamiliar. I glanced at Mr. Tambuki, who was studying me. I decided not to mention that my father had lost a leg on the Pacific front.

"They think you are rejecting their values?"

"Yes. My married sister with her husband, two kids, and a dog live less than a mile from them."

"And they'd like you to be more like her?"

"Yes, but that's her life. I want to be my own person." I swilled back my saké, and Mr. Tambuki poured me another one. He was still nursing his first cup.

"And if you are successful, you believe they will accept your choices?"

I had to think about the answer to this question. I wanted to believe that my parents would eventually understand why I'd chosen the route I had. "I hope so, but to be honest, I don't know."

"What is success to you, Gina?"

Again, I paused to think. "Being good at what you do, getting recognition, being well compensated, I guess." I wondered if Mr. Tambuki would challenge my definition, but he didn't.

"And you feel confident you can achieve these things?"

"Of course, there are always challenges. If it was that easy, everyone would be successful."

"And what are your challenges?"

I took a deep breath. "At the moment, my biggest one is money."

"Business school is very expensive in America, isn't it?" he observed.

I was constantly surprised at how much Mr. Tambuki knew about life in the United States. "Yes, it is."

"I am sure you will find a solution."

I felt this sudden surge of gratefulness at how much Mr. Tambuki seemed to understand me and how supportive he was.

I'd always been attracted to him, in the hypothetical way one might be attracted to a movie star. His formality, experience, and self-confidence made me feel like we lived on different planes of the universe. Now, he seemed within reach. I remembered seeing his art supplies in the trunk of the car. "Do you want to sketch me again? This room would make a lovely background."

"I would like that very much. I will get my materials."

He returned in a few minutes with his sketch pad, brushes, and inkstone.

I sat on one of the futons, my knees out to one side, my body turned in the other direction so that my neck was stretched out. My cotton robe opened slightly.

"Gina, what are you thinking?"

He knew damn well, but I wasn't going to spell it out for him. "I am thinking that you are a very smart man, though you have a strange sense of logic about some things."

"Is that all?"

"No. You are attractive, you know."

"Thank you." Mr. Tambuki's brush skipped over the paper. Then he turned the page of his pad to start another painting.

I undid the sash to my *yukata* and let it fall away from my shoulders. For the first time I looked right into his eyes and didn't turn away like a schoolgirl who has just left a Valentine for the boy she likes. He returned my gaze, the ends of his lips curling up almost imperceptibly.

He worked quickly, like he was using a camera rather than a brush, and I found myself changing poses every few minutes. I held my hair off my neck with one hand, my elbow in the air. I lay on my stomach on the futon and propped myself up on my elbows, the robe draped over my thighs, but revealing the dimples on my buttocks. I kneeled, my legs together, but my entire torso uncovered. Mr. Tambuki's expression didn't change.

After a dozen poses, each a fraction more suggestive than the previous one, but all within some unspoken boundary of propriety,

I felt warm. The heat rose into my face, and my breathing became heavier. I peeled off my *yukata*, bunching it up near my hip, and opened my legs ever so slightly.

"You are a good student," Mr. Tambuki said. He continued to paint.

I spread my thighs another couple of inches. "I'm thirsty, Tambuki-san."

As he brought me a glass of water, I could see his penis pushing up against the inside of his robe. He brushed my hair lightly with the back of his hand and went back to his perch on the cushion.

"Is there some pose you would like?" I asked.

"You are doing beautifully," he said. "Perhaps you could rest your right hand near the top of your thigh?"

"Like this?" My crotch felt damp.

"Yes." He furrowed his brow as he swept the brush over the page, taking a little longer than usual. When he was finished, he said, "I suppose that is enough for one evening." He blew on his last painting and then closed the sketchbook.

"Can I see them?" I asked.

"Yes. But not tonight. We need to get up very early in the morning if you are to appear at your internship on time." He stood up, his robe now flat against his torso. He walked over to the futon and kissed me on the forehead.

"You are an excellent model. Utamaro would have been proud," he said and let himself out.

I remained sitting on the futon, holding my last pose. What had just happened? It wasn't something I did very often, but I moved my fingers into the wet recess between my legs and brought myself to orgasm, imagining Mr. Tambuki's thick, straight penis deep inside me, milking waves of numbing pleasure with each bone-crushing thrust.

CHAPTER TWELVE

*T*he next day, the rain had subsided, but great puddles straddled the paths and the lingering moisture darkened every surface. Outside the *ryokan*, a car waited for me. The driver, who did not speak English, handed me a note that said, "I am sorry to have to leave early on a work emergency. I will look forward to seeing you on Tuesday. Here is a token of my appreciation." The "appreciation" was a packet that contained ¥50,000, I assumed for my advanced modeling poses. In the cool light of day, I didn't regret anything I'd done. Although I was puzzled by Mr. Tambuki's rejection of what I had thought was an invitation from me, I was also relieved that I hadn't yet crossed that line with him. His behavior increased my trust in him further.

At the Snack that evening, Chief and Mama-san came in together, a rare event. And even more unusually, they switched roles. Mama-san went back into the kitchen, and Chief sat down in the corner with the books.

"Gina, come over here a minute." I edged around the inside rim of the counter, keeping my distance.

"Mr. Tambuki is very pleased, very pleased," he said, as though there were an echo in the room. My face went hot. But Chief had on his businessman's hat, covered in yen. "Another man has also asked for you to escort him. A Mr. Bando."

I didn't know any Mr. Bando. "I am already coming to work late on Tuesdays and Thursdays because of Mr. Tambuki."

Chief put his reading glasses on and consulted his calendar. "No matter. Date Club pays extra. Better business for both of us. Okeydoke. All settled."

I didn't want Chief to see my dismay, so I started to walk away. But he managed to catch my attention again.

"Oh, and Gina, I'm thinking of starting up the Club again a couple of nights a week. I want you there. Businessmen like foreign ladies."

Now that the men were asking for me, I had suddenly become a hot commodity. Along with that popularity, I seemed to have lost what precious little freedom I had at the Snack. At least I seemed to be in control of my relationship with Mr. Tambuki.

"I like the Snack," I heard myself whine.

"Okay. Okay. We'll see," Chief said. There was little room for negotiation where Chief was concerned. He would say what he thought I wanted to hear if it would reduce my level of aggravation momentarily.

When I came back to the bar, Berta was calming herself with her usual schnapps. "So, the men are lining up now, huh? That Mr. Bando—he's one of the lion jacket guys. I'd sure like to be a fly on the wall for that date. Don't be afraid to kick him in his balls if he gets fresh."

"Oh, no. What am I going to do, Berta? Chief is not going to take 'no' for an answer." I began filling the big ice barrel with beer bottles. Berta pitched in.

"What's the big deal, honey? They're just men. Think of them like these beer bottles." She lined up a Kirin, a Sapporo, and a Heineken. "How different are they? Don't take it so seriously."

Berta never talked about her relationships. I wondered if there had been anyone else after the infamous military husband. "Did you ever do Date Club, Berta?"

She gathered up the three bottles in one hand and tossed them in the barrel. A couple of ice cubes chipped and flew out. "These guys don't want to go out with me, and I don't want to go out with them."

"But they seem to like you."

"Oh, yeah, I'm entertaining. I understand them, but they're not going to parade me around and show me off."

On Tuesday evening, I had another business dinner with Mr. Tambuki and some colleagues. As he was driving me back to the Snack, he said, "Gina. You are quiet tonight. What is on your mind?"

"Chief is acting like he owns me. He wants me to go out with someone new, and now he's talking about starting up the Club again. I am the victim of my own success."

"You see? You have taken an alien situation and made it your own. But I agree. You are too good for the Club. Do you remember that place I took you to with the gentlemen from North America?"

"Yes. The one with the hostess who came on to me?"

"She was just treating you with respect, as she would a gaijin man. She meant nothing. But, it was a pleasant place, don't you agree? Not like the Club at all."

I wondered why Mr. Tambuki even bothered with Chief's club if he didn't care for it, but I didn't ask. "No. It smelled better, that was for sure, and my feet didn't stick to the carpet."

"I know the owner of a similar bar," he said, as he rounded the final corner to the Snack, its winking sign announcing its presence. "I can get you a job there the three nights a week we do not see each other, and then Chief will not be able to bother you. How does that sound?"

"Won't he be mad if you try to take me away? Apparently, I'm his little gold mine."

Mr. Tambuki pulled the car up against the curb a few yards down from the entrance. A tabby cat scuttled out from the alleyway, with a mouse tail dangling from its mouth. "Leave him to me."

"Tambuki-san, I don't know what to say. You have been so generous. But do you think I am capable of being a hostess at such an upscale place?" I could never be as skilled as Nagomi in flattery. We didn't bother with those niceties at the Snack.

"Gina. Gina. You are pushing for compliments again. I would not suggest it if I did not think you were suitable. And of course, the pay and the opportunities will be much better."

"Thank you," I said.

He planted another chaste kiss on my forehead.

Of course, I was pleased at Mr. Tambuki's obvious interest in helping me. But I was puzzled. I always thought that sexual teasing was something women did. He had dangled the possibility of a paying liaison in front of me and cajoled me into seeing my thinking on the subject of paid sex was provincial. Yet, he didn't appear at all anxious to follow through.

Despite my confusion about Mr. Tambuki's intentions, my overall mood was positive. The next day I finished my self-appointed report on emerging American investment opportunities in the Japanese market that I had researched during my lunch hours and after completing my mindless tasks. It was a good melding of East and West. I made a copy of it, put the original in a large plain envelope, accompanied by a letter to Mr. Muriachi, and took it to Keiko.

"Could you please see that Mr. Muriachi gets this?" I said. "It's something he asked me to do when I met with him last week," I added, in case she thought I was trying to go around her.

"Certainly," she said, taking the envelope from me and putting it his box. "Oh, and Gina, I am glad you are here," she said, her voice like treacle. "You have done very well with the previous assignment, so we have a new assignment for you. A special one, so you can learn something different about the New Bank of Japan. Are you free this evening?"

"Uh. I have kind of an evening job to help pay the bills."

"That is a shame. You will miss such a good opportunity."

"I'll see if I can rearrange my schedule."

"That is best. Come back to my office at half past five," Keiko said. "In the meantime, here are some more numbers to check since you are so good at that." She handed me another sheath of papers.

I phoned Mr. Tambuki and explained my dilemma. He was obliging and even offered to serve as my cover for showing up late at the Snack that evening. Best of all, he said he'd arranged for me to start work at the new bar. I promised him a few free poses in exchange.

I rifled through the pages that Keiko handed me. To keep my attention on the work, I imagined the numbers swirling around and funneling down a drain.

At the appointed hour, I returned to Keiko's office. She rummaged through her desk drawer and pulled out a beautiful scarf.

"Here," she said, offering me the scarf. "I want you to wear this tonight for your assignment."

"Thank you. But just what is this assignment?" I took the scarf from her and tied it around my neck.

"You are going to accompany Mr. Muriachi and some very important gentlemen from Taiwan for dinner," Keiko said. She walked over to me and retied the scarf more artfully.

What a turnaround. I'd had my doubts about this internship, but at last I was being recognized for my talents. The initiative I'd taken had been worth it. I was thrilled. A few minutes later Mr. Muriachi's door opened, and he emerged along with two middle-aged Chinese gentlemen.

"Gina," Mr. Muriachi said, as though we had been on close speaking terms prior to this time. At least this time he knew my name, even if it wasn't my real name. "May I introduce you to Mr. Huan and Mr. Cho? We will be hosting them at dinner." I put my hand out, but Mr. Huan and Mr. Cho both ignored it and bowed instead. The three men left together, leaving me to march behind them. As Mr. Huan and Mr. Cho entered a large black limousine that had pulled up in front of the bank, Mr. Muriachi took my elbow and in a low, stern voice said, "Your job is to make sure my guests have a very nice time tonight. You want to learn about international banking? It is about personal relations."

We went to a restaurant that specialized in beef. Two other men and one woman I didn't recognize joined us there. The woman was tiny and wore an ice-blue dress with spaghetti straps, a fitted bodice, and a full, swishy skirt. At first, I assumed she was the wife of one of the men, but it was not long before she was flirting with Mr. Cho. One of the new men, a Mr. Kwan, and Mr. Huan both spoke English, and Mr. Muriachi arranged us at the table so that I was seated between them. The dinner began with a series of toasts. Mr. Kwan, the man to my left, was emptying his glass with each toast. Wanting to be on my best possible professional behavior, I sipped my drink slowly.

Through dinner, both men were happy to answer my questions about banking in Taiwan and how it differed from banking in Japan. Mr. Kwan touched me at regular intervals when he was making a point or responding to my comments. Mostly, it was just a hand placed lightly on my arm and then removed quickly. I didn't think much of it. He was a well-traveled man and had probably picked up some Western habits along the way. I also noted that the woman in blue did a fair amount of touching as well and at one point draped herself over Mr. Cho. During dessert, Mr. Kwan and I had an animated conversation about the American presidency. He particularly liked President Reagan and his economic policies. As I gave my opinion on the "trickle-down theory," I felt a hand resting on my leg. I didn't want to cause a scene and embarrass Mr. Kwan, but I couldn't just ignore this invasion. I casually put my left hand in my lap and then tried to nudge Mr. Kwan from his wandering path. With a strong grip, he grabbed my hand under the table and placed it directly over his hard penis.

"You are very attractive," he said in a hushed voice. "Will you come back to my hotel with me after the dinner? You will not be sorry."

"I am afraid there has been a misunderstanding, Mr. Kwan. I work at the bank. I have a boyfriend."

Mr. Kwan quickly let go of my hand. He put his own hands in his lap, with one clutching the wrist of the offending hand as though to restrain it. "Oh. Please forgive me. I am very ashamed."

"You didn't know," I said.

"You are not wearing a costume then?"

"This is what I wear to the bank."

"I thought you were like her," he said, nodding his head in the direction of the lady in blue, who clearly was going back to someone's hotel that night.

I excused myself and headed back to the comparative sanity of the Snack. On the train ride, I patted myself on the back for taking this latest episode in my stride. I'd become used to handling unwanted attention from drunken men. Perhaps it wasn't an accomplishment I would boast about in my MBA program, but here it was a useful skill.

The next day, when I went to return Keiko's scarf, she told me that my services were no longer needed. She thanked me for all my contributions and gave me the scarf as a going-away gift. She was polite, and I was too shocked to probe further about why I was let go. Had I said something out of line the previous evening? Had I been too assertive in seeking Mr. Muriachi's attention? I thought I had straddled the right line between doing what I was told and seeking opportunities. Now I was back to square one with my internship. At least I'd written a report on emerging American investment opportunities. On some level, I was relieved. Maybe I would just take a break from banking for a while and concentrate on my job at the new bar. I could catch up on my sleep, see a few sights. I went back to Wakoshi and took a long nap.

At seven o'clock, Mr. Tambuki showed up to take me to Bar Puss 'n' Boots. He'd instructed me to wear my sexy black dress as he said it suited the more sophisticated atmosphere of the bar. I told him about last night's dinner engagement and my subsequent dismissal from the bank. "They never really wanted me there. I tried, Tambuki-san. I really did. I feel like I let you down since you are the one who introduced me to Mr. Muriachi."

He patted my knee. "I am sorry it didn't work out. Perhaps you are right. Perhaps Mr. Muriachi thought he needed to do me this favor, but he did not know how to use your talents. I feel responsible."

"No. No. You shouldn't. I might not have even seen the inside of another bank if it weren't for you."

"I will give you another contact if you want. I know how important this is to you."

"Thank you, but it's not necessary."

"I insist, since I contributed to this problem," he said. "But were you not a little flattered that the Taiwanese gentleman wanted to spend more time with you?"

"I don't know. I suppose it was flattering, but it was a banking event, not a hostess bar."

"Men cannot resist your charms whatever the setting, Gina."

I saw my opening. "How about you, Mr. Tambuki? You seem to be resisting my charms."

He kept his eyes on the road. "Are you offering yourself to me?"

"I thought that was what you wanted, as part of the deal."

"Is it what you want, Gina?"

"I don't know. Perhaps."

We stopped at a red light, and he glanced over at me. "Are you still thinking it is wrong to take money for sex?"

I had started this conversation, but I felt confused. "I don't know anymore."

"You can have me for free if you prefer. I won't say no. As I told you before, I don't pay for sex if I don't have to."

Would I sleep with him for free? In Nikko when I desired him, I might not have thought about money.

"But I would like to help pay for your business school education," he continued.

Mr. Tambuki's proposal sounded less like a business transaction than a generous offer. I perked up. "When you put it that way . . . ," I said.

"I am not going to force the issue. You must want this of your own free will."

I nodded and changed the subject. "Before I forget, I thought you might like to read the report I wrote for Mr. Muriachi that he never had a chance to read." I pulled the copy of the report from my bag.

"Thank you. Perhaps it will help me to see better how that American mind of yours works." He winked at me. "Here we are at the bar."

He pulled over and I handed him the envelope with the report. He placed it on the back seat, for his "bedside reading," he said.

Bar Puss 'n' Boots was in a district with other bars, most of which were in the upper stories of buildings. There were three other bars on the tenth floor. Mr. Tambuki rang the bell, and a middle-aged Japanese woman, taller than average, greeted us both with a bow. She looked as though she had stepped out of an Utamaro print, dark hair in a knot, pale skin, brocade kimono with butterflies, edged in a deep purple. Mr. Tambuki exchanged a few words with her, and she took my hand. "Very beautiful," she said in English.

"I will come back for you at midnight," he told me.

"Welcome to Bar Puss 'n' Boots. You will like," Mama-san 2 said.

She guided me into her bar, gliding as though she were wearing tiny-wheeled roller skates. The bar was divided into many booths of a rich, dark wood. The cushions were a rich cherry. At regular intervals along the walls hung pictures depicting Western fairy tales and children's nursery rhymes. Snow White, with a lascivious smile and a short skirt, dancing with the seven dwarves. The prince fitting a big-busted Cinderella with her matching shoe, a strappy sandal. His other hand was up her dress. Puss wearing sexy high-heeled boots. Jack and Jill rolling down the hill cradled in each other's arms. A different Jack fondling a vulva-like pod at the top of the beanstalk. A few weeks ago, I might have been shocked.

Waiters in Robin Hood green belted jackets with red tights prepared the drink trays for the few customers who were there. Unlike the Snack, where the only brand of whiskey was Suntory, the bottle "keep" contained many kinds of liquor as well as various whiskeys. A young Japanese woman, who I assumed was also a hostess, sat with two middle-aged Japanese men in suits. Her blue sequined bodice twinkled as she turned.

"Very nice, yes?" Mama-san 2 asked. "You meet other American—Kat."

Mama-san sidled over to a woman with long, straight blond hair, her back to us. She had on a short, stretchy dress that showed off her long, slender legs and curved over a sculpted backside. I was envious. When she turned around, I saw that it was Victoria, who'd fed me that first morning at the Club.

"Oh my God!" she said. She hugged me as though we had known each other, not just an hour, but our whole lives. "I can't believe you're here, too. What fun!"

Mama-san 2 swiveled her head back and forth between the two of us. "Kat, you know Gina?"

"Yes. Gina," Kat, alias Victoria, said.

"You show?" Mama-san 2 asked.

"Yes, I will show her the ropes. No worries, Mama."

Mama-san 2 floated off to talk to a newly arrived customer.

"I thought you were a banker," Victoria said. "Look at you."

"I am doing banking," I said, resolving to put my two dead-end internships behind me. "I needed the money."

"There's money here all right," she said. "You done this before?"

"At the Snack where you worked."

"This is way better." Victoria twirled a strand of hair around one of her red-tipped fingers. She hugged me again. "Oh, I am so happy to see you. The last girl who spoke English left right as I started working here. It's been lonely."

"How are the clients here?" I asked.

"Rich. Does anything else matter?"

Mama-san 2 led us to a table with three Japanese men and introduced us. One of the men had fleshy lips and a scar over his left eye. Another had a shiny bald head. The third one had bushy eyebrows that hung over the top of his glasses. They all stood up and bowed. When we sat down, I noticed that Scarface was missing part of his little finger, like Mr. Yakumasei. One of the Robin Hoods brought over a tray, with a bottle of Chivas. Victoria poured.

"You drink, too?" Shrubbrow asked.

We thanked him, and Victoria poured two more glasses with lots of ice. The men couldn't have been more charming. With their limited English, there was no talk of breasts, no attempted touching. Shinytop asked me where I was from. They nodded when I said near Chicago. I told them about my interest in banking. They nodded some more and laughed.

"You banker, too?" Shrubbrow asked Victoria.

She shook her head. I tried not to stare at Scarface's missing finger, but he held his glass with his half pinky out like a Victorian lady with a teacup. Someone sang an off-key rendition of "(I

Can't Get No) Satisfaction" on the karaoke. After another couple of rounds of drinks, Shinytop asked me if I sang.

"Ooo, let's sing. It will be fun," Victoria said.

We did a duet of the Beatles' "She Loves You." Victoria stood up, caressed the microphone, and swiveled her hips. She received a few catcalls and whistles from one of the other tables.

After our number, Mama-san 2 split us up. She had me sit with a gray-haired gentleman and three younger men. Two of the men looked like twins, with identical dark gray suits and red striped ties. The Japanese hostess in the blue sequins, whose name was "Cindy," told an animated story in Japanese. Her hands mimed the parallel curves of a sculpture. The men laughed. I laughed, too, even though I didn't understand. One of the twins asked me if I spoke Japanese. I held out my thumb and first finger and said, "*Watashi wa nihongo ga mada heta desu.*" Very little. Hearty laughter.

"Very big breasts," the other twin said in English, looking around at the others for approval. Guffaws.

"Yes," I said. "Very big, like her," I added, pointing to the picture of Cinderella. Hysterical laughter.

"I am Cinderella. But no breasts," Cindy said, putting her hands over her smaller, but not insignificant bust. "Poor me."

"Nice breast," the older man said, gesturing to one of Cindy's breasts and leaning forward to touch it.

Cindy deftly met the oncoming hand and entwined her fingers in his.

"Nice breast, too?" Cindy asked, pointing to her other breast.

I guessed all bars were the same. After the men tired of the breast talk, they discussed their golf games, another favorite topic. They chatted in Japanese, but I knew the word for golf. One of the twins used a cigarette to demonstrate his technique.

Mr. Tambuki arrived at eleven thirty to pay his respects to Mama-san 2. She ushered me to his table, and I poured him a Chivas.

"So, my little Gina, how was it?"

"Not so bad. The men were more polite than at the Snack. The breast talk, more refined. Mama-san, saner. But what's with the over-sexualized fairy-tale theme? It's very kitsch for a fancy place like this."

"Ah. The bar is a fairy tale, is it not? Where, for a moment, men are made to feel like kings?"

Victoria came over to tell me that that next time I could get dressed in the back room so that I didn't have to wear my gown on the train. I introduced her to Mr. Tambuki, who stood up and bowed. We left just before midnight. On the way out, I noticed a painting of Dorothy, her frilly checked frock pulled up to her chin, sandwiched between the tin man fucking her in the front and the scarecrow in her rear. At least that was what I assumed they were doing. Toto nipped at her heels as the cowardly lion waved his paws.

"I thought I might turn into a pumpkin if I stayed much longer," I said, pleased at my little joke.

"Excuse me?"

Mr. Tambuki's English was so good I sometimes forgot that he might not know all my cultural references. "The Cinderella story. At midnight, she becomes a poor girl again."

"And will Gina be a poor girl tonight, or will she allow a wealthy man to make her rich so she can live happily ever after?"

I chuckled at Mr. Tambuki's reference to a storybook ending, but what I noted was his gentle attempt to appeal to my sense of practicality. Here was a decent man. Every time I needed help, he was there. I was learning so much from him, and he was growing on me daily. When I modeled for him, I even felt desire. What did it matter between consenting adults if I took his money? I didn't need fairy tales to justify my actions.

"Okay," I said. "Let's change that story."

CHAPTER THIRTEEN

We stopped at the Hotel Artemis, an ordinary-looking place without the garish signage of the Hotel Twist, my trysting spot with Baby Elvis. The carpeting was newer, the paint fresher. A vase of cut flowers rested on a wooden table in the lobby. Mr. Tambuki pressed a button on the menu board to select our room, and we went up in a modern elevator with mirrored walls.

Although the bed was the focus of the room, at first glance, it could have been a hotel anywhere. There were a few telltale signs that the purpose of the hotel went beyond a good night's sleep. The condoms in the nightstand, for one. The enormous bathroom, with a tub built for two, for another. And the bedside reading of a book of Japanese woodblock prints. As Mr. Tambuki fixed us a drink, I paged through the book and was surprised to see the familiar figures in some very unfamiliar poses. The men, elegantly garbed, were brandishing their imposing penises in preparation for entry into equally beautifully dressed women, whose bodies were twisted in unnatural directions that made me wince.

Mr. Tambuki brought me my whiskey. "Ah, *shunga*. Spring pictures. That one is by Hiroshige," he said, pointing to one of the unhappy couples. He put his drink down, removed his jacket and tie, and placed them neatly on a chair.

I stared at the print. "The Hiroshige of *Fifty-Three Stations of the Tokaido?* That Hiroshige?" I asked, remembering one series of masterful prints Mr. Tambuki had shown me.

"Yes, the same."

"More like 'One Hundred Views of the Impossible.'" I grimaced.

"Perhaps with a bit of practice, but not tonight. Don't worry."

"Is this some kind of satire?"

"Oh, not at all. These were very popular once. Many of the great artists made them."

"The porno of their day?"

"Not porno. They are very sensual. They capture the ecstasy of lovemaking." Mr. Tambuki smoothed his hand across the page as though caressing the image. He closed the book and put it back on the nightstand.

Sitting down on the bed, he gestured for me to do the same. We perched on the edge of the bed. Mr. Tambuki gripped his glass with both hands and ran one of his thumbs over the damp surface. He seemed as nervous as me. He picked up the remote to the TV, which was just a yard in front of us and clicked. On the screen, two naked bodies writhed in a pile of hay. Click. An unclothed man lay on his back, each limb handcuffed to a bed-post, so that he was splayed in an X shape. A nude woman knelt over him, tickling him with a large feather and bouncing up and down. She dug the spikes of her long black high-heeled boot into the man's thighs. Much sighing and moaning from both of them. Mr. Tambuki glanced over at me. I'd seen porn before but not in these circumstances, not that I'd ever been in these circumstances.

I didn't want to be aroused in this way, so I looked away.

"Some music?" Mr. Tambuki asked, as though we'd become bored watching a rerun of *The Brady Bunch*.

"Yes, please," I said, turning back to the screen just as blood appeared on the man's leg near the woman's high heel. They both grunted and screamed. Mr. Tambuki clicked off the disturbing image and found some big band music. The television pulsed with waves of color.

"Would you care to dance, Gina?" Mr. Tambuki jumped to his feet, holding out his hand. "Benny Goodman."

I was back at a high school prom of another era. I never attended my own. I took the hand he offered and placed my other hand on his shoulder, which was muscular and firm. He circled my waist, his palm and fingers pressing the flesh of the small of my back. As he brought me toward him, I could smell the earthy scent of his cologne. We were a good height match for dancing.

"My parents liked this music," I said as we swayed in rhythm. "I heard it a lot when I was young."

"It evokes good memories, I hope?" Mr. Tambuki asked.

I had to think for a moment. "Some," I said. I recalled my parents dancing at Carol's wedding, Dad dragging the leg with the prosthesis but reluctantly happy for once. That was the last positive memory I had of my parents. I was six, and from then on without Carol as a buffer, it was just us and Robert's ghost.

Mr. Tambuki sandwiched our joined hands between our chests. The tick of his watch and his heartbeat were in sync at a perfect sixty beats per minute. I wedged my head between his neck and shoulder. We held that pose through two numbers, still silent.

Mr. Tambuki's fingertips slid down under my waistband. My tummy fluttered, and I gave his upper arm a squeeze. From that trigger, our lips found each other. Our kisses delved deeper. Our hands traced each other's silhouettes. Mr. Tambuki controlled the pace, which was slow if not methodical. Clothes were peeled off, one by one, beginning with a button here, a zip there, until my dress fell to the floor and his shirt was off.

When we were naked, Mr. Tambuki explored me with his mouth, owning every inch. Tasting, sucking, nipping my neck, my breasts, my stomach until I moaned and went limp.

He led me to bed and placed me on the pink sheets. He

worked his way up from my feet, which he massaged one at a time. Then with his lips and tongue and fingers, he traveled the route up the sensitive flesh of my inside thigh, teasing my genitals, before devoting his attention to the other thigh. I squirmed and reached up for him, grabbing onto his arm, which was sinewy and felt like a tightly wound spring.

"Do not be in such a hurry, Gina. There is only one first time."

He got off the bed and returned with a large, ripe peach. As he approached me, I noticed his whole body. He was hairless and slim, but sculpted with a flat stomach and full thighs like a bicyclist's. It wasn't a body of a young person so much as one who had fashioned it at will for his own purposes. Different from round Hiro, pudgy Gabe, or slender and unmuscular Baby Elvis. My gaze stopped at his penis, which was long and thick in proportion to his stature. It was perfectly straight, just as I had imagined it. I wanted it inside of me.

I would have to wait.

"Here," he said, holding out the peach. I took a large bite, the juices running down my chin onto my chest. Mr. Tambuki lapped them up, finishing with my lips. He took his own strategic bite of the peach, drops slithering down toward his navel, and then two additional large bites so that the drops became rivers. I followed my cue and licked the sweet nectar from his hard stomach as it streamed toward his genitalia. His penis twitched up toward my mouth as I came closer. I circled around it until I enveloped it, swallowing as much of it as I could. Mr. Tambuki was silent, but he followed my motions with his eyes. I liked the feel of him in the cave of my mouth, but I stopped as he had. He was still holding the remains of the peach. I finished the peach, put the stone in the glass on the nightstand, and wiped my fingers on my erect nipples. I then sucked each of Mr. Tambuki's sticky fingers as Baby Elvis had done to me. It seemed like a light year ago.

"You are not such an innocent, I think," he said, a minuscule smile flitting over his lips. He took a condom from the nightstand, tore off the wrapper, and handed it to me to put on him. I did so slowly as I knew he wanted me to, but I was still eager for the next act.

Mr. Tambuki pulled me onto my back and probed my vagina, knowing where to find the extra pockets of wetness. He slid into me with ease and positioned himself above me. Our pelvic bones ground together with such perfect precision, I came within a few minutes. I had never before had an orgasm during intercourse the first time with someone, and certainly not in the "missionary" position. Mr. Tambuki stopped for a few seconds and then began to pulse again, my body instinctively responding to the motion. I came again, and then again. Each time he stopped, allowing me to experience the dissipating waves of pleasure. We continued for what seemed like an hour. I lost count of my orgasms, as one seemed to meld into the other.

Finally, as I was beginning to climax one more time, his pace quickened.

His penis spasmed, and he stopped just as I was almost at my peak.

He resumed, my vagina gripping, his penis pulsating, my insides bursting, neon colors flashing, until our bodies sighed.

I opened my eyes. Mr. Tambuki was staring at me. I thought I saw the lens of his eyes open, the shutter finally letting in some light through those dark pupils. He rolled onto his back, and we lay there for a few minutes.

He turned his head. "Gina, why do you keep your eyes closed?" he asked.

"I don't know." It's what people did.

"You should enjoy the whole experience with all your senses."

"I did enjoy it." My senses were bombarded to oblivion. "I thought Japanese avert their gaze."

"Very observant. But you are not Japanese."

"I hope I didn't disappoint you."

"No. You did well."

I was sore. I was tired. But he could have had me all over again. I was an open receptacle.

"Gina, I am sorry I have to leave. I am going to shower now." He disappeared into the bathroom.

I knew it was too good to be true. I wanted to prolong the most extraordinary sensations I'd ever experienced. I couldn't think about anything else. My fingers wandered to my vagina, still full and wet. I began to rearouse myself.

Mr. Tambuki emerged from the shower, towel wrapped around his torso. I whipped my hand away, but I thought he saw it. "I can drive you back to Wakoshi, or you can stay here," he said.

"Why do you have to go?"

"I have to get home to my wife and son sometime, you know."

I bolted upright. "You're married?"

"Of course. You knew that surely."

My stomach turned over. "You're married. With a child."

"Gina. I thought you were finished with the judging." He unwrapped the towel, and I turned away.

"I'm just trying to get my head around this."

"You and I had sex. Good sex. We have a business relationship—an exchange. I am not proposing to you." He put on his shirt and buttoned it.

"But your wife?"

"We have an understanding. I keep her in style, and she does not ask questions."

"I see."

"Once again, you are thinking too much."

"Perhaps."

"Did you not say you had a boyfriend?

"I said that?" I had forgotten about Hiro. I would be seeing him on Sunday.

"Yes. Let the pot not call the kettle black. We may be more alike than you suspect."

Hiro wasn't really my boyfriend, was he? Wasn't a boyfriend

someone with whom you potentially had a future? We hadn't sworn fidelity to each other. That didn't stop me from feeling guilty yet again.

"If you are coming with me, you need to get dressed," he said.

"I think I'll stay." I didn't really want to stay, but I didn't feel like talking to Mr. Tambuki during the long drive back to Wakoshi.

"Okay. I will pay for you to have the full night."

I let Mr. Tambuki kiss me on the lips, even though I was still annoyed at him. He tossed a fat brown envelope on the bed.

"Do not spend it all in one place," he said, obviously trying to shift my mood.

I decided I wouldn't open it until the morning.

I hadn't talked to Suki in a couple of weeks, but I felt like I needed to see her. We arranged to meet at her place and go to kabuki theater. I told her I wanted to treat her; I certainly could afford to do so after receiving ¥50,000 from Mr. Tambuki.

When I arrived at her home, the door was ajar. I heard raised voices. I peeked in and saw a large man, his entire bare back a canvas of colorful swirls—darting orange-red carp swimming in opposite directions in a sea of abstract blue-green waves, through which poked disembodied white-faced theatrical masks, the mouths turned down and the narrow eyes, squinting. I moved away and stood in the street until the voices quieted. Suki appeared at the doorway, a smile plastered on her face. If she wanted to tell me what had happened, she would.

On our way to the theater, Suki asked me how things were going. I told her about running into Gabe in Nikko, the end of my banking assignment, my new job at the Bar Puss 'n' Boots, and Mr. Tambuki. I was anxious when I got to that part.

"Mr. Tambuki has been very good to me, Suki."

"I'm pleased for you," she said.

"He said he knew you. You didn't tell me that."

"He used to come to the Club. I didn't know him that well."

"He implied it was in the biblical sense."

"Oh." She looked down at the sidewalk.

I waited a few moments to see if Suki had any explanation that would help me understand my own situation better. But she said nothing more.

"I'm sorry. You don't have to talk about this," I said. "But it kind of threw me, you know?"

Suki raised her eyes. "Are you and he . . . ? Not that it's any of my business."

"I'm finding this world a bit confusing."

"Yes, it can be. It's all right. You aren't doing anything wrong."

Although I wasn't angry with Suki for not sharing her brief history with Mr. Tambuki, I was no longer sure how reliable a source she was on moral matters. "He told me he's married, Suki. I've never been with a married man before."

"It's different here. Everything's different, isn't it?"

"He's certainly not like anyone I've ever met," I said.

"You're only here for a while. If you are truly open, you'll learn more."

"That's what Tambuki-san says. Gabe told me he could see the change."

"Does he know about you and Tambuki-san?"

"Not really."

"I don't think he knows about my life either. Me and Bento-san."

"And the shoes."

"And the price of the shoes."

Maybe I had wanted to believe in the innocence of Suki's relationship with Bento-san. I now grasped it for what it was. The price of the shoes wasn't just about his odd means of sexual gratification. In truth, I still didn't know what he actually demanded in that department. Rather, the cost was to her dignity, in having to rely on him for her livelihood. That would not happen to me with Mr. Tambuki. I saw myself as much more self-sufficient, but I was concerned for her. "Everything okay?"

"It's okay," she said.

I didn't push it further. We both understood each other. We didn't need to spell it out.

Near the theater, we passed a photo booth. Suki dragged me into it despite my protests that my hair was a mess. "Say 'bubbles,'" she said, and we both laughed as the flash blasted at our faces.

The kabuki was another new experience. Like everything else, it wasn't theater as I knew it. The heavily costumed and made-up actors spoke in a poetic fashion, like they were spouting *haiku*. Suki explained to me that the makeup was stylized, with emotions expressed through colors and design. It was hard to believe that the actors were all men. Several were so believably female in their body language and inflection of their voices. They were accompanied by flute, drums, and the shamisen, with offstage sound effects. Every so often an actor would strike a dramatic pose, and the audience would clap. People ate their box lunches. They came and went. The atmosphere reminded me of a baseball game. I was as interested in the crowd as the game at hand. I didn't understand all the rules, but I appreciated the spirit of it. There were good guys and bad guys. I wondered how I would have reacted a few weeks ago. Would I have thought it too forced and formulaic?

I was starting to forget some part of me. I was like a big chunk of ice breaking offshore into smaller pieces that were reforming into some new shape. After using all my energy to keep the chunk together, I was finally letting go, drifting a little, but relieved of my burdensome task. Was Mr. Tambuki one of the pieces, or the tidal force? I didn't have the new metaphor fully worked out, but the rolling stone image wasn't working anymore.

CHAPTER FOURTEEN

*I*f I was in the mood to be self-reflective, I didn't have the opportunity to indulge myself for long. Penny had left me a note asking me to meet her at the park before work. The note, written all in capital letters, was both childlike and urgent.

I found her sitting alone under a tree, legs crossed. I kneeled down next to her. Her eyes were moist and rimmed in red. As she started to talk, the tears began flowing again.

"I told Jimmy about the baby. He flipped out. He said I should 'take care of it.'" She stopped for a moment to catch her breath.

She hadn't said anything in the last couple of weeks, and I'd almost forgotten. "Penny, are you sure you're pregnant?"

She nodded. I found a tissue in my bag and gave it to her.

"He told me I had to keep quiet, or he'd be in big trouble," she continued between blubbers. "He said he'd be there for me, but we couldn't see each other anymore. What am I gonna do?"

"Does Jimmy know you're only fifteen?" I knew the answer full well.

"He thinks I'm eighteen, but not 'cuz I told him. He just assumed."

"Oh, God. That's rape. You're a minor. He could be court-martialed or worse." I didn't know for sure that was true, but it seemed plausible enough.

"I don't care. He broke up with me."

"Penny, listen to me." I wanted to shake some sense in her, but I was pretty sure I was no expert where men were concerned. "You have to think about what's best for everybody, especially you. I have money. I can help you."

"I don't want money. I want Jimmy back." Penny's waterworks began again. "I want his baby, too."

I reached over and held her. "I know. I know," I said as sympathetically as I could. I remembered how much I hated to be given advice as a teenager, and how easy it was to dish it out as an adult. "Penny, have you seen a doctor yet?"

She shook her head, looking down at the ground. "I don't want them telling Berta."

"You need to get yourself checked out. For the baby's sake. Will you go?"

Penny finally agreed. I promised I'd go with her. We didn't discuss her options. I thought we should take it one step at a time.

We walked back to the Snack together. Penny shadowed me as if to make herself invisible. When we reached the door, she was hesitant to enter until I gave her a signal. Berta's head was hidden by her own large rear end swathed in shiny purple taffeta. Bending down in search of something from a lower cabinet, she looked like a prizewinning eggplant. I motioned to Penny, who darted to the back, a thief with contraband. I went behind the counter and began the nightly setup. Berta rose up, empty-handed and scowling, with her cigarette hanging precariously from her lower lip.

"Goddam Mama-san. We're out of my favorite schnapps. Again."

"Hello to you, too," I said.

"You seen that little tramp of mine?"

"She's already in the back, working." I wanted to paint the

picture of the responsible Penny, not the one that had been knocked up by a married soldier. I felt protective of her as though she were my child, not Berta's.

"I swear she's getting moodier by the minute. I can't take much more of this. I got two jobs just to make ends meet." Berta raised her voice for Penny's benefit. "She should quit school and help out. What good is that local school anyway?" Then, more quietly, almost like a footnote to herself. "God, I hate this fucking country. And it's so fucking hot in here. Why can't they get air-conditioning like normal people?"

I knew that the last remark was rhetorical. It may even have been aimed at me for having deserted her for Bar Puss 'n' Boots. After my emotional roller coaster of the last few days, I wasn't ready to tackle Berta's pet peeves about Japan. I was going to stay positive, forward looking, on my ice floe.

Hiro and I planned to meet for lunch the next day near a parade. There was always a parade on the weekends, commemorating something or other. For me, the midday timing meant I wouldn't have to handle the issue of sex. If the deal with Mr. Tambuki was entirely business, then it shouldn't have mattered, but I'd justified our arrangement as being motivated as much by attraction as an interest in money. I told myself that I would be cheating on Mr. Tambuki if I slept with Hiro, rather than the other way around. My panties became damp every time I thought about the intense lovemaking session with him. And that was every waking minute since Friday.

When I spotted Hiro along the parade route, I smiled. He looked so fresh and full of anticipation as he watched the young boys with *happi* coats and the girls in the kimonos on their floats covered with flowers. By the time I reached him, he was crouched down in front of a young girl, a blue ribbon in her hair and a balloon in her hand. She talked and laughed. He made a funny face, his eyes bulging, his mouth contorted. The girl giggled. Then he waved goodbye to her and bowed to the woman standing next to her.

I tapped him on the shoulder. He grinned and embraced me like a long-lost love. Before I could even open my mouth to greet him, he kissed me rather intimately for such a public space. His kiss was familiar, different from Mr. Tambuki's, but nice in its own way. Fortunately, he pulled away first. Both of us had to catch our breath.

"Does this mean you did okay on the first part of your test?" I asked.

"No, not so good, I think."

"You seem awfully cheerful for someone who didn't do so well."

"I look forward to seeing you," he said. "I think you make me forget worry."

"I'll do my best."

"Already have."

I was flattered, but I felt undeserving. "I'll bet you did okay," I said, trying to make myself feel better.

"No, I pretty sure I do bad. Maybe need to practice more English for next part? I like it when you teach me." He winked at me, clearly enjoying his own little double entendre.

"Who was that little girl?"

"I not know her. I give balloon."

"That was nice of you."

"I like little childrens. I want to be father someday."

"I'll bet you'll be a good one, too."

"Yes. I will play with my childrens. I will see them every day." Hiro gazed off into the distance as though he were seeing his future life.

"Did your father play with you?"

"On Sundays. Not home very much other. Very busy salary-man. Make money for family. Your father play with you?"

"When I was very little, I would sit on his knee and we did

make-believe games. After that he wasn't around much either." In the flesh maybe, but not available to me. And his alcohol breath made me gag.

He nodded. "You want childrens?"

I guessed I probably would have kids one day, but I couldn't picture it. "I don't know. It's harder for a woman to be a good mother and have a career."

"Yes. Hard in Japan, too. But young men help now, I think."

I wondered about Mr. Tambuki's child and how often he saw his dad, whether he idolized him from afar, what kind of father the son would be when he grew older. Perhaps like Hiro, he would embody a different model of parenthood.

Hiro took my hand, and we strolled silently. After lunch at a stand-up noodle shop, we took the Funabashi-Minami Line to LaLaport, a brand-new shopping mall. Hiro wanted me to see (and I suppose be impressed) by this modern Japan. "No other thing like this," he said proudly. We didn't actually go into any of its many stores or its sporting complex. At the end of the afternoon, when we parted, I promised I would help him study his English again the following Sunday. I was hoping he would let us go back to being just friends.

The transition between Hiro's sanitized and cheerful Tokyo and Mr. Tambuki's murky night world might have been more jarring if I hadn't been so eager to play out my lust-drenched fantasies. As soon as I saw Mr. Tambuki, I erased his family from existence. I might never meet someone like him again, and sex might never be so good. As a bonus, my wallet was getting fatter. Or was the sex the bonus, and the money, the object?

Mr. Tambuki told me we'd be going to a studio he used. He wanted to paint me again in a different setting. Behind the gallery where he had shown me the woodblock prints was a small room furnished with a simple low table and cushions, a divan covered in sea-green silk brocade, a tall cupboard, and a two-burner stove.

A sideboard held a variety of brushes and inks. Rows of movable spotlights hung from the ceiling. After retrieving a gold-colored kimono with a butterfly pattern from the cupboard, Mr. Tambuki asked me to put it on. The silky lining was smooth against my bare skin and heightened the fluttering in my loins.

He heated up some saké, and we both sat cross-legged at the table, sipping from oversize cups and snacking on roasted edamame. I was happy to have something to crunch on and didn't say much. Mr. Tambuki sat behind me and massaged my shoulders and neck.

"You are tense, Gina. Are you anxious?"

"A little. I never know what to expect with you, Tambuki-san."

Mr. Tambuki stopped his rubbing but left his hands resting on my shoulders. "Expectations imply a past and a future, Gina. The past is no longer. The future does not exist. There is only now."

"But the future is what motivates me to do things, and the past allows me to see what might be possible and where I've made mistakes."

"You must live your life as though you were hanging onto the edge of a cliff. Be fully in the moment. No goals."

"Not even the goal of *not* falling from the edge of the cliff?"

"Not as a goal. Act spontaneously."

He stroked my neck, upper arms, and chest, his hands reaching down into my kimono. His fingers made a circle around my nipples without touching them. My breathing quickened.

"What do you want to do now, Gina?"

"Make love to you?"

"I am not part of this equation. Stay with the way your body is feeling now. Listen to it."

My body was saying, "Fuck me," but I was the student. Mr. Tambuki continued caressing me. How could he have learned so quickly what turned me on, how much pressure to use? My past boyfriends took weeks to discover these things, even with my guidance.

He slowly pulled his hands away. "Gina, why don't you go sit on the divan."

I assumed Mr. Tambuki would join me, but instead he picked up a brush, an ink block, and a sketchbook. "I want you to ignore me. I am going to busy myself so that you can continue your experience. You are on the edge of the cliff. Reach for the supreme pleasure."

"Without you?" I asked, puzzled by his odd request.

"Yes. I know you women don't really need us men."

"I'd feel a little self-conscious."

"It's not like I am photographing you. It's just a simple line painting."

"But why?"

"Because you are beautiful when you are aroused. I want to be a part of your experience, but not a part of it. Do you see?"

"You are a strange man, Tambuki-san."

"Indulge me in my strangeness then. You know you will be rewarded."

"But if I look forward to the reward, aren't I focusing on the future rather than on the present?"

"Very good, Gina. You learn quickly."

He came over to me, took my chin in his hand, and kissed me lightly on the mouth and traced his tongue along the inside edge of my earlobe. When he pushed the kimono off my shoulders, I arched my back instinctively. He stroked my stomach, allowing one finger to slip into my vagina and caress my clitoris on its way out.

"Do you want me, Gina?"

"You know I do."

"Then imagine us together in one of those *shunga* prints." He pulled his finger out and put it near my mouth. "Taste your own sweet nectar."

I sucked his finger, holding on to it with my lips, gums, and teeth. But Mr. Tambuki extracted it and returned to the table.

"Embrace your feelings," he said.

I let my hand wander to the wet and swollen spot he had abandoned.

Mr. Tambuki began to paint. "Go slow, Gina."

After a couple of minutes, he said in a hushed voice. "Stop. But stay with your feelings. Where else do they take you?"

I found my full breasts and circled them with my fingertips. I pinched my hard nipples.

"Open your eyes and watch yourself, Gina. Take it all in."

I saw that Mr. Tambuki was engaged in his painting, looking at me with a detached eye. I envisioned us in one of those contorted poses, panting, groaning, in a frenzy of exquisite sensation. Over the next few minutes or perhaps it was hours, he guided me on my journey. When he thought I was too close to coming, he would ask me to stop. I don't know how he knew what my body was feeling.

"Taste yourself again. Each finger in the honey jar," he said.

I had tasted myself before in that mingling of juices that happens during sex, but never so purposefully.

The fifth time he told me to stop, he asked me to close my eyes and assume the position of a cat. "Listen," he said.

I heard the rapid thudding of my heart, rushing in my ears like a tidal wave, the in and out of my shallow breaths, the swish of his brush across the page, the shush of stockinged feet, a muted yelp of a zipper, the rustle of cloth.

Then unfamiliar sensations. A finger rubbing the rim of my anus, stretching it, a jolt, hands on buttocks, the slapping of flesh against flesh, a bulge pulsing rhythmically inside me. In my heightened state, I writhed with each movement, straining to locate that spot that would meet my needs, but I couldn't find it. The bulge quickened its pace, throbbed, and shrunk. Wetness. Again, the rustle of cloth, the yelp of a zipper.

I didn't move for a minute.

"Thank you, Gina. You can relax now."

I sat down on the divan. Mr. Tambuki, a little pink, but otherwise looking as though he had just completed the Sunday crossword, handed me a full cup of saké. It was lukewarm, but I was thirsty. I gulped it down.

"Should I continue what I was doing?" I asked. Wanting to finish the job I'd started. Perplexed about what had just happened.

"No, I am quite satisfied. You can get dressed now if you wish."

"But I didn't come," I said, almost to myself.

"What did you say?"

I set the cup on the nearby table. "I didn't come, Tambuki-san."

"You weren't meant to, Gina. That was the point of the exercise. It was not about destinations."

"You came."

"This wasn't about me."

"That doesn't seem fair somehow." I could feel my face contort into a pout.

"You were enjoying yourself, were you not?"

"I guess. Except the last part, to be honest."

"You do not like that position, I take it?"

"I've never done that before."

"I am surprised. I assumed . . ."

"That's okay. It wasn't bad." In my aroused state, it was as though all my orifices had opened, not sure which one would serve as a receptacle. "Maybe more of a surprise."

"That was part of the idea, to jolt your senses, Gina."

Mr. Tambuki took me to an especially lovely restaurant that evening. Whether this was his way of apologizing, I wasn't sure. And what part would he have been apologizing for? Leading me unknowingly into what in retrospect felt like a degrading series of sexual acts? Using me for his pleasure, but not allowing me to satisfy my own needs? Treating me like his love slave? And why? To teach me one of his lessons about Zen? To fulfill some artistic impulse? I hoped this evening had been an aberration and that we would return to the extraordinary high of our first night of lovemaking. What could I really say? I was in this willingly, and I was handsomely compensated. I could walk out at any time. But I still believed that he was interested in helping me, even if he was getting something in return. He had a knack of making me feel that everything he did was for my own good.

He didn't speak much during dinner and seemed to savor every bite, commenting on the crispness of the vegetables or the subtle flavor of the sauce. I wished I knew what made him tick. I wished I had even an inkling of how much I could trust him, even as I wanted him in a way I had never wanted anyone before.

CHAPTER FIFTEEN

After I began working at Bar Puss 'n' Boots, my life became more compartmentalized. Each part—the Snack, my daytime hours as Dee Dee, Mr. Tambuki, and the Bar—had its distinctive characteristics, and each left a different imprint on me. Sometimes the edges of the parts would bleed into each other and leave me confused.

The Snack was the most familiar and comfortable. The only full evening I was there was Saturday. On Tuesdays and Thursdays, Mr. Tambuki would drop me off as late as ten o'clock. I became more cavalier and self-assured around customers. I still let Berta take center stage, to taunt them with her tart tongue, to curse them out, to punish the few obnoxious ones by ordering excessive drink and food to add to their bills. I was her sidekick, politer but still sassy. I sang; I danced; I laughed; I teased, using my meager knowledge of the Japanese language as bait to lure them in. I'd played my role so many times that I could sleepwalk through it, drunk. My equally inebriated customers didn't care as long as I paid attention to them. Even with my reduced hours, Chief appeared to be content with my performance.

Most days were a blur. My head didn't clear until the early afternoon. Often, I didn't leave my room until it was time to go to work. I no longer made any attempts at reconstituting my internship, other than the occasional trip to the library under the pretense of doing more research. Then I would settle in a comfortable chair and read an American newspaper to see how the White Sox were doing. Sometimes, though, I would wander into town and go to an exhibit, walk in a green space, or sit in a café. Small things surprised me—the intriguing or repellant taste of an unfamiliar food, the clean smell of the air after a rainstorm, the weird clothing combinations worn by teenagers. I savored those moments and would hold them in my memory as long as I could.

I saw Hiro once more before he went on vacation to Hokkaido with his family. I helped him study English again, this time in town so that I would not have to make excuses for our lack of intimacy. I was relieved he was leaving for a while, and I secretly hoped that in his absence he would forget about me. It was easier that way.

Mr. Tambuki filled too large a space for there to be anyone else of any importance. Oddly, I had difficulty remembering the order of events involving him and which experiences were attached to which settings. On one of our engagements, he made love to me again in that thrilling and deeply satisfying way of our first time. Had I posed for him that evening? On another, he was perfunctory and inattentive. Was that in a love hotel or in his studio? A third time, he was rough and demanding. Had we had a pleasant cocktail together just before, or had he arrived straight from work? Sometimes there was no sex at all. We would have a civilized dinner, and he would deliver me to the Snack at an early hour and even stay for a drink or two. Like Pavlov's dog, I could not guess when I would receive a sexual treat, so in the hopes it would be that night, I continued to do as he asked. My payments for our assignations varied as well, but they were always generous. Sometimes, instead of money, he would give me gifts—a green silk dress, a gold choker, and once, a Hokusai print of *Mt. Fuji in a Summer Storm*. In it, the big mountain, surrounded by puffs of clouds, is a deep orangey-red at the top of its cone. Mr. Tambuki said that the print had been made from the original woodblock.

I continued to model for him, although he never again asked me to arouse myself. Sometimes he had me hold a position for a long time until an arm or leg would fall asleep. He taught me some tricks to escape my discomfort. He didn't call them tricks, of course, but Zen meditation techniques. I didn't tell him that often I calmed down by conjuring up a vision of our two bodies meshed in perfect harmony to the point where I could come without touching myself. I think he could tell. After one particularly painful posing session, he took me to a room in a love hotel that had a variety of extra fixtures attached to the bed. In my hyped-up state, I allowed him to handcuff me to the bedposts while he tickled me with a feather. He knew all my sensitive spots, especially the inside of my thighs and the soles of my feet. I laughed, unable to stop even after the feather was no longer in contact with my body. "Now, Gina, see if you can refrain from laughing," he said. And I was able to do so. But as much as I desired him and as much as he intrigued me, I kept one of my antennae up. If I were able to peel away the complex layers to get close, I could see myself being consumed by him completely, by his huge appetites and needs, by his even huger ego. I couldn't afford to let that happen.

And then there was Bar Puss 'n' Boots. In contrast to the Snack, most of the regulars were in their fifties and sixties. Younger men generally accompanied their bosses, kowtowing to them, laughing too loudly at their jokes, buttering them up, just as the hostesses did. The Bar charged customers by the hour in addition to the liquor, food, and drinks for the hostesses, and visits could be expensive. Initially, I was relieved that the men were older than those at the Snack as I thought they would behave themselves better. But their talk, particularly after a few drinks, was just as sexualized, and "bad hands," as they themselves often referred to their roving fingers, had to be removed from unwelcome places.

Although I no longer felt personally harassed by the conversation or the groping, it seemed undignified from a people who were required to follow so many other rules of decorum. I soon realized that engaging in body dialogue was an expectation of the bar culture. However, whereas at the Snack we could say more or less what we liked to our young customers, at the Bar hostesses had their own unspoken code regarding appropriate responses. Berta, who egged the clients into being foul-mouthed and then berated them for it, would have been fired in a minute at the Bar.

Another expectation was that the hostesses would cultivate customers in the hopes that they would be taken on dinner dates, to be followed by a long session with the same customer at the Bar. The repeat clientele was the Bar's lifeblood. The *dohan* was the equivalent of Chief's Date Club, which had been strictly optional, but I was told that no hostess would last at the Bar if she couldn't attract a following. Not thrilled by the prospect of spending a whole meal with someone who had the equivalent of a schoolboy crush on me, I kept a lookout for the customer who didn't fit the usual mold.

I met one my first full week. One evening, a short man in a beige, open-necked shirt and black slacks came in by himself. Mama-san 2 delivered me to his table and bowed deeply. The man, whom she introduced as Akira-san, stood up and bowed in return. After Mama-san 2 left us, he glanced at me and then didn't say anything for a minute. I thought he might be shy. He was no more than thirty and handsome in a boyish way. In addition to the casualness of his dress, there was something not quite Japanese about Akira-san, something almost Western. I'd become so accustomed to Japanese features that I found myself staring at the round-eyed faces of white males when I saw them on the streets. I studied Akira, trying to figure out what made him different. The less than jet-black hair? The slightly deeper eyelids? I forgot that as a hostess I was in charge of starting a conversation.

When his bottle was delivered, I poured him a drink. He peered at me as though I were transparent.

"Gina. That's a beautiful name," he said in perfect English. His voice was soft and velvety. "Is that your real name?"

No one had ever asked me that before. "Uh, no, but it is easier to say than my real American name and less childish, I'm told, than my nickname."

"And what are those?"

His directness unnerved me, and I let it slip out without any hesitation. "Dorothy, or Dee Dee, but you won't tell anyone will you?"

"That will be our secret. Dorothy, are you searching for a way back home, or is Japan home now?"

"You know the story of *The Wizard of Oz*?"

"Yes, my grandfather was American. His family was English originally. He taught me all the stories that are on these walls."

I was happy to have the mystery of his appearance solved. One-quarter American, yet still Japanese. Not a bad combination. "Is that why you come here, Akira-san?"

"Just Akira. You don't need to be formal."

"Akira."

"Of course, the stories have been changed somewhat."

"Adulterated," I said, wondering if he'd understand my play on words.

He squinted at Snow White with her lascivious grin and laughed. "Yes, you could say that. But I come here because I like the company." He raised his glass. "Cheers!"

"Cheers," I said, hoisting my own cocktail, served in a tiny glass reserved for hostesses so that we could score more drink orders from our customers. "Are you a salaryman?" I doubted he was, but it was an easy conversational gambit.

"Oh, no. I am a monk."

I wasn't expecting that answer. Was he an ex-monk like Mr. Tambuki, or a real monk? Where were his robes? What was he doing in a bar? "A monk?"

"Don't be so surprised. We're not hidden away all the time. But why are *you* here?"

"To make money so I can pursue my goal of learning about international banking." This last bit sounded as hollow as bamboo to me. I changed tact. "Of course, my overall goal is to learn as much about the culture as I can."

Akira cocked his head. "And what have you learned?"

"That men behave differently in bars than in a bank and that everyone seems to accept this?" I laughed. I was both afraid of saying too much and happy to have the opportunity to be myself.

"Of course, I don't know banks." He smiled at me. There was a gap between his two front teeth. "What else?"

Clearly, Akira wasn't going to let me off too easily. "Zen influences in Japanese culture?"

"A big topic but one that I understand. Have you been to the tea ceremony?"

"When I first arrived."

"And what did you think of it?"

I could still remember my numb legs, my yawns, the bitterness of the tea. "I was rather new here. Maybe even a bit jet-lagged. But it was interesting."

"The tea ceremony embodies so much of what is good about the Japanese spirit. Personally, I also find it somewhat tedious." He chuckled and winked at me conspiratorially. "All that work for a cup of tea."

His irreverence delighted me. He reminded me a little of Gabe. Of course, I didn't go so far as to tell him about Mr. Tambuki's unorthodox teachings, but I didn't need to work to maintain a conversation. Akira asked me what I thought of American politics (much to my parents' chagrin, I was left-leaning), American baseball (again, to their horror, I wasn't a Cubs fan), and Japanese food (sometimes too salty, but otherwise I was enjoying it). With no pretense between us, not even my fake name, and no language barriers, I found myself drawn to Akira.

Perhaps he felt the same way because he promised he would come again soon.

Victoria, aka Kat, came over to me after Akira left. Her hair was swept back from her face into a messy bun. She wore long, sparkly earrings.

"He's nice, that one," she said. "You can talk to him, though he does like to ask questions."

"He's a regular?"

"Oh, yes. Never drinks that much. Very polite. No touching."

"He *is* a monk."

"That doesn't make any difference. In my last job, I went out with a monk. At least he said he was a monk."

"Have you been out with Akira?" I asked.

"No. He's yours if you can land him, but I doubt he has much money. See that guy saying goodbye to Mama-san?"

I looked toward the door to see three men, all dressed in identical navy-blue suits, bowing to Mama-san 2. "Which one?"

"With the red tie. He's super rich, and he likes gaijin women. I've already been out to dinner with him twice, and he's going to take me to Kyoto this weekend."

"Really?"

"Oh, they don't expect anything. But they have to dream."

I envied Victoria for her perpetual cheeriness and her ability to fit right in. She was a natural at hostessing. I began watching her to see how I could make my job easier. Customers loved her, and not just because she was tall, blond, and beautiful. Despite her youth and her minimal grasp of Japanese, she knew exactly how much to give someone and where to draw the line. When we jointly served a group of men, it was she who had them laughing with a silly story about how she once found a stray cat, which turned out to be a baby panther that someone had bought illegally as a pet. And then she tied the whole story back to her bar name, Kat, and they laughed some more. If a hand reached out to touch her, she would take it and hold it in her own, an intimate, yet innocent act. She accompanied this with agile flattery. "Rami-san, what strong fingers you have." "How young your hands look. Why, you have smoother skin than I do." "I'll bet these hands know how to swing a golf club." I was happy to engage the men in some primitive conversation, knitting together their English with my Japanese. These attempts won me accolades and bonus drinks, but I couldn't bring myself to practice the sort of worship that came so naturally to Victoria. On a slow night, Boopsie, a Filipino hostess who wore a push-up bra to show off her already gigantic breasts, sometimes performed a rudimentary striptease for the guests. Victoria cheered but never participated in that kind of stunt. We did have a costume night once. Victoria came as a fairy godmother, with a floor-length skirt, a high neckline, long sleeves, and a wand. The wand, which she waved ceremoniously over customer's heads as she told them to make a wish, caused more of a sensation than Boopsie's revealing miniskirted Dorothy with her low-cut, lace-up bodice that cinched in her already small waist. Her outfit left little to the imagination compared to Victoria's. Initially, I felt annoyed that Boopsie had appropriated my namesake Dorothy, but I had to admit that her costume was more adventurous than mine would have been. The small barking dog that accompanied her and nipped at customers' ankles was a particularly clever touch. But try as she might, Boopsie couldn't upstage Victoria. Not that Victoria was the least bit competitive.

When the inevitable breast or pubic hair drivel emerged, Vic-toria smiled and nodded, answering questions matter-of-factly in a cotton candy voice. If asked about another hostess's assets, she responded in a way that favored her colleague. Shrubbrow, one of the trio of yakuza I had met my first night at the Bar, seemed particularly enamored of the female form. He told her, "I think Gina's breasts are bigger than yours. You must have seen them. What do you think?" Victoria answered, "Oh, yes, you are certainly right." She neither goaded nor chastised customers, and soon they moved on to other topics, often at her initiation.

"How do you always manage to find the right things to say?" I asked her in the changing room after one especially busy night a few weeks after my arrival at the Bar. She had been hopping from table to table, stroking egos, soothing stressed souls, bolstering testosterone, juggling multiple hearts at once. She blew kisses, squeezed arms (commenting on their muscularity), allowed her fingers to be grazed by lips, and with a quivering sincerity urged them to "come back again soon." Each man must have left certain that next time he would be lucky.

"I don't know. I just tell them what they want to hear, and I don't promise too much. But sometimes, I follow through so they know that more is a possibility."

"What do you mean, you follow through?" I thought I knew what she meant, but I needed her to spell it out.

"You know, I go to a love hotel with them."

Even though she had professed that her relationships were innocent a few weeks earlier, I wasn't shocked. But I was surprised. "Don't you worry?"

"They're not strangers. I've talked to them here, maybe been out to dinner with them. Most of them are nice really, even though they are kind of old. I don't go out with the creeps."

"I'm sure they all want you. How do you decide?"

"If a man has kind eyes, or I feel a little sorry for him because he's had a difficult day, that sort of thing."

It seemed like Victoria was attracted to strays of all kinds. "I know that Mama-san likes us to go on dates, but does she encourage you to do this, too?"

"Not really. For her it's all about the business. Whatever keeps the customers. So, if you go too far with a guy and have a fight, that's not good."

"I thought if you fulfill their fantasies, the incentive to come here is gone."

Victoria shrugged. "I don't fulfill all of them. There's some mystery left. But don't say anything, will you? I don't want to get in trouble." Victoria glanced around nervously.

I was silent for a minute. *Is this common? Is this another unspoken rule?* I wondered. Instead I asked, "What do the men ask you to do at the love hotel?" Were they like Mr. Tambuki? Did they have enormous self-control and stamina? A penchant for experimenting with sensation? Odd quirks?

"Most are pretty normal, I guess. One guy did ask me to dress up as a character in a story or a movie like we did on costume night. That was weird but kind of fun. It's not like I do this every night. Just sometimes, when it feels right, and I think he might be generous."

I had to admire Victoria. She was forthright and unapologetic. She made her behavior seem ordinary, like buying groceries. Most of her regulars kept coming, and she soon managed to replace the ones that didn't.

After a month at Puss 'n' Boots, the Snack felt like junior high school to me. The boys behaved like teenagers who had found the key to Daddy's liquor cabinet and his stash of *Playboy* magazines. And having drained a cheap bottle of whiskey, they needed to have their mouths washed out with soap. I wanted to tell them to grow up, but that was Berta's job, and she wasn't much better than the customers. I enjoyed myself to a degree, but I was grateful to Mr. Tambuki for keeping my hours there as short as possible. At least he continued to be full of surprises, like a skilled tennis player whose variety of shots sent his opponent off guard. As he painted, he kept stressing the importance of practicing one's craft as the route to enlightenment.

"I don't have any craft to practice now," I said, stretched out on the divan, holding one white lily.

"I think you do, Gina. You are learning much about the client, are you not? How to talk to the client, listen to the client, please the client, be patient with the client, while maintaining your focus."

"I'm not sure I see the parallels between hostessing and business."

"Oh, but you are wrong, dear Gina. It is most similar in the importance of the client. Do you not see?"

"Mr. Muriachi said something to that effect once."

"It is not just my opinion then. But if you do not give yourself over to your craft, you will not make progress. You must let go of your ego, Gina. Become one with your craft. Seek its core."

Even after all these weeks, I didn't understand what Mr. Tambuki was talking about. But he seemed convinced that I could attain some higher state, and I didn't want to let him down. "I'm doing my best."

"Go beyond what you imagine to be your best, and you will find that egoless space. Let your spirit flow."

"Is it better than drugs?"

"You are not taking drugs, I hope?"

"No. I was just trying to make a joke. You are always so serious."

"Life is serious, but in that there is joy. The frog on the lily pad. The drop of dew on a blade of grass. You at the peak of your pleasure."

Mr. Tambuki slid his hand across my stomach, and I became instantly wet.

Maybe it was my quest for the egoless space, a space that was not so consumed by Mr. Tambuki's power over me, that made me agree to see Akira after hours. Or maybe it was a chance to pay attention to the moment. Or my curiosity about the potential sexual prowess of monks. After his third visit to Puss 'n' Boots, Akira asked me whether I "granted favors" to customers.

"What do you mean?" I asked, knowing full well.

"Bodily pleasure," he said. "I hope you do not take offense in my asking."

"No offense taken, but I need to think about it." I was flattered.

I spent the next afternoon at my favorite pond, watching the koi play with each other in the mottled sunlight. My intention had been to mull over this big decision, but I was already certain that I would "grant a favor" to Akira. I liked him personally. He felt trustworthy. Although I found him attractive physically, that I didn't lust after him made my choice easier. The sex would mean nothing, and it would be just this once to satisfy my curiosity if nothing else. And the prospect of money never hurt. If Victoria did this, I certainly could.

Akira did not care for the heavily themed love hotels. "I do not believe in charades," he told me. The room he chose at Hotel Bella Donna was simple, unadorned by plush fabrics or high technology. Two simple scroll paintings of blossoming trees, temples, and mountains hung at eye level on the champagne-colored walls. A large white futon with crisp white covers filled the middle of the tatami floor. Off to the side was a low table. On its center was an artfully arranged vase of twigs and flowers. In the windowless room, the only sounds were bird song and the rustle of trees from some unseen speakers. If the décor was meant to calm, it succeeded.

Not that I was all that anxious. I didn't even think of this as cheating on Mr. Tambuki. After all, wasn't it he who had urged me to hone my craft? And wasn't it he who had said, "Treat every time like the only time"? Plus, this was strictly business.

In this setting, Akira was a man of few words. When I tried to speak, he put his finger over my lips. Still fully clothed, he gestured to me to sit down on the futon in front of him with legs crossed. He stared into my eyes, and with delicate fingers flirted over the surface of my face, outlining the small mole near my lips. He smiled. Not Mr. Tambuki's fleeting smile, nor a tooth-filled grin, but a smile that emanated from his whole face, an uncritical smile. I gazed into his dark eyes and saw myself reflected back, features distorted by curved lenses. Yet, at the same time, like Alice's looking glass, his pupils appeared to open and let me in.

He brought my hands to his face. I traced the roundness of his cheekbones, the indentation beneath his lower lip, and the hollows and creases of his ears. He moved in closer and buried his nose into my hair. I could hear him taking deep breaths in through his nose. His fingertips brushed my neck, then kneaded the base of my head until he brought our mouths together. Lips, then tongues, tasting and tangling. His breath was sweet, untainted by cigarettes, garlic, shrimp, or whiskey. His kiss, though deep, was not the desperate foreplay of a man with more urgent goals.

When we both spontaneously drew back, he smiled again, rose gracefully off the bed, and took my hand to bring me to my feet. After removing each layer of clothing from me, he anointed each newly exposed part of my body with a lingering kiss. Standing naked in front of him, I took my own cue and undressed him. I was not sure what to expect of a monk, but he was lean and firm. He had a long torso and the strong legs of someone who must assume uncomfortable positions for prolonged periods. His penis was half-erect, as if waiting for an order from its master.

Akira led me into the bathroom with its tiled bath of steaming water, a handheld shower, two small stools, and a low platform, about the size of a single bed. Soft pink light bounced off the ceiling. The songbirds continued their enthusiastic chirping. After testing the water temperature of the shower, Akira aimed the nozzle at me, hosing me down methodically as though signaling the start of a spiritual cleansing ritual. He passed the showerhead to me so that I could do the same to him. After spraying the platform, until its edges dripped with miniature waterfalls, he sat down, rippling the slick surface, and gestured for me to sit also.

He unwrapped a large bar of fragrant soap and dipped it in a blue enameled bowl filled with water. As he coaxed a thick lather from the moist bar, the air filled with the perfume of roses. Twisting my body so it was turned away from him, he smoothed the lather over my back, massaging my shoulders, upper arms, and neck. Then he took each arm, covering it with soap and firmly rubbing my flesh as he did so, right down to the tips of my fingers. Returning the gesture, I picked up the cake of soap, which flew from my hands and skidded across the wet floor. Akira retrieved it, kissed me, and returned the soap to my hand. His broad shoulders became a smooth canvas for my foam painting. He turned around so I could lather up his chest, my hands skidding over his ribs and hard abdomen. He allowed me one sweep across his now erect penis, then took the soap from me. I was aroused and wanting more.

Pushing me gently down onto the platform, he smothered my stomach with suds, circling his way up to my breasts, my nipples stiff as he pinched each one between his thumb and forefinger. Circling down again, one finger ventured between my legs, probed deep for a moment, paused on my swollen clitoris, and retreated. Then supporting himself on his elbows, he stretched himself over me. The soapy layers on each of our bodies merged into one. Slick as seals, we slid over the filmy platform. I was aware of the platform's hardness, but more aware of Akira's penis, which felt enormous as it pressed against my pelvis, his balls slapping me with each grind of his body. Suddenly, he took hold of my shoulders and flipped me so that I was on top of him. I knew I could come in that position, rubbing against him, well lubricated inside and out.

But Mr. Tambuki's admonition that it was not about the goal hung over me in the steamy room. What about Akira? As a monk, did he subscribe to that philosophy where sex was concerned? It was his show after all. I realized I was thinking too much and allowed myself to drift back into the sweet sensations wherever they would take me. Here and now. Here and now. I found that perfect ridge of bone. I climbed that bolt of lightning, hot, bright, and sharp, resting to prolong the journey like Mr. Tambuki had taught me. Because the journey was all there was.

As good as it was, something kept me from climaxing. Akira flipped us again, and I felt as though we were on a barbecue spit. I thought this time he would try to enter me. I wanted him to. But he didn't. Instead, he reached for the soap and using both hands, smothered my calves and thighs with rich lather, skirting over my vaginal lips and re-soaping the rest of my body until I was frothy as a meringue. Still longing for release, I creamed him up from top to toe before slowly massaging his snowcapped penis and testicles. His eyes rolled back into his head. As I could feel him tense, he took my hand away, his lower body gently twitching. We lay there on our backs, the watery platform now cool. Then he took my face in his hands and kissed me, a deep and sexy kiss. A few seconds later I felt a warm fluid shoot onto my stomach.

We stayed there for a while watching the tiny soap bubbles on our skin popping silently. I began to shiver on the cold slab. Akira picked up the shower hose and sprayed me with hot water. The suds, mixed with his semen, escaped onto the floor and down the drain in the middle of the room. He rinsed himself and lowered his cleansed body into the steamy depths of the tiled tub until only his head bobbed on the surface. He ducked under quickly, a self-performed baptism.

I was waiting for a sign from him to join him.

Akira finally broke the silence. "Dorothy, come."

I stepped into the tub, relieved to be warm again. After fifteen minutes of stewing, we wrapped our pink bodies in thick terry cloth robes. Akira made some tea, and we sat cross-legged on the tatami mat.

"Thank you," he said, turning the cup around in his hands. "You are kind."

I wasn't sure how to reply to that. Was I kind to come here with him? To indulge him in his fantasy? Did my kindness go beyond this act?

"No. It is you who are kind." I had learned a thing or two during my weeks in Japan.

Before we left, he presented me with a white silk scarf, hand painted with green bamboo shoots. That was my entire compensation.

On the train ride back to Wakoshi that night, I tried to subvert my instinct to process what had happened. I chanted to myself, "Stay in the moment. The past is past." But I felt restless and incomplete, as I did when Mr. Tambuki left me unsatisfied. Then I felt guilty. Was it because I had allowed myself to become aroused during what I had thought was a business deal? That wasn't supposed to happen. Except it wasn't business. A scarf hardly counted as payment. Or was I feeling guilty because I was wondering what Akira would feel like swelling inside me? Had Mr. Tambuki made me into a nymphomaniac? But if that was the case, then why didn't I want Hiro, too? I had no answers.

I couldn't wait to get home so I could relieve my "itch" in private and guzzle a large whiskey. Maybe then I would become a rational person again.

CHAPTER SIXTEEN

When I reached Wakoshi after 1:00 a.m., I saw the shadow of a woman with a large brimmed hat sitting on the stoop. A tapestry bag lay at her feet. As I came closer, I saw that it was Suki.

"Suki, it's so late! What are you doing here?" I asked.

"I need a place to stay," she said, her voice flat.

I ushered her inside. In the hallway, she took off her hat to reveal a purple-and-blue bruise on her right cheekbone. Her lower eyelid was swollen, and her eyes were red.

"What happened?" I asked, afraid of the answer.

"Bento-san came over, drunk. He told me I had to leave. When I protested, he shook me. I lost my balance and fell on the table."

I studied her face a moment to see whether she was telling the truth. It was bad enough that he had manhandled her, but had he hit her? Was she protecting him or her own pride?

I brought her upstairs to my bedroom. "Now it's my turn to make you some tea. And I'm going to get some ice for that bruise." I forgot all about my original plans.

When I returned with the tea and ice, Suki was sitting on cushions, her left arm across her chest, the other elbow resting on her wrist, and her mouth and nose buried in her right hand. I set the tray down on the floor and handed Suki the small towel with ice cubes.

"I'm sorry this isn't more elegant," I said, as I removed the tea bag from a mug with a half-worn picture of a Coca-Cola symbol and handed it to her. "And all I have to eat are these." Four rice crackers sat unadorned on a chipped yellow plate.

"Thanks. I'm not hungry."

We sat and sipped our tea for a minute. "Do you think you'll go back to him?" I asked.

"I don't know. Without him, I have no means of support."

"Perhaps he'll be sorry?"

"Perhaps. But he won't come begging. I must give him an opportunity to save face, and I'm not sure I want to do that."

"You need to save your own face first," I said, trying to lighten up the conversation.

Suki managed a weak smile. "I look terrible, don't I?"

"I'd be lying if I said you looked your best. At least there's no blood," I said. From everything Suki had told me about Ben-to-san, he didn't sound like a bad person. But now I wasn't so sure. "You know you can stay here as long as you want. The room next to mine is still empty."

"Thank you. That's a big help." Suki sighed. "Do you have anything stronger to drink?"

"Now you're talking." I went downstairs to the kitchen to fetch the lone bottle of whiskey and two clouded and scratched glasses. I poured us each a large slug and rescued the last two ancient ice cubes from the tray in the small, overcrusted freezer compartment.

Suki chugged hers down, and I refilled her glass. She added a couple of ice cubes from her towel. Wanting to keep her company, I also tossed my first drink back.

"I think Chief is starting up the Club again. At least that's what he told me the other day," I said.

"Uh. Okay," Suki responded.

"Of course, you may want to look for something else."

"What else could I do? I haven't done any other kind of work in years."

"You're smart. You're bilingual. You know a lot about the arts. I'll bet you could find some other kind of work, if you wanted."

"That's easy for you to say. You've got an education, and a life to go back to in the States. Things aren't so easy here for women my age. We're expected to be married and have babies, not careers. Or to already have a career established."

"Have you thought about going back to the States?"

She started chewing on her thumbnail. "When I can get beyond my anger at my parents."

"Anger? What about?"

"For making me be a good girl. For not letting me go away to college. For protecting me from things they couldn't protect me from. For expecting me to live their dreams. For not being Japanese enough for them."

Except for the last part, her parents sounded like mine. "But you ended up in Japan."

"Ironic, isn't it? But I came here on my terms."

Suki was still pretty, and without the terrible bruise, her skin was smooth. But for the first time I saw that her eyes were old, even though she was in her early thirties. "Do you have contact with your parents?" I asked.

"I write to them, but I haven't seen them since I left home."

As angry and disappointed as I was with my own parents, I couldn't imagine not seeing them again. "You've told them about working at the Club and Bento-san?"

"Oh, heavens, no. I always sanitize my letters."

"I know what you mean." Without wanting to resort to outright lying, I had nothing I could say to my parents. "I send mine one-line postcards so they know I'm still alive."

We both laughed.

"Speaking of something I'm guessing you haven't told your

parents about, how is the new club?" Suki seemed almost cheerful now.

"Some of the customers are interesting. I met a monk, who doesn't behave exactly like a monk, at least not as I think of a monk."

"Oh?"

"Except he had his rituals." If I was guarded about Mr. Tambuki, I had no censor with Suki regarding my latest escapade.

"Involving?"

"Soap."

"Ah. The soapland fantasy?"

"Soapland?" Akira's fantasy had seemed so original.

"A kind of club where men go for suds and sex, in the form of a full body massage. A bit déclassé, but one of the many alternative venues for men to get their jollies."

"Oh. Good clean fun. At least this one isn't married," I said.

"Does it matter?"

"Maybe not. But I like him. I want to think of him as one of the good ones."

"Don't get too attached," she warned.

"I'm not. But if I like them, it seems okay, you know?"

Suki sighed. "It's no use trying to be rational about this. Just clear your mind."

"Tambuki-san says that, too," I said, picturing him in the middle of one of his short Zen lectures.

"He knows about the monk?" Her eyes widened.

"No. Should I tell him?" I was fairly sure I knew the answer to that one.

"No. No," she said, almost alarmed, but confirming my instincts. "Better to keep some things to yourself."

Suki stirred from the place she had been rooted for some time. When we were both on our feet, she gave me a hug. In retrospect, I think the hug was less from gratitude for taking her in than from an acknowledgment of yet another new line I had crossed.

On Sunday, I was awakened not by the sun, but by a persistent knock on the Club's front door. Suki's bag was on the floor of her room, but there was no sign of her. I threw on some shorts and went downstairs to answer the door. It was Hiro, with a big sack of books. He grinned ear to ear when he saw me. I had completely forgotten that he was due back from his vacation.

"We study for my English test tomorrow," he announced.

I was happy to see him, but he felt like an alien in my world. I gave him a perfunctory hug and offered him some food to stall the trip up the stairs to my room. Unfortunately, the refrigerator contained only seven pots of yogurt (my week's worth of breakfasts), a half-eaten bun of Suki's, and a jar of aspirin. Hiro told me he wasn't that hungry, and we could catch a bite later. I removed the aspirin bottle and put it in my shorts pocket, in case. I'd slept off most of my Saturday night hangover but still had a dull ache on one side of my head and slight nausea. I poured us both a glass of water and asked Hiro about his holiday.

"Very pretty place, but I miss you," he said.

I felt panicky, and my empty stomach did a flip. I hoped he was just saying what he thought was the right thing. "Maybe we should go to the park to study? It's very warm in here," I suggested, eager to change the subject.

"Look like rain maybe. Better here."

I momentarily considered the main room of the Club, but with its imminent reprisal, it was even more a symbol of my other self. Resigned, I let Hiro follow me up the worn stairs. My room was a mess. I hadn't put away the futon, and my dress, shoes, and underwear from the previous night were strewn around randomly on the tatami mat, looking like seaweed on a beach. Hiro swept the room with his eyes but didn't say anything. As he was getting settled, I scooped up the clothes and threw them in the closet. I left the futon where it was in the middle of the floor.

We sat across from each other, and for two hours I grilled him on vocabulary, corrected his grammar, and had him write out sentences that I dictated. "My teacher went to university in the United States. Now she works in Japan." *Your teacher gets paid for sex,* I thought to myself, as I waited for Hiro to complete the assignment.

"My teacher is very pretty, and she is nice person," Hiro said, grinning.

"A nice person," I corrected, feeling like a fraud.

"She is a nice person," he repeated dutifully. The words reverberated in my head, back and forth, like a ping-pong ball, bouncing against my skull bones.

"Okay. Very good. Maybe we should get some lunch now," I said, weary.

Hiro started writing the sentence down.

"No, I mean it. Let's go eat something." I was still feeling nauseous, but I'd learned that food was the best cure. Besides I needed some fresh air.

Although it had rained, the air was still thick and moist. We bought some *yakitori* from a cart near a small park, where mothers pushed strollers, and young children teased and chased each other. Unlike most of the parks I had visited in Japan, this one was devoid of charm or any memorable feature. It was just a patch of grass with a couple of benches and a small dirty pond, all set in the middle of a jumble of colorless buildings. We sat at the edge of the pond. A young boy was about to torpedo his blue toy boat into his friend's red toy boat.

I'd brought along a raggedy cloth so that we could picnic. Otherwise, eating outside seemed to be frowned upon. Hiro devoured his *yakitori.* I nibbled around the edges of mine.

"You very good teacher," he said and leaned over to kiss me. I felt self-conscious among the mothers and babies, and even the dogs, but I let him kiss me. His lips were soft and tasted of the chicken we'd just eaten. For a second, I let myself relax into it before my head told the rest of my body to be on guard. I pulled back.

"Not here, Hiro."

"Okay."

It was about 5:15 p.m. when we returned to the Club. We studied for another half an hour. Then Hiro ceremoniously closed the big textbook we'd been using.

"One more vocabulary test," he announced. "What is this?" he asked, as he took a strand of my hair and ran his fingers through it.

"A strand of hair."

"What are these?" He painted his fingers across my lips, then took my hand and did the same with his lips. As I did so, he kissed my fingers.

"What are these?" he asked as he cupped and began fondling my breasts. When he discovered I wasn't wearing a bra, he put his hands up my T-shirt and moved in closer for a more intimate kiss. His touch was much gentler than Mr. Tambuki's. But it had been a while since we'd had sex, and his urgency frightened me. I couldn't sleep with him, and I stiffened.

"Dee Dee. I so want to make love to you. You not want me anymore?" he asked, his voice tinged with sadness.

I felt beads of sweat form on my forehead. "No, I do. I just can't. Not tonight. Chief has opened the Club again."

"On Sunday?"

"Yes. You really need to go. I'm so sorry, but I have to get ready."

Hiro packed up his sack of books, and I followed him downstairs. There was a rat-a-tat-tat on the front door. I froze on a middle step, and Hiro bounded down and opened the door. If Mr. Tambuki was surprised at his greeter, he didn't let on. He stood expressionless in his handsomely cut suit with a big bunch of flowers in various hues of pink in one hand and a large beautifully wrapped box in the other. Framed by the doorway, he looked like an advertisement for Mother's Day. Hiro stared at him and then turned back to me expectantly.

"Mr. Tambuki. You're early," I said. I was in shock. How would I explain this man to Hiro? I felt the blood drain from my face.

I saw Mr. Tambuki open his mouth to reply, but before he had a chance to speak, Suki, all dressed up, flew down the stairs past me. She must have come back while Hiro and I were out.

"Mr. Tambuki, how lovely," she gushed. "You brought me flowers. Shall we go into the Club?" She took his arm and guided him swiftly into the main Club room.

"You very white," Hiro said to me. "You okay?"

"Yes. I'm just a little tired from all the heat." I sighed audibly, but to myself I thought, *Thank God for Suki.*

"This is not good man. I think he yakuza," Hiro said in the sort of low voice that is meant to be a whisper but actually carries. He chopped the air with the edge of his hand to punctuate his point. "You want me stay?"

Correcting his English now would seem patronizing. "No, I know him. He's not yakuza. We'll all be fine. You should go. Good luck on your test." I gave him a peck on the cheek and attempted a smile. Hiro hesitated and left.

I went upstairs to change. I put on the brocade shift, which I hadn't worn in a while. I had to strain to get the zipper done up, the result of eating too many chicken legs and French fries bought by customers. But I didn't really care what I looked like. When I entered the Club room, Suki and I traded places. She bowed to Mr. Tambuki and then smiled and winked at me as she passed by. Mr. Tambuki was seated at a table with the flowers now arranged in a vase. I remained standing.

"So, my little Gina. Suki tells me you have been tutoring this young man in English. How noble of you. I hope it has done him some good."

"I'm sorry I didn't have time to introduce you."

"Yes. Suki was quick to the rescue, was she not? She wanted to save you any embarrassment from having to explain your two lives. It is good to have friends who look out for you. But, come, why are you standing?" He patted his knee in an almost paternal manner.

Instead, I pulled out a chair, but as I did so, my zipper burst open, loosening the cloth across my stomach.

"I need to get changed if we're going out for dinner," I said, wondering if Mr. Tambuki had noticed any of this.

"I was thinking we could spend time together here first and then go out after my required Club appearance."

What I wanted was to be left in peace to recover from my fright. "As you wish."

"Is that what you would like?" he asked, with a tone somewhere between teasing and menacing.

"It's fine. We'll stay." As I started up the stairs, Suki passed me going down. She had her handbag with her.

"I'm going out for a bit. I'll see you at eight." Chief had welcomed her return as a hostess and was fine with her staying with me. "Will you be okay?"

"I'll be fine," I lied.

As the door closed, I heard Mr. Tambuki behind me. He caught up and put his hand on my bare back.

"A new fashion perhaps?" Now that we were alone, he unhooked my bra, which had become exposed. I sprinted up the stairs to avoid any further ravaging.

Once inside my room, he handed me the large wrapped box and removed his jacket, folding it neatly in the corner of the room. "Aren't you curious to open it? It is not going to explode."

I carefully peeled off the paper, both because it was too exquisite to rip and because I didn't want any more surprises. Mr. Tambuki removed the lid and pulled back the tissue paper. There hugging each other in a sixty-nine pattern was a pair of black leather high-heeled boots. I held one up on each side of me, as though I were handling two unwanted and misbehaving animals by the scruffs of their necks.

"Look inside them." I put one down and fished inside the other to find a black lace teddy. In the other a black garter belt nestled against silky black stockings. Mr. Tambuki took a step closer and brought me tight against his body. I half expected him to say something like, "I am going to fuck you like you've never been fucked before." But even with his sometimes rough and tumble lovemaking, Mr. Tambuki's language always remained refined. His use of the vernacular would have been jarring despite its pitch-perfect match with his gifts.

"I'd like to paint you in these. They are very sexy, yes? But I did not bring my paints here, so we shall have to amuse ourselves in another way." He kissed my neck, sucking the flesh with each kiss. One hand meandered down the back of my panties, which were now very accessible from my open dress. One finger inserted itself inside my anus, a signal I was now familiar with. I wasn't feeling sexy, but I neither resisted nor reciprocated.

Suddenly, the door flew open and slammed against the wall. Before we had time to separate, Hiro leaped into the room, poised for attack.

"You let her go," he hissed in Japanese. "I mean it!" He moved in to striking distance.

"What's going on?" Mr. Tambuki asked me in English, as though I had personally ordered in the troops.

Hiro was coiled tight. Bristling with fierceness and resolve, he looked like a completely different person from the young student who earlier was practicing his English. Mr. Tambuki did not seem impressed. In fact, he appeared almost amused. At that moment, I was rooting for Hiro, but I also wasn't ready to deal with the consequences of his victory. What if he hurt Mr. Tambuki? Would Mr. Tambuki retaliate? Would he feel his manhood was offended? I had to stop this confrontation.

"He has a black belt!" I blurted out.

Mr. Tambuki paused for what felt like an eon, but was maybe only a few seconds, and then released me from his hold. I realized then that I knew nothing of Mr. Tambuki's own martial arts skills. He was clearly fit; perhaps he was a warrior, too.

"Hiro, be careful." Having quickly reassessed the situation, it was all I could think to say.

Mr. Tambuki sized up his enemy. "What do you want?" he asked Hiro in Japanese.

"You let her go, or I'll kill you!"

"And who is she to you?"

"She's my girlfriend."

My Japanese had become sufficiently proficient that I was able to understand these simple exchanges. Hiro had taught me the word *kill* after seeing the martial arts films. Mr. Tambuki may not have realized how much I understood because he made his offering in English.

"Take it easy. No one is going to hurt anyone." He backed over to his jacket as though Hiro was shoving a rifle butt in his chest. As he picked up the jacket, he looked at me, and said, "I'll see you later, Gina."

Hiro remained on guard, pivoting to keep his eye on Mr. Tambuki as he left. When the door slammed, he relaxed his stance and directed his attention to me.

"I knew he bad man! Definitely yakuza. He man we saw in Club one night. Doing bad business. Drugs, I think. Very dangerous."

I started shaking from the shock of the event, from relief, from fear, from confusion. I clenched my jaw, and my teeth clicked uncontrollably against each other. I couldn't deal with Hiro and Mr. Tambuki in the same room.

"He hurt you?" Hiro asked.

I shook my head, unable to speak. Hiro moved in closer. He noticed my open dress.

"He do this?" For a moment I thought that Hiro was going to bolt out the door after Mr. Tambuki.

"No. The dress was too tight. It ripped open on its own."

Although it was true, it sounded like I was trying to cover up for Mr. Tambuki. Hiro looked at me strangely.

When I was finally able to connect my brain with my mouth, I asked, "Why did you come back?"

"I not go. I wait near house. When Suki leave without bad man, I worry. I slip in before door lock."

"Why would you risk the trouble he could cause you if he's so bad?"

"I not think about that. I not afraid. I just think about you. But maybe I get you in trouble with bad man?"

"No, what you did was very brave." I was overwhelmed with his selfless courage. "Thank you. I'll be okay."

"I stay here by door all night and protect." He moved in to hug me.

Encircled in Hiro's round arms, I felt both safe and claustrophobic. "You need to get a good night's sleep for your test," I said.

Whether the thought of the test triggered Hiro's mental processes rather than his instinctual ones, I couldn't say.

He frowned. "Why he call you Gina?"

I was about to tell him that it was my hostess name, but he had more questions.

"And why he give you boots?" Hiro's view over my shoulder was a direct line to the boots, the box, and the lingerie, all of which were lying on the floor. He disengaged from me and picked up the black garter belt as though it were a used condom. "You know bad man! You want bad man!"

"No," I protested weakly, my guilt trumping my current annoyance with Mr. Tambuki.

Hiro stared at me in horror and then tore down the stairs. I followed him as far as the upstairs landing.

"Hiro, it's not what you think," I shouted, as he raced out the front door. But of course, it was probably even worse.

Before I returned downstairs, I changed into something looser and tidied up. Although I had been ambivalent about Hiro's feelings for me, I didn't want our relationship to end this way. Why was he so quick to blame me as the temptress and not the "bad" Mr. Tambuki? What could I have said or done to help him see the evidence in a different light? I could juggle the capricious Mr. Tambuki and the audacious men at the Puss 'n' Boots. But I didn't know how to fit the gentle Hiro into my act. I felt sad and inadequate. At the same time, I was relieved I no longer had two lives that needed to be kept separate.

That night, although the Club was officially open for business, no one came. Chief had been expecting Mr. Tambuki, as had I. I covered for him by lying that some important business engagement had come up.

Hana, Suki, and I sat around trying to piece together a conversation in which we could all participate. Suki translated when necessary. I'd never taken the time to talk with Hana before. She was sweet. I learned that her father was dead and that she helped to support her mother. Three days a week, she sold handbags in a department store. She told me she could get me a discount. Chief prepared us his special barbecued chicken. We drank and laughed at each other's sauce red lips. Then, we played cards until Chief deemed it time to close. I weaved my way up the stairs.

After Suki said goodnight, I went to my room and undressed. The new boots beckoned me from the cupboard. I stroked the soft Nappa leather, sat down on the futon, and pulled them on. They hugged my calves like a second skin. I felt very sexy wearing them while naked. I put on the black lace garter belt. Standing on the middle of my futon, I found my sweet spot and imagined Mr. Tambuki's, or was it Akira's, firm abdomen against mine, thrusting his engorged penis deep inside me until I came again and again, insatiable.

CHAPTER SEVENTEEN

ow that I thought I'd never see Hiro again, I missed him. I
phoned him several times. Sometimes, he'd hang up when
I announced myself. Other times, a woman would answer—I
assumed it was his mother—but when I asked for Hiro, she
would tell me he wasn't there. I wrote him a couple of postcards
with simple messages, such as "Please phone me," because it was
too difficult to apologize or explain myself in writing. I resigned
myself to the fact that he'd be just one more pleasant memory
in my journal. He represented my daytime Japan, and with him
went the last vestiges of any pretense about addressing my other
daytime desire—to find another banking internship. Each time I
tried to muster up the energy to search for another opportunity, I
found some excuse. After the Mr. Muriachi debacle, Mr. Tambuki
made a weak effort to help me, but I didn't follow up, and he never
mentioned it again.

With my daytime associations abandoned, the nighttime
became more alluring. I gave it my full attention, my star performance. Akira was only the first of multiple lovers I met at Bar
Puss 'n' Boots. I went on dates at least two of the three nights I
worked there.

Although the money was important, I derived even greater
satisfaction from being wanted. I had the power to decide whether

I would grant these men "favors," as Akira had put it so delicately. They weren't all as handsome as Akira or as sophisticated as Mr. Tambuki, but every man I chose had some intriguing quality. Victoria and I traded notes so we wouldn't step on each other's territory. She was more tempted by the businessmen, whom we nicknamed the "shiny shoe brigade." They lavished her with gifts—expensive necklaces and bracelets, designer handbags, a set of silk sheets—mostly just for going out to dinner with them or accompanying them on the occasional weekend jaunt. Since they made up the bulk of our clientele, I, too, went on *dohan* with business executives. But I found the innocent dalliances even more stressful than having sex. Meeting the physical needs of my customers, no matter how quirky, was easier than maintaining the illusion of romance through conversation and body language. Besides, I didn't care to be reminded of my own business failings.

My tastes ran more to the eccentric. Big Sumo-san certainly fit that category.

One night about a week after my tryst with Akira, this giant of a man, accompanied by three comparatively diminutive companions, squeezed through the front entry. Mama-san 2 practically scraped her head on the floor bowing. I knew this symbolized a person of importance, and I felt flattered when she chose me along with Cindy to entertain the entourage. Big Sumo-san, his hair pulled back in a topknot, wore a loose green tunic with matching pants that looked like hospital scrubs. The only English phrase he appeared to know was "thank you," which he pronounced "tanku," so for translation he relied on one of his buddies, Tadao, a reed of a guy, whose whose black-framed glasses overwhelmed his narrow face.

Tadao immediately fell into the role of public relations man. In fluent English, he made sure I knew that Big Sumo-san was an up-and-coming star in the sumo wrestling world. He had recently won an important bout, and his big break would be coming "any day." I couldn't picture Big Sumo-san dominating his opponent. He reminded me of a sweet-natured, overfed pussycat, which lumbered along and occasionally rubbed your leg. It also never occurred to me that someone of Big Sumo-san's girth might even want an intimate relationship. I assumed that his "practice," as Tambuki-san would have called it, consumed him. I was wrong. When, through Tadao, he made his interest in me clear after his third visit to the Bar in two weeks, I envisioned myself being smothered by his pillows of flesh. How could I be attracted to someone whose work gear consisted of an oversize diaper? But for some reason, I didn't want to offend this gentle colossus. And a part of me was curious. It took four straight whiskeys before I had the courage to satisfy that curiosity.

Tadao drove us to a love hotel affiliated with Bar Puss 'n' Boots. Big Sumo-san indicated through Tadao that I should choose among the several themed rooms revolving around storybook characters. These rooms were available only to patrons of the Bar. I considered it strange to have a go-between arrange such a personal encounter, but as I was to learn, Tadao never left Big Sumo-san's side. I selected the Cinderella room, partly because the concept of Big Sumo-san being my Prince Charming was so utterly ludicrous and partly because of the laugh I'd had about it my first night at the Bar. It couldn't be any more kitsch than the Elvis room I'd shared with Baby Elvis.

The room looked like a medieval torture chamber, with leather handcuffs hooked up to the bed, pulleys and harnesses dangling down from the ceiling, and a wooden box filled with an assortment of whips, chains, dog collars with studs, oversize strap-on dildos, and other props designed to inflict pain. Except for the one handcuff incident with Mr. Tambuki, I'd only heard about such items, never seen them. Big Sumo-san gave me a wide grin, revealing a set of chompers stained bluey-yellow with one missing tooth near the front. I feared I'd made a huge mistake.

Short of bolting, I had no idea what to do next. Big Sumo-san was obviously capable of hurting me without these accessories if he wanted to.

Apparently, what he wanted was a cup of tea. Tadao prepared it, but Big Sumo-san insisted on pouring it since I was his guest. He presented me with my cup, bowing as he did so. I bowed back. We sat cross-legged on cushions on the floor. With each sip, Big Sumo-san turned his cup just a fraction of an inch. I could tell by the distinct pattern of the glaze that he downed the last drop just as he had revolved the cup 360 degrees. Nervously, I wondered what other rituals he enjoyed.

As he disappeared into the bathroom with Big Sumo-san, Tadao instructed me to change into one of the costumes in the cupboard. Five dresses, identical except for their color and size, hung in a neat row. The minimal bodice fitted in such a way as to push up and exaggerate the fullness of my breasts, revealing them so entirely that I really did look like the overly endowed Cinderella on the wall of Bar Puss 'n' Boots. The feathery lace at the edges tickled, and the stiff satin of the skirt rustled with the slightest movement. In the box of sex toys, I found some silky scarves that I knotted to produce one bigger scarf. I arranged it around my neck so that it covered my chest.

As I waited on the edge of the bed, I heard muffled sounds of running water, splashing, and grunting. I practiced my deep breathing, trying to erase all thoughts about the past or future. About twenty minutes later Big Sumo-san emerged, three towels tied together around his waist. His skin glistened with beads of moisture, and the flesh of his stomach fell in folds, like saltwater taffy before it cools. Tadao trotted after him.

"*Yoi-desu,*" Big Sumo-san said when he saw me and let out a hearty laugh. It's good. He looked at Tadao as though he needed to be reassured that he'd said the right thing. Tadao nodded and said something about *chibasu*—breast.

Big Sumo-san plodded toward me, whipped off my makeshift

stole, and put it around his own immense neck. My hands instinctively covered my naked bosom.

"Relax," Tadao said. "I've seen it all, and I'm not going anywhere. You want a drink?"

"Please," I said.

As he poured me a drink from a small bottle, Tadao directed Big Sumo-san to lie down on the bed, which he completely filled.

I gratefully took the pale brown drink, which turned out to be a plum wine, and swilled it down, keeping one hand strategically placed over my breasts.

Big Sumo-san gestured for me to come over and patted his voluminous tummy.

"He wants you to stand on his stomach," Tadao said.

"What?"

"His stomach. You won't hurt him."

I climbed up on the bed, stood on the small edge of mattress that was not taken up by Big Sumo-san's body, and then tentatively put one foot on his fleshy middle. The top surface was soft. As I put my weight on it, I reached a shelf of rock. Big Sumo-san took hold of my ankle to steady me as I lifted my other foot. His large hand easily circled me as though I were a twig. I felt silly as I hovered over him, trying to maintain my balance.

"Walk on him. He likes that," Tadao said.

I took baby steps up his chest, my dress swishing across his acreage. Big Sumo-san grabbed the hemline and stuck his head inside. His arms followed, and in the hollow darkness, he yanked down my panties and lifted each leg so I could step out of them. Peeking his head out and grinning at his triumph, he waved the panties around like a trophy from a frat boys' nighttime raid. Then he brought them to his nose, sniffing at them and rubbing them over his face. Back he disappeared into the tent of my dress. I don't know what he could see in there, and he didn't try to touch me. After about five minutes, he reappeared and gestured to me to sit on his stomach. His flesh was warm as my now exposed vagina suctioned against him.

He lay back down.

Tadao came over, took one of Big Sumo-san's treelike wrists, and secured it inside one of the leather handcuffs. He moved over to the other side of the bed and affixed the other wrist. Big Sumo-san grinned again.

"*Chibasu*," said Big Sumo-san. There was nothing salacious in his tone.

"He wants to see your breasts. Lean forward," Tadao said.

I put one hand on Big Sumo-san's shoulder and bent forward at the waist. My breasts hung down, like fruits waiting to be plucked.

"Don't let him have it right away," Tadao said. "He needs to work for it."

Big Sumo-san sat up partway, his mouth open. I jerked just out of reach. I leaned in again. This time his lips grazed me, leaving a wet streak. The third time, he wrenched his wrists hard, snapping the handcuffs off their moorings. With his leather-braceleted hand, he grabbed my right breast and steered it into his gaping mouth. At first, he sucked like a hungry baby seeking milk. Then he added teeth and tongue, nipping and licking, pausing to observe my tightening nipple. He gave my left breast equal attention.

Arms wrapped around me, the broken chains of the handcuffs dangling against my back, he smothered his face with my bosom. Babbling and cooing with obvious delight, he crashed back onto the pillow.

I turned around to look at Tadao, who sat in a chair watching us. I could see his penis twitch underneath his trousers. "Does he want anything else?" I asked.

"He will let us know when he is through."

Big Sumo-san's snores announced his status.

"You can get down now," Tadao said. "Please come over here."

I extracted myself from Big Sumo-san and went over to Tadao. He unzipped his pants and pulled down his underwear to release his surprisingly large, erect cock. I thought I'd done my duty and did not expect this turn of events.

"He can't satisfy you, but I can. You will be well compensated."

I looked back at Big Sumo-san, lost in slumber.

"He doesn't care. You gave him what he wanted," Tadao continued.

What difference did it make at this point? I was expecting to have intercourse. Did it really matter with whom? Tadao was nice enough, and at least he could speak English. I was too drunk to care.

I shrugged my agreement. Tadao stood up and shook off his trousers and pants, which pooled around his ankles, revealing his lean and strong legs. With his shirt still on, he fetched a cushion from the bed and threw it on the floor near me.

"I like it from the rear. Please."

I got on my hands and knees. Tadao sheathed himself with a condom, bent over me, and pulled up my long skirt. He slipped three fingers into my vagina and expertly massaged my clitoris. My hips responded to the pressure.

"Is that good?" Tadao asked.

In my inebriated state, the bizarreness of the situation was almost a turn-on. "Mmmm."

Tadao's penis slipped easily into me. He thrust in and out, continuing to use his fingers. With each push, he muttered "*Hai*" more loudly. "*Hai, hai. Hai!*"

Big Sumo-san snorted once.

I found myself moaning loudly, almost in harmony.

A third voice joined us. "Go, go, go," it said in Japanese. Tadao's penis pulsed, and one last time, he shouted, "*Hai!*"

When he pulled out, I twisted my neck around to see Big Sumo-san watching us, his hand pumping inside his big, white nappy and his mouth stretched wide in a smile of bliss. "*Iki, iki, iki,*" he said. His arm grew still.

"Tanku," he said to no one in particular.

Big Sumo-san and the half-naked Tadao disappeared into the bathroom. I lay down on the bed and shut my eyes, the layers of the stiff skirt bunched up around me. I reminded myself that this was business; it wasn't about me. I practiced my even breathing and drifted off. About a half hour later, the two men emerged, clean and dressed. After my own quick shower, we had tea again as though we'd just finished watching the day's races at Ascot.

Following Suki's advice, I didn't tell Mr. Tambuki that my list of customers had grown beyond him. I had no idea what his reaction would have been—jealousy? Anger? Pride that he had trained me so well? I felt more in control not relying on him to define my life in Japan and my understanding of the culture. Now I was even more certain I'd made the right decision to keep my lips sealed. Did I really know him? Where did his money come from? Was his erratic behavior a part of his teaching techniques, or did he have a mean streak? Despite Hiro's insinuation, I didn't believe that Mr. Tambuki was a yakuza. He wasn't anything like the yakuza I met at Puss 'n' Boots. For one, he was a loner. He had a couple of colleagues, but they seemed more attached to him than he to them. Mr. Yakumasei, with his missing finger, was possibly a yakuza, but there didn't appear to be any others. Unless he was operating on his own. For another, he seemed too cultured and refined, with his artistic talents and inclinations. I surmised that the full body tattoos that some allegedly sported were the closest yakuza got to visual expression. Of course, what did I know except what I'd seen in the movies and the odd fact or prejudice picked up here or there, especially from Hiro? Even if Mr. Tambuki was a yakuza, I had no real reason to be worried. Victoria, who was turned on by elaborate full body tattoos, told me the yakuza were gentle—"real teddy bears"—and Suki said that they restricted their violence to rival gangs. The occasional non-gang-related incident got blown up in the news because they were so rare.

Having grown up in a country where crimes against people were commonplace, I found it difficult to shed all my beliefs and stereotypes. But my new open self was certainly willing to try, and I had no shortage of opportunities. Initially, I couldn't tell the yakuza apart from the salarymen who frequented the Bar. But with time, I noticed that in addition to suits that weren't as conventionally cut, more jewelry, and a larger variety of hairstyles, they carried themselves with more confidence.

On several occasions, Victoria and I hosted the trio of men who'd been there my first night, the ones I had christened Scarface, Shinytop, and Shrubbrow. Scarface seemed interested in Victoria, and she laid on the charm for him. He always wore a Rolex watch and a thick gold chain around his neck. Shrubbrow had a perpetual grimace and didn't laugh as much as the other two. I liked Shinytop the best. I thought he was the brightest of the bunch, and he wasn't as pretentious as Scarface or as sullen as Shrubbrow. He was also better looking than his colleagues, although his head was large in relation to the rest of his body. He was solidly built, but compact.

One evening, two weeks after the confrontation between Mr. Tambuki and Hiro, the three came in again. Mama-san 2 directed Victoria and me to their table.

As I approached, Shinytop addressed me. "Banker is beautiful tonight."

"Thank you," I said, twirling around playfully to show off the tight midnight-blue sequined dress I'd found in the dress cupboard. I was feeling more cheerful again. After a period in which Mr. Tambuki seemed preoccupied and had even canceled one of our dates, we had spent a pleasant evening together, with no unusual demands. He was almost boring.

"Too young to be banker. More like schoolgirl, I think," Shinytop said. He patted the space next to him, and I sat down.

Japanese men had an odd obsession with schoolgirls. "Not that young," I said.

Shinytop pulled my hair into a ponytail. "With horse tail, see how young?" He looked at his companions for agreement. Shrub-brow nodded.

"Kat—she is most young. So pretty with yellow hair," Scarface said, flicking Victoria's hair with the hand that was draped over the back of the booth.

"Gina look good with yellow hair—more young, too," Shinytop said.

"What do you think, Kat? Should I go blond?" I asked, jumping into their game.

"What fun!" Victoria said. "We could be twins." She pulled her hair back in a ponytail. "Schoolgirl twins."

"At top of class," Shinytop said. "Best students."

The trio left around eleven o'clock. Later Victoria cornered me in the dressing room. "Adachi-san is taking me out tonight to a late dinner." Adachi was Scarface's surname. "He is really rich, you know."

"That missing finger doesn't creep you out a little?" I asked. Apparently, she had moved on from the businessmen.

"I think it's almost as sexy as the tattoos. Anyhow, it shows he has been repentant for doing something wrong, doesn't it? I think the one you call Shinytop likes you, if you're interested."

"He prefers blondes. Young blondes," I said.

"So? You could bleach your hair."

"Just for a guy?"

"No. For you. To do something different."

The idea took root quickly. The customers certainly salivated over Victoria. Maybe as a blonde, I'd be rewarded monetarily. But more importantly, I thought it would make a public statement about my willingness to take chances, and privately, it would make me feel more in control.

The next day I enlisted an expert.

When I reached Berta's house, I almost lost my nerve. Berta

brought out the schnapps to relax us both. Before long, we were giggling like a couple of girls at a slumber party.

"Do blondes have more fun?" I asked.

"Honey, I haven't had this much fun since I told that toad of a boy to go fuck himself with a chicken wing."

"That was just a couple of nights ago."

"Like I said, it's all fun, all the time. You sure you want to do this? What's your Mr. Tambuki going to think?" Berta was standing behind me, studying me in the mirror.

"I don't give a shit," I said. "He'll either love it or hate it." The schnapps had done its work. And at that moment, I didn't care what Mr. Tambuki thought. This act was a symbol of my independence.

"That's the spirit. Be your own person. Men are just a bunch of fucks, and some of them aren't very good at that."

It wasn't a perfect job. There were patches of orange, but in low light it wasn't bad. After Berta gave me some curls, I looked even younger. We decided to leave my eyebrows alone. It was obvious I was a fake blonde. But I liked that. It was all part of my great act.

That evening I wore the boots Mr. Tambuki had given me, a thigh-high blue mini, and a tight top. I had fun playing a strumpet at the Snack. With the blond hair, I felt free.

"Who the new girl with sexy legs?" Licker asked.

"That not new girl. I know Gina tits," One Eye said.

"Fuck me!" Licker said.

"You want me to fuck you?" I asked Licker, as I leaned across the counter, pointing my breasts at him.

"Fuck me?" Licker asked, acting confused at having his bluff called. He took a large swallow of beer.

"Yeah, you and your dick."

"Dick?"

"Yeah. Right here. Right now. In front of your friends to show them what a man you are."

"Now?"

"I'm all ready. I'm not even wearing any underwear." I started to pull up my short skirt.

One Eye laughed and pointed at his hapless friend.

I turned to him and squinted into his one visible eye. "If you think this is so funny, how about you? You wanna fuck?"

"Me?" One Eye squirmed on his stool and pushed his hair back off his face, revealing his green eye.

"Yeah. Both of you. Together."

Licker and One Eye mumbled something about having dates and scurried from the Snack, like two beetles about to be crushed.

Afterward, Berta said, "Honey, I don't know what was in that bleach, but you were really hopped up tonight."

I felt like Samson. With this blond hair, I thought I could do anything.

CHAPTER EIGHTEEN

*T*wo nights later, I dressed for my date with Mr. Tambuki. I wore a simple shift as well as the boots he'd given me, as I thought that would please him. I met him at his studio.

"Gina, what has happened to your hair? I do not like it," Mr. Tambuki said when he saw me.

I touched my head. It felt strange, like straw. "I wanted to do something different. It's just hair."

"I have not helped to make your life interesting enough?"

"I didn't mean that."

"It is your choice. But I can offer you something different as well."

"Oh?"

He unfurled a hand scroll of *shunga* pictures, like the ones he'd shown me first at the love hotel. "Do you think you are capable of this?" He pointed at two twisted bodies, their colorful robes parting sufficiently to leave little to the imagination. "Or this?" The woman's back was arched like a bridge, her head turned unnaturally too far to the side, her toes curling. The man's oversize penis penetrated her at an odd angle.

I winced. "I don't know, Tambuki-san. It looks painful."

"Pleasure-pain—how far apart are they really? Of course, you can do it."

I laughed nervously. "Aren't they just inspirations for sex, to be imitated at one's peril?"

"We shall live dangerously, then. Just a practice session. You will be well-rewarded. Are you up for the challenge?"

Despite my initial reaction to the strange contortions in his hand scroll, I wanted to experiment.

Mr. Tambuki was remarkably flexible; I, less so, even though I was so much younger than he. I could approximate some of the positions. Others I could hold for just a few seconds after much urging. Still others were not within my reach. After more than an hour, I was exhausted and sore but excited from the novelty. Neither of us had come. He brought me on top of him, a rare event, and we reached our peak together. I had just one orgasm, but it was magnificent, with wave upon wave of sensation.

Afterward, as we lay on the futon, he said. "I would like to paint my own *shunga*."

"But it takes two. How can you paint if you're doing it?" I had visions of him using a movie camera.

"Ah. That is so. I will need a stand-in."

"A stand-in?" This solution hadn't crossed my mind.

"I have a nice young man in mind. You will like him." He turned to me and stroked my cheek with uncharacteristic tenderness.

I recalled the odd threesome with Big Sumo-san and Tadao. My relationship with Mr. Tambuki wasn't exactly wholesome, but it had always been private. "Oh. You mean you watching me doing it with another man?"

"Of course, you will not actually be 'doing it,' as you say. It will be simulation."

"Not stimulation," I said, to add a note of humor to this new twist in the ever-bending, unpredictable road I was on with Mr. Tambuki.

On our next Sunday date, Mr. Tambuki took me to Hotel Venus, where he'd set up a temporary studio. He had me change into a kimono and don a black wig swept back into a bun "to increase the authenticity." My partner, Nobu, was indeed handsome, with a shaved head and even features. He was not as young as promised but still younger than Mr. Tambuki. He also wore a kimono-type gown and held a black wig in his hand.

We all sat on the floor and drank whiskey together. Nobu did not appear to speak English. Mr. Tambuki spoke to him only in Japanese, and he showed no signs of following the conversation between Mr. Tambuki and me. From time to time, he smiled at me close-lipped.

"Has Nobu modeled for you before?" I asked, chugging back my third glass of whiskey. I was going to have to be good and drunk for this episode.

"No, but he is very strong and agile, and he is an experienced *shunga* model." Mr. Tambuki stood up and prepared his inks. "You should both go on the bed and become acquainted so that you are ready."

"This feels very odd, Tambuki-san." My wig was heavy and made me sweat.

"Do not worry," Mr. Tambuki said, his tone more dismissive than reassuring. He turned to Nobu and said something in Japanese that I didn't understand. "Nobu will know what to do. I will give you two some privacy."

Mr. Tambuki left the room. Alone with Nobu, I felt awkward and virginal. He led me to the bed, and we kneeled, facing each other. He untied my robe's sash and then his own to reveal a swirl of tattoos on his upper chest, back, and biceps. Rather than just a series of random designs, they formed an unbroken bolero of ink. On either well-sculpted pectoral muscle, matching frowning heads of angry kabuki characters with down-turned mouths glared at me. The heads appeared to rest on a background of stylized blue clouds, but two pale hands held upturned swords, curving against each other to form the outer edges of the tattoo jacket. It was as though Utamaro had carved his woodblocks directly on Nobu's skin. Was Nobu a yakuza? I stared, fascinated and apprehensive.

Nobu laughed. It wasn't a mean laugh, but it seemed patronizing, perhaps a response to my disconcerted wonder. I looked up at him. He smiled at me, his eyes softer and less opaque than Mr. Tambuki's. I relaxed. He slid his hands over my body, tentatively at first and then with more sureness. He motioned to me to lie down. I was surprised when he spread my legs and used his tongue to explore my inner crevices until I was wet and wanting him. It was as though Mr. Tambuki had told him exactly what I liked. He grabbed his own flaccid penis and gave it a few yanks until it was stiff and waiting for orders. Erect, it was both thick and long, with a small black tattoo of a bee at its tip. I'm sure I stared at his penis even harder than I had at his body art. I wondered how it would feel inside me. Then I realized I hadn't turned Nobu on. Perhaps he, too, was a monk who had perfect control over his body. Were he and Mr. Tambuki part of a special clan of yakuza monks? It was an incongruous notion, but not out of the question in this country of odd juxtapositions.

When Mr. Tambuki returned, he busied himself setting up his chair and lap easel. "We will start with something easy."

Because of my previous practice session with Mr. Tambuki, the first few positions weren't too much of a strain. Then, they became more convoluted and bizarre. Nobu was lither than Mr. Tambuki. His body and his penis bended in unnatural ways, with never more than its mushroom-shaped tip inside me. He stayed hard throughout, responding to the briefest commands. We were required to hold one uncomfortable pose after another while Mr. Tambuki glanced up and sketched, expressionless. I needed all my concentration to keep still. But, as on other occasions when I modeled, I was aroused. Was it from this tortuous teasing or from Mr. Tambuki's gaze and its promise of potentially mind-blowing sex?

After an hour, Mr. Tambuki put down his brush. "Thank you," he said. "That will be all for today."

I stretched to unknot the kinks in my tired muscles and pulled my robe around me.

"Gina, what would you like now?" Mr. Tambuki asked.

"To see the pictures you've painted?" I was curious about how he'd rendered us. Would he have made Nobu's penis outlandishly supersized as it often appeared in *shunga*? Would my vagina be a tufted cavern? "Not yet. They need additional work. But surely you would like something else?"

"What do you mean?" I wasn't going to say outright in front of Nobu that I wanted Mr. Tambuki to make love to me, even if Nobu didn't know English.

"Would you like Nobu to give you an orgasm? He will do what I ask," he said.

I was stunned. This had to be a trick question. Surely Mr. Tambuki didn't need me to say how much I desired him? That only he could satisfy me? Or was this another one of his Zen teaching sessions, and I was supposed to indicate indifference to his proposal? Or did he actually want me to get off with another man? I had to admit I was curious about Nobu's capabilities. "What do *you* want?" I asked.

"I asked you first."

"You taught me that the end point doesn't matter. That sex shouldn't have a goal." Of course, I didn't believe that for one minute, not when the goal was so delicious.

"So I did, but were you not aroused just now?"

I was stumped, but I came up with the best answer I could. "Was I meant to be aroused by someone other than you?"

A flicker of a smile passed over Mr. Tambuki's lips. "I am not interested in sex right now, but Nobu will oblige." He began to pack up his gear.

Nobu was sitting patiently on the bed, his wig by his side, his robe still open. His shrinking penis twitched as though the tattoo bee had irritated it.

"You have my permission. Go on. I will disappear." Mr.

Tambuki didn't bother to wait for another response from me. "I have paid for a full night." He nodded at Nobu and left without acknowledging me.

His methods were so infuriating. Did he expect me to run after him?

Nobu patted the bed and took off his kimono. I pulled off my wig, relieved to free my now matted hair. I was annoyed at Mr. Tambuki for manipulating me, and I felt rejected. I would have sex with Nobu out of spite.

I let my robe slip off and lay down on the bed. Nobu treated me to some of his expert tongue work. I closed my eyes, focusing on the pleasurable feelings and pushing out everything else as Mr. Tambuki had taught me to do. Then before I knew what was happening, Nobu had fastened my wrists to the bedposts with handcuffs. I opened my eyes. He was squinting at me, and his lips were curved down into a sneer, as though he were channeling the mean kabuki characters on his chest.

Then he laughed and said in English, "You have a big juicy pussy." He flopped down next to me.

"I didn't think you spoke English," I said, at a loss. Where was this going?

"You Americans think we are dumb because our English isn't perfect. I hear the gaijin speak when they think I don't understand."

"I don't think Japanese are dumb at all."

"You say that because you are in handcuffs." He laughed again.

"No!" He was right. Even if I had thought Japanese were dumb, I'd hardly admit that in this vulnerable position.

"You're afraid of me, aren't you?" He flipped his agile body so that it hovered over mine, his weight resting on his hands, the evil eyes of the kabuki men appearing magnified.

My heart started to race. "No," I lied.

"I think you are." Nobu stared at me. He lifted one hand and dangled the key to the handcuffs in front of me. "Tambuki-san is very generous, isn't he?"

I raised my eyebrows. I didn't want to do or say the wrong thing.

"Not only did he pay me for the modeling. He paid me to fuck you good and hard. He said you liked that."

Those didn't sound like Mr. Tambuki's words. "I'd like to go home now."

"Before I fuck you? You know you want it." He slid a finger from his other hand into my still wet vagina, which had not yet moved in sync with my mind.

I tried not to betray any further emotion as I knew it would not help my cause. "Please unlock the handcuffs," I said as firmly as I could.

"Maybe *I* don't want to fuck *you*," Nobu said. "But I've been paid, and that's not honest, is it? What would Tambuki-san say if he knew?"

"He doesn't have to know."

"That I didn't fuck his girlfriend or that I did fuck her? Which do you think he'd prefer?" Nobu laughed a third time, tossing his head back triumphantly.

These questions with unknowable answers sounded like more Zen mumbo jumbo than I was able to tackle. Both fear and the effects of whiskey battled for supremacy, but the fear was winning and sobering me up too quickly.

"Unlock the handcuffs," I said again. "And I'll do what you want." If I was going to have sex with this madman, I wanted it on my terms, with my hands free.

Nobu paused, as though considering this question. "Hmmm. What do I want?" He sat back on his heels and tapped a finger on his lips. "I think I'd rather fuck Tambuki-san."

It hadn't occurred to me that Nobu might be gay.

"He's very good in bed, isn't he?" Nobu continued. "That delectable cock. Such control. He can fuck me for hours. Is it that way for you, too?"

I could feel the blood drain from my face. "You're lying. Mr. Tambuki isn't gay."

"It doesn't matter what you call him. He likes boys, too. Especially me." He played with his penis until it sprang to life again. "You can see why. I give it as good as I get it."

"Why are you telling me this?"

"Since we share a boyfriend, I thought we could get to know each other. Maybe we should fuck after all." With his now hard penis, he flipped back on top of me again, his tattoo swords appearing to aim for my face.

"I want to leave *now*!" I said firmly, but I was terrified that he would try to take me by force.

"Okay. Okay. I'll be nice *this* time. I'm not in the mood anymore." Nobu unlocked the handcuffs, and I scrambled off the bed. I desperately wanted to shower, but I didn't want to take my eyes off him. I slipped on my brocade dress.

"You forgot your panties," Nobu said, waving them in the air. "Or are you hoping to get lucky elsewhere?"

When I returned home, I washed my crotch as best I could in the small downstairs sink. I didn't know how much to believe Nobu about Mr. Tambuki. Were they lovers? Did Mr. Tambuki tell Nobu what I liked? Why was Nobu so unpleasant, and did Mr. Tambuki know his true nature? I would need to make it clear that I was not doing that again. I had other sources of income now, and I didn't have to put up with that kind of abuse. But how could I even face Mr. Tambuki now? My life felt as tangled as bodies in a "spring" picture.

CHAPTER NINETEEN

I slept fitfully, dreaming about strange men entering my room, taking me against my will, laughing at me as I struggled. I was awakened by the phone. It was 1:00 a.m.

In response to my cautious "hello," a muffled, frightened voice replied.

"Gina. It's Penny. Something's terribly wrong. I need your help . . ." Her voice trailed off, and I heard whimpering.

Since I'd started working at Bar Puss 'n' Boots, I hadn't seen Penny much. She seemed resigned about not seeing Jimmy, and I thought that the whole pregnancy thing appeared to be either a false alarm or something she'd made up to get Jimmy back.

"Where are you?" I asked.

"In the park. I'll be in the lav. Hurry. Please. Don't tell Mom." Before I could ask any other questions, she hung up.

I threw on shorts and a T-shirt, not bothering with a bra, grabbed my purse, and ran into the street to hail a taxi. By now, I was able to convey instructions in my broken Japanese. When we arrived at the park, I asked the driver to wait and gave him a few extra yen to make my point. He nodded.

I made my way in the dark to the lavatory and found Penny, sobbing uncontrollably, crouched down inside one of the stalls, which she'd left unlocked. Her hair, damp with sweat, stuck to her cheeks; her mascara dripped dark lines down her face. Fresh red blood pooled on the floor near her. Her underpants, which were down by her ankles, were also stained crimson. I stifled the urge to throw up.

"Penny. Omigod. What happened?"

"It hurts so much," she said, sucking in gulps of air.

"We have to get you to the hospital. I have a taxi waiting."

"I want to die. Just let me die," she said unconvincingly.

"Penny, did you do this to yourself?" I had to ask.

"*No!*" And then more quietly, "It was Jimmy's fault."

"Jimmy did this to you?" I couldn't believe my ears.

"No. Ooooh," Penny moaned.

I could see I wasn't going to get much more of an explanation. I yanked hunks of toilet paper off the roll and stuffed them into her pants.

"Can you stand if I help you?" She nodded.

I reached under Penny's armpit as I had seen my mother do with my elderly grandmother and helped her to her feet. She hung on to me like a frightened monkey, hands gripping my neck, while I pulled up her soiled underwear. Her legs were rubbery, ready to collapse under her if she let go. I reached behind her to flush without looking. I didn't want to see what was there.

With her arm around me, I guided her to the taxi. She was wearing only a very short, somewhat sheer dress. Before she sat down, I pulled a plastic bag out of my purse and put it on the seat. I'd gotten in the habit of carrying it in case I felt like vomiting after drinking too much. This time my Girl Scout preparedness came in handy.

"Penny, what's the word for hospital?" But we didn't need it. The taxi driver turned around and said something in Japanese. Penny nodded. He drove quickly through the narrow streets and within minutes was at a hospital entrance. I had no idea where we were.

With my help, Penny staggered in. The receptionist at the

hospital desk looked contemptuously at the young, blond Penny with her mascara-striped face and thin minidress and me in my tatty shorts, nipples showing under my T-shirt. She gestured at an empty row of seats without taking any information. I think she assumed that because we were foreigners, we didn't speak Japanese. It also occurred to me that she thought we were a couple of doped-up gaijin hookers. Penny slumped into a chair, arms wrapped around her belly. She winced once or twice and shivered. I put my hand on her arm.

After what seemed like ages, but might only have been ten minutes, a young man in a white coat came out. I assumed he was a doctor. The receptionist pointed at us, and he came over.

"What is the matter?" he asked in clipped English.

"I think my sister lost her baby," I replied. I thought they were more likely to listen to me if I pretended I was a close relative. We were both bottle blondes with big breasts.

"No baby here."

"No. No. She was pregnant." I explained about the toilet and the blood.

"Ah," he said. "Perhaps you could come back tomorrow? We are very busy tonight." I looked around at the empty room and felt anger bubbling its way through me. But I was calm at first.

"Please. We really need to have someone look at her."

"Come back tomorrow. More people will be on duty then."

"You have to see her. She lost a lot of blood," I burst out. Penny's chin lifted suddenly from where it had been resting against her chest, and her eyes widened for a moment. Then she sunk back into her stupor. "She could be dead by tomorrow!" I was starting to sound hysterical. I would be the ugly American if I had to be.

"I am sorry," the man said. Sorry that she was dying? Sorry that he couldn't accommodate us? Sorry he was being such an asshole or that I was losing control? I wanted to cry myself, but somewhere from deep within, I found a new cache of strength.

I inhaled and spoke in firm, measured sentences. My voice was about an octave lower than usual.

"Apparently, I have not made myself clear. We are not leaving until you or some other doctor sees her. If she dies here in your waiting room, I will hold you personally responsible. Her father is a very important person in the military."

Penny babbled something in Japanese. I could not make it out. The doctor startled. This woman child spoke his language, and he looked at her now as though she were a human being, if not deserving of compassion, at least worthy of acknowledgment.

"I will see what I can do," he said. "It is very busy," he repeated to underscore his original argument.

A few minutes later he came back with an older woman in a white coat. He said something to her in Japanese. The woman knelt to Penny's level.

"What is her name?" the woman asked me.

"Penny," I said.

"Penny." The woman took Penny's hand. "Penny!" she said more insistently. Penny opened her eyes a little, and the woman spoke to her in Japanese. Penny mumbled. The woman said something in a firm tone to the other doctor, and he disappeared. Moments later, he and an orderly came back with a wheelchair. After positioning Penny carefully in it, the female doctor and the orderly pushed her through some double doors and disappeared. The seat where she had been sitting was soaked red.

"I'd like to be with her," I said to the male doctor, who, looking bewildered, remained planted in one spot staring at Penny's bloodstained chair.

"That is not possible," he said. "Someone will come for you when she has been seen."

"Thank you for your help," I said, infusing sarcasm into my tone. Who did he think he was? Maybe he wasn't a doctor after all but just a flunky without any real power.

He nodded, looking down at the floor, and trotted away as quickly as he could.

No one had asked me for personal information about Penny. I was sure she'd tell them if asked. For someone who did such outrageous things and had such unrealistic expectations, she could be oddly honest, except to Berta, whose anger she chose to avoid.

I found a pay phone and called Berta, but she didn't answer. It was the middle of the night after all. Someone came along with a bucket and cleaned up the mess. I sat at the edge of my chair and cried silently. What was Penny doing all alone in the park at night? Not that it was dangerous as it might have been at home. I could only imagine the terror she must have felt as her insides poured out. If Nobu hadn't been such a jerk, I might still have been with him at the love hotel, lost in boozy slumber, far from my home phone. Or worse, if I hadn't stood up to him, I might still be there in handcuffs or perhaps in need of medical care myself. What would Penny have done then? Who would she have called? I didn't like the phrase "It was meant to be." It was so passive, as though we had no free will. But as I waited, my jaw clenched and my teeth chattering, I thought, *It was meant to be.* I just hoped I'd found Penny in time. If I were a better student of Zen meditation, I would be able to clear my mind of these negative thoughts. And maybe if I wasn't so sober, I wouldn't be thinking at all.

Two middle-aged men entered the reception area carrying a third man by his arms and feet. He was passed out. Drunk to oblivion, no doubt. I saw men like that all the time when I was out late. They stretched him out on the carpet, and one of them went up to the counter. A few other people straggled in over the next half hour—a woman with an infant who was coughing incessantly, an elderly couple holding hands, and a guy who limped in. I was the only non-Japanese person.

Finally, a nurse came out and chatted briefly with the receptionist, who pointed in my direction. "Your sister rest."

I leaped up. "Will she be all right?"

She guided me to an empty corridor. "We not know yet. She lose baby. Much blood from wound. Maybe infection? Your mother know?" Her tone was kind and nonjudgmental.

I told her I'd tried to phone Berta, and I asked if I could see Penny. She told me I could, but that Penny needed to sleep. Then, she led me to a ward with a half-dozen beds, three of them occupied, and parted the curtain separating Penny from the other patients. I sat down on the one chair. With her eyes closed and her face clean of its smudged makeup, she looked very young, almost angelic, the previously pinched face now relaxed. She was hooked up to a machine that sent a clear liquid through a thin tube into her veins.

I watched her breathe rhythmically. Why hadn't I asked her recently how she was doing? It was easier to play ostrich. How selfish could I be?

She finally opened her eyes. "I lost Jimmy's baby," she whispered.

"I know. I'm sorry." I took one of Penny's hands and held it. With my other hand, I stroked her forehead.

She gazed at me, her eyes filled with tears. "You could have let me die."

"I would never do that."

"Berta would have. She's gonna kill me."

"She loves you, Penny. She just has a tough time showing it."

"You didn't tell her, did you?"

"Not yet. She didn't answer when I phoned."

"You can't let her find out!"

"I have to let her know where you are and that you're okay. I'll be back in a minute."

"Don't tell her anything," I heard her say.

Because I still had no luck reaching Berta, I asked the woman at the front desk if she could try for me.

Penny was fast asleep when I returned. I stayed with her all night, tossing fitfully in the uncomfortable molded chair. I couldn't leave her alone again and have her wonder where she was.

At 7:00 a.m., a nurse checked her vital signs and changed the drip bag. Penny barely stirred. I must have dozed off again. An hour later a nurse and doctor woke me up and shooed me out of Penny's area while they examined her again. Rumpled and stiff, I went in search of a cup of tea from a vending machine. As I reentered the lobby, I saw Berta, in loose magenta pants and matching tunic, talking animatedly to a new receptionist.

"What the fuck is going on?" Berta asked me. No "hello" or anything. "This idiot won't tell me. And are you my 'other daughter'?"

"Everything is okay now, Berta." I steered her away from the desk. "I had to pretend I was a relative, or they wouldn't have let me stay with Penny."

"Where the hell is she?"

As we walked along the corridor to Penny's room, I gave Berta my summary of what had happened. I had to tell the truth—that her daughter had been pregnant—but I feigned ignorance about who the father was. I was thankful I didn't know any more details.

"That little tramp," Berta said. "She's been lying to me."

"She thinks you're going to kill her."

"You bet I'm going to kill her, and I'll kill him when I find out who he is."

Bile rose in my esophagus. "Berta, I know it's not my business, but she's had a big scare. Maybe you could tone it down for the moment?"

"Yeah, yeah. Thanks for helping her. But why didn't she call me?"

I assumed it was a rhetorical question.

The nurse and the doctor were just leaving. Berta said something to them in Japanese, and the doctor responded. Berta's eyes widened, and she put her hand over her mouth. "No!" she said, as though she didn't believe what they were telling her. I'd never seen her so distraught.

Berta burst into the curtained cubicle, a giant swirl of magenta chiffon. I stood back so that she could have time alone with Penny, but I hovered close enough to intervene if I needed to. I could see through the parted curtain that Penny was fully awake.

"My baby! My baby! Why would you do such a thing?"

"Mother!" Penny was clearly startled by Berta's appearance.

Penny's narrow bed groaned as Berta plopped herself down on it. "Why would you try to get rid of it? Why didn't you tell me?"

"I don't know what you're talking about," Penny said. "Where's Gina?"

"The doctor told me. *He* didn't do this to you, did he?"

"Who?"

"The shit who knocked you up in the first place."

"No, Mu-ther," Penny said in that exasperated tone she used to respond to Berta's accusations, no matter how true.

"I promised Gina I wouldn't yell at you now. Are you okay?"

"No, Mother."

"I'm here now. I won't ask any more questions, baby. Just rest."

Berta took Penny's hand and brought it up to her lips. It was a strange truce, and I wondered how long it would last.

"Tell me just one thing. It wouldn't have been Japanese, would it?" Berta asked.

"No." It was clear that Penny wasn't going to volunteer any information.

Berta didn't say anything. I wondered if she guessed that the barracks was the source of the father. *The apple doesn't fall far from the tree,* I thought.

Since it was obvious that Berta was not about to kill Penny, at least at that moment, I decided to leave. Later, I'd try to find out the whole story from Penny.

When I arrived back in Wakoshi, exhausted and ready for sleep, I found Suki in the kitchen making a pot of tea.

"Hello, stranger," she said. "You look a little pale. Are you all right?"

"I don't know."

"Do you want to tell me about it over a cup of tea?"

I nodded, more for the warm liquid than the opportunity to talk. Suki poured tea into two mugs, and we went to the Club to sit down in the tattered booth. The table surface contained several sticky patches embedded with salt and pepper. A green glass ashtray was full of half-smoked cigarettes, sticking out at odd angles, no doubt the artistic attempt of a well-lubricated client. Suki pushed the miniature sculpture to the edge of the table. I told her about my adventure with Penny, but I didn't give too many details. It was my business, not hers, and my problem now as well.

"Poor thing. I'm glad to hear she's okay. How lucky for her that you were available."

"I guess." I didn't want to discuss Penny anymore. Some hero I'd been. "How are you doing?"

"Trying to keep it going with Bento-san. He feels terrible about the apartment. He's just having some business troubles and can't afford to find me another place."

"Is that okay with you?"

"As quirky as he is, I do love him. He means well. It's hard with me working. We can't see as much of each other, and we have to meet in love hotels." Suki opened a packet of biscuits. She didn't look at me.

Here was another Pandora's box waiting to be opened. This Bento guy was a piece of work. But unlike Penny, Suki was an adult, and she had to make her own decisions. I would try to be more available to her after I'd had some rest.

"How are things with you and Tambuki-san?" she asked.

I wasn't sure I wanted to open my own Pandora's box, but I had to tell someone. "Honestly? He's into some weird stuff."

"Oh?" Suki perked up. "I know about weird stuff."

"I really don't want to describe it, but it's freaking me out."

"That's not good." She dunked her biscuit into her tea until a piece broke off, crumbs floating on the surface of the steaming liquid, like abandoned lifeboats.

"I'm thinking of breaking it off with him." I was surprised to hear myself say those words since I hadn't expressed that thought to myself.

"Are you sure? Is it really that awful?" Suki touched me lightly on the arm.

"He's so full of surprises."

"Surprises aren't always bad. They make life interesting."

After tonight, I was tired of surprises. "You think I should stay with him?" Suki was hardly in a position to judge my relationship with Mr. Tambuki, but I was curious about what she thought. She had strong opinions about a lot of things, although she sometimes buried them in ambiguous language.

"I can't tell you what to do," she said. "You have to weigh the benefits against the downsides. Remember your dream of graduate school."

"Yeah. Graduate school." I hadn't thought about the MBA in weeks. "But I'm wondering if it's all worth it, you know?"

CHAPTER TWENTY

O n our next Sunday date, I met Mr. Tambuki at Harajuku Station near the mock-Tudor clock tower. He wanted to take me to the outdoor market in Togo-jinja. I thought it was interesting that he chose a public place. Did he know that I had an issue with him?

As we walked through the aisles of old crockery, I said, "Tambuki-san, I found it very strange that you would offer Nobu to me."

He examined an old jar, turning it over in his hands. "He is very handsome, yes? Did you enjoy him?" He set the jar down and continued to walk.

I trotted behind him. "He wasn't very nice to me. Did you really want me to be with another man?"

"Does it matter what I want?"

"Of course it does."

"So, if I want you to be with other men, you will be with other men?"

"No. That's not what I meant."

"So, it does not matter what I want." He stopped in front of another stall of crockery. They were all various shades of green.

"You're twisting my words. I guess I'm wondering why you would want this."

He ran his finger around the inside of a paper-thin bowl. "You should consider yourself lucky that I have not been possessive. I have not asked you what you do when you are not with me."

"I appreciate that."

"Should I be wondering what a beautiful woman decides to do when she is not with me?" He looked right at me.

"No." I knew he wasn't talking about visiting art galleries.

"I should not be wondering, or there is nothing to wonder about?"

I wasn't good at lying to him, so I said nothing.

"I see," Mr. Tambuki said. He continued walking rapidly down the aisles filled with goods of all kinds.

I almost said something about working on "my craft," but I thought that would be offering too much information. When I caught up with him, I tried diversion instead. "Was Nobu yakuza? He had a lot of tattoos."

"Perhaps. Does it matter?" He sounded impatient. "There are good yakuza and bad yakuza as there are good and bad men and good and bad women."

I expected greater profundity from Mr. Tambuki. "He said you told him to, and I quote, 'fuck me good and hard' because I liked that. Did you tell him that?"

"That is not language I use. You know that."

"So maybe it was different words, but did you tell him something to that effect?"

"Gina, I do not like you accusing me of things. I am sorry you did not enjoy Nobu. Apparently, he does not feel the same way. He likes you. He said you were spirited. I feel you are misrepresenting him."

"He's one of the most unpleasant people I've ever met." And it was true.

"You have lived in a fairy-tale world, then."

"We didn't have sex, you know." I took in a deep breath. "But he said that you and he had been lovers."

"Did he?" Mr. Tambuki sounded surprised. "What else did he say?"

"Some things I don't want to repeat. His English is very fluent and quite colorful."

"He is a talented man with an active imagination." He was trying to sound matter-of-fact, but I could tell I'd hit a nerve.

"Please don't be angry with me for bringing this up. I just thought you should know what he was saying about you."

"Apparently, he is not the only one who talks too much. Discretion is a virtue, Gina."

"I'm sorry. Can we just drop this? I've said what I wanted to say."

We were now in front of a rack of old kimonos. They were arranged by color and intricacy of design. Mr. Tambuki selected one in robin's-egg blue and held it against me.

"This one looks nice with your blond hair," he said as though we had just been discussing the lunch menu rather than his sexual preferences.

The kimono had a pattern of large yellow flowers and dragonflies with green bodies and lacy golden wings. It was one of the loveliest ones I had seen, and I am sure that my eyes must have lit up.

"Would you like it?"

"It's beautiful, but I don't need it." I did want it, but I felt I was being bought off again.

"Nonsense. You should have your own kimono, not just borrowed ones." Mr. Tambuki turned away from me and began negotiating with the seller.

Afterward, we went to the nearby Ota Memorial Museum of Art to look at the ukiyo-e prints displayed in small galleries on two levels. We were required to replace our shoes with slippers. I removed the tall black boots hidden under my pant legs. Mr. Tambuki glanced my way.

By now, I had seen many examples of ukiyo-e in books, in Mr. Tambuki's private collection, and at the Tokyo National Museum, where I had been with Suki on several occasions. The sheer variety of subject matter and detail never failed to enchant me. One print might depict a peaceful village scene; another, people escaping from a humongous dragon. Or in one a beautiful woman would be playing her shamisen, and in another a fierce warrior in a colorful costume would be locked in battle with a demon. I loved being lost in these other worlds. Out of the corner of my eye, I saw Mr. Tambuki study me as my eyes wandered over the surfaces of the prints.

Later, we ate in the attractive courtyard of an Italian restaurant. I was surprised at Mr. Tambuki's choice of cuisine, as he tended to prefer Japanese food, but he seemed as comfortable here as anywhere and knew his way around the extensive wine list. We shared two bottles of a red wine from Montepulciano. I felt mellow and had all but forgotten my earlier annoyances. I also savored the creamy tiramisu.

"I see you are wearing the boots I gave you. Do you like them?"

"Very much. It was a generous gift." I scooped the last bite of the dessert and licked the spoon clean. "And thank you for the kimono as well."

"Have you forgiven me?"

Mr. Tambuki hadn't sought my forgiveness since the time he put the moves on me in front of the love hotel.

"I can't figure you out sometimes, Tambuki-san."

"If you could figure me out, I would be a dull person, would I not? And why do you want to figure me out? It is enough that we are enjoying this moment together, yes?" He took my hand in his and gave it a squeeze; with his other hand, he lightly grazed along my thigh, sending shivers through me.

"Do you want me to 'fuck you good and hard' now?" He chuckled after he said this.

His use of this incongruous expression aroused me further. I wanted to stay mad at him, but I couldn't. "Yes, please."

It wasn't Mr. Tambuki's fault that Nobu was a jerk. And what if he had slept with Nobu? Who was I to judge? If he could ignore the fact that I had other men, I suppose I could forgive him again. No harm had been done.

I wasn't disappointed that night. At first, he asked me to keep the boots on as well as wear the kimono draped open, an odd merging of East and West. But I removed the boots when they interfered with our pleasure. I came more times than ever before and in many different positions, including a few of the strange *shunga* postures. I twisted my body, draping one leg over Mr. Tambuki's shoulder, and curling my toes around his neck. I felt my vagina open wide. And although I kept having orgasms, it was never the goal. It wasn't even about me. I was floating above myself, removed from my ego at last. Perhaps all that extra practice had paid off. When we were lying there after the last incredible mutual spasm, our bodies synchronized, and for a moment, I became one with the universe.

Now that Mr. Tambuki knew about or at least suspected the nature of my extracurricular activities at Puss 'n' Boots, I felt even less inhibited about whom I saw.

In particular, Shinytop intrigued me, but I couldn't get beyond the fact that he was a yakuza. He had asked me out twice, and I didn't reject him outright. Once I hinted that I had "woman's troubles." He had nodded knowingly. Of course, I could never use going out with someone else as an excuse. Each man had to think that his chosen hostess had eyes only for him. While Penny was still in the hospital, I told him that I was taking care of a sick friend.

Victoria had dated Scarface on several occasions. "Adachi-san has been so good to me. Look what he bought me." She flicked her diamond-covered wrist at me. "They're real, too. Can you imagine how much this is worth? And he was such a gentleman."

One night, both Scarface and Shinytop came in. Shinytop seemed more relaxed without Shrubbrow around. He proposed a drinking game—Ping Pang Pong—that involved saying one of those words in the right order and pointing at someone else to say the next word. Anyone who messed up the routine had to slug back a shot. I was good at these games if I started sober, but I'd already had a couple of rounds by the time the men came to the Bar. Both Shinytop and I lost badly to Victoria and Scarface. After Scarface proclaimed his victory and the game ended, the two of them engaged in intimate conversation.

Feeling a little giddy, I asked Shinytop, "Do you think I still look like a schoolgirl?" I remembered his earlier observation about me and pulled my hair back into a ponytail. I also pursed my lips into a pout.

"Gina is very sexy schoolgirl." He leaned in a little closer. "Is she bad schoolgirl?"

"That depends on what you mean by bad," I said, letting my hair back down.

"Does she do naughty things with the teacher?"

"To get good grades, she might," I said, twirling a strand of hair around my finger, as I had seen Victoria do. "Of course, it depends on the teacher."

"I am teacher," he said. "You like?"

Shinytop took me to an unfamiliar hotel, punched his room selection on the smoky screen, and led me down a sterile corridor. Through the open door, the décor screamed early American schoolroom. The edge of the room was lined with old-fashioned desks, the kind with beige metal legs and wooden tops that lift up. On one wall was a large colored map of the world, and on another, a chalkboard. A slide projector flashed kanji onto a blank third wall. In the center of the room, on a large platform overlooking the desks was a bed, a mock version of a teacher's desk, except for the ever-present handcuffs hanging from the ceiling. The bed was covered with a brown sheet and bedspread, simulating wood.

Shinytop directed me to a cupboard for my "uniform," a short, pleated skirt, white shirt, knee socks, and clunky black shoes. There was even regulation underwear—a cotton undershirt and cotton panties. As costumes went, this was somewhat hokey, even perverted, but I looked forward to losing myself in my part.

"You like disco?" Shinytop called out.

"Whatever you like," I replied from the bathroom where I was changing. The big tub was clean but stained. The entire room smelled like bubblegum meets Lysol. I pulled my hair back into a ponytail and secured it.

"I got 'Saturday Night Fever' on Friday." Shinytop chortled at his little joke. The insistent rhythm of the Bee Gees bounced off the tile walls.

I entered the bedroom to find Shinytop lying back on the bed, fully dressed except for his trousers. A welcome drink of saké sat on a table that pulled out from the desk-bed. The whiskey from the drinking game was wearing off.

"Class in session," he said. "Miss Gina, come here."

I stood above him. My pleated skirt barely covered my butt, and my shirt was so short it exposed my tummy.

"Miss Gina, lesson is to dance."

"Can I have a drink first?" I asked.

"No. Dance first. If you pass, you get drink."

The heavy black shoes made it hard to move. I wasn't used to shoes inside hotel rooms, but Shinytop had insisted that I put on the whole uniform. I began to sway to the music. Shinytop clapped. Then he stopped and frowned.

"Dance not sexy," he scolded.

I started to shimmy. My breasts flapped around inside my braless undershirt. "Is that better?"

"Better, but take down hair."

I removed the rubber band and shook my head. Hair fell over my eyes like a curtain. Shinytop turned up the volume with the remote.

"Do strip."

This wasn't the first time a man had requested me to do a personal striptease. In one case, that was all the customer, an older businessman, had wanted.

I kicked off one shoe and then the other. I turned around and pointed my right arm in the air in imitation of a disco dancer. Then I undid the buttons of my shirt, trying to stay with the beat. Shinytop kept his eyes riveted on me and resumed his steady clapping. I tried to peel off my shirt but became tangled in my sleeves because I had forgotten to undo the buttons on the cuffs. I felt ridiculous, and I lost my rhythm.

"Bad lesson. Do over."

"You want me to put my shirt back on?"

"You argue with teacher. Go to board."

I extricated myself from my shirt and ambled over to the chalkboard.

"Write. Gina will be good girl."

I wrote the sentence but added an *a* before good.

"Nine more times."

I did as I was told, writing in an even cursive script, put the chalk down, and turned around. "Is that okay? Now what would you like?"

"Come here." He sat up and perched at the edge of the bed. "Strip me."

I came to him and started to undo the buttons on his shirt. As I reached the last one and started to tug on one sleeve, Shinytop yanked his arm away.

"Why you undress teacher?"

"You told me to." I was feeling impatient at Shinytop's conflicting commands, but I tried to keep in mind that he was the client.

"You are very bad. Come here for punishment."

I approached the bed. Shinytop snatched my arm and brought me across his bare legs. "Bad girl need spanking."

He tugged at my panties and slapped me hard on my buttocks. I could feel his penis grow hard under the thin layer of his briefs. The smack took me by surprise. I braced myself for more, but he seemed content with this one quick display of sadism.

"Watch me. I show you how to dance." Shinytop sprang off the bed and began gyrating to "Stayin' Alive." He wasn't graceful, but neither was he heavy on his feet.

"Oh, oh, oh, oh . . ." he sang off-key to the thumping beat. He slipped one arm and then another out of his shirt and swung it around his head, managing to keep time to the music. His entire torso and arms were covered in intricately inked paintings, mingling gentle images of silver frogs, green lily pads, and full-blossomed peonies with coiled, hissing snakes and fire-breathing dragons. What did it all mean?

He pivoted around so I saw the full effect of the tattoos. Then he flung the shirt into the far corner of the room, continuing to swivel his hips, now clad only in his diaper-like briefs with their twists of cloth connecting the back to the front. He was a ludicrous sight. Was this supposed to turn me on? I had to stifle a laugh.

"You see right way to do?" he asked, huffing from his exertion. He walked across the room to retrieve his shirt, which he hung up in the cupboard. "You do," he said in Japanese.

I thought to myself, *I can do this. It's dumb, but harmless. It's what he wants, and it will all be over soon enough.*

I stepped out of my plaid pleated skirt and whirled it around my head like a lasso, swiveling my hips in time to the thumping beat of the karaoke machine. The skirt reminded me of my Catholic school uniform. I conjured up visions of Sister Archangel snapping a ruler on a textbook as some poor girl butchered the holy Latin language. I imagined Sister's face contorting when I confessed to her that I often exchanged sex for money and gifts. I smiled.

"More sexy," Shinytop ordered me.

I gyrated faster, pretending that I was trying to keep a hula hoop spinning around my hips. I searched Shinytop's face for approval, but I couldn't look at him for long. His damp scalp reflected specks of light from the slide projector, giving him a diseased appearance. And the swirling, almost psychedelic tattoos that covered his arms and torso made me dizzy.

"Naughty student!" Shinytop scolded in an ambiguous tone.

Was he praising or berating me? I lost my concentration. The skirt slipped from my fingers and plopped in a sad heap at Shinytop's feet. He picked it up and meticulously draped it over the arm of a nearby chair.

"Stupid yellow-haired American girl," he muttered under his breath in Japanese.

I wasn't stupid, was I?

Shinytop reached up to touch my breasts. A striped snake curled down his bicep, its mouth open as if preparing to engulf the frog near his wrist. I closed my eyes to avoid the images, hoping I would come across as coy.

"Oh, sensei, please don't," I said. Now dressed only in a prim white undershirt and panties, I crossed my hands over my chest, believing he still wanted me to play the ingénue.

"Teacher is always right. You are very bad student. Show me breasts."

He sounded angry now, but I assumed he was just acting as well. I cautiously inched my undershirt up over my boobs. Shinytop stared at my chest. For a moment, I felt powerful.

"Stop! Gina is seducing teacher. More punishment."

I pulled the undershirt back down, deflated. This game was getting tiresome, and I was starting to regret that I'd agreed to go out with Shinytop. I needed another drink. It was the only way I could tolerate him for much longer. I reached for the cup of saké next to the bed and swigged it down. It left a strange, bitter aftertaste.

"Not yet!" Shinytop roared.

Apparently, I had deviated from his script. He hurled himself at me so that I toppled backward onto the mattress. The cup leapt from my grasp. He pressed a knee against my stomach to hold me still and swung my arms above my head. After securing my wrists with the handcuffs, he straddled me like a cowboy who has just brought down a prize steer. Sweat from his scowling face dripped onto my neck.

"What do you want me to do?" I asked. I wasn't used to such roughness from clients.

"Silence, you whore."

My pulse quickened. Whore. I was not a whore. Whores were common prostitutes flaunting their wares in the streets. The men I saw were classy.

Shinytop pushed his hands under my undershirt, his fingernails digging into the tender flesh of my breasts. His bloated rump still encased in briefs restrained my legs. He hovered over me. The green scaly dragon festooning his wide torso lashed out its long, forked tongue and exhaled a stream of red fire.

"Please don't," I whimpered for real. "Tell me what you want."

"Shut up, I said." Shinytop shifted his weight to his rear end and yanked off my underpants.

The elastic stung as it ripped down my legs. I yelped like a small dog that has been stepped on.

He stifled my cries by stuffing the pants in my mouth. What was happening?

My heart banged against my chest. I forgot how to breathe through my nose. I felt like I was falling down a deep well. The water surrounded me.

I tried to recall what Mr. Tambuki had taught me about calming myself. I shut my eyes and pictured a rock garden with four large oddly shaped stones of black and blue and a carefully raked bed of gravel. *Kare-sansui* is supposed to be a place of composure for finding one's source of strength, perhaps even some cosmic meaning or insight. I held the image for as long as I could. But a tongued tsunami of water, like the one in a Hokusai print, surged over the gravel and surrounded the rocks.

I realized then why the saké had tasted strange. I'd been drugged. Why? I was cooperating with Shinytop's every whim. I willed my eyes to open, hoping to rid myself of the hallucinations, and found myself fixated on the leaping silver frog on his arm, which appeared to be frozen in midair.

Then the rocks sprouted silver frogs. They slid down the slippery surfaces into the well with me.

I remember thinking it was okay, though. The cool water was comforting, soothing even. The frogs seemed content, didn't they?

A bolt of lightning. The water turned crimson. Its temperature rose.

Sister Archangel appeared above us, the arms of her black habit fanning out like wings. What was she doing here? She reached down into the well and pulled out one frog. The water bubbled violently; steam spiraled up.

Sister tossed the frog back in. How could anyone be so cruel? But the frog jumped out. Why didn't the other frogs budge? Were they stupid? *If they stay here, they'll die,* I thought. "Can't you save them?" I called out to Sister.

Then, the tsunami engulfed the nun, and she melted like the Wicked Witch of the West.

Her black cloak whirled around, forming a massive charred log, its rough bark still glowing. The log burst through the well's distant opening and pummeled me over and over like a hot poker. I was too weak to fight back.

As I sank deeper into the darkness of the fiery hot well, the sky no longer visible, I turned into a silver frog. A tarnished silver frog.

CHAPTER TWENTY-ONE

When I woke up, everything hurt, especially my head. Where *was* I? I struggled to sit up and extract my arms from the shit-colored sheet wrapped around me as though I were a cadaver. I propped myself on my elbows. A crack of light from a door faintly illuminated a row of school desks. Draped over the arms of a swivel chair were a plaid pleated skirt and a white shirt. Next to the wheels lay a pair of clunky black shoes, one lying on its side.

When I mustered up the courage to pull back the brown sheet, my knee socks mocked me with their primness. The only other thing I had on was an undershirt. I gingerly picked up the cotton panties balled up near my elbow. They were clean but punctured with two gaping holes. If it weren't for my pulsating brow, I'd have sworn it was a dream, a twisted memory of Catholic school.

I lay back down and stared at the ceiling. Dangling at arm's reach were two ropes with handcuffs at the end. Then, scenes flooded my mind. Shinytop. My botched striptease. The strange-tasting saké. The frightening hallucinations in which his tattoos came to life. The silver frogs in the boiling well. Sister Archangel.

And the charred battering ram. I shivered.

Wanting to dislodge the images, I turned my head. At the top corner of the mattress, I saw a large wad of money and a small gift box. The wad was larger than usual and the gift box, smaller. I sat up again and had to shut my eyes for a minute to keep the room from spinning.

I reached for the box. It was exquisitely wrapped in a beautiful blue paper with a repeating pattern of white flowers flecked with gold and silver and topped with a narrow pale blue ribbon. Was Shinytop trying to compensate me for his rough treatment of me?

I carefully removed the ribbon and peeled back the paper to reveal a tiny golden bowl with a lid. I lifted off the lid. Inside, something lay shrouded in a double layer of pale blue organza. I took the parcel from the bowl and unfolded the fabric.

There, on a bloodstained piece of beige velour sat the top of a finger, complete with fingernail.

Reflexively, I threw the ghastly object in the air. It landed on the bedsheet, still on its blotched rug, the demi-finger pointing at me accusingly. Although I didn't dare touch it, I studied it for a minute. It was definitely real, not one of those rubber models you find in a novelty shop.

For what seemed like an eternity, I perched at the edge of the bed. My heart raced in preparation for flight, but I felt paralyzed. I conjured up Mr. Tambuki's voice as he instructed me in Zen teachings. I couldn't go back. The future was unpredictable. There was only now. I tried to locate that space inside my head that should lead to calm. I took ten deep breaths. Resisting the urge to gag, I held the eleventh breath, returned the cloth with its amputated part to its miniature coffin, and replaced the lid. I glanced at my own fingers, just in case I'd missed something in my fright. Still intact. I exhaled, but the relief was temporary.

If this was now, I wanted it to go away. Questions roared through my pounding skull. Was this some kind of a sick joke? A message with a hidden meaning? A warning of what could happen to me? Was Shinytop coming back? Had he raped me? Was it rape when someone paid you?

And whose finger was it?

This was definitely not a dream. It was a nightmare. Or I was dead and in hell.

Suddenly feeling the urge to vomit, I rushed to the bathroom. As it had been hours since I ate, my heaves produced nothing substantive. But the act felt like a symbolic purging. After hanging over the toilet for a few minutes, I rose slowly, the white tiled wall whirling around me like a colorless kaleidoscope. I wet a washcloth and pressed it to my face. Its welcome coolness wakened my senses further. My eyes popped open. Over the edge of the washcloth I stared in the mirror at the girl with the yellow hair. She had my features, but she was an imposter.

Without showering, I slipped into my smoke-stamped evening clothes. Every muscle was shouting. As odious as it seemed, I decided to take the finger, money, and punctured panties in case I needed evidence. I could always dispose of them later. I threw the rest of the costume, including the socks and undershirt, in a hamper designed for that purpose, trying not to imagine some other young woman donning them to satisfy a horny man with a schoolgirl obsession.

I shuffled to the door, opened it a crack, and peered into the empty hallway of the lifeless hotel. I grabbed my high-heeled sandals and ran barefoot down the six flights of stairs.

As I stepped into the blinding, sun-drenched day, I realized I didn't want to go back to Wakoshi just yet, back to the center of this strange stew of a life I had concocted. After finding out where I was, I took the subway to Shinjuku. Hobbling through the cool, vast halls of the Takashimaya Department Store, I bought a plain pair of black slacks, a long-sleeved white blouse with a ruffle, ballet flats, a new bra, and modest light blue underpants. A sales clerk directed me to the nearest *ofuro*.

Stripped of all reminders of my night, I scrubbed and rinsed myself and plunged into the hottest of the three steaming tubs. A few months ago, I could barely stand the first and coolest of the tubs.

My physical tension eased, but my mind still raced. Was I really in danger, the damsel in distress from one of Hiro's martial arts films? Or was last night a fluke? The men I saw fell into two categories. Some, like Akira and Big Sumo-san were basically contented people, for whom sexual games with me were just an extension of that contentment. Others, especially the salarymen, seemed frustrated and unhappy, sex a temporary release from that condition. Perhaps I had been lucky that up until last night my clients' fantasies had been harmless. Were there more unhinged and malicious Shinytops out there? I didn't want to find out.

My thoughts wandered to Mr. Tambuki. Where did he fit into my theory? Some days he was thoughtful and attentive to my needs; other days, boorish, arbitrary, and demanding. I realized how little I knew him, given how many hours I'd spent with him. I didn't even know what he did for a living. What did he want from me aside from sex? Did he have some nefarious plan for me? If it weren't for him, I wouldn't have been working at Bar Puss 'n' Boots or sitting in this tub with a bruised body and the top of a finger in my bag.

But then there were all the things he was trying to teach me about his culture. I reminded myself that if he were here now, he would tell me to enjoy this moment, to feel the gentle heat of the water as it soothed my muscles and soaked through to my bones, to see the way the light caught the top of each silver ripple, to inhale the fragrant scent of soap and shampoo, to listen to the changing timbre of the splashes from the taps, here hitting a plastic bowl, there a hard tile. For him, there would be no Shinytop, no severed finger, because yesterday was no more. Tomorrow may never be.

And that was what worried me.

That evening, Berta greeted me with motherly concern. Penny had spent the week in the hospital fighting an infection from her self-inflicted abortion. Berta didn't talk about it, but I could see she was shaken at the thought of losing her own "baby."

"Gina, honey, you look as pale as vodka this evening, and that blond hair ain't helpin' any. You okay?"

I loved her dearly at that moment and wanted her to fold me in her massive, taffeta-covered arms. I wanted her to tell me that everything would be all right, that the finger meant nothing, that sometimes a drink just doesn't sit right, that nightmares are just the mind's way of releasing anxiety. But all I said was, "I'll be fine." She had enough to worry about.

Berta took care of me anyhow. She made sure I had the nicest, least offensive customers to serve. Her wisecracks were more restrained, less raw.

"You can't finish all those French fries, can you?" she taunted Licker, who on a bet with One Eye had ordered three plates. But when One Eye disappeared to the men's room, she told Licker, "Let me help you out. I've got more room than you," patting her rotund middle. After One Eye returned, Berta swooped up and ingested a mass of fries, like a friendly vulture, whenever he turned his head. Licker won the bet, and Berta winked at him.

Close to midnight as I wiped down the counter, Mr. Tambuki strode in with the confidence of a cowboy ready to settle a score. I froze when I saw him and bowed my head, ostensibly out of respect, but more because I was afraid to look him in the eye. I felt brittle, and I didn't have the energy to handle him. He sat down on a stool. Hana and Mama-san, who had long since left sobriety behind, stopped chattering for a moment, noted his presence, and then resumed their lighthearted conversation. I was about to retrieve his marked bottle of whiskey when he waved his hand "no."

"So, Gina, I have competition, do I?"

I wondered what prompted this question as I thought he understood by now that there were other men. I searched for some hint of emotion from him—scolding, anger, jealousy, even curiosity—but there was none.

"No one can compete with you, Tambuki-san. You are in a class all by yourself."

"Do I not pay you enough?"

"You are very generous. I've said that."

"You are letting yourself get distracted from your study. I do not think it is a good idea."

After my ordeal with Shinytop, I certainly had my own doubts about the direction I'd taken, but I found Mr. Tambuki's rationale somewhat strange. Was he covering for his need to own me completely?

I kept silent for a moment, and then asked him the question that had been foremost on my mind. "Tambuki-san, are you a yakuza?"

The smallest smile unfolded across his lips. "If I tell you I am a yakuza, will you then do what I want? And if I tell you I am not, will you walk away and go to the others? Would it not be prudent for me to say I am a yakuza, even if I am not?"

My head reeled from Mr. Tambuki's hypotheticals. "You are toying with me, Mr. Tambuki," I said, stamping my foot.

The smile disappeared. "On the contrary, Gina. It is you who are toying with me. You have not been honest. And yet, I have been entirely honest with you where it counts."

I was confused. "Then you are not a yakuza?"

With a blank face, Mr. Tambuki pulled out his wallet, removed a large, crisp bill, and set it on the counter.

"We will have dinner Thursday." Mr. Tambuki swiveled off his stool and left, without even a glance backward. Moving quickly, he almost knocked down Chief, who was on his way in. Chief bowed. Mr. Tambuki gave him an almost imperceptible nod.

"Everything okay with Mr. Tambuki, Gina?" Chief asked me, agitated. Then he noticed the money and sighed with relief.

"No problem," I said as I pocketed the bill, but my hand felt unclean where I'd touched what felt like a bribe.

It rained the next day, the large drops banging against my windows like strangers trying to get in. I decided to try calling Hiro again, but there was no answer. It was just as well. What would I have said? That I missed his friendship, his enthusiasm, his openness; that I wanted to be with someone not associated with the murky world that was encasing me in its hard shell? Even if I saw him, I couldn't tell him about the finger. I knew his tendency to sensationalize, and I didn't need to be reminded that I could be in a fix—me, who had always been so deliberate, so clear about what I was doing. Suki was not around. She was still trying to patch things up with Bento-san. I wondered what Gabe would say about my situation. Perhaps I'd phone him.

I never considered calling in sick at Bar Puss 'n' Boots. Although I was somewhat anxious about the possibility of running into Shinytop, I felt as safe within the Bar's fantasy-laden four walls as I did at the Snack. I looked forward to seeing Victoria. I decided I'd share some tidbits about my escapade with Shinytop, maybe not the whole story, but enough to have her nod in sympathy with the crazies out there. Maybe she would tell me about her date with Scarface and assure me that it was all a game.

But Victoria didn't show up to work that night and hadn't left word to explain her absence.

Cindy and I handled the breast men and the golfers, and I managed to avoid the one table that could be yakuza. Shinytop didn't make an appearance. I willed myself to drink less than usual, and in what felt like semi-sobriety, I even turned down a potential customer. I couldn't face the shadowy after hours alone with a man I barely knew.

I wasn't particularly sanguine about my date with Mr. Tambuki either. What big announcement was he planning for tonight? I dressed in my new conservative wardrobe. I would have worn my hair in a ponytail, but it reminded me of my recent night as a "schoolgirl."

Mr. Tambuki was talkative, chatting about the weather and other irrelevancies while I stared at the impressive menu in the opulent restaurant that was all overstuffed velvet. I couldn't decide, so I let him order for me, perhaps to allow him to continue to feel superior. When my plate of large shrimp arrived, I nibbled at the edges of one.

"Not hungry tonight?" His look could have been mistaken for concern.

"No." I took a large swallow of my wine to steady my nerves.

"That is too bad. The shrimp are delicious." He deftly scarfed one up with his chopsticks and popped it in his mouth, chewing earnestly.

"Gina, I have decided to get you an apartment so you can quit your job at the Bar." I wasn't exactly surprised at this turn of events, but I was offended by its presumption. "With all due respect, Tambuki-san, as you know, I am leaving soon to go back home to business school." As soon as it left my lips, that statement felt as false as my praise of a customer's sexual prowess. I'd heard nothing from Wharton, and it was already the middle of August.

"With all due respect, I do not think that is such a good idea for you."

"Mr. Tambuki! How can you say such things? I thought you understood me . . ." My voice trailed off. I waited a moment for my anger to continue rising, but it didn't.

"Oh, but I do understand you, dear Gina. It is you who don't understand yourself. What are you doing here? You came here as Dorothy to study banking. You never even contacted Mr. Watanabe, the man whose name I gave you. You gave up so soon. Why?"

Mr. Yamaguchi, the men in their identical dark suits at the large table, the terse dismissal from the first bank, the circular logic of the human resources person who told me I couldn't get a job without experience, Mr. Muriachi and the patronizing Keiko all paraded across my mind in orderly succession. I thought I'd put up a pretty good fight, but it hadn't netted me my goal of a decent internship experience. "I don't know." I felt completely deflated.

"My point. I think you like being Gina, but you can't admit it to yourself. So, now I am giving you the opportunity to be my mistress, exclusively. You can spend your days as you like, taking up whatever activities suit you, just as your friend Suki did. I will give you whatever you want." Mr. Tambuki paused.

For a moment, his offer seemed appealing. No need to prove myself. I could be a permanent student of Japanese culture, maybe even learn the language properly, not the bastardized masculine bar version I'd picked up in my nighttime jobs.

"If you want to continue working at the Snack a couple of nights a week to amuse yourself, I will not object. But, of course, I don't want you being a whore."

There it was. That word again. Shinytop had used it. The very sound of it was hard. Was that how all my clients saw me, even as I fulfilled their fantasies by acting out a role?

I didn't respond to Mr. Tambuki's last comment because I couldn't deny what I'd been doing, but neither was I ready to admit it out loud. "Whatever I want in exchange for what you want," I paraphrased to be sure I understood him correctly.

"But of course. And your delightful company." No hint of sarcasm.

Maybe I was being too harsh in my assessment of Mr. Tambuki. He had called me a whore, and yet he still wanted me. Maybe he had a heart after all. But to be his permanent mistress? "What would I tell my family?" Not that it mattered anymore. With my lackluster communications with them, I was probably as dead to them as my brother. Maybe even more dead because at least they had loved Robert, and anyway, he died before he could disappoint them. I bit my lip and forced back the tears.

"I am sure you are capable of concocting some believable story about international understanding." It was the kind of comment that should be accompanied by a conspiratorial wink or a chuckle, but it was not.

"And if I don't accept?"

"You will have to roll your own dice on that one. You have no doubt heard that yakuza men have ways of getting what they want."

Was he now admitting he was a yakuza? I started to feel ill. A minute ago, he'd made me an interesting offer, but now it felt more like a demand. "I could leave the country."

"You could, but I could stop you. Yakuza have their loyal allies."

"Even freelance yakuza?"

"Oh, you know about that, do you?" He stared at me with opaque eyes.

"No tattoos of belonging." I parroted something I remembered Hiro saying.

"Yes. That's right."

"If you are a yakuza, why didn't you cut down Hiro that night?"

"Small potatoes, you might say. Not worth the trouble." Mr. Tambuki lifted up another succulent shrimp to his mouth, and neatly devoured it. "And not in my best interest at the time."

I stared down at my plate, hoping to see small potatoes. Instead, the glistening headless shrimps, which had escaped with only their tails intact, lay inert in their juices.

"Gina, I will give you until the weekend to decide. But I must ask you not to discuss this with anyone. It is between you and me. Are we clear?"

"You're serious about this?" Not that I ever considered anything Mr. Tambuki said to be a joke. He played games, but he had a limited sense of humor. Even when he was mocking me, I now realized it was more with malice, an attempt to bring me down a peg or two so he could manipulate me better.

"Deadly serious."

If I tried to leave Japan, how would he even know? I had the money to fly home last minute, even first class. Maybe I was crazy, but I didn't want to go. I didn't even know exactly why, except that I didn't want to prove him right—that I didn't have the stuff it took to be successful in international business. And what would I be going home to? Anyhow, I thought he was bluffing about being a yakuza to unsettle me. I was just an investment to him, and he wanted his money's worth. He was too used to getting his way. But what if he was a yakuza?

Victoria didn't show up at work a second evening. Now I was concerned for her and for myself. I cornered Cindy in the back room and asked her if she knew anything about Victoria—"Kat" to her. Her hair was pulled back tightly into a bun. On anyone else it would have looked severe, even schoolmarmish, but on her it was sexy.

Cindy stopped applying her mascara and knitted her brow. "Kat is in some kind of trouble, perhaps? I think she went out with that man with scar, but the big boss man, he not like that?"

"The man with the bushy brows?" I asked, pointing to my eyebrows. The one I called Shrubbrow.

"Yes. He is very powerful man."

"What kind of trouble?"

"Perhaps he like Kat, too?"

Men and the green monster. "All the men like Kat," I said.

"Yes. She is very pretty. But she go out with too many men after bar shut at night. Not a good idea, I think." Cindy's voice dropped to a whisper, and she glanced around. "She talk about dates too much."

It was true. Victoria made no secret of her extracurricular life. I believed I'd been subtler, more selective. I wondered about Cindy. I had assumed that she, too, had dated the customers beyond the expectations of the *dohan* system. Now I wasn't so sure.

"You don't go out with the men here after the bar closes?" I asked, realizing I might be stepping out of line. But I needed to know.

"Oh, no! Only for dinner before. I have nice boyfriend." She sounded shocked. "You do not go out with the men, do you?"

"No," I lied. "I have a boyfriend, too." I was relieved that Cindy hadn't noticed or didn't let on she'd noticed that I saw men after hours, but then I became aware that Victoria and I might be the aberrant ones. Unless Cindy was covering for herself the way I was.

"Oh, I am happy." She beamed at me, apparently forgetting all about the reason for this conversation.

"But what about Kat?" My stomach churned. "Should we call the police?"

"The police? Oh, no. We cannot. If something happen to Kat because she have sex with customer, Mama-san not want to know. Very bad for bar."

"Do you think something might have happened?" I whispered. A few days ago, this thought would not have crossed my mind. Until Shinytop and the severed finger, weirdness had no relationship to danger.

"Perhaps she is sick. She will be in when she is better. We must go to work now." Cindy licked a finger and rubbed one last invisible imperfection from her face.

I looked up at the wall of fictional characters. The Dorothy from the mural on the wall seemed to beseech me from her precarious spot sandwiched between the tin man and the scarecrow. "Rescue me!" I plastered a smile on my face, but I felt the veins in my neck throb every time the door opened.

CHAPTER TWENTY-TWO

After another sleepless night in which every gust of wind and rattling window, every car tire and headlight set my heart pounding, I phoned Gabe to ask if I could come to Kyoto for a couple of days. He didn't ask me why, and I didn't offer. I had to leave town and clear my head. Berta agreed to cover for me at the Snack.

On the smooth ride on the Shinkensan train, I fell asleep and dreamed. Men, missing whole limbs and faceless except for the inky blue tattoos where features should have been, were taking turns thrusting their oversize penises into me as I lay helpless with my hands and feet bound with writhing snakes to the bedposts.

I awoke with a start when the train pulled into Kyoto and was surprised to see everything looking normal. Instead of a man with a bloody stump where a finger should be, I saw Gabe's welcoming round face with a couple of days' worth of stubble. He wore a striped short-sleeved shirt, open at the neck, and his usual khakis. At first, he didn't appear to recognize me as I'd forgotten to tell him about the blond hair. I walked right up to him, and his eyes widened.

"Good God. What do we have here? Marilyn Monroe on downers?"

"Nice to see you, too." I leaned in for a much-needed hug, and he encircled me with his bare arms. I buried myself in his neck, which was faintly moist from the high humidity and smelled piney. We stood entwined like a couple of lovers who had been separated by war. Gabe kissed the top of my head and pulled back first.

"Are you okay?" he asked, searching my face.

"I guess it depends on your definition. I am here, and I am in one piece."

"And these are your highest expectations?"

"One day at a time, Gabe. One foot in front of the other."

"You looking to forget your troubles or share them?" He took my overnight bag from me and heaved the strap onto his shoulder.

"Yes, I'd love a drink," I said, my recent semi-resolve to lay off the booze having dissolved with my nightmare on the train.

"Good start. With a food accompaniment, I think."

He was right. I hadn't eaten much the last few days. A customer had ordered me a plate of Chief's chicken, and I barely choked down a bite. Normally, I wouldn't have left a scrap.

Although Kyoto was both modern and old, it felt rooted in its past. Its green spaces and endless temples enchanted me. In contrast to sprawling Tokyo, it appeared to be a manageable, compact city, with a simple subway system.

We strolled through a lovely garden with stone statues and red *torii* gates. Gabe recounted a funny story about how one of his students brought him an apple every day, but by the end of each class the apple disappeared. After two weeks, Gabe noticed that the apples were becoming increasingly bruised, and he realized the student was recycling the same apple. "How could he think I wouldn't catch on?"

"Sometimes you believe what you want to," I said.

In a small, bright café, over a couple of bottles of beer, he finally said, "So spill."

In the train, between naps, I'd considered carefully how much I would reveal to Gabe. But I was so comfortable with him and so elated to be away from Tokyo that the words just flowed. "I think I may be in trouble, Gabe. That Mr. Tambuki you met in Nikko? He wants me to be his mistress. I trusted him at first, but now I think he may be a yakuza, and I've had two really negative experiences with yakuza men, so whether I say yes or no, it could be bad news."

"Take a breath, Dee Dee, and back up. Tell me about the bad experiences with yakuza."

"I'm afraid you're going to judge me if I tell you."

"The guy who can't remember half the things he did five years ago doesn't judge."

A needle-thin waiter with spiky hair brought our burgers and fries. Gabe thought I might want some comfort food from home. This place wasn't cheap, but the burger was a respectable size even by American standards. I took a big bite, and the juices ran down my chin. Gabe leaned forward with a napkin to blot the greasy trickle before it reached the collar of my new blouse, which had become my symbol for this transformed life I intended to lead.

"Thank you," I said, after swallowing.

"It's good, isn't it? I come here when I need to indulge my American heritage." He chomped into his own bun for confirmation and let me eat several more bites before restarting his questioning. "So, the yakuza men?"

"Yes. It's hard to know where to begin. I was short of money, and Mr. Tambuki offered me this arrangement to see him regularly, and one thing led to another, and then he got me this job in a fancier club where an Australian girl I'd met when I first arrived just happened to be working. And she was making a lot of extra cash by seeing customers after hours, and at the time it didn't seem like such a terrible idea." Describing this chain of events, I wondered how I could have been so naïve. I felt my face heat up in shame.

I looked down at my plate, not wanting to see Gabe's reaction. When I reached for a French fry, I glanced up. He wasn't registering shock or disgust, so I continued, French fry poised between my fingers like a pointer. "I mean I was already accepting money from Mr. Tambuki, so it didn't seem like a big stretch, you know? And most of the men were nice enough. I only went out with guys I had some sense of, and the money was mostly good. Then there was this weird stuff with Mr. Tambuki."

After devouring a handful of fries, which were crisp on the outside and soft on the inside, I told him about the *shunga*, and Nobu, and the severed finger, and Victoria. The only part I left out was about Suki and her tussle with Bento-san. Gabe nodded sympathetically.

"Wow. You've got me beat for foreign adventures," Gabe said with what sounded like a tinge of envy. "Who would have predicted this from the girl who pledged celibacy? And oh, the cultural adaptability points you've racked up." He added quickly, "I'm not dismissing the seriousness of all of this, you understand. But whatever happened to the banking internship?"

"A whole separate saga, full of failure, I'm afraid." Although Mr. Tambuki had been blunt enough about my lack of persistence in pursuing the internship, this was the first time I used that particular f-word to describe my pathetic experience in that department. It was liberating. "I have more pressing issues to deal with now." Trying to sound lighthearted, I added, "Like my life!"

Gabe raised his eyebrows. "I guess that excuses it." He stared at me. "What do you think is going on?"

"I was hoping you could tell *me*."

"The finger sounds like someone could have been disloyal to a superior, but I don't know why he would give it to you. And I've heard that yakuza don't do that finger-cutting thing so much anymore. Sure it wasn't a rubber replica?"

"Oh, it was real. And don't forget I was drugged."

"Look. If that guy wanted to do anything more than scare you, he could have. You don't even know whose finger it is, or who left it."

I'd assumed it was Shinytop who left it. "But what about Mr. Tambuki's proposition, which he told me not to reveal to anyone?"

"Now you're in deep shit. You just told me. How do you know I'm not a yakuza?"

I felt my face drain of blood. "Gabe, I'm spooked and confused enough already."

He reached across the table and took my greasy hand. "I'm sorry, Dee Dee."

"Tell me what to do." I felt like I was treading water with land nowhere in sight.

"I can't do that, but I'm glad you trust me enough to ask. What do *you* think you should do?"

"I don't know. I've never been so unsure about anything."

Gabe kept holding my hand, and I began to feel as though he'd handed me a life preserver.

When I told him that I found parks and gardens calming, he took me to Nijo Castle and led me to a garden adjoining the Ninomaru Palace. It wasn't a traditional garden but rather a pond with three islands all connected by bridges to the shoreline. Dozens of rocks and many forms of greenery around the edge cast reflections in the still pond so that it almost didn't seem like water.

"Is Suki still with that Bento fellow?" Gabe asked.

I was glad he had taken the focus off me, but I didn't want to betray Suki. "You know about him?"

"The guy who gets his jollies from feet."

Gabe probably knew more than Suki thought he did. "It's kind of up and down with him at the moment," I hedged.

"She could do better."

"I thought you didn't judge."

"Not to people's faces."

"Now we find out."

We stopped in front of a mini-waterfall cascading over one moss-covered rock. The large stones near it were dry, but their

arrangement, their seams of color, and the shadows from surrounding trees created the illusion of a bigger waterfall.

"She's really smart, like you," Gabe said. "Did she tell you how
we met?"

"In college."

"Yes, she was my chem tutor. Chemistry! The only chemistry
I knew was mixing drugs and alcohol. She was a junior when I
was a freshman. Premed, and then she dropped out."

"She never told me that."

"I'm not surprised. Being a doctor was her parents' dream for
her. The immigrants' American dream."

"She said something about that once. What was your dad's
dream for you?"

"To graduate. He didn't expect much," Gabe laughed. "I
delivered."

"I've been nothing but a disappointment to my parents.
They've probably disowned me by now, that is, if they even care
enough about me to bother."

"They care," Gabe said with confidence. "More than you
might ever know."

When Gabe heard I was studying Zen, he took me to the famous
rock garden at Ryoanji. The garden contained only fifteen rocks
of different sizes arranged in small groups on a bed of white sandy
gravel raked in straight lines.

"No matter how you look at this garden, you will never see
more than fourteen rocks, guaranteed, unless you have attained
spiritual enlightenment," Gabe explained.

We walked around. I squinted. I cocked my head. I stood on
my toes. I couldn't see all fifteen rocks at once. "I guess I have a
way to go before I'm enlightened," I said.

It was late in the afternoon. We sat on the edge of the garden
watching as the shadows of the rocks lengthened, creating new
patterns and enhancing the space between the rocks. I noticed

the way the rake marks made circles around each rock group, with the straight lines abutting right up to the circle and continuing on the other side. The rocks were like islands in the sea of sand. Such perfection. But a changing perfection. How could that be?

We sat in silence for a long time. Out of the corner of my eye, I could see Gabe look my way from time to time. Then he reached over and took my hand. The sun was low in the sky now, and I felt a breeze. I was as near to contentment as I had felt in a long time.

We ended up at Gabe's apartment, which was cozy and surprisingly neat for someone who'd received short notice about company coming. I had him pegged as a messy bachelor with a sink full of dirty dishes and last week's laundry drying on chairs. The décor was nothing special, but neither was it random. The various pieces of furniture felt like they belonged together. A large bookcase filled with both paperbacks and hardbacks dominated the living room.

Gabe fetched a bottle of plum wine, and we settled on his couch, feet up. I rested my head on his shoulder. When the familiar alcohol buzz took hold, lowering my inhibitions, I kissed him, and he reciprocated. His kisses were soft, but sexy. I'd forgotten how nice that part of attraction could be. After a while, my hand migrated to Gabe's crotch. I thought it odd I even wanted a man after all I'd been through, but it was more like unfinished business with him. I caressed his already hard but still clothed penis. He moaned and put his hand on top of mine.

"Are you sure this is what you want?" he asked.

I knew my judgment hadn't been so good recently, but this time it felt right. "It's like getting up on a horse again when you've been thrown," I said, pleased I could still make a joke. But there was a certain truth in it.

Gabe pulled away from me slightly. "So essentially, you want to use me." He threw me a couple of fake punches.

"No. Yes. Maybe you're right. I hadn't thought of it from your point of view."

"I don't mind being used, but I wonder if it's a good idea?"

"Afraid you're going to catch something from me? I am careful, you know." I dismissed the unknown nature of my final encounter with Shinytop, vowing I would schedule a medical checkup when I returned to Tokyo.

"I bet you are."

"You're being a tease, then, aren't you?"

He tickled me. I screamed and squirmed from his fingers. My body released its last ounce of tension, escaping like trapped air from a plastic bag being flattened. I'd forgotten what normal could feel like.

"You're a really good friend," I said when I recovered my composure.

Lying against a stack of cushions on the floor, we polished off the wine. Gabe turned on the television. We watched four busty girls in bras and short skirts take turns performing tricks to show how well-endowed they were. One of them bounced a ball off her breasts; another put a glass in her cleavage and poured water from the glass into a bottle.

"Ugh! That's disgusting," I said.

"I think it's very educational."

"You've been in Japan too long."

"Okay," he said with fake resignation. He aimed the remote and surfed through the channels.

I caught a glimpse of a young woman with long blond hair. "Go back to that one."

The woman looked like Victoria, but it was a Japanese woman with a blond wig. It didn't take much to make my fears resurface. Gabe put his arm around me.

"You can stay here for a while if you want to," he whispered as though he might be overheard.

"That's nice of you. I'll sleep on it." Like Mr. Tambuki's offer, it was momentarily attractive, for very different reasons.

Later, we cuddled in bed, with my head on Gabe's hairy chest and my hand on his round belly.

"You know, if I were you, I think I'd probably go back home," he said, breaking our silence.

I sat up, taken aback by this belated advice. "You would?"

"Probably. If I were you."

"You don't think I can handle this?" His remark annoyed me.

Gabe smiled and gently pulled me back down. "On the contrary. But why do you want to? You're way too good for this kind of life, Dee Dee."

He didn't say anything else. He didn't need to. A part of me knew he was right. I was smart. I was educated. Had I, like the other Dorothy from the Oz story, always had the power to get to where I needed? But somewhere I'd lost the road, and I didn't have any magic shoes to whisk me to my destination. In truth, I no longer had a destination. Or a home.

Gabe's rhythmic and reassuring snores eventually lulled me into slumber. My dreams were vivid but abstract this time. Bright bursts of color, loud music. Then heavy streams of water aimed at me until I couldn't breathe anymore. I woke up with a start, sweating and gasping for air.

"It's okay," Gabe said as he wrapped his arms around me.

I managed to fall into a deeper sleep. In the morning, with my head hammering from all the wine, I quietly gathered my things. As tempting as it was to hang out with Gabe, I had to take care of my other unfinished business with Mr. Tambuki. I also wanted to go with Berta to fetch Penny from the hospital, to provide some support for both of them. I needed to feel like I had a purpose. I wrote Gabe a brief note, thanking him for being there for me, and left, gently pulling the door shut so as not to wake him.

CHAPTER TWENTY-THREE

As I sat on the train pondering my next steps, my eyes locked with those of a Japanese man in a seat behind me on the other side of the aisle. He looked away. Perhaps he was one of my clients, but I didn't recognize him. His black suit, with matching shirt and tie, contrasted to his white, brimmed hat, which cast a shadow over part of his face. As a blond gaijin, I had been attracting notice, but I guessed that I didn't appear my best this morning. My long hair was lifeless, and my jeans and T-shirt were hardly alluring.

From my tote bag, I retrieved a novel Suki had lent me, sneaking another glance at Whitehat before opening it. Again he was watching me, but when I caught his eye, he returned his attention to the newspaper in his lap. Had Mr. Tambuki sent one of his minions to follow me? It was a silly thought, and I knew I was working myself up over nothing. I would have moved except that every seat was taken. I shut my eyes, placed my wrists loosely on my thighs, and concentrated on my breathing. After a few minutes, my muscles untangled and my head cleared. No bad thinkings, as Hiro would have said.

Still, I didn't want to fall asleep and risk more nightmares. I tried reading but stared at the same paragraph over and over as though the words were in Japanese kanji. I swore I could feel

Whitehat's gaze burning the back of my neck. I didn't dare look. Eventually, I nodded off, thankfully dreamless, and woke up as the train jerked to a stop in Tokyo. Passengers flooded the aisles. Whitehat had disappeared. Perhaps I'd imagined him.

As I headed for my second train bound for Wakoshi, I saw Whitehat in front of a newsstand. He peeked at me over the top of his newspaper, which covered the lower half of his face like a veil. Then I saw a bloodied white bandage wound around one of his little fingers. That sight triggered the image of the severed finger in its shiny bowl, an image I'd managed to suppress for a day. Whitehat was a yakuza. Was it his finger I'd been given? Was he after me now? My heart raced.

I walked briskly to the ladies' room, where he couldn't follow me, and sat on the toilet for at least twenty minutes, hoping he'd catch his train while I missed mine. I tried my deep breathing exercises and hyperventilated instead. All I could picture was a cleaver slamming down. I imagined the sharp shock as it tore through skin, muscle, veins, and bone, blood spurting everywhere.

When I was sufficiently composed to emerge from the restroom, I headed straight for my platform. Whitehat was buying something from a vending machine, his newspaper tucked under his arm. He didn't seem in any particular rush. I wasn't even sure he noticed me, but how could I be certain? What if he followed me to the train? He hadn't made any attempt to speak to me, so I could hardly complain to anyone of harassment. I knew by now that hysteria, especially from gaijin, only drew stares if it didn't seem warranted. This time, I wouldn't turn around and indulge him. I walked as fast as I could without actually running.

Then, wham! I was so focused on my getaway, I smacked right into someone. Embarrassed, I mumbled an apology in Japanese and then looked up to see Hiro, who was holding a long, skinny package. He squinted at me, puzzled. Then his face erupted into a big grin.

"Dee Dee with yellow hair."

"Hiro. What are you doing here?" I threw my arms around him. He had appeared from nowhere, like a genie out of a magic lamp.

Hiro returned my hug but pulled back. I held on with one hand, afraid that if I let go, he would vanish in a puff of smoke.

"I come to see you. I worry about you. You phone me many times. I feel bad I not answer."

"You're on your way to Wakoshi to see me?"

"Yes." He waved the ticket in his free hand. "Train leave soon."

Hand in hand, we ran down the platform to the front of the train. When we took our seats, I was out of breath. Hiro seemed perfectly relaxed.

"I am happy to see you. I've missed you, you know," I said.

"I miss you, too."

I remembered that he was due to take the exam the day after the disastrous encounter with Mr. Tambuki. "How did you do on your second exam?"

"I not take it."

"Because of me?"

"Not your fault. Head okay, but heart not want."

"So, you don't blame me?"

"No. I thank you."

"Thank me?"

"Yes. I not want to go to Tokyo University and be salaryman."

I wondered how I had been involved in his decision-making process, but I didn't pursue it. "So, what will you do?"

"Study *kendo* more. Teach maybe." Hiro sliced at the air with an imaginary sword.

"And your mother is okay with that?" I asked.

Hiro shrugged.

"You are a good teacher. She should be proud of you," I continued.

Hiro glowed. "Thank you. You good teacher, too. Good English teacher."

"Thank you. I enjoyed it." I stared at my hands for a while. They were dry and cracked from handling ice at the Snack. "Hiro, do you still think I am a bad person?"

"I sorry I act mad that night. It not my business. You were good to me. I think later, maybe you not understand Japan?"

I certainly didn't understand how he could be so forgiving. "No, I don't. I know that now. It's a complicated place."

A man in black walked by us and turned to look at me over his shoulder. It was Whitehat. He sat down three rows ahead of us on the other side.

I held my breath and slouched down, wishing I could disappear. I could see only the top of the white hat. I fixated my eyes on it.

Hiro glanced at me and then at the direction of my gaze. "You still see the bad man?" he asked, obviously referring to Mr. Tambuki.

"You were right. He is bad." The hat fell from my view for a moment. I tensed up.

"He hurt you?"

"Not physically. He played games with my head, you know?" The hat popped back up.

Hiro followed my sight line and nodded toward Whitehat. "You in trouble with that one?" he whispered.

"I don't know. I may be." I hesitated, wondering how much to tell Hiro, afraid he might do something that would endanger us both.

Then Whitehat angled his body and looked directly at me, expressionless like Mr. Tambuki. I trembled. Hiro stared back, narrowing his eyes. I grabbed Hiro's hand and squeezed it.

"I think that man is following me, but I've never seen him before," I whispered.

"Yakuza," Hiro said definitively, confirming my suspicions.

"You think so?"

"You safe with me."

I felt like we were reenacting a scene from Hiro's favorite martial arts film. I wanted to believe I was safe. I hoped Hiro's skills matched up to those of the star of that movie.

We walked from the station back to my neighborhood with no signs of Whitehat. I let Hiro carry my bag, but I felt unworthy of his attention.

"Hiro, tonight I have to see that man you had the fight with."

"I come with you," he said. "I not afraid of him."

"No. I don't think that would be wise, but you can wait here for me. I won't be out late."

After eating at a tiny place that had only one meal option—a very bony fish with rice and some greens, we headed for our favorite little park. Hiro presented me with the long package he had been carrying. It was my very own practice sword. He spent time reviewing the routine he had taught me weeks ago as well as some new moves. His performance was like a ballet. In contrast, I was clumsy, and the sword felt heavy. Eventually, I completed the routine without any major mistakes. Hiro applauded.

I wished I could erase these last few months and start over. Where had I made my first truly wrong turn? But I had to keep going forward. Maybe I had made a small difference to Hiro, at least that was what he said. Maybe that counted for something. Even if I was a whore and not a very good girlfriend.

I took a deep bow, but I was painfully aware of what a clueless gaijin I was.

When we reached my place, I went upstairs to change for my "date" with Mr. Tambuki, taking my *ken* practice sword, which I propped against the cupboard. Again, I put on the plain outfit I'd bought in Shinjuku and pulled my hair back from my face, securing it with some pins. I didn't put on any makeup. We were going to discuss a business proposition after all, even if I was the commodity to be brokered.

As I did up the last button, I heard a piercing cry from below—more like a battle cry than a call for help. I peered down from the top of the stairwell.

The front door was open. A white hat lay on the ground. In the hallway, Hiro kicked a man in black; the man ducked and lashed out with his fist. Hiro sprang away. They disappeared into the larger, dim space of the Club, and for a moment I couldn't see anything. I didn't want to seek help for fear of distracting Hiro. I'd seen enough films with that story line.

I heard the crack of a chair being thrown, loud grunts. I caught a glimpse of Hiro still on his feet and then a flash of black.

Who was this man? My mind raced through possible scenarios. It all added up. Mr. Tambuki had Whitehat follow me all the way to Kyoto to make sure I didn't escape. Maybe Whitehat had been disloyal to Mr. Tambuki, who'd chopped off his finger and given it to me. Maybe Victoria's disappearance was also Mr. Tambuki's doing. Maybe he had her hidden away somewhere, or maybe he'd killed her as a lesson to me. And now I had involved innocent Hiro.

The shouts and the crashes became more frequent. As the fighters reappeared in my frame, I saw a flash of something shiny in Whitehat's hand. The light from the door highlighted the point of a knife with a mother-of-pearl handle. The knife vanished for a second. I heard another cry, but this one sounded different from the others. The knife, now covered in red, came into view again.

Suddenly, a foot struck the hand with the knife, which flew into the air before landing on the floor. Hiro and Whitehat circled around it, neither taking his eye off the other. If Hiro was hurt, he wasn't showing it.

I took a few deep breaths, and from somewhere deep within, I felt strength I didn't know was there. I fetched the *ken* practice sword and returned to watch the continued standoff. I noticed a dark patch on Hiro's thigh. Hiro was closer to the knife than Whitehat was, but he wasn't able to pick it up.

Barefoot I crept down the worn stairs, careful to stay flattened against the wall and out of view. Whitehat had his back to me. Then I flew down the remaining steps and swung the dull sword with all my might at the center of Whitehat's spine. "Get the knife, Hiro," I yelled, as Whitehat tottered.

Hiro grabbed the knife just as Whitehat regained his stance. But now he had to face two of us—me with the *ken* sword and Hiro with the knife. When he saw me, he looked confused. Hiro jumped on him, knocking him down. His head hit the wall hard, and he slumped, out cold. Hiro held the knife like he was about to plunge it into Whitehat's heart.

"Hiro, no! Let's call the police."

As I rushed to the phone in the kitchen, Suki walked in the open door. She saw Hiro standing over the seemingly lifeless Whitehat, knife still in hand, and screamed.

"Bento-san! Have you killed Bento-san?" She looked at Hiro and then back at me, bewildered, and fell on the still body. She put an ear to his chest and picked up his wrist.

"He's alive," she said. "That fucking pig." She stood up again.

"That's Bento-san?" I asked, trying to process all of this. "So, he's not a spy?"

"What?" Suki asked.

"Never mind. I'm just trying to get my head around some stuff." I needed to revamp my hypothesis about this man being Mr. Tambuki's stooge. "What was he doing *here*?"

Suki sat back on her knees, her words tumbling out. "He came over to try to win me back, but I'm finally onto his game. All those lies about a mother-in-law who wanted the apartment. He was up to his eyeballs in debt from gambling, and he owed his boss all this money. Of course, he couldn't admit he was in trouble, so he managed to make me feel like I was at fault."

Hiro moved close and put an arm around me.

"But I did a little asking around," Suki fumed. "I know he went to Kyoto to see his boss, who's a very traditional man. He believes in the old customs of loyalty." She picked up the limp hand with the bandaged finger. "Serves him right, the prick."

"How do you know he wanted to win you back?" I asked.

"He left me a note saying that he was sorry he treated me so badly, that he still couldn't pay for the apartment, but he wanted to see me anyway. What a big baby." Suki glanced around the room until her eyes landed on a Mitsukoshi store shopping bag lying on its side. "Ha! He thinks I'll be satisfied with another pair of shoes."

Hiro kept his eyes on Bento-san, but he was obviously trying to follow what Suki was saying. She uttered a few things to him in Japanese, and he stepped away from Bento-san.

"Hiro, I'm so sorry to have put you through this," she added, in English, so I would understand. Then, fixing on the bloody patch on Hiro's leg, she said, "You're hurt." She instructed me to fetch a wet cloth and the emergency medical kit from the kitchen.

"I know a little first aid," she said as I handed her the requested items. She spoke again in Japanese to Hiro, and he pulled his trousers down. It was a clean wound, and the bleeding had subsided. Suki administered to it expertly. I held his hand as Suki prodded and dabbed.

"What are we going to do with him?" I asked, pointing to Bento-san. "Shouldn't we call the police or get him to a hospital? Maybe he has a concussion."

Bento-san moaned, showing some signs of life.

"I'll take care of him," Suki said.

I thanked her, grateful to have one less burden. But before we left the scene, I asked Suki, "When I was on the train with Bento-san and later in the station, he kept staring at me. I've never met him."

"He probably saw that photo of us I had in my house, and he couldn't quite place you because of the blond hair."

"Oh." I turned to Hiro. "I have to go now. Everything is going to be fine." I wasn't convinced, but I had to deal with Mr. Tambuki myself. What could he do in a public place like a restaurant? "Are you going to be okay?"

"I okay. You were spectacular." He beamed as he used the word I had taught him when I first saw him break a board with his hands.

"No, you were spectacular." I kissed him on the cheek. We both surveyed the Club. Chairs were strewn around like so many bodies, with their dismembered legs lying nearby. The wall had a big hole. I would have to concoct some explanation for Chief. "You should go home and get some rest."

"No, I stay here if you need me."

"Okay. But I'm not worried." I was very worried, but I didn't want Hiro attacking Mr. Tambuki again. Bento-san may have been an even match with Hiro, but I wasn't so sure that Hiro would come out so well in a contest with Mr. Tambuki, who in my mind was turning into a monster with multiple heads and tentacles.

Just I was walking upstairs to change, the phone rang.

"Penny's fever is worse." It was Berta. "She keeps calling your name along with someone called 'Jimmy.' Can you come to the hospital?"

I'd never heard Berta sound so helpless. I assured her I would be right there. I phoned Mr. Tambuki and explained that I would have to postpone our dinner to another night. He was polite, obviously not wanting to alienate me, but was quite firm about seeing me the following evening.

I told Hiro about the change of plans. He insisted on taking the train with me as far as Ikebukero. I didn't say much during the journey. I was both exhausted and exhilarated after the battle. My role had been small but significant. It was a good dress rehearsal for my upcoming match with Mr. Tambuki.

When I entered the hospital room, Berta was holding a damp green cloth to Penny's forehead. Penny, hooked up to an IV again, was twitching and mumbling something.

I barely recognized Berta. Instead of her wig of platinum curls, thin, mushroom-colored strands barely covered her pink scalp. Her makeup had worn off, revealing blotchy skin. I was shocked by her appearance, more than by Penny's wan face.

"Thank God you're here," Berta said. "She had a terrible nightmare. The nurse gave her a sedative, but it hasn't kicked in yet."

"Jimmy. Don't go, Jimmy," Penny moaned.

Berta snatched her hand with the washcloth away from Penny's head. Her nostrils flared, and her eyes widened, exposing a full circle of white around each iris. "Is Jimmy the bastard responsible for this?"

I shrugged. What good would it do either of them for Berta to know the truth? I could imagine her trying to get Jimmy court-martialed, and Penny running away from home. "I have no idea who Jimmy is."

Berta continued to regard Penny with suspicion. She rinsed the washcloth in the nearby sink and pressed it again against Penny's head.

I hovered nearby. "Berta, would you like to get yourself a cup of coffee, and I'll sit here with Penny?"

Berta nodded. "Thanks. I'm about to pee in my pants. Let me know if she says anything else." She grabbed her big purse and shuffled out of the room.

I moved to Berta's vacant chair, happy to feel useful by taking over her role with the washcloth. I could feel the heat of Penny's fever through the thick fabric.

She opened her eyes but seemed to look right through me as though I were a ghost. "Jimmy. You came back," she said.

"Penny, it's Gina, not Jimmy."

She ignored me, raking her nails down the sides of her face, leaving red marks. "I'm sorry, Jimmy. I didn't mean to. I love you." Then, she closed her eyes again, and in a few minutes, her contorted face relaxed. The change in her behavior was so dramatic that for a moment, I thought she was dead. Terrified, I put my head to her chest and heard the steady thump of her heart. Her breathing became more even.

I perched at the edge of my chair and quietly prayed, although it had been years since I'd done so. Even back in Catholic school I'd only gone through the motions, not believing. I said a couple of Hail Marys. The familiar and repetitious words soothed me and felt more appropriate for the occasion than my Zen meditation techniques. As I mouthed the prayers, a beatific smile crossed Penny's lips, and her golden hair framed her face like a halo. She looked so innocent.

And compared to me, she was, misplaced love for Jimmy and all.

But she was also her own person in a way that I never was.

Maybe Mr. Tambuki was right when he suggested I didn't understand myself. Could I assume an identity only when someone else assigned it to me? The good daughter, the stellar student, the overachieving employee, the obliging bar hostess, the seductive model, the responsive mistress, the kinky blond whore. Even my plan to go into international business, the rationale for my actions since coming to Japan, was Mark's idea. I was just one of those cooperative Bunraku puppets, who gave the illusion of life but whose sophisticated movements were shaped by multiple puppeteers. And where had trying to please everyone else gotten me? On a twisted road, heeding the commands of a possible con man.

Penny nudged me, snapping me from my self-flagellation. "You're here," she said, her voice low and croaky. "Where's Jimmy?"

I put my hand on her head. It was still warm but no longer like hot coals. "Jimmy isn't here, Penny."

"I thought he was here. I killed his baby." She looked up at me, eyes moist.

"It's okay, Penny." What else could I say? That she nearly died? That Jimmy didn't have a clue about what had happened and wouldn't want anything to do with her if he had?

"I wanted to punish him," she whispered. "He's mad at me, isn't he? That's why he left."

It's funny how real hallucinations seem, I thought. But hers seemed so rational. Would it hurt to build on them? "Jimmy said to tell you he's very sorry. He knows that none of this is your fault." I held her hand, which, although bigger than mine, felt soft as a child's. "He said that he was wrong to take advantage of you. He said he hopes you can forgive him." Sister Archangel would scold me for lying, but I didn't care.

Penny smiled. I wondered whether she would remember any of this conversation when she recovered or at least internalize it.

Berta waddled back into the room. She'd applied some lipstick and blush but still looked weary. "Baby, you're awake." She stood by Penny's bed and felt her nightgown. "She's very damp." Taking charge, she called for the nurse, who came in and changed Penny's gown and bedsheets. Berta helped by cradling Penny in her big arms. The nurse took Penny's temperature again and reported that it had gone down.

After the nurse left, Berta smoothed Penny's clean hospital gown and pulled the sheet and blanket up around her chest as though she were tucking in a toddler. Penny fell back into a restful sleep.

"Did she say anything while I was gone? Anything about that Jimmy?" Berta asked.

"She said she hoped you would forgive her." I knew I was pushing it.

"I know I haven't been able to give her everything she needs," Berta said. "I've done my best. I don't run around."

I nodded. "She's going to turn out all right." And I meant in the long run, too.

"Thank you for being there for her," Berta said. "I don't know what I'd do without her."

I smiled. I envied the love they had for each other.

CHAPTER TWENTY-FOUR

*N*ow I knew what I had to do when I saw Mr. Tambuki. I would break it off with him, of course, but I would do it in a civil way. I wrote down what I would say and rehearsed it so I wouldn't become tongue-tied in the moment. I put on my black slacks and white shirt and stuffed the envelope with the remaining money Mr. Tambuki had given me into my purse.

He took me to an upscale Japanese restaurant. We had a private room with many cushions, a low table, and sliding paper-screened doors. Despite its traditional style, the restaurant had an extensive wine list. Mr. Tambuki ordered champagne, which he knew I liked. When it arrived, he took the bottle from the waiter, uncorked it so it didn't froth over, and filled two glasses.

"So, Gina, do we have something to celebrate?"

"I believe we do." I'd hoped to buy even more time to refine my words further, but as usual, Mr. Tambuki was in control. I searched for that place I'd found the day before when I'd picked up the *ken* sword and attacked Bento-san.

"You were right," I began slowly, keeping composed and trying to sound confident. "I do like being Gina. I like the Snack and to some degree the Bar and helping people forget their troubles. I like the money. And, I have to admit I like being seen as sexy. That was new for me. And I even like being challenged, and you have certainly done that, Tambuki-san."

A smug smile flashed across Mr. Tambuki's face.

I took a dainty sip of champagne and let him bask in my ambiguous praise of him. "But maybe what's kept me here are the people I've met. Hiro, whom you called 'small potatoes,' was willing to put his own safety on the line for me. No one has ever done that before. And Berta who has a big heart, even if she won't admit it. She's helped and protected me. And Suki. I love her, but in her, I saw what I could become if I didn't use my brains. And Gabe, who accepts me for who I am, without judging."

Mr. Tambuki stared at me, not moving a muscle.

I kept going. "And yes, you, Tambuki-san. You taught me about art, about being mindful, and about getting a response from my body. I'm very grateful. Maybe all of that is a little corny, but I don't think a bank could have given me those things. At least, no bank I know. So, if that's Gina's life, then maybe it isn't so bad. Even if I can't put it on my resume."

"Dorothy . . ."

"Please, let me finish," I said, afraid that if I stopped for long, I would lose my way and that yellow brick road, which was straighter and wider than it had ever been, might disappear altogether. "I am not proud of the decision I made to take money from you in exchange for sex. I confused something that should have been personal with business. And then I believed I had become this other person. So, I lived that to the hilt. Yes, Mr. Tambuki, perhaps more than you suspect even."

Still no reaction.

"I got sucked into a degrading world, and for a while I left behind my soul. And then some things happened that made me think I was in danger. I thought you had orchestrated it all. But today I realized you don't control me. I may not know who the real Dorothy is, but I'm ready to find out. On my own. I suppose I should be thanking you for pushing me to that discovery."

I swallowed hard. Mr. Tambuki waited silently.

"That's it. I'm done," I said. I reached for the champagne glass again, not quite ready to look Mr. Tambuki in the eye.

Then he started to clap, slowly at first, and then quicker and louder. "Bravo! A fine performance."

I was momentarily relieved, thinking I'd impressed him, when the sliding door opened and in lumbered the grotesque Mr. Yakumasei, who'd made my first evening in Chief's club so uncomfortable. He bowed in my direction and talked so rapidly to Mr. Tambuki that I couldn't follow. Then Mr. Tambuki reached into his pocket and retrieved a small penknife.

"Be quick," Mr. Tambuki said, "and leave here right away. Right away!"

My heart pounded so hard, I thought I could feel the floor shake. I balled up my hands and placed them protectively in my lap.

Mr. Yakumasei nodded and bowed to Mr. Tambuki. He opened up the knife, and then glancing in my direction, he dropped it. He muttered something I took to be, "What will you do with her?"

"Give me the knife. I'll do it," Mr. Tambuki said sternly but with no hint of impatience.

I leaned forward on my cushion, wanting to make a run for it, but I was frozen to my seat, unable to draw a breath. I had angered Mr. Tambuki, and now he was going to punish me for it. He was a yakuza after all. In what seemed like slow motion, Mr. Yakumasei bent over to pick the knife off the floor, grunted, and handed it back to Mr. Tambuki with another small bow. Mr. Tambuki wiped the knife on his napkin.

Just as I was ready to take back everything I'd said, to swear total allegiance, Mr. Yakumasei handed Mr. Tambuki a small brown package wrapped very tightly several times in string. Mr. Tambuki gripped the package firmly, and with one swift move, cut the string, snapped the knife shut, and returned it to his pocket. He then gave the now unbound parcel to Mr. Yakumasei, who nodded to both of us and exited in disgrace. In one big puff, I released the breath I'd been holding.

"You look pale, Dorothy. Is anything the matter?" Mr. Tambuki asked in a cloyingly solicitous voice.

I sucked in as much air as I was able. "Mr. Yakumasei . . ." was all that came out.

"Ah, I apologize for the interruption. It seems like I must always do business."

"The packet . . . the knife."

"I keep forgetting that Mr. Yakumasei is scared of knives since an unfortunate sushi accident some years ago. Pity. Now, where were we? Oh, yes." Mr. Tambuki resumed his slow clapping. "Your speech. Magnificent. From the heart."

"I could say the same," I retorted.

"What?"

"The knife. Making me think you were a yakuza. That you were going to cut off my finger." I unfurled my hands and stretched my fingers out.

"What? Surely you did not think I am a yakuza, my little Gina, and that I would do such a terrible thing to you." Mr. Tambuki reached over and patted one of my hands. "However did you get such an idea?"

"What about the shady deals in back rooms, your designer suits, all your money, your connection with Nobu?"

"You have watched too many films. I am a simple businessman, who has been fortunate to be somewhat successful. I know many people."

"How about the fact that Chief is quite scared of you and keeps referring to you as an important person?"

"How flattering. But I am important to him. I financed his Club and the Snack. He is still in debt to me. He likes to keep me happy."

"That's all?" I wasn't convinced.

"But of course. And now we have this behind us, I think you

and I could be great friends. You have spirit. You see, I am not like those men in the bank. The ones who told you that Mr. Yamaguchi had been transferred to Dubai. That is not the true story."

"The true story? How do you know about that?" I asked. I could see that Mr. Tambuki was determined to have the last word.

"I have my sources. Mr. Yamaguchi could not tell you himself that his superiors did not approve of his taking on a young foreign woman for that internship. And I apologize for your negative experience with Mr. Muriachi. You are right to shun international banking. Unfortunately, it is a man's world still."

"Those men had to save face?" I was catching on at last.

"Precisely. Mr. Yamaguchi was honoring a promise he made to his Wharton friend, and Mr. Muriachi was just doing me a favor. But you have rejected my offer, and I am not embarrassed. In fact, I would have been disappointed in you had you accepted. I am pleased I was right about you in the first place."

I pondered this for a moment, rose off the floor, and looked down on Mr. Tambuki. "And who is saving face now? This is just a big game to you, isn't it?"

"You misunderstand me. And by way of 'coming clean,' as you might say, I will admit that I had a role in the gift of the finger. But it was for your own good. You were living a dangerous life as Gina."

Even though the thought had crossed my mind that Mr. Tambuki was involved with the finger episode, I was still surprised that he could have stooped so low. My face grew hot with anger. "You! How?"

"That young man Nobu—the one who you say mistreated you—I made sure that the proper authorities were informed of some of his illicit activities. He got only what he deserved."

The pieces were starting to make sense. "And you have some connection with the love hotel I stayed in that night?"

"I own it along with the Bar Puss 'n' Boots. And you are lucky I do. You were in over your head. So, you see, I did you a favor."

Every muscle in my body throbbed. He must have known everything. "I never asked you to interfere in my life like this, to spy on me. You know, I was prepared to come here today to thank you and move on. At one time, I thought you understood me, but now I realize that you used your insights to take advantage of me. What a waste of a gift. You're nothing more than a petty, egotistical, misogynist lowlife who cheats on his wife." I had to get that last dig in. "You're as conniving and as empty as . . . as the Wizard of Oz."

"I am sorry you feel that way," Mr. Tambuki said, his eyes uncharacteristically downcast. "How can I make you think better of my motives? Would you like me to tell your boyfriend that there was never anything going on between us?"

"I can take care of my own misdeeds, thank you."

"What if I pay for you to attend classes of your choosing? I will expect nothing in return. I could even continue to teach you if you wish." His voice cracked slightly.

"You want me to stick around so you can manipulate me some more? No thank you. I'd like to leave now."

"But we haven't had our supper yet."

He sounded almost desperate, and I felt pleased to have the upper hand for once. "I'm not hungry."

"The duck is excellent here. But whatever you wish," he said, calm again. He set his napkin on the table.

I let Mr. Tambuki take me home. I probably should have taken a taxi and ended it there. He didn't have any other surprises for me and played the car radio so we didn't have to talk. I faced forward the whole ride, my hands clasped in my lap. But out of the corner of my eye, I could see him glance at me every now and then. When we arrived in Wakoshi, I opened the car door without waiting for him. He hustled out his side and met up with me at the door of my house.

"Let me pay you for your escort services tonight," he said, as though nothing of consequence had transpired.

"No, I don't want your money," I said. I just wanted to be rid of the man. Then I remembered the bulging envelope I was carrying with me. I reached into my purse. "In fact, I don't want this either." I thrust the envelope toward him.

He made no move to take the money. "No, it's yours. We made a deal, and you earned it. I'm sure you can find a use for it."

I kept my arm out, but Mr. Tambuki just shook his head. I thought of stuffing it ceremonially into his pocket, but I didn't want to create any more reason to prolong our interaction. I lowered my hand.

"Well then. You win, I guess. I hope you're happy. Goodbye, Mr. Tambuki."

Mr. Tambuki took a deep bow. "Good luck to you, Miss Falwell. I hope you find what you are looking for."

The next morning, I was awakened by a rustling in the hallway and a long ray of sun shining across my futon. I felt rested for the first time in days, perhaps weeks, and my head felt clear. I realized that other than a few sips of champagne I hadn't drunk any alcohol since I'd left Gabe, and I hadn't wanted any. In fact, the thought made me squeamish.

I wandered out to find Suki emptying her room of dozens of shoeboxes.

"Good morning," she said brightly. "You want some shoes?"

She handed me a couple of boxes.

"Thanks, but they're not my size. Anyway, what are you doing?"

"Wiping the slate clean. You want to help?"

"Whatever you need," I said.

I changed into jeans and a T-shirt. Suki gave me a large stack of boxes and marched down the stairs with her own teetering stack.

When we set the boxes on the curb, I peered in a few. There were shoes for every occasion and in every imaginable color. "These are nice shoes. Are you sure you want to do this?" I asked.

"Quite sure. I'd rather go barefoot from now on than wear any of these."

"Most of them look brand-new," I said.

"Oh, I wore most of them just once, right after we bought them, and then only around the apartment."

"I thought that Japanese didn't wear shoes inside their homes."

"That was part of the titillation for Bento-san." She laughed.

"Can I ask you something, Suki? Was your physical relationship with Bento-san just the foot thing?"

"I guess I rationalized that this foot stuff wasn't really sex because we didn't have intercourse. But it was sex to him. He had me parade around with nothing on but the shoes. Then he basically made love to my feet. He said they were the most beautiful feet he had ever seen." She shuddered.

I tried to imagine what that act must have looked like.

She continued, "Now I'm thinking there are some things I'm not going to do for money anymore."

"You're giving it all up?"

"Yes. It's easy to get caught up in that life when you see others around you doing it, isn't it? The money. The gifts. You almost forget that it's not an acceptable way to make a living."

I nodded. "Do you think it's dangerous, too?"

"Sometimes. When I was working at a club in the city, a Canadian woman got involved with one of the yakuza men. He took her on expensive holidays, got her a luxurious apartment, bought her gorgeous clothes and jewelry. One day she decided she'd had enough. She tried to leave. They never even found her body."

I remembered Victoria and silently said a prayer for her.

"It doesn't happen all that often," she added.

I raised my eyebrows.

"Really, it doesn't," she said. "It just causes a sensation when it does."

"If Bento-san was a yakuza, why did you stay with him?" I asked.

"Most of the time, he treated me very well. He didn't involve me with his yakuza life."

I plucked another pair of shoes from the box and examined them. They were ruby-red round-toed pumps, with a hint of glitter, like the ones Judy Garland wore as Dorothy in the film version of *The Wizard of Oz*. I closed the lid. "Mr. Tambuki isn't a yakuza, is he?"

"He could be, I guess. I don't know him very well. I wasn't Caucasian enough for him. Are you still with him?"

"No. It's over."

"Oh. Are you sorry?" Suki asked.

"That it's over or that I ever was with him in the first place?"

"Either or both," she said.

"I don't know. I'm still angry with him."

"Because underneath his charm, he's human, warts and all?"

"Yes." I didn't regret what I'd said to him, but I was still confused about him and all that had happened between us. I changed the subject. "What will you do now?"

"I don't know. But not this life." Suki set down the last of her shoeboxes and rubbed her hands together.

"I guess we both have something to celebrate," I said. "A past past and an unknown future."

I hesitated a moment and then placed the box with the red shoes on the curb with the others. As we turned to walk away, I heard high-pitched gabbling. I looked over my shoulder and saw two young women descend on the collection like birds of prey, ripping off the lids and hoisting their new trophies high into the air.

When we returned to the Club, I tramped upstairs and grabbed both pairs of my high- heeled sandals from the cupboard. I slipped into the silver ones. They were powerful shoes. They'd netted me a lot of money. But magical? For fun, I clicked my heels together three times.

When I passed Suki, now in the kitchen, I waved the sandals by their straps. "I have something to add to your collection. I won't be needing these anymore."

I skipped out the doorway and almost tripped on a long, thin package left on the front steps. I deposited my shoes with what remained of Suki's and stooped to pick up the parcel, which was addressed to me. I ripped off the outside paper to find a box of polished wood. Inside the box, a scroll. I unfurled it. On a beige textured silk background with a patterned border was a delicate painting of a kneeling woman holding and sniffing at a pink long-stemmed rose. She wore a blue kimono with yellow flowers and green dragonflies, their lacy wings lovingly detailed. Her robe drifted sensuously off one of her pale shoulders. The scene and the kimono were familiar. When I looked more closely, I realized that the woman was me. The painting was as beautiful as many I'd seen at museums.

A brief note on high-quality vellum accompanied the picture. It read, "A rose greets each day being the best rose it can be. You are the rose. Norio Tambuki."

I wandered back into the house, dazed.

"What is it?" Suki asked.

"The last word," I said. As with many of Mr. Tambuki's pithy proverbs and comments, I wasn't sure what the message meant and whether he had written it to stimulate me or annoy me. Maybe I had been too rough on him last night. Maybe in his own way he was trying to teach me about his culture. I handed the note to Suki to decipher along with the picture.

Suki studied both and looked up at me, her eyes wide. "He was in love with you, I think."

I was stunned. The thought had never occurred to me. "He had a very strange way of showing it."

"Love makes us so vulnerable to hurt, we can be afraid of it and behave in strange ways, to the point of acting the opposite of love."

We both studied the scroll. The woman in the kimono appeared confident but tender. The painter believed in her.

"He's very talented, isn't he?" Suki continued. "Look at this exquisite brushwork. Who would have guessed?"

I rolled up the scroll, tucked it under my arm, and returned to my room. I pored over the note for a long time. All these months of sexual intimacy, and I had never known Mr. Tambuki's first name. A wall always stood between us. He was my sensei, and I, his student. In this final present of the painting and the name, he had revealed something of himself, some crack of vulnerability. Had he shown me any of that earlier, maybe I could still bring myself to like him, despite his unorthodox and sometimes manipulative ways. After all, if Suki was right, he loved me despite the monster I'd become. He'd been generous with his gifts—his talents and his money—and I had spat in his face. Yet he could still write, "You are the rose."

Maybe I was a rose, thorns and all. And maybe that wasn't so bad for a previously nerdy Catholic girl. As metaphors went, I preferred it to the fairy tale I'd been inhabiting. But I was through with metaphors and costumes. From now on, I was going to experience the world as Dee Dee—not a rolling stone, a drifting ice floe, a leaping frog, a slutty schoolgirl, a flower in bloom, or even that other Dorothy from Kansas.

CHAPTER TWENTY-FIVE

I thought about what Suki had said regarding love and how it makes us do strange things. I thought about Gabe's insistence that my parents did care about me. I sat down that night and wrote my parents a long letter, apologizing to them for choosing to come to Japan, of all places, and asking for their forgiveness. I said that by going so far away, I hadn't intended to abandon them, but rather to test out my wings. I gave them a sanitized version of my activities ("waitressing") and described some of the places I'd been and all the interesting people I'd met of all ages and backgrounds—people who welcomed me, helped me understand more about myself, and made me value family. Finally, I told them that I loved them and appreciated all they'd done for me and that no matter what I decided to do, I would write to them regularly and include them in my life. I came on a little strong in places, but the basic sentiments were from the heart.

I gave my notice to Chief without much fanfare. He was annoyed with me, of course, since he saw me as a big draw for the customers. If he had known that Mr. Tambuki was no longer my patron, he would have found a way to give me the boot indirectly. This way, I allowed us both to save face. I didn't want to return to Bar Puss 'n' Boots with its distorted caricatures of beloved childhood stories, so I left one note for Mama-san 2, thanking her, and another for Cindy, telling her how to contact me if she heard from Victoria.

Now back home, Penny was bouncing back to her former adolescent self, much to my relief. If she was sad, she was hiding it well. She was even able to make fun of herself. Mischievously, she told me that she was sorry she wouldn't be able to show off her big, fat belly. She pulled up her strappy top and thrust her stomach out, eliciting stares from the passersby in the park, where we perched on the picnic table. In return, she gave them her "what are you looking at" scowl. I wondered how she would recreate her story in her own mind.

"How are you and Berta doing?" I asked.

Penny alternately swung her long, bare legs. She wore checked sneakers with orange laces. "She's grounded me forever. At least with a baby she would have had something else to occupy her, so she'd be off my case."

"I think given what happened, she might have a good reason for being on your case?"

"Hey, she got knocked up at eighteen. Anyway, I'm through with married American soldiers. It's strictly Japanese boys from now on."

"That sounds like a better plan, but it's not going to make Berta happy," I said.

"Nothing will make her happy except me being a nun," Penny chuckled.

"Explain something to me, Penny. If Berta hates Japan and the Japanese so much, why does she stay?"

"Oh, Mom would be lost if she didn't have something to bitch about. She'll never leave."

"Even if you left?"

"Why would I leave? This is my home. My friends are all here."

I looked at blond, blue-eyed Penny. Was she a gaijin in Japan, or just one of the girls? Apparently, it was not an issue for her.

"Are you going to stay?" she asked.

"I don't know," I answered. The question had been hanging in front of me for these last few days. I was painfully aware that I knew little of Japan.

"You should. You've hardly been here any time at all. I could show you stuff."

"Thanks for the offer." The eight years between us felt like a chasm.

"But if you stay, dye your hair back to brown. You suck as a blonde."

On my last night at the Snack, after the clients left, Mama-san gave me a going-away party and even managed to stay sober for it. Everyone was there but Chief, who watched from the kitchen window. Penny surprised me with a Betty Crocker–type chocolate cake emblazoned with "Good luck, Gina" in rainbow-colored frosting, and a book with Japanese stories translated into English. Mama-san proudly presented me with a *yukata* in the traditional blue-and-white printed cotton. It was a simpler garment than the ornate kimono Mr. Tambuki had bought me, but more practical, for everyday use. She motioned me to try it on. I put it on over my street clothes and twirled around. She beamed approval.

Then it was my turn to give everyone gifts. With Suki's help, I had chosen small tokens of appreciation for each person. For Berta, there was a turquoise chiffon scarf; for Penny, a T-shirt that said, "one world," and pictured a globe surrounded by people of all different colors; for Hana, a slender bracelet; for Mama-san, a mother-of-pearl barrette to hold back her long hair; and for Chief, a tie clip. Berta cried and gorged on cake. Chief stayed hidden.

Afterward, I bought everyone drinks and poured myself a coke. Penny trotted to the karaoke machine, punched in a selection, and gestured for me to come over. I gave Berta a shrug and joined Penny on the small dance floor. She picked up the microphone, and we gyrated as we sang "Lady Marmalade," the song that had embarrassed me my first night at the Snack. Everyone applauded. I bowed and gave all the women a final hug, knowing I would probably not see any of them again after tonight. As it was late, Chief was forced to drive me back to Wakoshi. Hana sat in front, and I sat in the back with Mama-san, who stroked my hair, which I had dyed back to its normal color. Chief silently handed me my last week's wages minus what I owed him for rent. I thanked him, and he nodded.

I went to Nikko with Hiro, as I had long ago promised him, and we wandered up the same path Mr. Tambuki and I had trod. Although it had rained earlier in the day, enhancing the apple red of the *torii* gates, the skies had cleared, and shards of blue sparkled between the thick canopy of trees. The piney earth filled our nostrils and lungs, energizing us better than a jolt of caffeine.

As we walked by the souvenir stands, Hiro stopped and picked up a little statue of a Samurai. He handed it to me. "You like this one?"

"He looks a little like you would if you had less hair. My warrior!"

"I buy it for you."

He paid the stall keeper, and we headed back to our *ryokan*.

Later that evening after we finished our Japanese dinners and the American ones the staff brought as well because I was a gai-jin, I lay back against the cushions and groaned, the little samurai statue sitting on my belly. Hiro was still full of pep. He brought out his *ken* practice sword, which he took everywhere, and danced through a long, graceful routine. I applauded.

Sitting back on the cushions, his brow knitted, he said, "Dee Dee, I have made big decision. I go up north to study at special *budokan*."

"That's wonderful news, Hiro. I'm sure you'll do really well there."

"You inspire me," he added. "I look up that word in dictionary."

"Oh?" I never thought of myself as the inspirational type.

"Yes. You come all this way from America and take chances. I can leave home, too."

"That's nice of you to say. I hope you make fewer mistakes than I did."

"Mistakes are good. We learn from mistakes, yes? Otherwise, just do as people say. Learn nothing."

He really was a sweetheart in more ways than I had appreciated. "I have something for you to remember me by," I said.

I leaned over and kissed him on the lips. He eagerly reciprocated and pulled me down on top of him. After a while, we made love for the first time in many, many weeks. I was not constrained by expectations, nor propelled by alcohol. It felt right but also like the parting gift it was meant to be.

I took a room in a small hotel while I figured out my next steps.

When I picked up my mail at the American Express, there were three surprise items. The first was a letter of acceptance from Wharton, along with various forms for me to complete. The program was due to start in less than two weeks. Since I never sent any follow-up materials about my dubious internship experiences, I wondered whether my acceptance was yet another one of Mr. Tambuki's doings. His final attempt to make himself into the good guy or to give me the illusion of choice? I should have leaped for joy, but in truth, I found myself no longer excited by the prospect of a business career.

The second item was a postcard from Victoria. She was staying in a cheap resort in Goa. No apology for leaving without a goodbye. No explanation. But she sounded content, and I had to admire her for following her instincts. We exchanged a couple of letters after that. I told her what Cindy had said about possibly getting in trouble with Mama-san 2 for having sex with customers. She replied, "I never had sex with customers. Just pretend romance. But they thought it was real." If that was true, she had me fooled, too.

The third was a long letter from my mother. Most of it was about mundane things—the barbecue they attended at the church, their grandson's baseball games, the hot weather they'd been having. But near the end, she thanked me for my letter and said she'd been worried she'd said something to upset *me*. She was glad I was having a valuable experience and seeing the world, something she never had a chance to do, since Dad had no interest in travel (or much of anything else for that matter). She said there wasn't an hour that went by that she didn't think of each of her three children with the greatest love. She and Dad missed me a lot and looked forward to hearing of my adventures but urged me to be safe as they couldn't bear the thought of anything happening to me.

I read the letter five times, marveling at how dumb I'd been. Had I ever even tried to have a conversation with my mother about how she felt about her life? Living with Dad couldn't have been a picnic, and losing her firstborn? I couldn't begin to imagine. Of course, there were many more conversations we needed to have, but for now, we'd both gotten what we'd needed.

Tambuki-san was often in my thoughts. Sometimes, late at night, I would conjure up my own pretend world where the two of us were doing what we did best together, meeting each other's physical needs. I'd bring myself to a full throttle orgasm. Afterward in the darkness, I felt empty. I wondered whether he, too, despite his exhortations to live in the present, pined for me, just a little.

Gabe returned to Tokyo for a few days, and he, Suki, and I hung out together. Gabe and Suki wanted to take me to a tea ceremony, and I relented despite my memories of my first time. But this occasion was different. I studied the tools, admired the brown-flecked glaze of the bowl, and followed each deliberate movement of the tea master. My pulse rate dropped as I relaxed into the hypnotic flow of activity. I couldn't say I fully understood it all, but I was fascinated down to the last drop of the tea, prepared with care and precision, for me, the honored guest.

With encouragement from Gabe and me, Suki decided to visit her family, who had moved to California. She even considered returning to college to finish her degree. As a going-away present, I gave her a first-class ticket. It was a good use of part of the money I'd earned. I still had plenty left. To purchase the ticket, I asked Gabe what Suki's whole name was and discovered it was Susan Kitao. Gabe had said that Suki was a grade school nickname, based on both her first and last names and on the dish, sukiyaki. At one time, it had been used to taunt her, a stranger in her own country, and I wondered why she had embraced it. At the airport, I asked her.

"Suki is who I am—a one-pot meal—with both Japanese and American ingredients, and I will always be that no matter where I live. It's a good name, don't you think?"

I thought of my own dual identity as Dee Dee and Gina— and what separate lives those two had led. "It suits you," I said. "But doesn't it also mean 'to like' in Japanese? I think that's an even better meaning."

After the hugs, Suki waved goodbye as she walked toward the gate.

"Gabe, keep Dee Dee out of trouble, will you?" she called out.

"You're asking the wrong guy," he said. "I introduced her to *you*, remember?"

"Yes, and I'm very grateful," I shouted, before she disappeared out of sight.

Gabe put an arm around me and gave me a peck on the forehead.

We bought two expensive cups of coffee at the airport café. I treated.

"So, what are your plans now?" he asked.

"You know, I haven't the slightest idea!" We burst out laughing.

He took my hand and gave it a squeeze. "Well, that narrows the field a little."

"I know more than I ever wanted to know about Japan and not nearly enough. But it's all good."

"Very philosophical of you and quite a shift from the Dee Dee I met at the youth hostel—the determined banker."

"But I'm not changing my name again," I said.

We went back to my hotel. Gabe had to leave that evening for Kyoto, but he accepted my invitation to come upstairs. I brewed us some tea, and we sat on the futon with our backs against the wall.

"I've been thinking," he began. "I know a nice guy. Teaches English. Might be able to help you get a job in Kyoto. Learn about that *other* Japan. No strings."

I remembered how much I'd liked Kyoto. I could live a normal life there, learn the language properly, see some more art, and maybe figure out what I wanted to do with my life. "No strings? No hidden puppeteers? No curtains hiding the Wizard?"

"All up front," he said, putting his hand up his shirt and patting his ample belly.

I watched him and felt the familiar flutter of desire. "I thought you said if you were me, you'd go home."

"But I'm not you," he said.

"No, and I'm not that other Dorothy—the one who said, 'There's no place like home.'"

"Ah, but what is home?" Gabe asked. "Isn't that the crux of the question?"

"I don't need another Zen master, thank you." I kissed him on the nose. Once again, he was right.

He took my hand and placed it where his own had been. His flesh felt warm, and without thinking, I let my fingers slip a little lower. I was pleased to find I wasn't the only one on the verge of arousal.

"So how about it? You interested?" he asked.

"What? In this?" I asked, giving his crotch a gentle squeeze.

"Now that you ask . . . But I was talking about my other offer."

"I might take you up on it." Or maybe I wouldn't. I could do whatever *I* wanted. And right now, I had other things on my mind.

QUESTIONS FOR DISCUSSION AND REFLECTION

1. In what ways does "the floating world" serve as a metaphor for Dee Dee's life both before and during her stay in Japan?

2. How has Dee Dee changed by the end of the story?

3. What role do each of the major characters play in her journey?

4. How do Dee Dee's feelings for Mr. Tambuki shift over time? How about Mr. Tambuki's feelings for Dee Dee/Gina?

5. The novel depicts norms of speech and behavior within the bar culture that nowadays we would consider to be sexual harassment. How did you react to these incidents?

6. Dee Dee is aghast when Victoria, the young Australian, says that "the rules don't apply," referring to the sexual activities that some of her friends engage in while they

are traveling. Yet, Dee Dee herself eventually seems to embrace this same philosophy. What allows Dee Dee to justify her own behavior?

7. This story is told in the first person by a young, naïve narrator. What did that viewpoint add to the story? Where did you question the narrator's reliability?

8. How well does Dee Dee fare in her quest to show her "culturally adaptability" to Japan?

9. What role do Japanese arts, both performing and visual, play as the story unfolds?

10. What parallels do you see between *Gina in the Floating World* and *The Wonderful Wizard of Oz*?

11. The novel is set in 1981. If it were set in the current day, how might today's communication methods have made the story play out differently?

12. What do you think Dee Dee's life might look like over the next few years after the story ends?

ACKNOWLEDGMENTS

Gina in the Floating World has its own coming-of-age story, beginning with its conception in Japan so many years ago. I am indebted to the scores of people who helped foster its development from its birth as a screenplay, through its turbulent adolescence as a novel-in-progress, to its eventual arrival into adulthood as a published book. I owe special deep gratitude to:

Lawrence Pruyne, who taught me the basic elements of narrative structure in a character-driven screenplay course at the Cambridge Center for Adult Education, and classmates and critique group members, Paul Peacock, Jacque Sullivan, and Jonathan Kharfen, who helped me to breathe life into the original screenplay version of my story.

Michael Neff, at the Algonkian Novel Writers' Workshop in Tucson, for his excitement about the premise of my first novel draft, his crucial recommendation to heighten its dramatic arc, and his publishing of my short story featuring my same protagonist.

The many authors of fiction and nonfiction whose work related to Japan I researched to provide authenticity as my story took on more ambitious directions.

All the writers and readers who gave me feedback along the way, especially my late sister, Beth Brett, for her original ideas based on her regular travels to Japan; Jane Jewell, Susan Goodrich,

Michael Graves, and my niece, author Pippa Goldschmidt, who provided suggestions on early drafts; Donna George Storey, whose beautiful, erotic story set in Japan gave me the courage to write more explicit sex scenes and who helped me with Japanese language and culture references; Buki Papillion, who read chunks of my evolving manuscript and provided invaluable critique and encouragement over cups of tea; my biweekly writers' group, Shellie Leger, Lisa Birk, and Burns Woodward, who embraced Gina with love and honesty over several years and many beers; Chris Erb for her careful review of one of my last drafts; Jackie Stefkovich for her thoughtful, final proofread; and all the friends who've given me access to their networks and provided ideas as I approached publication.

Grub Street in Boston, where I have taken many classes to improve my writing, especially to instructors Michelle Hoover and Lisa Borders, whose intensive, year-long Novel Incubator program provided me with the tools to kill my darlings and produce the final, leaner version of *Gina*; to my Novel Incubee colleagues, especially my nine classmates, who are a continual source of support and information about writing and publishing.

Brooke Warner and the team from She Writes Press for including me in their book pantheon and for shepherding *Gina in the Floating World* into publication, with special acknowledgment to Julie Metz for her exciting cover design, my project manager Samantha Strom for being on top of the details, and my She Writes Press sisters, especially Anjali Duva, Jeanne Blasberg, and Cheryl Suchors, for their advice, example, and support.

Crystal Patriarche, Ashley Ann Alfirevic, and the BookSparks team for helping to make my novel more visible through their publicity efforts.

And most of all my loving husband, John Heymann, not only for his superb editorial skills but also for his enthusiastic support of me and this project every step of the way.

ABOUT THE AUTHOR

Belle Brett is a graduate of Grub Street's intensive Novel Incubator program. After a career in education as a teacher, career counselor, and evaluator of educational programs, she is now an artist and a writer, contributing to her own and others' blogs and writing fiction that deals with coming of age across the life span. She holds a doctorate of education in human development and psychology from Harvard University. A lifelong traveler, in her twenties Belle served as a bar hostess in a working-class Tokyo suburb after a six-month trip across Asia. She now lives with her photographer husband in Somerville, Massachusetts. *Gina in the Floating World* is her first novel.

SELECTED TITLES FROM SHE WRITES PRESS

She Writes Press is an independent publishing
company founded to serve women writers everywhere.
Visit us at **www.shewritespress.com**.

Beautiful Garbage by Jill DiDonato. $16.95, 978-1-938314-01-8.
Talented but troubled young artist Jodi Plum leaves suburbia for the
excitement of the city—and is soon swept up in the sexual politics
and downtown art scene of 1980s New York.

The Tolling of Mercedes Bell by Jennifer Dwight. $18.95, 978-1-
63152-070-9. When she meets a magnetic lawyer at her work,
recently widowed Mercedes Bell unwittingly drinks a noxious
cocktail of grief, legal intrigue, desire, and deception—but when she
realizes that her life and her daughter's safety hang in the balance,
she is jolted into action.

The Geometry of Love by Jessica Levine. $16.95, 978-1-938314-62-9.
Torn between her need for stability and her desire for independence,
an aspiring poet grapples with questions of artistic inspiration, erotic
love, and infidelity.

Fire & Water by Betsy Graziani Fasbinder. $16.95, 978-1-938314-
14-8. Kate Murphy has always played by the rules—but when
she meets charismatic artist Jake Bloom, she's forced to navigate
the treacherous territory of passionate love, friendship, and family
devotion.

In a Silent Way by Mary Jo Hetzel. $16.95, 978-1-63152-135-5.
When Jeanna Kendall—a young white teacher at a progressive urban
school—becomes involved with a community activist group, she
finds herself grappling with issues of racism, sexism, and oppression
of various shades in both her professional and personal life.

Pieces by Maria Kostaki. $16.95, 978-1-63152-966-5. After five years
of living with her grandparents in Cold War-era Moscow, Sasha
finds herself suddenly living in Athens, Greece—caught between her
psychologically abusive mother and violent stepfather.